"So. What have you decided?"

My heart raced a million miles an hour.

*Wait.* What *am I doing trying to seduce this man?* I was Penelope Trudeau. A normal, everyday person, with normal, everyday looks. I worked for minimum wage plus tips and lived in a world so different from his. Not to mention he was shopping for a "baby mama." This was silly. I stood up. "I made a mistake coming here."

Within the space of a breath, his large body caged me, and his full, delicious lips were over mine. His hot, sweet tongue slipped in my mouth, instantly sending a delicious current of flutters and tingles straight down the center of my body, between my legs.

A tiny moan escaped my lips as my core did wild cartwheels. Image after image of how I wanted to explore his body, of how I wanted him to take me, pummeled my mind. It was so damn intense that I needed to catch my breath.

"What was that?" I panted.

He nuzzled my neck. "I believe it is what people call . . . *chemistry.*"

# PRAISE FOR MIMI JEAN PAMFILOFF'S ACCIDENTALLY YOURS SERIES

"The story really made an impression and she definitely makes me want to continue on with her series... witty and catchy."

—BookMaven623.wordpress.com on
*Accidentally In Love With...A God?*

"*Accidentally Married to...A Vampire?* remains one of the funniest paranormal novels I've read in a long time."

—IndieBookSpot.com

"It was fun, the pace was fast, there were laugh-out-loud funny lines, plenty of pop-culture references, and lots of very sexy moments. I am *definitely* going to be reading the author's other books!"

—SarahsBookshelves.blogspot.com on *Accidentally Married to...A Vampire?*

"Hot sex, a big misunderstanding, and a shocker of an ending that made me want the next book in the series now! I can't wait to go back and read the other books in the series."

—Romancing-the-Book.com on *Accidentally...Evil?*

"If you're looking for a read that's a little bit silly, a little bit sexy, and a whole lot of fun, you need to pick up *Accidentally...Evil?* I'm off to pick up the other three now. Damn, it was a funny one."

—HerdingCats-BurningSoup.blogspot.com

"Give me some black jade and a god for the weekend. No Payals or Maaskab need apply. P.S. Someone please find Cimil a garage sale and something pink to keep her out of trouble. Maybe."                                              —Dy

"Who needs a man, when you can have a god!"
                                              —Ally K.

# SUN GOD
## SEEKS...
# SURROGATE?

# SUN GOD SEEKS... SURROGATE?

MIMI JEAN PAMFILOFF

FOREVER

NEW YORK   BOSTON

Copyright © 2012 by Mimi Jean Pamfiloff
Excerpt from *Vampires Need Not...Apply?* © 2013 by Mimi Jean Pamfiloff

Forever
Hachette Book Group
237 Park Avenue
New York, NY 10017

www.HachetteBookGroup.com

Printed in the United States of America

Originally published as an ebook

First mass-market edition: February 2014
10 9 8 7 6 5 4 3 2 1

OPM

Forever is an imprint of Grand Central Publishing.
The Forever name and logo are trademarks of Hachette Book Group, Inc.

The Hachette Speakers Bureau provides a wide range of authors for speaking events. To find out more, go to www.hachettespeakersbureau.com or call (866) 376-6591.

The publisher is not responsible for websites (or their content) that are not owned by the publisher.

This novel is dedicated to Javi (God of All Things Manly), Seb (god in training), and Stefano (dictator in training). You make it all worthwhile. Now, please, please, stop breaking everything. Naughty boys!

# Very Special Thanks To

Naughty Nana (spiritual cheerleader extraordinaire), Team FOREVER ROMANCE, Phoenix (my writing buddy who's now come over to the dark side of PNR! Yes!), Cassie (for ensuring my pop culture references were relevant to twentysomethings: Ninja Turtles, Günther... really?), Vicki Randall (thank you for the abundance of enthusiasm, input, and watching my back), MY FACE-BOOK buds (OMG! I don't know you, but I love you—in a non-creeeepy way, as Ashley would say. Not only do you crack me up, but you wow me with your '80s sitcom knowledge), and all of the NICE, NICE PEOPLE (like you, Ute Carlin and Kim McNicholl!) who beta-read, sent e-mails, tweeted, and posted reviews (you ROCK!).

# Warning

This book contains sexual content (for some of you, not enough. I know. I'll try harder, I promise), adult language, hot men with unrealistically large physical characteristics, female whining (whaaat? I whine all the time. It's a healthy form of venting!), silliness, snarkiness, sarcasm, and blatant abuse of the English language.

# Cimil's Mandatory Pop Quiz

Well, hello again, my little People-Pets!

Now, I know you've been patiently waiting for this sequel to BOTH Books 1 and 2, but you must first pass my fabulous little pop quiz.

Oh yes. The gods have spoken. And by gods, I mean me. Because I'm the only one who counts. No, really. The gods can't count or do any sort of math. Don't ask. Leprechaun curses aren't funny.

Anyhooo, no cheating! (Especially you, Ashlee...) And I will know if you do. Because I know everything. Except how this story will end...

Demon crackers!

Cheers to me,
*Cimil, Goddess Delight of the Underworld*

1. **An ancient society of warriors and scholars who serve as the gods' eyes, ears, and muscle.**
   A. The Smurfs
   B. The were-Smurfs
   C. The Uchben

2. **A female descendant of the gods. Not immortal but does carry the gods' bloodline.**
   A. Snooki
   B. Betty White
   C. A Payal

3. **An evil cult of dark priests, descending from the Mayans.**
   A. The Republican Party
   B. The Democratic Party
   C. The Maaskab (aka Scabs)

4. **Evil vampires whose favorite flavor is innocence.**
   A. The Obscuros
   B. The Osmonds
   C. The Osbournes

5. **Now that Chaam, the God of Male Virility, is locked away, I lead the Maaskab army.**
   A. The Dos Equis "Most Interesting Man in the World"
   B. Kathy Griffin
   C. Gabriela, Emma Keane's grandmother

6. **Mimi Jean's favorite slang term for a man's private parts.**
   A. Man-treat
   B. Man-sicle
   C. Man-fritters

**SEE ANSWERS IN BACK**

# SUN GOD
# SEEKS...
# SURROGATE?

# *Prologue*

⌒

Wondering which screw in her head had come loose *this* time, twenty-four-year-old Emma Keane strapped a parachute to her back in preparation for another fun-filled jungle mission.

"Dammit! Stop wiggling!" she barked over her shoulder. "And that had better be your flashlight!"

Well, actually, it was a cranky, rather large warrior named Brutus strapped to her back and wearing the parachute because she had yet to find time for skydiving lessons.

*Dork.*

In any case, looking like a ridiculous, oversized baby kangaroo wasn't enough to stop her from making this nocturnal leap into enemy territory—Maaskab territory. She had scores to settle.

Emma sucked in a deep breath, the roar of the plane's large engines and Brutus's growls making it difficult to find her center—the key to winning any battle. And not freaking out.

Funny. If someone had told her a year ago that she'd end up here, an immortal demigoddess engaged to the infamous God of Death and War, she would have said, "Christ! Yep! That *toootally* sounds about right."

Why the hell not? She'd lived the first twenty-two years of her life with Guy—a nickname she'd given her handsome god—obsessed with his seductive voice, a voice only she could hear. Turned out, after they finally met face-to-face, their connection ran blood deep. Universe deep, actually. A match made by fate.

Emma rubbed her hands together, summoning the divine power deep within her cells. One blast with her fingertips and she could split a man right down the middle.

"Careful where you put those," Guy said, cupping himself.

Emma gazed up at his smiling face and couldn't help but admire the glorious, masculine view. *Sigh.* She knew she'd been born to love him, flaws—enormous ego and otherworldly bossiness—and all.

His smile melted away. "Please change your mind, my sweet. Stay on the plane, and let me do your fighting."

"Can't do that," she replied. "The Maaskab took my grandmother, and I'm going to be the one to get her back. Even if I have to kill Tommaso to do it."

Guy shook his head. "No. You are to let me deal with him."

Emma felt her immortal blood boil. She'd trusted Tommaso once, and he'd betrayed her. Almost gotten her killed, too. But she'd known—well, she'd *thought*—it wasn't Tommaso's fault. He'd been injected with liquid black jade, an evil substance that could darken the heart of an angel. That's why, after he'd been captured and mortally wounded, she had begged the gods to cure him.

Then she did the unthinkable: she'd put her faith in him again.

Stupid move.

He'd turned on her a second time, the bastard. Yes, his betrayal—done of his own free will—was her prize on that fateful night almost one year ago, when her grandmother showed up on their doorstep in Italy, leading an army of evil Maaskab priests, her mind clearly poisoned.

"If Tommaso hadn't helped her escape, we could've saved her," she said purely to vent, because she really wanted to cry. But the fiancée of the God of Death and War didn't cry. Especially in front of the hundred warriors riding shotgun on the plane tonight.

*Okay, maybe one teeny tiny tear while no one's looking.*

"Do not give up hope, Emma." Guy clutched her hand. "And do not forget...whatever happens, I love you. Until the last ray of sunlight. Until the last flicker of life inhabits this planet."

Brutus groaned and rolled his eyes, clearly annoyed by the sappy chatter.

Emma elbowed him in the ribs. "Shush! And how can you of all people be uncomfortable with a little affection? Huh? You bunk with eight dudes every night. That's gross by the way. Not the dude part. I'm cool with that. But eight big, sweaty warriors all at once? Yuck. So don't judge me because I'm into the one-man-at-a-time rule. That's messed up, Brutus."

Brutus growled and Guy chuckled.

In truth, Emma didn't know what Brutus was into or how he and his elite team slept, but she loved teasing him. She figured that sooner or later she'd find the magic words to get Brutus to speak to her.

*No luck yet.*

Accepting a temporary defeat, she shrugged and turned her attention back to the task at hand. She took one last look at her delicious male—nearly seven feet of solid muscle with thick blue-black waves of hair and bronzed skin. *Sigh.* "Okay. I'm ready," she declared boldly. "Let's kill some Scabs and get my granny!"

She glanced over her other shoulder at Penelope, their newest family member. Her dark hair was pulled into a tight ponytail that accentuated the anger simmering in her dark green eyes. Pissed would be a serious understatement.

Emma didn't blame her. What a cluster.

"Ready?" Emma asked.

"You better believe it," Penelope replied. "These clowns picked the wrong girl to mess with."

Guy frowned as they leaped from the plane into the black night.

*"A true friend is one soul in two bodies."*

—**Aristotle**

*"A true friend is two souls in one body."*

—**Kinich Ahau, God of the Sun**

# *One*

---

*Penelope. Approximately Three Weeks Earlier*

"Sorry, but did you just say...? You want me to *what*?"
I stared at the flaming redhead who'd trotted into the
crowded café off the snowy New York street, helped
herself to the chair across from me, and swiped her finger through the creamy froth of my eagerly anticipated
cappuccino.

*Rude!*

Didn't matter that the woman was disturbed, which she
clearly was; the pink scuba mask on her head was a dead
giveaway, as was the hot-pink mink coat.

"You heard me, Penelope," she said, rapping her glittery pink fingernails on the tabletop. "Five hundred thousand dollars—okay...I'll make it one million. But not a
penny more!"

How the hell did she know my name? And had she

really offered me money for what I thought? Was today April Fools'? No. It was November 30.

Then it dawned on me. I was being punk'd. Wait. That show was canceled. Yes, Ashton had moved on to corny camera commercials, a sitcom, and a very unflattering Ringo Starr beard.

Well, double dammit, whatever was going on, I didn't have the patience for this today; I'd just received bad news. The worst kind of bad news.

I dog-eared my book, *Spanish for Linguistic Tards*— never too late to learn another language, you know— and slapped it down. "I don't know which of my friends orchestrated this crappy prank, but I've got work in twenty minutes, and it's going to be a long, long night—"

"Hold your jicama!" she interrupted, shoving her index finger in my face as her phone squawked. She quickly dug through her oversized pink fuzzy handbag and pulled out the device. "Wassup? Yeah. Yeah. Oooh my…" The odd woman, who appeared to be in her thirties, continued her egregiously loud banter while stroking the lapel of her furry coat.

I glanced over my shoulder, wondering if anyone else inside the bustling café was witnessing this obnoxious display. Oddly enough, not one person was.

Whatever. Didn't matter. I'd already decided to go find my pre–night shift triple-skinny cappuccino (hold the weirdo finger) elsewhere.

I pushed away from the table, and she latched onto my wrist, instantly igniting a surge of numbing static through-out my entire body. Every muscle ground to a halt. Except my pounding heart. That worked fine.

She narrowed her eyes and then made a little no-no wave with her scrawny, pale finger.

"Yeah. Uh-huh. Oooh. Nice," she continued, chatting on her phone while I experienced the world's quietest panic attack. "I'm thinkin' we go with the chicken fingers." She shook her head a few times. "No, silly. Real ones. I love crunchy food." Pause. "How the hell should I know what to do with the chickens? Make them some special shoes." Pause. "Yup. Yup. Clothing is optional. Except for the clowns. They get too carried away with the ball jokes. Seriously. It's disturbing. Even for me." Another pause. "We can talk about it later, Fate. I gotta take care of this girl before she throws a hissy." Pause. "Yes. It's *that* girl. This is gonna be dramalicious!"

She ended her call and sighed happily in my general direction. "Gods, I rock. I should be a ride at Six Flags. They should name a country after me— Wait! No. The planet. They should name the entire planet after *magnifique moi*!" She suddenly snapped back her head and locked her eyes on the ceiling. "Oh yeah? You just try it!"

I couldn't move my head, but from the corner of my eye, I noticed a little black dot.

*A fly? She's talking to the fly?*

She then pointed right at the little bugger. "That's right! I'll take you down. I'll cut you, bitch!"

The fly buzzed away.

The woman shrugged and then leaned into the table. A wide, evil grin stretched across her elfin face. "Okillee-dokillee, Penelope. Let's not play games—for the next five minutes, anyway—Pin the Tail on the Donkey is my favorite, though. Just in case you were wondering." She snorted. "I like it when they squeal."

Her paralyzing grip didn't allow a response, but I was all ears; this woman scared the crappity crap out of me.

"I know everything about you," she continued. "You're Penelope Trudeau. You were raised right here in good ol' NYC. Your mother has been fighting a mysterious illness for the past year, which is why you've put off going to grad school even though you've been accepted to several excellent programs."

Who the hell was this woman? She recited every fact about my life, including how I was a size 8—or size 10 after the major holidays and sporting events—had a black belt in karate, was afraid of spiders, and had no intention of celebrating my twenty-fifth birthday tomorrow. Birthdays freaked me out.

"My brother and I mean business, Penelope. This isn't a joke. Though…" She snorted twice. "…Did you ever hear the one about the porcupine who married the sheep?"

She released my wrist.

Ever so slowly, my body sparked back to life. Terrified, I blinked several times before nodding no. She was insane. Truly. Unequivocally. Bonkers. And she apparently knew how to do that Vulcan grip thing. Not a good combo.

"Well, their children were able to knit their own sweaters!" She chuckled loudly and slapped her knee.

Then, for no apparent reason, her expression transformed into a void of human warmth. It sent shivers deep down into the pit of my stomach, which was now telling me to run. Run far, far away. I didn't know if her offer to pay me one million dollars was genuine or the ramblings of a madwoman, but God save me, I didn't want anything to do with her.

"So, you in or out?" she asked, crossing her arms.

"One million dollars, honey. It will solve all your problems: help your mother, pay for school...What's one little egg and nine months of your life?"

The insane woman continued staring as I realized I had full control of my body again.

The words "My womb is not for rent!" exploded from my mouth, and the entire café fell silent. Everyone stared with gaping mouths.

"Oh, sure. *Now* you're all paying attention," I mumbled.

I turned my attention back to Ms. Nut Job and slowly stepped away, preparing to make a mad dash for my life. "I'm not interested."

"Great!" She popped up from her chair and flicked her hand in the air. "You'll get half the money now—just for showing up to the party. I mean that figuratively, by the way—'cause you're not invited to my *actual* party. Friends and family only. Plus a few people who won the raffle. And some clowns. And my unicorn—don't ask."

I felt my face involuntarily contort. She wasn't just disturbed, she was batshit crazy.

"Come to my house tomorrow morning, nine a.m. sharp." She began digging in her purse again. "My lawyer slash Twister coach, Rochell, will have the papers ready along with a Welcome Handbook. I suggest you read it. There will be a pop quiz, and Rochell doesn't mess around."

I stepped away from the table toward the door. "I don't know who you are, but I said no, and I meant it. Stay the hell away from me!"

That something in my gut, which had told me to run, now screamed at the top of its lungs.

I listened.

I bolted onto the bustling street filled with evening

holiday shoppers making their way down the snow-covered sidewalks. But when I glanced over my shoulder, back toward the corner café with its floor-to-ceiling windows, the madwoman wasn't inside or on the street.

I stopped in my tracks and shook my head.

Had I dreamed the entire thing? Had some deranged woman dressed like pink cotton candy, using a scuba mask as a headband, just propositioned me to be the surrogate mother of her brother's baby for one million dollars?

*Nooo.*

I seriously needed some sleep. Or therapy.

# *Two*

For the record, I've never been one to look down on a hard day's work. I come from a long line of hard workers despite my hoity-toity French last name. But truth be told, I couldn't wait for the day I'd leave behind waiting tables in exchange for a real career. My dream was going to grad school to get my master's in political science. Eventually, I wanted a PhD and to teach. Unfortunately, that dream was far off, some untouchable horizon beyond the daily grind of my current life that consisted of taking care of my sick mother during the day and working two back-to-back night shifts at Carmine's Trattoria seven days a week.

What about my dad? We didn't talk about him much, but I knew he'd studied at the same university as my mother and hadn't been ready for fatherhood. So that left us two girls and a few random cousins out West.

Mind you, I didn't complain about taking care of my

mom because she was the sort of person worthy of any sacrifice—kind, generous, always finding the silver lining in everything. Still, that didn't mean our situation wasn't hard. Her condition was a medical mystery with only one real symptom: She suffered from a crippling exhaustion. She barely stayed awake long enough to get in one meal a day. And not one of the dozen or so specialists I made her see knew what caused it.

Regardless, I wasn't giving up. Even if the cards seemed stacked against us.

Case in point, this morning I'd received a call from her doctor. I wanted to get her on a new European immune-boosting drug, but found out her insurance wouldn't cover the eighty-thousand-dollar-per-year prescription. Now she'd been turned down as a candidate for FDA trials.

"Miss? May I have some more water, please?"

I glanced up from the polished cement floor I'd been staring at while deep in contemplation. *Table nine.*

"Right away," I replied with an apologetic smile. I trotted back to the drink station and promptly returned to fill glasses and clear away empty plates. All the while, my mind wasn't far from that one nagging question: What the hell was I going to do?

*You'll figure this out, Penelope. You always do. You just need some sleep so you can think clearly.*

I squared my shoulders and made my rounds, remaining cheerful for my customers. After all, they weren't at the famous Carmine's spending their hard-earned money to watch me sulk. No, they deserved all the joy they could have. Life is short.

I displayed a bottle of Chianti for uncorking to my regular at table five, and my mind drifted back to the bizarre incident at that café before my shift. Had it been real? Sure felt that way. Or maybe the sleep deprivation finally had me by the big toe.

*But what if it was real? You wouldn't be the first woman on the planet to be a surrogate mother.*

Then an image of the crazy redhead popped into my mind. "My womb is not for rent! Okay?" I slapped my hand over my mouth. "Sorry, Mr. Z, I have a little brain baggage today."

Mr. Z, who thankfully dined alone, smiled graciously and nodded at the bottle. I reached into the pocket of my black slacks for my corkscrew, but instead of finding the slim, plastic-covered tube, I felt paper.

"Oh. Jeez. So sorry. I must've left my corkscrew in the kitchen." I held up one finger. "Be right back." I scurried toward the kitchen, distinctly remembering having put the corkscrew in my pocket.

I smiled at the line of three chefs working their steaming skillets as I headed to my locker toward the back of the cramped kitchen. I popped open the lock and then dug through my purse. Sure enough, there it was. This particular corkscrew with a large gripper was the only professional model that didn't require me to place the bottle between my thighs. Funny to watch, yes. Professional, no. Not many diners wanted to see their wine wedged in my crotch.

Picky, picky.

I pulled the paper from my pocket to deposit it in my bag, but the moment my eyes registered what it was, my heart stopped.

Paper-clipped to a small business card was a cashier's check for five hundred thousand dollars drawn on the Bank of New York.

"Holy crap," I whispered, my hand trembling. The check seemed official enough—watermark, signature from the bank president.

*But...but...it was just a dream, wasn't it?* I stared at the card. It had the name Cimil and an address near Central Park written on the front. On the back, a handwritten note said:

> *9:00 a.m. sharp. Don't be late. Have garage sales to hit.*

No. It most certainly hadn't been a dream.

Okay. So I get how in this situation, especially for someone with my particular set of challenges, the proper reaction might be to ignore how the check ended up in my pocket and then jump up and down in gleeful hysterics. One might even fall to his or her knees and thank the angels above for such a gift. Five hundred thousand frigging dollars. It *would* solve all my problems. I could go to the bank in the morning, cash the check, pay for my mother's treatment, and go to school.

But the fact was, an ugly cloud of bizarre hovered overhead along with an equally bizarre string attached to the money. And on the other end of that string was some crazy woman with a fetish for hot pink.

*A baby? She really wants me to have a baby with her brother?* What I couldn't figure out was why. Why would anyone believe I'd go for such an insane idea? And why would anyone think I'd make an ideal surrogate? Was it the four Big Gulp–sized cappuccinos every day? How about my addiction to mochi ice cream and sourdough bread with extra butter? Oh, I know. It must've been the four hours of sleep I got each night. Yes, I could see how anyone would want to rent my womb.

My mind raced. I felt so damned cornered. Yes, I needed the money, but I didn't want to have kids yet. Someday, yes. When I found the right man. Not now. Not like this.

That's when it hit me. Anger. How dare this strange woman...

I glimpsed at the card. *Cimil*.

*How dare this...Cimil pop into my life and throw money at me.* She obviously knew about my horrible situation and was taking advantage. How did she know? Good frigging question! I wasn't going to stand for it! My eggs and body weren't for sale! No way would I have a baby with some stranger and then give it away to a bunch of crazy, rich people. What sort of person would I be?

"You'd be a bad bumper sticker waiting to happen." I huffed loudly and shoved the check in my purse. After work, I would give Cimil a piece of my mind. I'd find some other way to get my mom her medicine. I could go to private organizations for funding. I'd also petition the Swedish company directly. I bet they gave away dozens of grants each year. It would take time, but with a little luck and lots of persistence, I'd find a way.

*You'll figure this out, Penelope. You always do.*

Chock-full o' determination and hell-bent on defending my honor, I stomped up the steps of the insanely gorgeous brownstone located in the exclusive Carnegie Hill neighborhood. Despite the late hour, salsa music and laughter poured outside through several cracked windows.

*What kind of people would want to party with a depraved woman like her?* I wondered.

I leaned over the side of the porch and tried to catch a peek inside through a tiny gap in the noxious pink curtains, but could only make out the shapes of a few bodies.

"Some seriously messed-up people, that's who," I mumbled to no one.

The door flew open. A very large, fierce-looking man with spiky, dark brown hair, wearing leather pants and biker boots, filled the doorway. He looked me over with a glare that could melt the half inch of snow right off my parka. Despite the death sneer, the fact that he held a baby—dressed in a girly Santa-style outfit, chewing a cracker, and slung over his hip—sort of ruined the tough guy image he was going for.

He frowned and waited for me to say something.

"Oh. Um. Is Cimil here?" I asked.

"Name?" He sounded like a soldier working a checkpoint.

"Penelope. Penelope Trudeau." I don't know why I suddenly felt guilty, like I was trying to crash the party, so I offered, "I have an appointment with her in the morning, but it can't wait."

He looked me over once more and then stepped aside to let me in.

I brushed the snow from my shoulders and slid past him. The adorable, cherubic blonde baby with enormous green eyes cooed and then reached for me.

"Oh, hi, honey," I said and shook her plump, little hand. "I'm Penelope. What's your name?"

The baby opened her mouth and leaned forward. I could swear I saw a full set of gleaming, white teeth.

The man swept my hand away and moved the baby to his other hip. "No, no, Matty," he said lovingly. "No biting."

I gasped as I noticed little red puncture marks all over his hand.

*Yikes!*

He must have read my thoughts because he shrugged. "She's teething."

I made an uncomfortable little laugh and refrained from cracking any *Addams Family* jokes. Instead, I unzipped my coat and wiped my damp feet once more on the waterhog rug.

"Wait here," he said and then headed to the end of the opulent foyer, disappearing through a large doorway.

I scanned the room quickly and noticed an ornate crystal chandelier overhead, decorated with streamers—pink, of course—hanging down in uneven strips. Two shimmering suits of armor were situated on each side of the entryway, and the high-polish white marble floor displayed weird little circular mats that ran down the middle of it like stepping-stones. Each mat had a large word printed on it. "Just. Say. No . . ." I frowned. "To. Naked. Clowns?"

Beyond a doubt, these were the worst holiday decorations I'd ever seen and this was one of the strangest women I'd ever met.

I stood there for several minutes listening to cheers and the clinking of glasses coming from the other room. I was dying to see inside. Was her entire house pink, too? I moved a few steps closer to what I assumed was the living room doorway, wondering if the man had forgotten about me.

I paced a few times before deciding how ridiculous I was behaving. I didn't want to make a scene in front of her guests, but I wasn't going to wait around all night. I wanted answers. Like how she knew so much about me. Or how she'd managed to put a check in my pocket. And where she'd learned that Vulcan paralysis trick.

I took a deep breath and approached the end of the foyer. The crowded room with gold-leafed moldings and vaulted ceilings was in fact decorated in pink, including a hot-pink Steinway in the corner next to the extra-large fireplace.

*And...clowns.*

Really, really unhappy-looking clowns.

Was it because Cimil had made them wear clothes?

Then I noticed everyone else. They were dressed to the hilt in tuxes and ball gowns.

Was this a party for the obscenely rich and gorgeous? I could swear every man measured at least seven feet tall and every woman had fallen out of the Victoria's Secret catalog.

With friends like these, why in the world would Cimil's brother want me? Couldn't he find a better surrogate within this gene pool?

I suddenly felt like a skuzzy, little bug, the kind you might find living beneath your refrigerator stuck inside a cluster of dust bunnies. I'd come directly from work, so I still had on my white button-down shirt (complete with spaghetti stains) and black slacks, with a giant black parka to complete my ensemble. My long, dark hair was pulled back into a tight bun at the nape of my neck. Though I didn't consider myself a slight woman at five foot six, I felt two feet tall in comparison to the stylish crowd.

I started to back away from the room, thankful no one had taken notice of me. My fury and I would come back in the morning when all of the Greek gods were gone. I know—a totally spineless move.

I was almost home free when a man, who stood with his back to me, talking to a leggy blonde, turned around. We locked eyes, and the air whooshed from my lungs. I'd never seen anyone like him. Pure male magnificence.

Like the other men in the room, he wore a tux and was close to seven feet tall, but his eyes...they were a mesmerizing turquoise green. His skin was smooth and deeply tanned, like he'd just flown in from the Bahamas. And his shoulder-length hair resembled silky caramel ribbons streaked with rays of sunshine.

Images suddenly flashed in my mind like an erotic slideshow of sweat-slicked skin, of steel-cut muscles intertwining with the soft limbs of my eager body, of flesh on flesh writhing in a primal rhythm under moonlit shadows. With one simple glance, he'd made me feel empty inside. Deprived. Hungry. And the look in his eyes promised salvation from the burning hole deep within my clenching stomach.

I swallowed hard, feeling my mouth go dry while every other nook and cranny of my body turned into a hot, syrupy mess.

At first he studied me, narrowing his eyes, but then a quick smile flashed across his full, delicious lips.

My knees began to wobble, and I was about to tip over when Cimil came from behind and spun me.

"Penelope! What are you doing here?" she hissed.

"I...I...um." Why the hell was I there? I could no longer remember.

"Dammit, girl! You'll ruin everything!" She yanked me in the opposite direction of the gawking crowd, back through the foyer toward another doorway. She dragged me down a long hallway with blond hardwood floors and several life-sized portraits of...well, they looked like... *pirates holding small jars?* before she shoved me inside a room and slammed the door behind us.

"Hell in a handwoven Easter basket!" she barked and began pacing in front of a large, mahogany—not pink—desk situated in the center of the room.

Her study was filled with floor-to-ceiling bookshelves and a few leather armchairs. For all intents and purposes, it seemed like the study of a fairly normal person. I wondered if she just hadn't gotten around to decorating this part of the house yet.

She quickly plucked a thick leather-bound book from the shelf and slammed it down on the desk.

*Now? She chooses now to catch up on her reading?*

Cimil flipped through the pages and ran her pointy little finger over the text. "No! It was here when I checked last week. I know it was. You weren't supposed to come until tomorrow morning. This is bad. Bad! Something changed! Why didn't I recheck the book? I always recheck." She shook her head and covered her face. "Damn you, *Love Boat* and your sinfully delightful marathons! I shall shun you for eternity!" She swiveled in my direction. "You have to go. Right now! I need to figure this out. Something's gone wrong." She ushered me back to the door. "Come tomorrow. I'll have the answer then."

I had no clue why Cimil was in hysterics or why anyone would eternally shun the cheesy goodness of *Love Boat*—I mean, who could resist Gopher, Captain Stubing...Charo? *Cuchi, cuchi, cuchi*—but the insane didn't need a reason.

In any case, her sitcom issues weren't my problem. I pulled the check from my pocket. "I'm not coming back. I'm not interested in your money or having a..." I winced. "...baby. And, to be honest, I have serious issues with you being around *any* child, let alone any of mine—not that I want one. Yet. Seriously, have you spoken to anyone about your problems? I mean, has anyone told you that—"

"Did you say you're...not doing it? You're rejecting my offer?" Cimil tilted her head and then glanced at the check in my hand.

"My eggs and womb aren't for sale, and I resent you trying to take advantage of my situation. I have no clue how you're even aware of it! And what kind of person does this? For Christ's sake, my mother is sick. She could die."

She frowned, regarded her feet, and then glared at my face.

I was a good six inches taller than her, yet for some reason, I felt small. She radiated a sort of massive darkness despite her brightly colored clothing (hot-pink evening gown, of course) and flaming red, Cleopatra-style hair.

She unexpectedly burst out cackling like a madwoman on a mad, mad mission. "You drive a hard bargain, but okay. You can keep the five hundred g's just for showing up. All you have to do is meet with my brother and hear him out. 'Kay?"

I was *this* close to stomping my feet like a three-year-old. "No. The answer is *no*!"

"Great! Come back in the morning, and we'll finish this. But you need to leave now. You can't be here."

*Oh. My. God! She's frigging insane!* "No! I said no!"
Stomp. Stomp.

A rancid expression swept across her face. "No?
Nobody ever says no! And...did you stomp your foot at
me? That's my move!"

I crossed my arms. "It's mine now, honey." Stomp.
Stomp.

She closed the gap between us. "You're supposed to
take the offer," she snarled. "I give you the money. You
use it to save your mother and you end up mated."

*Mated?* I moved one step back toward the doorway.
"Don't even think of doing that Vulcan thing on me again!
It won't change anything. I'm. Not. Interested."

I shoved the check at her, but she refused to take it.

"Fine. I'm leaving." I let it fall to the floor. "I don't
know why you've decided to stalk me—which I'm pretty
sure is illegal in most states—but I'm warning you to
stay the hell away. I know people." I really didn't, except
the owners of Carmine's who were Italian. Maybe they
knew people. Or maybe I could find some people on
Craigslist.

I reached for the door, eyeing Cimil cautiously, afraid
she might jump on my back and pull out my hair. She
seemed like the type who fought dirty.

I turned and ran straight into a wall. My palms quickly
assessed the barrier and discovered it wasn't brick or plas-
ter but a very firm set of abs cloaked in very fine fabric.

I snapped up my head, and staring down with a surly
expression was the man who'd turned me into a mindless,
sex-starved heap moments earlier.

Once again, my knees wobbled, and I felt myself tipping over.

He grumbled something and then grabbed my shoulders to steady me before shifting his gaze to Cimil.

"Cimiiil?" he said, his voice filled with authority and disapproval.

"Son of a beach ball!" Stomp. Stomp. "You're not supposed to be in here!" she barked. "Do you have any idea what I went through to align the events correctly? Out! Out!" Cimil practically knocked me over while attempting to extract the exquisite, irate man from the vicinity.

He didn't budge an inch. Instead, he studied me with his intense aquamarine eyes.

"I think I'll show our guest to the door." He grabbed my elbow and pulled me down the hallway toward the foyer. My entire body lit up like a slot machine that had hit the big one. I could swear beeps and sirens went off, too, but my mind was scrambled from his electrifying touch. One thing I did grasp, however, was the howl of Cimil's voice as she cussed up a storm, ranting about stars, planets, and all sorts of random garble.

We were almost to the front door when the man finally released me. "I'm sorry about that," he said in a deep voice that threatened to undo my equilibrium permanently.

Like a brainless fool, I simply stared up at him, unable to speak. His eyes were the most amazing swirls of tropical greens and blues. Being near him made me feel like I was on an exotic beach, bathing in the warmth of the sun.

I sighed.

"Can you hear me?" He snapped his fingers in front of my nose. "Penelope? That is your name, yes?"

I realized he was talking to me, but I lacked the cognitive agility to respond verbally, so I bobbed my head instead.

He narrowed his eyes for a split second. "Good. I suggest you do not return." He ushered me out the front door. "My sister is not to be trifled with."

*Huh? Did he just say*...I pivoted on my heel as the door slammed shut in my face.

"*You're* her brother?"

# *Three*

That night, I tossed and turned for hours, obsessing over the beautiful man.

Something about him...mesmerized me.

His full, sensual lips perhaps? I imagined they could do things I'd only read about and kiss in ways I'd only dreamed of. And his size. Did men of such enormity occur naturally? Or were they grown on farms where they were fed raw buffalo and worked out from sunup to sundown?

*Outside. Nude. Sweating.*

I kicked off the blankets. *Boy, it's hot in here.*

Why couldn't I purge him from my brain? Maybe I didn't want to. What I really wanted was to see him again. In my bed. In the shower. Ironing naked in my living room. Folding my undies—the pretty ones I reserved for special occasions, of course.

I sighed deeply and rolled over for the fiftieth time.

I hadn't had a case of lust this bad since Jimmy Roberts

in the fourth grade. He had *the* coolest BMX bike—
Ninja Turtles motif with flag, bell, the works. Jimmy also
resembled the blond guy from *Saved by the Bell*. I followed him around at recess, offered him my cherry Capri
Sun every lunch, and had his name written twenty times
inside my Care Bears notebook. Oh yeah, I'd had it bad.

But this...this thing with Cimil's brother was far
worse. I could practically feel my eggs shaving their legs
and painting their toenails—hooker red—in preparation
to meet him.

*Ugh. Stop it. You don't even know the man. And
Cimil...double ugh! Anyone with a sister that twisted
has to be bad news.* She screamed "dysfunctional family."

I glimpsed at the glowing green numbers of my clock
on the nightstand and sighed. In only twenty minutes, it
would shriek.

I rolled onto my other side and continued the mental
Ping-Pong match. *See him again? Not see him again. See
him. Not see him.*

*I have to.*

*No. If you go back there, you'd be deceiving the poor
guy. You'd never have a baby with a stranger. And there's
nothing he or his sister could ever say to change your
mind.*

*I bet he* could *say something. Something like, "I will
make steamy, steamy love to you with my hard-as-steel,
muscled body all night long if you agree to have my
baby."*

I swallowed. *Yeah, that actually might do it.*

*Really, Pen?* I countered to myself. *Come on. Don't be
ridiculous.*

Bringing a child into the world was a serious matter,

and giving it up to strangers was in another league altogether. Not that I knew from personal experience, but anyone who had a heart could figure that one out.

I suddenly felt a warm, gentle hand on my back.

"Oh," I said, "you're up..." It wasn't my mother coming to see if I'd woken up yet. It was...

*Shit! Cimil's brother.*

I sat up so fast I almost head butted him. "Christ! What are you doing here?"

It was still dark outside, but since I'd left my curtains partially open, my room glowed with a faint silver hue from the streetlamps outside.

He reached out and swept the hair from my forehead. "That doesn't matter. What is important is that you listen to me." His deep voice washed over me like a calming tropical wave.

I was about to say something. It was...

I'd already forgotten.

His hand cupped my cheek, and when he stared into my eyes, the expression on his divinely handsome face was unreadable. Warmth. Suspicion. Acceptance and determination.

*Me sooo confused.* I sighed inwardly while my mind floated in a pool of dopey bliss.

"Penelope, please focus," he said affectionately.

I nodded dumbly. "Okay," I whispered.

*Why can't I think straight?*

"Good," he said. "Because you're not thinking this through properly. Not everything in life is a question of absolutes, love."

*He called me "love."* I liked the sound of that.

"Not an absolute?" I asked.

He traced his finger along my jaw. "No. This is why you must keep an open mind. This is why you must come to see me."

"See you. Uh-huh," I responded, my mind feeling rich with a hormone-induced fog.

He leaned forward and pressed his lips to mine. A soul-shattering surge of elation rocketed through my body. I wanted him with every cell in my body, every molecule of oxygen in my blood, and every beat of my heart. I never wanted to be without him, his touch, or the sweet, rich, exotic scent of him that filled my lungs.

"Ah. Now you're catching on." He made a deep, hearty chuckle.

The screech of my alarm clock pierced my ears and jolted me to life like a defibrillator. I blinked and found myself faceup on the floor next to my bed.

I clenched my fist over my chest as the adrenaline fueled my palpitating heart. "Son of a beach ball," I said in a breathy voice. "What the hell was that?"

*Oh, great. Now I'm talking like that crazy lady.*

"Are you all right, Penelope?"

The thin silhouette of my mom in her pajamas appeared in the doorway.

"Must've fallen out of bed," I replied.

She flipped on the light, causing me to wince.

"Oh, Penelope," she sighed. "You look like you haven't slept in days. I told you, no more double shifts."

I smiled. "I'll sleep when I'm dead."

She didn't laugh at that.

"Sorry." I rolled over and crawled back into bed, flopping facedown. "I have a lot on my mind."

"You know, baby"—the bed sank when she deposited

herself next to me—"I've been meaning to talk to you about all this. About me."

I flipped onto my back.

My mom's frizzy blonde braid and bloodshot hazel eyes broadcasted her exhaustion, and her posture—sagging shoulders and head hung low—reeked of surrender.

Well, maybe she'd given up. I hadn't. Not yet.

"Penelope, I can't keep letting you sacrifice your life for me. I'm your mother. I'm supposed to take care of you. Not the other way around, sweetie."

I mumbled a few angry words and got up to collect my clothes for the day. I knew what speech was coming next: her backup plan. I'd heard it fifty times, and I'd rejected it fifty different ways. She had a cousin, a holistic healer in California, who'd offered to take her in and treat her. Although the probability of success would be extremely low, it was fine by me. But she didn't want me to go with her, and that was ridiculous. She insisted I stay in New York and move on with my life: apply for financial aid, finish school, get a boyfriend . . . live. What she really meant was she planned to wither away out of sight from me.

I stared at her face. Despite the hollow cheeks and dark shadows under her eyes, she still held a youthful appearance with barely a wrinkle. In perfect health she could pass for my sister. She was beautiful and strong, and I loved her with all my heart, which is why I blurted out, "I got the money. A private grant."

Her eyes filled with tears. "How?"

"It's one of these trust fund charities. Sorry I didn't say anything last night when I found out, but you were asleep. Didn't want to wake you."

She hugged me with as much energy as her weak body could muster. "I love you, Penelope. You truly are an angel." She pulled away. "I almost forgot! It's your birthday. Now we have two things to celebrate."

*Ugh.* I hated celebrating my birthday. It was one of my many quirks. Something about getting older made me feel...old. And now that I had to see Cimil again, I felt even less like celebrating.

She left the room and returned with a small box. "I hope you like it."

"Oh my God, how did you find the energy to buy me something?" Sometimes it truly is the thought that counts.

I unwrapped the shiny red paper covering the box. Inside was a small silver ring with tiny black cabochons.

"Do you like it? I got it from an antique shop. The woman said it would bring you good luck."

It was lovely. "I'll wear it forever."

# *Four*

⌒

At a quarter to nine that same morning, I found myself pacing the sidewalk across from Cimil's house with giant spoon in hand, ready to chow down on a heaping helping of crow. My mother's health was well worth a few kicks to the ego, but I still needed to go in with a game plan.

I'd agreed to listen. Just…listen. *Five hundred thousand dollars.*

I blew out a quick breath and watched the steam billow from my lips. The air outside had to be in the teens, though it could have been one hundred and eight for all I knew; my body, riddled with adrenaline, felt like it was on fire. Maybe because I felt like an animal about to be caged.

*Yes, here's the yummy carrot, bunny. Jump! Jump!*

*No. You agreed to listen, to consider their proposal in exchange for a boatload of money your mother desperately needs. Nothing more. There is no obligation to share your eggs.*

Not that my eggs would mind. Little traitors. They were already creating decoupage memorial plates in her brother's honor.

In any case, the chances of Cimil saying anything to convince me were slim to... never, ever, ever. I mean, who in their right mind would consider this sort of scheme, aside from those weird people who show up on the cover of the *National Enquirer* between articles titled "I Was Carjacked by a Yeti" and "Aliens Are Living in My Shampoo Bottle."

I took a quick sip of my extra-strong coffee, taking comfort in its fortifying bitterness.

*See. You could never say yes to Cimil. You'd have to quit coffee if you had a baby.*

I stared at my constant companion for the last year. Coffee and I had done things. Been places. My bud. I ran my finger lovingly down the side of the paper cup. *No, I could never give you up.*

*Still, that dream... You can't deny there's a subliminal somethin' somethin' going on.*

My mind quickly replayed the imaginary conversation. What did it mean?

*"Not everything is a question of absolutes..."*

Were they somewhere in between? Areas of gray?

*What's your gray, Penelope?*

I bit my lower lip and took a sip of my rapidly cooling coffee.

"You know, Penelope," said a deep male voice at my side, startling me from my personal force majeure. "Sometimes it's best to treat fate like a Band-Aid."

The man who'd answered the door the evening before stood next to me. Only this time he wore a black turtleneck (not a baby) and a full-length leather jacket.

His breath was thick as smoke when he said, "I am Andrus."

He held out his leather-clad hand, and I immediately wondered if the gloves were meant to mask the creepy bite marks rather than shield his fingers from the formidable cold. He didn't seem like the kind of man who got chilly.

He gave me the once-over while we shook hands. "You're going to catch a cold standing out here in that," he pointed out.

I'd worn my jeans and faux fur–lined boots with a white sweater. My parka was tied around my waist. "Not really the high nail on my list of worries."

He nodded and then shifted his gaze toward the front door of Cimil's house. "Take it from me, life never turns out as one expects. The sooner you let go of what should be, the sooner you'll see the forest through the trees."

"Great," I said, "just what I needed . . . life lessons brought to you by the bumper sticker."

He laughed at that.

"Who is she?" I asked.

He smirked and rubbed his black stubble-covered jaw. "She's someone extremely powerful. And someone who knows what you need even before you do."

Well, la-di-da! Didn't that make it all better?

"And what exactly did *you* need?" I asked, wondering why anyone would choose to have someone like Cimil in his or her life.

He scratched his sprouting beard again. "To heal a piece of me that was broken long ago."

"How's that workin' out for ya?"

He smiled a bright, glowing, heartfelt smile. "Well. Really, really well."

"Sorry, buddy. Not drinking the Kool-Aid."

"Kool-Aid?" he asked.

"Never min..." I turned to fully face him. It was then that I noticed his eyes were an inconceivable amalgamation of light blues and greens, almost iridescent.

*Just like Cimil and her brother.*

I swallowed my shiver. Something about these people felt...different. Very, very different. "I'm not in Kansas anymore, am I, Andrus?"

"No, Dorothy. You are not."

# Five

⁓

"What do you mean, he's not coming?" I said. "I came to hear him out, like you asked."

Cimil sat at her desk, flipping through the pages of the same thick book she'd been reading the night before. "You will meet with him tonight *before* you say yes or no. That is my one condition to your keeping half the money."

"Fine." That would be easy enough. And I had to admit, the part of me that craved to see him again was Hula-Hooping.

Her finger carefully skimmed a page and then stopped on a word. "There's more. How could I forget?" Her head snapped up.

*Here come the strings. I knew it!* Would she ask me to ride a pink pogo stick to this meeting? Perhaps I needed to be escorted by clowns. Clothed, of course.

"Yes?" I replied.

"I've got something for you." She reached to her side and began fishing through a drawer. "Oh, pickle. Where is it?" She pulled out a Slinky, a Taser, a pack of Bubblicious gum, and a pink Troll—the kind you put over a pencil eraser. "Ah! Here it is." She plunked down a large three-ring binder labeled "Handbook." "You must read this before tonight."

She'd been serious about the handbook? "You're not telling me there's really going to be a pop quiz, too?"

Cimil's eyes glowed with wicked joy. "You're off the hook. Rochell, who handles that little tidbit of fun, is resting after an unfortunate Twister mishap at last night's party." She shrugged. "Strippers. Policemen. They all look the same to me. Especially after you steal their clothes and grease them up. Yanno what I mean?"

I blinked as my mind tried to form a cohesive connection between those thoughts. I was coming up blank. "No. No, I don't." *Moving on...* "What sort of handbook is this?"

"The kind that will give you answers, silly. For things." Long awkward pause. "What else?"

Well, that was vague. And weird. Just like this entire depraved situation. "Okeydokey. Anything else?" I asked.

She laughed hysterically for several moments and then shook her finger. "You! You're a firecracker. Kaablam! Pow! Fire! Cracker!" She paused and stared at the ceiling, completely checked out.

Damn, she freaked me out. "Are we...done?"

She burst back to life. "Yep. Here's the address and time." She handed me a slip of paper from the pocket of her pink satin jumpsuit.

I snatched it from her hand, swiped the handbook,

and prepared to flee. I wanted to skedaddle before this got any weirder or she tied any more strings to this little bunny.

"Penelope," she bellowed as I was almost home free and out the front door.

I cringed and turned to find her scampering after me.

"Aren't you forgetting something?" she asked.

*Oh, jeez.*

"The check." She shoved it at me. "Buy yourself something nice for tonight. It's your birthday."

*Thanks for the reminder.* I put the check in my purse and gave her a polite smile as I reached for the door. Then I paused, fighting the urge to kick my own tuchus.

*Dammit.* I couldn't leave without saying something. As awkward and ludicrous as the situation might be, she was about to help my mother.

I took a deep breath and faced her. "Cimil, I know you're not doing this to help my mom, but I wanted to thank you anyway."

She flashed another wicked smile. "Don't mention it. Helpful is my middle name—except on Saturdays. Then it's Jaaaasmine..." She waved her hand in a semicircle through the air.

It was actually Saturday, but I thought it best not to say anything.

"Anyhooo"—she shrugged—"you'll pay me back someday. They always do."

I didn't like that answer one little bit. In fact, my body lit up with tiny adrenaline-fueled tingles. Why did this woman evoke the fight or flight—mostly flight—response?

I scrambled out the door.

"And Penelope," she called out when I reached the bottom of her front steps.

*No, no, no. More strings.* I reached for the wrought iron railing at my side to steady me.

"There are three rules..."

*"I ask you to leave here tonight,*
*you knew it was planned*

*When the world takes your heart from the fight*

*You do what you can*

*You're living here lost in this land*

*So brother, don't force my hand*

*Please let's see the forest for the trees*

*'Cause it's time to rise up, it's time to rise up*
*from your knees"*

—Pilot Speed

# *Six*

*Kinich. December 1, 9:30 p.m.*

Grinding his teeth, Kinich watched his brother, the infamous God of Death and War, stroll into the trendy Manhattan hotel bar with an expression on his face that could—well, kill. The maître d' took one look at the towering mass of muscles in an Armani suit and thick, black hair wild and loose, and practically dove out of the way. The crowd parted like the Red Sea, leaving a trail of gaping-mouthed females in this muscled man's wake. Like all gods, if he did not leash his energy, humans of the opposite sex—sometimes of the same sex, too—turned into rioting, sexually flustered mobs.

"Good evening, Kinich." Votan took the barstool at his side.

"Nice of you to come, brother, but must you always flaunt your powers in public?" Kinich scolded to hide his uneasiness. Votan was the one brother whom he admired and respected above all others. But this was not a conversation either would enjoy. Kinich could only hope that Votan's sense of duty would prevail over his anger.

"Can't help it. It is impossible to contain such strength inside this humanlike body." Votan stretched his neck from side to side.

"Perhaps you need to return to our realm for a vacation," Kinich suggested.

"I cannot. Emma has forbidden it until things are"—Votan cleared his throat—"settled. So what's your excuse? Why haven't you returned?"

"I have been spending time with an old friend—a very old friend. One who may help us with the Obscuro problem."

"Who is he?"

"I am unable to discuss the details, Votan—"

"I no longer go by that name," Votan snarled.

"Ah yes." Kinich stifled a laugh. "You've chosen a new name. What is it that Emma calls you?"

Kinich knew, but enjoyed egging his brother on.

"Guy. She calls me Guy."

"Very modern," Kinich said teasingly.

The bartender tiptoed over like a gazelle about to serve two hungry lions. Kinich ordered a bottle of Chateau Petrus 2008.

Guy raised his two dark brows. "Yes. I bloody well like my new name. Nick, is it?"

"Touché." Only his brothers and sisters called him Kinich. Everyone else called him Nick. But the gods had many, many names, depending on the culture. Votan, on the other hand, now had just one: Guy. Guy Santiago. Not very deity-like, but whatever. Didn't change his gifts: killing and fighting.

"And why are you trying to butter me up with a three-thousand-dollar bottle of wine this evening?" Guy asked.

*No use in beating around the bush.* "This." Kinich held out the black jade amulet Cimil had given him and each of the gods at her party.

Guy sneered. "Thanks, I'm flattered, but I have several already . . . and a mate."

Kinich growled deep in his chest. "This isn't a fucking joke, Guy."

The bartender quietly crept up and served them each a glass of wine.

Guy thanked the man and then swilled the ruby-red liquid in his mouth before responding. "I'm well aware of your feelings, Kinich; Cimil warned me, though you are mistaken in your point of view. Chaam did not turn evil because of the black jade. He was already fucked in the head when he discovered it."

Chaam was the God of Male Virility who'd found the black jade mines in southern Mexico. The jade had the ability to absorb and blunt the gods' powerful energy in the physical world. With it, Chaam discovered he could be intimate and procreate with humans; both acts were an impossibility for any deity up until that point because prolonged contact with a god overloaded a human's circuits, so to speak.

However, no one knew for certain what caused Chaam to turn against humanity. Kinich still reeled with horror every time he thought of the hundreds of women Chaam had used to provide him with female offspring called Payals. Eventually, he would slaughter his female descendants and harvest their divine energy to fuel his apocalyptic weapons. A complicated, horrific mess.

"You are correct; the jade is not to blame for what happened to Chaam." Kinich sipped his wine. He much preferred a fine tequila or cognac, anything that burned, actually. "However, even Cimil admits she does not know the consequences of our using it. She thinks screwing humans is a recreation, like driving her latest new car."

"I assure you, screwing my fiancée is infinitely more enjoyable than a new Pagani—and trust me, I know. I have three. Paganis that is. Not fiancées. Emma would kill me if I ever looked at another woman."

Emma, one of the surviving Payals, was Guy's new fiancée and the love of his existence. His devotion to her went beyond disturbing and disgraceful. Guy pranced around like a sappy, lovesick fool.

*Sad. Simply . . . sad.* Kinich shook his head in disgust.

"What?" Guy barked defensively, misinterpreting Kinich's reaction. "I won the cars in a poker game from Cimil. Damn her, if she hasn't taken every automobile, carriage, and horse I've owned for the last three centuries. It was about time I won."

"Idiot. Cimil sees the future. She let you win."

"Who cares?" Guy shrugged. "They're Paganis. Still, nowhere near as enjoyable as a night with Emma."

"Yes, Emma is indeed special, brother. There will be consequences for bringing more Payals into this world. This black jade is nothing but a test—if we were meant to bear offspring, the Creator simply would have given us the ability."

Guy ran his hand through his long black hair. "We're hardly in a position to guess the Creator's intentions.

Who's to say this is not fate playing its hand, guiding us into a new era of our existence?"

"Or leading us to destruction," Kinich argued. "The universe is in a state of cataclysmic imbalance. If we do not intervene, the Maaskab will overrun the planet."

The Maaskab, a cult of dark priests, descendants of the Mayans and secretly ruled by Chaam before the gods managed to imprison him, grew more powerful by the day. Kinich suspected the Payals were somehow linked.

Guy sighed with irritation. "What is it that you want, Kinich?"

"I'm going to call it to a vote in the next summit. Creating offspring will be forbidden, punishable by banishment to the human world for eternity."

"Fuck you, sunshine boy," Guy growled under his breath. "You're not getting my vote. Emma's nesting, and if I don't give her a baby, she'll have my balls."

"Since when does a female, or anyone, decide your actions?" Kinich challenged.

Guy narrowed his luminescent aqua eyes. "I still decide. And I decide to make her happy. After everything that happened with her grandmother, all the suffering she's endured, I owe her this much."

Emma's grandmother, one of the first Payals, had disappeared several years ago and was believed killed by the Maaskab. Emma, Guy, and others later learned the hard way that they were wrong when she turned up on Guy's doorstep in Italy, leading an army of Maaskab. Obviously, her mind had been poisoned.

When the dust finally settled, they'd killed the Maaskab and captured the woman. Before they could cure her, she escaped. A traitor named Tommaso had made sure of it.

"Besides," Guy added, "have you ever seen Emma when she doesn't get what she wants? Now that she's been honing her powers and we've given her immortality..." He shivered. "No, thank you. She could make my life a living hell for eternity. I would rather face banishment."

Guy glanced at his watch. "Christ. Speaking of, I'm supposed to meet Emma and her parents for dinner. I'm late. She'll have my head." Guy promptly swallowed the last of his glass and gave Kinich an overly sharp slap on the back, thrusting Kinich forward on his stool.

"Good luck," said Guy, "but unless you can prove that having a child with Emma is detrimental to humanity, I'm sticking with marital harmony. And sex. Lots of sex."

Kinich swallowed hard, partially from the pain of the slap and partially from his current confusion.

How was it possible that a god as dedicated as Guy, who had sacrificed so much of himself throughout his existence to safeguard humanity, would say he'd rather be banished than displease a woman? He might expect such a response from mortals—their lives were fleeting and they were known for being overly obsessed with love. But Guy was the infamous God of Death and War. He was ruthless. A goddamned beast of destruction.

*Good gods, what is happening to us?*

If Kinich was going to convince the gods that procreation with humans would ultimately lead to their demise, then he needed to understand what he was truly up against.

# Seven

⌒

Almost twelve hours after I'd left Cimil's home, I stood across the street of yet another building, staring at its ornately carved stone entrance and revolving glass door. Only this time, it was a posh boutique hotel named Eden situated in Manhattan.

I'd managed to walk through the snow the entire eight blocks from the subway in three-inch heels and a tight black silk dress—the only suitable outfit I owned for a formal restaurant. Five hundred thousand dollars richer or not, I could never throw away money on frivolous comforts, even on my birthday. Not when there were so many people going without.

So there I was—10:00 p.m. on the dot—perfumed, plucked, slightly frozen, and ready for a meeting with a man I didn't know, was inexplicably obsessed with, and determined to leave behind forever once I'd upheld my part of the bargain: listening.

*And drooling.*

I slipped my mirror from my black handbag and made one last check. The walk and sprinkle of snow hadn't undone my sleek bun or makeup. I'd done a fantastic job of masking the circles under my dark green eyes, which now appeared greener than usual due to my red-tinged whites.

I sucked in a deep, fortifying breath and plowed across the street, with my knees wobbling, toward the hotel. A thin man in a black suit immediately greeted me at the door. He reached for my no-frills parka, and I slid it off while reminding myself that breathing mattered.

He returned quickly with a smile and a claim ticket. "Here you go, miss. Do you have a reservation?" he asked.

"I'm meeting someone." My eyes swept the formal, candlelit room to my right filled with cozy couples sipping wine, eating, and laughing. To the left, through a large open doorway, was a dimly lit bar decorated in a Deco style—mirror-covered walls, paintings of swanky 1920s flappers, and high-polished maple floors—packed with elegantly dressed patrons.

My eyes immediately gravitated toward the far end of the room. With his size, he stood out like a high-def, larger-than-life giant among a sea of washout gray.

I lost my breath for multiple heartbeats.

It seemed odd for such a magnificent man to be sipping wine alone. I expected to see a posse of adoring women groveling at his feet, perhaps nibbling on his ankles and kissing his toes. A tiny part of me rejoiced. I didn't want to share him with anyone, a realization that instantly scared the hell out of me.

*Sigh.* Who was I kidding? I wasn't there to listen. I was

there to gawk and fawn. Who could blame me? *Double sigh.* With eyes that pierced your very soul; those strong, full lips—the kind you wanted to run your tongue over and suck on or watch as they did delicious things to the most intimate parts of your body; his stratospheric height, wide shoulders, and thick caramel-colored hair hanging just past his collar...*triple sigh*...he was simply a specimen of divine masculinity.

I shook my head, realizing the bizarre truth. *Devil crackers, I want that man.* He was a complete stranger, yet I'd already had one erotic dream and played ten rounds of imaginary house with him.

I forced the breath into my lungs and willed my feet to make the journey.

Weaving through the crowd, I caught several brief glimpses of the male morsel in question as he stared into his wineglass. A prominent frown occupied his sublime face, and he clenched something in his fist. Whatever it was, he seemed troubled by it.

So there I was, facing his back and ready to wow him with my brilliant wit, when I realized I didn't know his name. Cimil had said it once, but I couldn't recall.

*Ugh.* I groaned inwardly. *Well, why not make the situation extra-extra-awkward?*

"Hi," I said.

Cimil's brother continued staring at his glass.

"Hello?"

Nothing.

He was completely checked out—*a family trait?*—and now several people to my side noticed I was being ignored by the delicious, brawny man sitting at the bar who everyone was desperately trying to avoid staring at.

Now I felt like an idiot.

I poked the back of his shoulder. "Hey—um..." Hell. Why couldn't I remember his name? "You."

With an irritated, deliberate slowness, he turned on his barstool, apparently ready to unleash a fury on whomever had disturbed his wine-templation.

His angry eyes settled on my face. "Oh. It's...you."

*Me? It's...me? Is that how a man greets the future mother of his child?*

*Whoa! Penelope! You're here to listen. Remember?*

*Yes, yes.*

Lucky for him, I wasn't going to hold a little thing like sorry manners against him, because I was frightfully close to losing my cerebral skills once again—*holy hell, a man has no right being that good-looking*—so I was pretty sure my own manners were about to fall off a cliff.

*Is groping a stranger in public considered bad manners?*

"Yep. It's me." I shrugged, grasping my evening bag in both hands.

He stared.

I stared.

He stared some more.

*Is this the standoff at the okay-we're-going-to-have-a-baby corral?*

*Penelope! Listen! Just listen!*

*Oh! Yeah.*

I finally decided to make the first move. A smile. Wasn't that the most original icebreaker? It was a timeless classic.

His intense turquoise eyes examined my face for several moments before a forced smile shaped his lips. "Care to sit?" He stood and held out his hand to offer me his seat.

*His large...strong...manly hand. Sigh.*

"Thanks."

"You look...nice," he commented in a slow, hypnotically deep voice.

Trying to ignore the sensuality embedded in his timbre, I flashed another polite smile and slipped past him. His gaze slid down my body, all the way to my black heels, and then swept up over my bare back as I lowered myself onto his barstool.

I lifted my chin a little higher then; he'd taken a detailed inventory.

"What would you like to drink?" he asked, wedging himself sideways in the space between me and the man next to us talking to his date.

The warmth of his touch made my insides light up and spin like a disco ball, but I played it cool. "I'll have a double, extra-dirty vodka martini."

He raised one brow.

*Well, jeez. I'm not pregnant.*

*Yet.*

*Oh, stop that!*

*But we want him! We want him!* my tiny eggs cheered in unison.

It was then that I noticed how his dark, tailored pants and gray sweater displayed every masculine bulge of his insanely ripped body. To be clear, he wasn't overbuilt like those artificially enhanced TV wrestlers who spend every waking moment pumping iron. No. This man was all hard, lean muscle, more like a champion stallion or a jaguar. Raw power draped in fine, expensive fabric.

Speaking of, where did a man of his girth and stature find clothes? Well, whoever was responsible for clothing him should be shot; he looked too perfect.

*He'd get cold if no one sold him clothes.*

*I'd warm him up.*

Just like he was doing to me. He was so darn tall that from a sitting position, I was at eye level with his nipples. No, I couldn't see them, but I knew they were there. Did they want to meet me as much as I wanted to meet them?

I cleared my throat. "I like a good stiff nipple"—*gasp!*—"I mean...*drink!* I like a stiff *drink* every once in a while. I'm not a big drinker if that worries you."

Ignoring my mental blip, he leaned over and planted his elbows on the bar. "And why would that worry me?"

*Okay. Because I'm sure you don't want the mother of your child to be a lush.*

*Pen! You're not on a job interview.*

"I don't want people getting the wrong impression, that's all," I clarified.

He ordered from the bartender who apparently knew him well because he scrambled to bring us our order ahead of everyone else.

"So," he said, his face a brick wall of seriousness, "what brought you here?"

Wow. It was such a complex question to answer straight out of the gate. My mother's life? A nagging little voice that told me I had to see him again? My awe-inspiring ability to ignore the weirdness of the situation? Take your pick. Something told me we weren't yet ready for a deep dive into Honesty Land.

I gave him my brightest smile. "They make the best dirty martinis in town. And you?"

I still couldn't understand why a man of his caliber needed a surrogate. Unless...unless he was the kind of man who was afraid of commitment.

*Then why have a child? Isn't that the biggest commitment there is?*

I mentally gasped. *Oh no! He's gay! Dammit. No!*

It all started to make sense. He was beyond gorgeous. He was also well dressed and wealthy.

*Yep. Totally gay. The best ones always are, Pen.*

Gravity gripped hard and pulled me crashing toward Earth while my secret little fantasy of making him all mine deflated with a whiz.

He gave a little chuckle. "Why am I here? I am staying here, of course." He raised his wineglass toward me and then took a sip.

"How long are you and your"—I mustered a polite smile—"your boyfriend in town for?" *And where is he? I'll scratch the bitch's eyes out!*

He hacked on his wine, but managed not to spit any out.

"I am...alone," he finally said. "And while I appreciate humanity in all its shapes and sizes, I place infinitely more value on the female form." His eyes traveled down to my breasts and lingered for several shocking yet exhilarating moments.

*He's not gay! He's not gay! Glory be thy name! And he just looked at my tatas!*

*Penelope. Focus. You're here to listen. Then you should definitely leave. You don't want to get mixed up with these people.*

Yes. What I needed was to get the conversation moving so I could get out of there. I'd promised to listen to his pitch, and I would. I'd even keep an open mind—I owed him that much—but in my heart of hearts, I knew he couldn't do or say anything to convince me to move forward with this transaction.

*Right. So let's get this show on the road.*

But how could I? My swooning was getting in the way. Maybe I needed to remind myself that men like him didn't go for girls like me. Any interest he might've shown was simply the male libido flashing its little tail feathers.

*Boooo! Booo! Quitter!* screamed my eggs.

Oh my God, I so needed to get out of there.

What could I say to get things rolling and break the ice? It wouldn't be easy when Cimil had given me three very, very weird rules.

One: I could not ask why they'd chosen me. That alone was a monumental sacrifice because the question burned in my gut like a festering ulcer. There had to be a reason. Perhaps something to do with the genetic testing I'd volunteered for when a group of specialists researched my mother's illness? It was plausible that my information ended up in one of those databases.

Two: I had to let her brother bring up the topic du jour first. He apparently felt very sensitive about the surrogate subject and found it difficult to discuss. She insisted I start out by getting to know him a little and waiting for him to open up.

Then there was demand number three: Under no circumstances could I tell anyone about our arrangement. Doing so would land me in "a very hot and dark place," she'd said.

*Cuckoo. Cuckoo.*

I cleared my throat and rallied my determination to see

this meeting through. "So, you live here? All alone?" I asked the beautiful man whose name I still couldn't recall.

"No. I am here for several weeks on business. My summer home is in Arizona. My winter home is in southern Mexico. I'm a sunshine kind of guy."

Well, that explained the killer tan. But having a summer home in Arizona? Wasn't that where people usually had winter retreats? He must really like hot weather.

*Who cares? Get him to start talking. Ask him something personal, though not too personal.*

I bit my lower lip. "Listen. I hope you're not insulted, but..."

He seemed surprised. Maybe a little suspicious, too. "Yes?"

"What's your name? Cimil told me, but I can't remember."

He tilted his head to one side. "Kinich. Kinich Ahau. My friends call me Nick. You may call me whichever you like."

*Now* it was official; I was gaga over everything about this man, even his two names. One was exotic. The other masculine and strong. "Those are...um...nice names."

He slid back the sleeve of his sweater and glanced at his watch.

Hmm. Was that a hint that he wanted me to leave? Or maybe he had a date later? And was that a Hublot?

*Crispy crackers! That watch is a year's worth of rent.* The only reason I knew was because it had been in the news recently, and I'd wondered what sort of man actually bought a watch like that. Well, now I knew. *A really, really sexy man who wants a baby. With me.*

*Listen! You. Are. Here. To listen!*

Okay. Now I really meant it; I needed to get out of there. Something about this man struck every irrational, horndoggy note in my body.

Perhaps if we went somewhere he felt more relaxed, he'd get to the meat of the matter. There was a quiet café around the corner.

"Kinich—um—Nick, do you want to go somewhere a little less crowded?"

He blatantly glowered. But why would he be annoyed with me?

Then, as if I'd imagined his initial reaction, I watched his gaze travel from my face down to my toes and back again.

"Yes. I think I'd like that." His voice was above a whisper, but its depth made my girlie parts quiver.

Without warning, he reached out and ran his thumb over my lower lip. "Why don't we go up to my suite." It wasn't a question.

*Sweet devil's food cake. He hit on me?*

*Me?*

*For real?*

If he had, then I was sooo over my head. One touch, one look, and I was ready to agree to anything he might ask. Dye my hair electric blue? Suuure. Rob a bank armed with a Twinkie? Anyyything you want. Have your baby? Ten of them? You betcha!

Oh, and his scent. It was an olfactory delight. I wanted someone to bottle it and put it on my fabric softener sheets so I could wear it.

I dipped my head slowly, meanwhile my mind swam in a lusty fog named Nick, um, Kinich.

I removed myself from the barstool, and when I felt his

toasty warm palm brush across the base of my bare back, I was pretty darn sure I'd somehow acquired an addiction to him. And that meant I'd do almost anything to have him touch me again.

We entered the suite, and I tried to keep from gawking like the middle-class apartment dweller that I was. Expensive things, wealth, they never mattered much to me—I was too busy worrying about things that really mattered, I suppose—but this hotel was truly beyond the luxury I'd ever known: gray-and-red modern furniture; expensive-looking paintings; large, open living room; and flat-screen TV the size of my entire apartment. All overlooking the city.

An awkward silence filled the elevator ride to the penthouse while my mind did a few laps around the logic tree. It kept landing on the same exact branch: This man turned me into a ball of hormones, where logic had no clout. I wanted him. I wanted him in a way that defied rational thought or a need for self-esteem.

*Danger, Will Robinson. Danger.*

He proceeded to the bar in the corner. "Make yourself comfortable."

*Got a Snuggie and some Old Navy Uggs knockoffs?*

I made my way to the couch facing the panoramic window overlooking the shimmering city dusted with snow. With as much grace as I could muster, I sat and tried to hide how nervous he made me.

He quickly returned and handed me another dirty martini. "Hope it's to your standards."

I took a tiny sip. It was god-awful. "It's perfect.

Thanks." I flashed a forced smile, thankful that I'd finally found at least one teeny-tiny flaw in the man.

"So." He sat down next to me, incredibly close. I felt my heart begin to thump wildly in my chest. "I sense I make you anxious, Penelope. Are you certain you wish to be here?"

I took a large swig, feeling the vodka sear its way down my throat. I turned my body to more easily see his face.

Mistake.

He made me absolutely tongue-tied. My reaction to him, simply put, was unknown territory for me.

Yes. I'd dated men before. I'd even managed to have two relationships. One when I was seventeen and the other when I was twenty-two. Each lasted about a year, but even in the I'm-so-into-you phases of those relationships, I'd never felt so lacking in control over my emotions. Maybe that's what excited me about Kinich, Nick, *still can't decide*—he made me feel like...like...*not me.*

Escape.

I craved it.

"Yes," I finally replied after several moments of silence. "I want to be here."

He reached out with his hand, but then jerked it away when the door buzzed. He made a little growl. It was so sexy that my nipples instantly perked.

He got up and headed for the door. I heard the low rumble of voices before the door closed.

Kinich returned with a bottle of Dom Pérignon in a silver wine bucket and placed it on the glass coffee table in front of us.

"What's the occasion?" I asked.

"A debt being paid."

"Sorry?"

"I bet my sister that she could not have a party without the police being called."

"You mean the party last night?" I recalled Cimil mentioning something about a policeman Twister mishap.

"Fifty arrests this time. She topped her record."

Somehow, I wasn't so surprised. Nor did I really care for details; I didn't want to talk about his crazy, scary sister.

He gestured toward the bottle. "Would you like a glass?"

Since his martini could melt the chrome off a bumper, I accepted. I'd actually never tried Dom Pérignon.

He poured two glasses and took his spot next to me. *Close. So very, very close.* Once again his eyes set on my face and he stared.

The intensity made me squirm. "Why do you keep looking at me like that?"

He narrowed his eyes. "Like what?"

"Like you can't decide if you want to throw me out or kiss me."

*Crap! I can't believe I said that. Dork.*

He didn't flinch. "Because that is exactly what I am thinking."

A lump stuck in my throat. I looked away as I tried to clear it.

I took a large sip of my champagne and then met his gaze pound for pound, note for note, unspoken word for word. "So. What have you decided?"

He sipped his champagne and nodded at the glass, approving its taste.

My heart raced a million miles an hour.

What would he say?

*Wait.* What *am I doing trying to seduce this man?* I was Penelope Trudeau. A normal, everyday person with normal, everyday looks. I worked for minimum wage plus tips and lived in a world so different from his. Not to mention he was shopping for a "baby momma." This was silly.

Suddenly, panic overtook me. I stood up. "I made a mistake coming here."

Within the space of a breath, his large body caged me, and his full, delicious lips were over mine. His hot, sweet tongue slipped in my mouth, instantly sending a delicious current of flutters and tingles straight down the center of my body between my legs.

I wanted this. I wanted this so badly. It was better than my dream. Every cell and nerve ending lit up with a tension I knew wouldn't abate until I had this man deep inside me. It was primal and needy and liberating all rolled into one erotic mess.

A tiny moan escaped my lips as my core did wild cartwheels. Image after image of how I wanted to explore his body, of how I wanted him to take me, pummeled my mind. It was so damn intense that I needed to catch my breath.

I planted my palms on his hard chest and pulled away. "What was that?" I panted.

He nuzzled my neck. "I believe it is what people call... chemistry."

He pulled me closer, and I had no doubt that the hardness jutting from his groin was anything but chemistry. It was the timeless, primal call of biology.

His mouth, hot and demanding, returned to mine as the room began to spin.

The next morning, I slowly stretched my deliciously sore body while luxuriating in the softness of the silky sheets beneath me and the warm, oh-so-very-naked, well-built man snuggled to my side.

My heart fluttered when I opened my eyes and found Nick sleeping next to me, his bed-play-mussed, golden-brown hair sweeping to one side across the pristine, white pillow. His heavenly eyes were closed, allowing me to study the golden lashes fanning out against his bronzed face, looking like tiny threads of caramelized sugar. He was a picture of exquisite male perfection.

I sighed and resisted the urge to kiss his exposed, chiseled chest—yes, yes, perfectly tanned like the rest of him (*nude sunbather?*)—and stroke the perfectly formed swells of his biceps, one of which was attached to the arm draped over my waist.

Last night had been the most . . . the most . . .

I sprang from the bed in horror. "Oh, crap!"

Nick's eyes instantly popped open. A warm smile swept across his face. "Oh, you're up." His large frame stretched across the length of the extra-long, king-size bed.

I stared at him, wondering what to say; somehow screaming, "Oh my God! Oh my God! Oh my God!" didn't seem appropriate.

*Okay. Breathe, Penelope. Breathe. Just ask him what happened!*

I didn't want to insult the guy. Because from the look of his delectable body, it had to have been the best night of my life.

*That is . . . that is . . . if we did.*

*Of course you did! Look! Even your eggs are smoking a cigarette.*

*No! Demon crackers, no!*

He rolled onto his side and propped his head up with his arm. "Why are you standing there naked? Come back to bed."

I glanced down at my body. Oh, crappity! I *was* naked.

I scrambled to the bathroom, a large, modern affair of stainless steel and glass, and grabbed a fluffy, white towel.

*Oh, shit. Oh, shit.* What was going on? I needed to go out there and ask him, point-blank, what happened. *Not with your iguana breath. You might melt the man's face off.*

*As long as I get to keep his rockin' body.*

*Pen!*

I quickly found a bottle of mouthwash in the cabinet and swished. Then I checked the mirror and noticed I was wearing an odd-looking necklace with a large, shiny black stone dangling in the middle. Had he put it on me last night?

Darn it! Why couldn't I remember what had happened? *Don't be a child, Penelope. Ask him.*

Yes. That's what I would do.

Again I glanced in the mirror. "Oh no," I hissed at my reflection. My dark hair resembled a beehive, but without the symmetry. I ran my fingers through the mess a few times, but it was useless. I'd have to make a polite exit, go home, and ensure I looked hot enough on our next date to erase any memories of my current discombobulation. *Is that even a word, Penelope? And do you really think he wants to date you? You're a one-nighter for a guy like that.*

Christ. What had I gotten myself into?

I took three quick breaths and opened the door. My heart ignited from the sight of him still propped up on one elbow and lying in bed with a smug, male smile stretched across his face. He looked frigging perfect, practically glowing. *Dammit. So unfair!*

"Everything okay?" he asked.

I smiled sheepishly. "Yeah, I needed to wrangle the tornado." I pointed to my matted hair.

"You look sexy as hell." He patted the empty space next to him. "Come here."

Mischief sparkled in his eyes, and though I didn't know him well, I knew what that look meant: encore.

I held up my hands. "Whoa. I think we need to talk."

His lower lip stuck out in a slight pout and his shimmering eyes seemed to glow against the backdrop of his toasty-almond-colored skin. Damn if he wasn't the most irresistible man on the planet.

And he wanted me. Wow.

I slowly padded over to the bed. "Please don't take this the wrong way, but what happened last night?"

He cocked one brow. "You don't remember?"

I shook my head and gave him an apologetic smile. "I'm sure it was...great. The best toe-curling sex ever— but...no, I don't remember a thing."

His smile melted away. "Bloody Christ! Neither do I."

From the living room, I heard Nick scream the f-word in fifty different languages and then, "I'm going to fucking kill her!"

That got my attention. I hoped he didn't mean me.

Nick appeared nude in the doorway, holding the bottle of champagne upside down.

Now I desperately wanted to hear what he had to say, because, let's face it, this was a serious situation. Nonetheless, I found myself dumbstruck by his perfectly chiseled abs that rippled for miles. My eyes traveled over his belly button and lower stomach, not a strand of hair to be found until they reached nirvana: a patch of dark brown hair just above his...

*That can't be real. Can it?*

It was long and thick and larger than any penis I'd ever seen or imagined.

Nick cleared his throat.

My gaze darted back to his face.

"Sorry, I was just...just..."

*...ogling your giant man-sicle.*

*Change subjects! The bottle. Look at the bottle. Why is he holding it up?*

"I've had a lot more than that before but didn't black out," I offered.

"That's because our champagne had something extra in it."

He rubbed his finger over the opening of the bottle and then sniffed the drop of liquid. His sour expression drove the point home.

"Someone roofied the champagne?"

He ranted as he stalked over to the dresser and pulled out some clothes. "Typical fucking Cimil. I should have known better than to trust her. That manipulative, conniving, heartless, fucked-up..."

As he delivered every expletive known to man, my

brain did the mental math. This situation was beyond bizarre. I mean, why would his very own sister drug us? And if he thought she was so insane and untrustworthy, why would he ask her to help him find a mother for his child?

*Unless…unless…Holy. Frigging. Hell. Unless she really is crazy.*

"Nick, why did you ask Cimil to help you?"

If gorgeous looks could kill, I'd be a pile of dust. "Help me?" he fumed. "You think I asked her to drug you?"

"No. I mean…with that other thing."

"*What* other thing?" His tone signaled that he teetered on the edge of massive rage.

Oh, this was bad. Really, really bad.

I plunked down on the edge of the bed and threw my hands over my face. "I knew it didn't make any sense. Why didn't I listen to myself?" I whispered.

"What the devil are you talking about, woman? What did my sister do?"

"Idiot! You're an idiot, Penelope." I shook my head from side to side, berating myself aloud. "How could I have been so stupid? Attractive, intelligent, wealthy—not that I care—but he could have any woman he wants, probably most men, too."

Nick crouched down in front of me and tipped up my chin to meet his glare. "I repeat. What in the devil's name are you talking about, woman?"

A lump of dread stuck in my throat. "Your sister? The baby?"

"Bloody hell." His hand snapped back as if I had cooties. "Baby?"

I had the distinct feeling my entire body was about to shatter into a million pieces. "The one she said you wanted to have with...me?" I gulped.

His eyes moved to the black stone pendant around my neck. "Son of a bitch! I'll bloody kill her!"

"Wait!" I screamed. "Where are you going?"

"To wring Cimil's neck!"

Holy shit. Had this dream just turned into my worst nightmare? "Are you telling me you didn't know anything about this? Or the one million dollars?"

Shirtless, he swiveled to face me. An intense heat exuded from his direction. Was it my imagination?

"One. Million. Dollars?" he growled.

"Yes! How can you *not* know about this? I get five hundred thousand for showing up. The other if we actually have a baby." I slapped my hands over my mouth. "Oh, God. That came out all wrong."

"She paid you to sleep with me?" His roar rattled the windows.

I adjusted the towel, making it tighter around my body. "First of all, you and I aren't sure we actually did the deed. Besides, it wasn't like that." I reached for him, but he pushed my hand away. "Hey!"

He took two steps toward me and leaned down, putting us nose to nose. "Then, like what?" he snarled.

Was this really happening? And where did he get off snarling at me? At *me*!

"I agreed to hear you out, not sleep with you. Christ!" I snarled back.

"You set me up! Admit it!"

"Oh my God! You actually think I had something to do with this? How can you say that? She came to me! She told me she was helping you. There was never any talk about sex. Ever!"

"Then why the hell did you come up here?"

"I told you . . . to listen to you. That was all! I agreed to keep an open mind."

"No! You came here to obtain my seed." His voice reverberated in my ears.

*Oh my God! What a barbaric jerk! What kind of man calls his semen his "seed." What a frigging ego!* I stood in front of him, refusing to let his size intimidate me. "I came up here because I thought you would be more comfortable talking somewhere in private."

His unblinking stare called my bluff.

"Okay! I admit I wanted you! Are you saying you didn't want me back? 'Cause it sure the hell felt like it!"

"I-I . . ." He blinked. "I would have used precautions."

At least he threw me that bone.

"Well, we don't even know if we . . . you know," I mumbled.

He narrowed his eyes again.

"Okay," I admitted, "odds are slim we didn't go to Lambada Land considering how we woke up, but we really don't know—"

"Drop the act," he scolded and then reached for a neatly folded navy-blue sweater in his dresser drawer.

I held the white towel to my chest, wishing to God I had on a suit of armor to protect me from this painful conversation. Or had at least used a condom last night—if we'd even done it. Not that I was afraid of getting any diseases; that welcome handbook Cimil had absurdly given me yesterday morning included her brother's latest blood work and physical results. It was almost as odd as the list of dos and don'ts.

**DO NOT ever open the door for anyone who refuses to identify himself or herself.**

*Hello. I'm from New York City. How naive do you think I am?*

**If you smell the stench of rotting animals, DON'T walk the other way...RUN!**

*Okay, that is just weird.*

**DO tell Cimil how fabulous she looks when you see her.**
  **DON'T hide behind garbage Dumpsters.**

The bizarre and useless list went on and on. At least, the stupid handbook gave me the assurance that Nick was disease-free. Now, if only it had told me...

*What the HELL is going on!?*

He pulled the sweater over his head. "You're obviously a part of Cimil's absurd scheme," he grumbled. "And she paid you, no less."

My blood officially boiled then. He'd insulted me in every way possible, short of calling me a whore.

*No, actually, I think he just did!*

I felt my face turn a shameful shade of red. That made me even more livid. I wanted to throw something at him. Something big, heavy, maybe even sharp. Oh yeah.

I threw the only thing I had: the towel. "You and your crazy sister can go to hell!"

Nick's body froze, and his eyes locked on my breasts. Before I could regret my decision to throw—yes, of all things—a soft, fluffy towel to demonstrate my anger, he had crossed the room and pulled me into his body. He dipped his head but held his lips one centimeter away from mine. I wasn't sure if I should be afraid or extremely turned on.

He huffed in frustration, released me, and grumbled at the pendant.

The last thing I heard was Kinich slamming the front door behind him.

I tore the necklace off and threw it. "Take it! I don't want your stupid necklace!"

# *Eight*

*Two Weeks Later*

What a difference a few weeks and a substantial amount of money can have on someone's life. Mine, for example, had changed in ways I thought only possible in dreams. My mother had left the previous day for Sweden to begin her treatment. I'd quit my horrible, backbreaking job and taken a position as a karate instructor at our neighborhood martial arts academy. I'd missed the deadline for the spring semester at NYU weeks ago, but planned to apply for a third time and start in the fall.

For the first time in years, it seemed my life was looking up. Except that I couldn't forget my night with Kinich, nor could I remember it—a thought that preoccupied me every second of each day. Even when I slept, I dreamed about the man, especially his smell—like a tropical beach filled with fresh, clean ocean air, coconuts, and exotic plants. He smelled like sunshine.

Then there was his body. I couldn't stop fantasizing about the hard lines of his golden skin or the sound of his voice as he groaned my name. I repeatedly saw images of his fierce eyes boring into me as he pushed himself deep inside my body.

That was a dream, not a memory.

Wasn't it?

For as many hours as I'd racked my brain, trying to remember any smidgen of detail from those missing hours, I came up woefully short. The only evidence of my conduct had been my slightly sore body, but not sore in places one would expect after having a wild night with a man as well-endowed as Nick—umm—Kinich. *Still can't decide.* Could it be possible that we'd simply had a wild, kinky make-out session with heavy petting, and then passed out?

If only I could remember something. Anything. Because at this point, the only thing I knew for certain was that the darn man had embedded himself in my mind, and I hated him for it. Not only him, I hated his lunatic sister, too.

I'd actually stopped by Cimil's several times to tell her so, only to be turned away by her grumpy maid—a short, sassy woman in her sixties—who insisted her boss was away indefinitely, and not hiding as I suspected.

In any case, now that my anger had subsided somewhat, I wasn't sure what I'd say if I finally saw her. "I hate you for changing my life?" Because as painful as the situation might be, I couldn't ignore the fact that my mother meant everything to me. And now, she might live. That was a fact. *That* made everything else water under the bridge. Everything except...I was late. Twelve days late. Oh yes. My night with Nick had been at peak ovulation.

"What were you thinking?" I said aloud, spinning my ring, the one my mother gave me—damn thing wouldn't come off—while I stared at the little white plastic stick sitting on the edge of the sink. The two minutes had passed, but I couldn't bear to look.

*Chicken! Go over there and pick it up.*

The phone rang, and I practically jumped from my skin. It was almost 9:00 p.m., just about the right time for my mom to be checking into her hotel.

I scrambled to my bedroom and answered. "How was the flight?"

"Penelope?" said the deep voice on the other end.

My heart dropped to the floor. *That voice. Oh, demon wafers, that voice.* I wanted to weave it into a blanket and wear it wrapped around my naked body.

"What do you want, Nick?" I responded.

Awkward silence. "To apologize."

*Too little, too late.* "How very big of you." My mind flooded with images of his face. I couldn't help but start to feel pliable and needy.

Thankfully, my rational side kicked in, countering, *He treated you like scum, Penelope. He called you a liar. He had zero sympathy for how his sister manipulated you.*

"I have to go."

"Penelope. Wait."

I didn't respond.

"Are you...?" he said.

I knew what he was asking. I had the same question,

and the answer was in the other room displayed in that little clear-view window with a plus or minus sign. And if it showed a plus, then what? I certainly didn't know how I felt about the situation, but I knew two things: he had no interest in having a baby, and I was a full-grown educated woman who was ready to accept the consequences of her actions.

It was true that Cimil had treated us to a lovely bottle of Dom Roofie, but I couldn't overlook my contribution to the situation. I'd decided to go to his hotel room. Me. No one else.

"Penelope, my treatment of you was less than honorable. However, you should know that I returned to the room almost immediately to tell you so. You were already gone."

*Sure. Right.* I thought *I* was a bad liar.

"And then you waited two weeks to call," I chided.

Silence.

"Look," I finally said, "you don't need—"

"Cimil has been unreachable, and I did not know your last name or where to find you so I had to hire someone. I was given your number ten minutes ago. Apparently, Penelope is a very popular name."

He'd gone looking for me? I felt my anger tick down by about ten notches. "Oh." Now I didn't know what to think or exactly how to feel.

*Um... that's called confused, genius.*

Yes. Confused. He'd come looking for me, wanting to apologize, and I had to admit it made me feel...good. A little too good. But that didn't change my situation or the fact that I wanted nothing to do with him and his psycho family.

"To answer your question, there's nothing to worry about, if you know what I mean," I lied. Or maybe I wasn't lying. Wouldn't really know until I faced that little white stick.

"Are you still wearing the necklace?"

*So that's why he's calling? To find out about his stupid necklace?*

My anger dialed right back up again.

Well, if he hadn't found it lying in the middle of the floor where it landed after I hurled it at him, perhaps it had grown legs or walked away with the hotel maid. *Serves him right!*

"No. I left it at your hotel."

"I see," he said, sounding mildly disappointed, followed by a long pause. "May I see you?"

Wait. He still wanted to see me? So this wasn't about the necklace? I felt so...

*Confused?*

"Why? Why do you want to see me? I'm just some seed thief." Dammit. I hadn't meant to sound that bitter, but I did. Oops.

"I bought you flowers," he grumbled.

"Flowers? Why?" This is when I'm supposed to say that flowers wouldn't buy him a ticket to forgiveness. However, my ego said otherwise.

"I am told this is how men apologize."

"What kind of flowers?"

*Idiot. I can't believe you asked him that.*

Okay, but this was important. Red roses were a world apart from begonias.

"Monkshoods," he replied.

What the heck was a monkshood?

*Wait. Penelope, are you seriously worried about what type of flowers he bought you? Let's do a little fact-check. Crazy sister. He treated you like garbage. Men like him don't date women like you.*

*This, my dear, is a booty call.*

*Gasp!*

"I'm going to have to say no," I replied.

"The word *no* only counts if it comes from me."

There was a loud knock at the front door.

*Smug jerk! He's already here!*

We lived in a secure apartment building, so I assumed he'd snuck in while someone was leaving.

"How dare you! You can't just come here uninvited!" I threw down the phone on the bed and marched to the front door. I yanked it so hard it flew open and practically walloped me in the shoulder. By the time my brain registered that it wasn't Nick, it was too late.

So I screamed instead.

⌒

Kinich's shock from Penelope's refusal to see him was still reeling in his head—*what? She doesn't want to see me? Me? I am a god, for Christ's sake!*—when he heard Penelope's gut-wrenching scream erupt in the background.

"Penelope!" he roared into his cell and immediately ran for the door of his hotel room. It was the one and only time in his entire existence that he would have exchanged all his powers to be a vampire who could sift. She was a good twenty minutes away by car, ten without traffic.

Wearing nothing but a pair of jeans, he scrambled barefoot to the elevator and jabbed at the call button.

*Fuck!* He couldn't simply stand there, waiting for a goddamned elevator.

He slammed his fist into the wall, leaving wires hanging from the gaping hole. "Fucking hell." He bolted for the stairwell, descending ten steps at a time. When he finally reached the lobby, he was unnervingly close to losing control and unleashing his power. Not good. That would have left the few thousand people within a four-block radius looking as though they'd been sizzled in a microwave.

Kinich roared instead. Penelope was being murdered by whom or what, he did not know, but there was nothing he could do to save her.

Dammit! He was a fucking god! He channeled the power of the sun. He could compel any human with his voice! But he wasn't powerful enough to save one goddamned mortal? A mortal he'd now become reluctantly fascinated with, a fucking first for him at a really bad fucking time.

When the yellow cab pulled to the curb, he focused his energy on four simple thoughts: the traffic would clear, all of it; the driver would obey him; he *would* save Penelope; and come hell or high water, he would never, ever be stuck in this fucking situation again.

"Drive or I'll castrate you!"

Kinich burst into Penelope's apartment through the front door, which was left ajar. A broken potted plant lay in the center of the living room floor next to her Italian mosaic tiled coffee table. All of the lights were on, and a purse had been left sitting on the armchair in the corner of the room.

"Penelope!" He ran into what had to be her bedroom; it smelled like her.

*Empty.*

"Bloody hell."

Kinich closed his eyes and opened his senses. He hoped to feel or hear anything that might indicate which direction she'd been taken. If he could figure out that much, he had a chance of catching up.

*Unless she's been taken by an Obscuro.* Which he prayed wasn't the case. Obscuros—dark vampires— were multiplying like cockroaches, and missing persons reports were through the roof. It was believed they were turning their victims, building an army to prepare for the Great War that Cimil had prophesied.

This was the reason he'd come to New York in the first place; he'd been spending some quality time with an old—very, very old—friend who might help with this problem. For a price, naturally.

Kinich sensed a small disturbance in the air to his side, like a void or an absence of light. Once again, he closed his eyes and allowed his mind to drift into the atmosphere, hoping to catch a tiny whiff of her essence in the air.

*There!*

His eyes flew open, and he darted for the door. He almost reached the threshold to the outer hallway when his eyes caught another glimpse of the broken potted plant. A tiny clump of bloody hair stuck to one jagged edge of a large piece of the pot.

His heart skipped exactly three beats. "Holy saints."

He picked up the shard and gave it a whiff. He immediately tossed it back to the floor when the foul stench permeated his nose.

*Not an Obscuro.*

"Fucking Maaskab."

Why would they want Penelope?

# Nine

You know that scene in *Alien vs. Predator* when the woman stands right in front of Mr. Predator, almost pees in her pants, and then decides to team up with him to avoid becoming alien chow? Well, facing that monster standing at my door had been exactly like that. Only without the teaming-up part because I was pretty dang sure he'd viciously murder me on the spot.

*No. Not going to be sci-fi BFFs.*

The hulking beast occupied my entire doorway with his deadly looking, soot-covered body clothed in a black leather loincloth of sorts. His hair was unlike anything I'd ever seen: long black ropes of crusty dreads down to his midsection. He looked like he'd shampooed, rinsed, and conditioned it in a slaughterhouse, and then, for good measure, did a little spritz with evil stench behind the ears.

I immediately gagged from the smell and sprinted to

the kitchen where the only weapon in the apartment lay tucked away in a drawer.

The man, monster, demon—whatever—caught me by my hair, and I flew back with a snap that nearly broke my neck. My body arched painfully backward as he fisted my hair and pressed my head against his foul-smelling chest. Snarling and growling, his black-and-crimson eyes drilled into me.

"What do you want?" I managed to croak.

He said nothing, but an unmistakable sense of doom crept into my bones.

He lowered his head ever so slightly and took a long, hard whiff. His eyes rolled back in his head.

*Holy hounds of hell.*

At such an angle I felt the muscles in my back stretching and pulling in an unnatural direction. I had to do something. Anything.

Across the back of my arm, I felt the tiny tickle of my giant, feathery philodendron that sat on the center of my coffee table. I reached out my hand and grasped a bundle of leaves close to the roots and swung hard. I landed a blow on the side of the monster's head.

He stumbled for a moment and released me to the floor.

I righted myself and bolted to the kitchen, where I yanked open the knife drawer and sent its contents scattering across the floor. The giant Chinese cleaver landed an inch from my big toe.

*That was a close call, little piggy!*

I swooped for it and then quickly reached for something else to hurl.

*The cookie jar on the counter!* Empty, of course. Snickerdoodles. I ate them.

The moment the monster appeared in the doorway, I smashed the jar in the center of his face. Blood gushed from his nose, but he simply smiled and flashed his blackened teeth.

I raised my cleaver and swung. He jumped to the side, catching my wrist. How had he moved so frigging fast?

He lunged for me, but I quickly twisted my body and used his momentum to throw him off-balance. He did a face-plant. I took advantage and slammed the entire weight of my body into an elbow thrust at the back of his neck.

"That's right, asshole. Black belt!" I bounced up and gave him a kick in the ribs for good measure.

Then he started to get up.

"What are you? Voodoo Terminator?"

I wasn't going to stick around for an answer to that question. I bolted for the front door, swiped my boots, and didn't stop running until I was at least ten blocks away. In the back of my mind, I'd planned on going to the nearest police station, another ten blocks, or throwing myself in front of the nearest patrol car.

But fantastic miracles do happen! *No traffic?* Of course, for me, at the wrong time. The one day ever that I wanted to see an abundance of people and cars, and the street was vacant? Normally, at this time of evening, there would be traffic aplenty.

Okay. The best plan of action was to get as far away as possible, then go to the police.

I started running again, my bare feet ice-cold and wet, toward the subway station. I rounded the corner to my right. The monster emerged from a side street directly ahead with his back to me. How the hell had he ended up in front of me?

I made a split-second decision to turn back the way I'd come. I ran one block, then hooked to my right down an alley.

*Shit. Shit.* It was a dead end. Why had I gone that way?

I turned around and darted back out to the street, thinking I'd simply continue running until the next block. The moment I emerged from the alley, the bastard was there again. *Again! How?*

I dashed back into the alley, stopping halfway down its length, panting and on the verge of an epic freak-out. *Where do I go? Where? Where? Think dammit. Think, Penelope!*

It was a dead end for Christ's sake. There was only one choice: hide behind the Dumpster in the middle of the alley.

I bolted toward my sanitation sanctuary, crouched, and tried to calm my breathing. With the city's eerie silence, a mouse scratching its privates could be heard for ten blocks.

*Oh, please, God. Oh, please. Help me,* I prayed silently with my hands clasped.

*You're agnostic, Penelope. Think that's gonna really work?*

*Doesn't hurt to try . . .*

Then it struck me. Cimil's handbook.

It had read not to open the door for people who don't identify themselves. Run in the opposite direction of rotting stench. Do not hide behind Dumpsters.

What the hell was going on? Was she some sort of psychic?

Now what would I do? I was hiding behind the Dumpster. Just like Cimil had instructed not to.

*Hide inside the Dumpster.*

No. I can't. This was New York City—there could be anything in there: rotten food, broken glass, a dead body.

*You idiot. You're going to be the dead body if he finds you.*

*Oh, hell.* What had I done to deserve this?

I slowly peeked around the edge of the Dumpster toward the main street. The coast was clear for the moment. I slipped on my boots; lifted the heavy, plastic-molded lid; and slipped inside.

The stench was—*freaking instant-gag-reflex smells of hell!*—the most god-awful thing my nose had ever witnessed. Old fish and rotten eggs mixed with something dead. Thank the universe for small favors such as winter, because had it been summer, my tossed cookies would be joining those smells.

Regardless, I pinched my nose and clamped my eyes shut.

*Find a weapon. Anything. A glass bottle, a lid to a tin can, anything.*

*Oh, I hate you,* I argued with myself, *and your practical advice!*

I reached out my hand, instantly finding something squishy and wet.

*Ew, ew, ew.*

I stretched my hand a little farther and found something long and hard. I wrapped my fingers around it and—

The lid flew open. My reflexes instantly took over, and I sprang from the Dumpster, swinging with everything I had.

An arm reached out in midair and caught my wrist. "Penelope? What the hell are you doing inside there?"

Kinich's towering mass stood before me, barefoot and shirtless.

*Kinich!*

I was never so happy to see anyone in my entire life. I jumped and flung my arms around his neck. "Oh, thank God!"

I instantly felt my body hum with delight. His smell, his warmth ... Touching him felt like being bathed in a euphoric tropical wave complete with magical sea horses and mermaids and ... *endless orgasms*?

He gently pushed me away and crinkled his nose. "Jeez, woman. You smell awful." He glanced at my hand. "And why are you holding that?"

"What?" I looked at my right hand. Yes. I was indeed gripping a stale baguette.

How very deadly.

I dropped it to the ground and began rattling on about what had happened. Kinich stared at me like I was insane.

*But wait.* "Not that I'm ungrateful—hell, I'm so happy to see you, I would name my first child after ... I can't believe I said that."

He frowned.

"How did you find me?" I finally asked. "And what happened to your clothes? Are you okay? You must be freezing."

Kinich considered my questions, clearly thinking long and hard about his answers. "I heard your scream and—"

It happened so fast, my brain simply couldn't process it.

Kinich flew to one side and landed with a smack on the cement. The monster was on top of him, trying to wrap some sort of bumpy-looking rope around his neck. Kinich grunted with pain for a moment and then screamed, "Penelope, get back in the Dumpster!"

"But..."

"Do it now, woman!"

I didn't know what else to do, so I obeyed.

As soon as the lid thumped down, a burst of blinding light flashed outside. My eyes instinctively squeezed shut, and I turned away to shield my face from the heat seeping in through the tiny gap of the heavy lid.

Then it was over, and I heard Kinich moaning.

I slowly peeked out and saw him lying on the cement. A pile of ash covered his half-naked body, and the monster was gone.

# *Ten*

My mind shuffled through all the possible explanations of what I'd just witnessed. Someone had put LSD in the public water supply, hoping to create the next Steve Jobs?

*No.*

*Matrix* the movie was real, and I'd lived through a binary blip?

*No.*

Asleep?

*No.*

Deep coma? *Not on your life.*

*Well, poop! This can't be real! Give me something. Anything! I don't want the only plausible explanation to be that I'm crazy. That would suck. Badly.*

*Penelope, maybe now's not the time to figure it out.*

Kinich writhed on the ground.

"Oh, hell." I climbed from the Dumpster and rushed

to his side. "Are you okay? What's wrong? How do I help you?"

His anguished expression seemed only to worsen. "Just...ahhhh"—he rolled to his side, then back again—"give me a second."

"Oh, okay." My hands hovered over him, eagerly awaiting any instructions.

After a minute, his face relaxed and his breathing steadied. "Help me up."

"Um—sure." I stood and latched onto his hand—it was boiling hot—and began pulling him up. With a few awkward grunts and heaves he was up, steadying himself on my shoulders.

"We need to get you somewhere safe," he said, his voice low and raspy. "More might be coming."

*Demons on whole wheat toast! There are more?*

He yanked me by the hand and started for the nearby street. He muttered something unintelligible under his breath.

"Sorry?" I said.

"Get in."

*Get into what...?*

A cab pulled up directly in front of us.

*What the...?* "There were no cars a minute ago. It's the weirdest goddamned thing..."

Kinich yanked open the door and shoved me in. He quickly gave instructions to the driver and then closed his eyes.

*He's closing his eyes? Of all the possible ways to react to this situation, and this guy wants a nap?*

"Would you care for a blankie and a graham cracker?"

He didn't move an inch.

"Excuse me. But mind telling me ... What! The! Hell! Is going on!"

Kinich cracked open one turquoise eye, gave me a "don't mess with me" look, and then snapped it shut again.

"Excuse me," I screamed, "I get that whatever happened back there was very rough on you! And that you're probably suffering from frostbite on your toes and nipples"—*look at that chest. Holy shit, he's so damned built*—"but I just had some Medusa-haired monster who smelled like cooked innards show up to my apartment to kill me."

"He wasn't there to kill you," Kinich interrupted. "Not yet anyway."

"Thanks. Thanks for removing the turd from my punch bowl. But it still smells like shi—"

"Penelope!" His eyes snapped open. "Please be silent. I am trying to think."

*How. Dare. He!* I poked his bare arm—*oh ... so strong.* "Don't you ever talk to me like that again. Do you hear me?"

He sighed. "Damned humans. Never listen." He focused in on my eyes. "Sleep, Penelope. Sleep."

Like I'd been hypnotized into thinking that was exactly what I wanted to do, my eyes closed and my brain slipped into the abyss.

# Eleven

⌒

"Not going to happen, buddy," barked Andrus through the cracked door. "I already have two females to look after. And what the hell happened to your clothes?"

"Who needs clothes when you're as hot as me," Kinich replied with a grin. Holding Penelope in his arms made him feel like a dopey kid with a new, shiny toy. "Now open the door."

Andrus began shutting it instead.

Kinich shoved his bare foot in the opening and then pushed his shoulder into the door, careful not to crush Penelope.

Andrus stumbled back several feet. "Gods dammit! Goddamned gods never goddamn listen!"

Kinich marched through the living room, making a beeline to the guest quarters. "You know that makes no sense. We cannot damn ourselves. And just be grateful; not only am I in a good mood, I've got an important meeting tonight. Otherwise, I'd stick around merely to fuck with you," he called out as he disappeared down the hallway.

Kinich stopped at the second set of doors and pushed. Like the rest of Niccolo and Helena's lavish penthouse overlooking Central Park, the furniture was modern and white. The only splash of color came from the red pillows on the large king-size bed in the middle of the room.

He was about to set Penelope on top of the pristine, white comforter but realized she was covered head to toe in...

He took a whiff and winced. "She smells like rotten cabbage." He glimpsed at the doorway that led to the private bath, then cast his gaze on Penelope. He wondered, would she mind? He'd already seen her excruciatingly sumptuous nude body.

*You may have done more than that.* He would give anything to remember what had occurred that evening. Unrelenting images hounded him day and night: Penelope's naked, sweaty body pinned beneath him as he pumped his hard cock inside her, lost in her smell, her groans, her moist heat. A heat that had matched his own in every way—something he'd never fathomed. He'd been obsessed with seeing her again for that very reason.

Kinich began to grow hard.

*Gods be damned!*

"Down boy."

In any case, once he got a hold of Cimil, he would decapitate her for her little prank. Idiot. Sex with mortals and having offspring were not recreational activities— okay, perhaps the sex part was, but not the procreation. Definitely not that.

Thank heavens Penelope had not conceived. Not that he knew for certain if they'd had sex, but she'd removed the black jade necklace the morning after their night together. To be clear, he had nothing against children. In fact, the notion of being a father delighted him. It was one of the many aspects of human life from which the gods had been deprived. Still, his wants and desires were simply not on the table, and the matter boiled down to one truth: The universe demanded balance; it constantly strived for it. Life could not exist without it.

This was his belief, and he needed only to observe the world around him to see the evidence—the changing of the seasons, the food chain, Newton's laws of motion. For every action, there is an equal and opposite reaction.

Balance.

This meant that for each Payal created, the universe would create a counterbalance—something dark, something evil. And as of late, evil had been busy. The Maaskab had been honing their skills, amplifying their powers. They could send the universe into a tailspin of self-destruction if they were allowed the upper hand for even one second.

*Not on my fucking watch. Not even for . . . her.*

No. He would not deny he wanted Penelope or that he eagerly wished to understand what drove his bottomless craving for the mortal's body. But there was no endgame, and he knew it.

Mortals belonged with mortals. Gods belonged alone. That was the natural order.

*Still, you can't deny you want—you need—just one more taste . . . or . . . a first taste?*

He lay Penelope on the thick, cream-colored carpet

next to the bed and began untying her boots. They were thick and clunky with a fur lining. He half expected her to have on wool socks, but as he slipped the boots off, he saw she wore none. Her little toes were raw and frozen.

He clasped both hands around her delicate foot and directed warmth into each cell. The circulation quickly returned.

He continued rubbing her toes and noticed they were painted pink.

Hmm. What sort of underwear might she have on? Would they match?

He beheld Penelope's serene face. She looked stunning lying there with her dark hair fanned out on the floor. Her pink, heart-shaped lips...he couldn't forget their taste or silky texture. He wondered how they might feel if she ran them over the tip of his pulsing, hard—

"Nick! What do you think you're doing to that girl? And what the hell happened to your clothes?"

Helena stood behind him with one fist parked on her hip. Her golden spirals were piled into a ponytail atop her head, and ribbons of black swirled in her bright blue eyes.

She was pissed.

Considering she was wife to the most powerful and feared ex-vampire ever to exist—Niccolo DiConti—meant she was one tough cookie. Thank goodness Niccolo and Helena were good friends of his.

Kinich stood and beamed at his prize, Penelope. "My clothes are resting comfortably back in my hotel room. As for her, I was merely going to bathe her. Then perhaps rub her down with scented oils."

"Oh no, you won't. I'm not letting you take advantage

of some poor unconscious girl. Not in my house," she scolded.

Kinich grumbled. "She is far from being a 'girl,' and I was planning to behave like a perfect gentleman."

*Sorta.*

Helena wagged her finger. "Uh-uh. Unless she's written a note specifying you as her official spokesperson or personal bather, you're not touching her. What the hell happened, anyway? Is she hurt? She'd better not be."

"She was attacked but is uninjured. I thought she could do with some rest so I voiced her. Should wear off in about an hour. Or twenty. I'm not sure; I was a bit distracted."

"I don't like the sound of this. Attacked by whom?"

Kinich didn't wish to see Helena's face when he spoke the words, so he focused on the ceiling instead. "A Maaskab."

"Oh, shit!" Helena cupped her hands over her mouth and then whispered, "Maaskab? Here in New York?"

Kinich nodded.

"Does Niccolo know?"

"Not yet," he replied. "I planned to call after I tend to Penelope, a task I am greatly looking forward to. So if you do not mind—"

"Oh no, no, *señor*! I'll take over from here. You go call the general. This minute!"

Helena grabbed Kinich's arm and urged him toward the door. "Use the phone in the study. Dial pound three."

"But—"

"Stop acting like someone took your favorite new car, you big baby."

That's exactly how he felt. He growled. "Okay. No biting."

"Out! I can handle her myself!"

About one year ago, Helena, who'd been told by Cimil she was going to die saving Niccolo, cheated death by becoming a vampire. And for an added fun twist, Niccolo had been unknowingly turned from a vampire into a demigod—compliments of Cimil. They now had a baby girl, little Matty, who was half-vampire.

He shook his head. *Soon we're going to need a species scoreboard to keep track of this mess.*

Especially since Cimil seemed to delight in turning people's lives upside down. Her guise of "Hey! Just keeping the wheels on the universe's bus" really meant, "I'm so bored! Let me entertain myself by watching some poor souls jump through hoop after hoop, only to find their darkest fears become reality. If they don't play nice, I'll turn them into an insect with irritable bowel syndrome."

Sure, it was fun to watch when Cimil's victim was some vile filth and phlegm of humanity—a rapist or thug—but sometimes she went too far to prove a point. It was only a matter of time before the universe invoked another law of balance: karma. Payback would be a substantial bitch for someone like Cimil.

Helena's hissing snapped him back from his vengeful thoughts. "Just because *you* don't know the meaning of restraint doesn't mean I don't. Besides, I only like nibbling on my hubby, Niccolo." She licked her lips. "However, if you don't do as I say, I could be persuaded to try a new flavor. You'd be surprised how hungry I get on this new blood-only diet"—she stepped forward parting her lips—"and I bet a full-fledged god tastes pretty damn good."

Kinich backed away toward the door. "I am told my blood is very spicy. Fire hot, actually. You would not enjoy it." He regarded Penelope once again, taking in her beauty. "I leave her in your care, but if a hair on her head is—"

"You *really* like her, don't you?" Helena's jaw dropped.

Frankly, he wasn't sure what he felt. It was all very... foreign.

"I'm a god," he replied. "We're hardwired to care for humans."

"Sure. Right. I saw that look." Helena shut the bedroom door in his face.

Sulking, Kinich marched into Niccolo's office and picked up the phone.

General Niccolo answered immediately. "Hi, my sweet. Are you missing me? Because I'm missing not only you, but those silky, soft thighs, too."

Kinich cleared his throat. "Wow. I'm flattered, though I assure you my thighs are neither silky nor soft. They are, however, firm, muscular, and untouched by male hands. I intend to keep them that way."

"Who the fuck is this?" said Niccolo.

"Nick. And before you say any shit you might regret, your wife made me call you."

"What the fuck for?" Niccolo responded.

"Maaskab attacked my woman," Nick said, and then rebuked himself instantly. Why the hell had he called Penelope his woman?

"A Maaskab? You sure? Wait... You have a woman? Is the end of the world here already?" Niccolo responded.

"Fuck you, vampire. And yes, I'm sure it was a Scab. I don't make mistakes, unlike you," Kinich fired back.

"I'm no longer a vampire, you fuck. I'd also be damned careful with that tone of yours," Niccolo warned.

"I'm pissing myself, demigod." He chuckled. He loved taunting Niccolo and could normally go on for days, but the situation was serious. "I need to find out why they are after her."

"Can't help. I'm here with your Uchben, training them on the subtle yet exhilarating art of decapitating sifting Scabs and Obscuros."

That was the reason he'd wanted to talk to Niccolo in the first place. Normally, Kinich would call on the gods' human army (and all-around eyes and ears), the Uchben, for this sort of work. But Cimil had recently advised everyone that the kickoff for the Great War grew near. If their side did not win, it would mean the end of civilization as they knew it. The apocalypse.

"Yes. I'm aware the Uchben are occupied. That's why I'm calling you. I need you to send someone to track down a Maaskab and bring him to me. I will torture the truth from him."

Niccolo made a deep, rumbling sound. "What happened to the one that attacked her?"

"He met with an unfortunate fate."

"You cooked him, didn't you? Fucking gods. Will you ever learn? A prisoner is worth more than revenge."

"The Maaskab caught me off guard. I had no choice," Kinich lied. He knew he'd had a choice and he chose to cook the motherfucker for attacking Penelope.

"You could have tried to knock him out," Niccolo grumbled.

"You going to help me or not?" Kinich said.

"I cannot. I am under orders from your brother to have every able warrior preparing for war."

"Then I will go myself and catch one," Kinich stated.

There was a long pause. "Why?"

"Why what?" Kinich asked.

"Why take a risk for this woman?"

Again, Kinich didn't actually know why. He simply felt... needs. Lust-driven, obsessive sorts of needs. "That is my business."

"I see," Niccolo replied, followed by another long pause. "He's going to kill me for saying anything, but lucky you, I enjoy pissing people off. Guy has someone on the inside now. Perhaps his spy can help."

*On the inside?*

"Thank you," Kinich responded dryly.

"Don't mention it."

"One more thing," Kinich added.

"My daily quota for helping useless deities is filled."

Kinich ignored Niccolo's jab. He had more important things to worry about at the moment. Plus, he really liked the bastard. "I need to leave Penelope here for a few days. There are some urgent matters I must address. Your man, Andrus, can he handle her?"

Niccolo growled. Then again, he growled every time he heard the name Andrus. Andrus had kidnapped Helena once, intending to use her as a bargaining chip to get his hands on the now-deceased, evil vampire queen. To make matters worse, Andrus had also made a play for Helena. It chapped Niccolo's hide to have Andrus under his roof guarding Helena and his daughter, little Matty. But Cimil had foreseen an attack where Andrus saved their lives. The decision to swallow his pride was a no-brainer. Helena was also madly in love with Niccolo, which helped keep his jealousy in check.

"Is she going to be trouble? Because I'm guessing if you've taken an interest in her, she's a pain in the neck," Niccolo said.

"I haven't taken an interest. She's in danger, and I can't help wanting to protect mortals. But, yes, she's no pushover."

In fact, he found her bravery to be one of her most fascinating traits. She seemed afraid of nothing, not even him. How arousing.

"I'll send Viktor to the penthouse," said Niccolo. "He is in New York taking care of an issue. I'm sure he'd planned to visit with Helena, anyway."

Viktor, a very old vampire, was Niccolo's right hand and best friend for the last millennium. He'd also been the one to turn Helena, which is why she'd grown quite attached. It was yet another relationship Niccolo had to come to grips with.

It was truly a goddamned immortal Mexican soap opera.

"Thank you, this means a lot," Kinich grumbled.

Niccolo howled with laughter on the other end of the phone. "Wow. Sun God showing kindness? She must be something if she can make *you* civilized. Can't wait to meet her."

"Fuck off." Kinich hung up the phone, irritated about the whole situation. He knew he cared more than he should about the human, but that didn't mean anything. It was sexual. Nothing he couldn't handle.

He would figure out why the Maaskab came for her, get her somewhere safe, and then go back to his life of being a god. After all, they had a war to prepare for, humans to save, and the issue of restoring balance to the universe—starting with putting a stop to the gods breeding with the humans. Although he could be persuaded to make an exception for bedding them. That part, he again noted, was a diversion worthy of the gods.

# Twelve

⌒

Vaguely aware of the unfamiliar yet incredibly soft sheets and fluffy-as-a-cloud pillow cradling my head, I rolled over in the bed. Some mysterious force made it nearly impossible to coax my mind from the transcendent state of relaxation, despite the unsavory snippets swirling aimlessly in the back of my mind—monsters with black teeth, garbage, flashes of light, and...

"Kinich!" I sprang from the bed, trying to gather my wits, my head whipping from side to side.

The room, decorated in pristine white, reminded me of those high-end European resorts—not that I'd ever been to one, but I had it on my to-do list. Right there along with renewing my passport, taking salsa lessons, and getting a Brazilicide (getting hammered on suicides—a schnapps-and-vodka drink—before getting a Brazilian bikini wax) my best friend, Anne, recommended.

I pulled up the thick, cream-colored blinds, shocked

to discover I was in a very tall building. The city seemed daunting and glacial with its hazy winter air. The sun was just dipping below the skyline, bathing each and every gray building in an even gloomier gray hue.

*Christ!* How long had I been out if the sun was setting? It had been night when Nick...Nick...

*He put me to sleep after voodoo Terminator attacked.*

*Son of a...what is going on?*

Waves of dread undulated beneath my skin. Ironically, however, I didn't feel afraid. No. Quite the opposite. I felt resentful. I felt like kicking ass and taking names. Because whatever inexplicable bizarreness was occurring—monsters, the strange things I'd witnessed Nick doing, his crazy sister's psychic handbook—I didn't appreciate the intrusion in my life. Good or bad, it was my life. Mine. And nobody got to drive the Penelope-mobile except for me. How dare these *people? Creatures? Funky beings?* How dare these funky beings get in my car and drive.

*Oh, so you think you can control everything, huh?*

*Yes.*

*Ha! Good one.*

*Shut the hell up!*

A baby crying off in the distance caught my attention. I cracked open the door and found the brightly lit hallway empty.

I tiptoed in my pink, fluffy socks toward the sound.

*Pink, fluffy socks?* I looked down. *Oh my God!* I was wearing a Hello Kitty nightie. "What the...?" I moved my hands over my various parts and then lifted up my gown.

*Speaking of intrusion.*

"Kitty underwear, too? Damn him! How dare he touch me."

*And Hello Kitty? Seriously?*

"Anything I can help you with?"

I spun around to find a shamefully attractive, well-built man with spiky, dark hair and turquoise eyes casually watching me or, really, watching my bottom half. I gasped and dropped the nightie.

"Wait! It's you!" I pointed. "You're . . . you're . . ."

He bowed his head. "Andrus. So we meet again, Dorothy."

Oh, oh, oh. This little traveler knew damn well she wasn't in Kansas anymore. *Because Kansas doesn't have men who hex you with sleeping spells and then dress you like a kindergartner.*

"Where am I? And where is that SOB, Nick?"

He smiled. "SOB? I see that you and I will get along famously."

I narrowed my eyes and tightened my lips, waiting for my answers.

He cleared his throat. "Come with me."

Fuming, I trailed behind him and his leather pants. As we rounded the corner, the wide-open living room came into view. It had floor-to-ceiling windows and the most breathtaking view of Central Park I'd ever seen. A chubby, blonde baby sat in the middle of the floor on a large blanket next to a set of multicolored blocks.

My memory clicked. "That's the baby you were holding at Cimil's. Right?"

He nodded with a glowing smile.

"Dat sweet wittle baby," he said in baby talk as he pranced over to her, "is our wittle Matty." He plucked her off the floor and nibbled her ear. She instantly stopped crying and gave a little giggle.

Okay. That was weird. The large man appeared deadlier than sin, like he ate bullets for breakfast and drank gasoline martinis, but turned into a mindless ninny for this baby?

*Oh, stop! That's totally adorable, and you know it!*

*No! You stop! You're in deep shit, and here you are judging the man's domestic divaness. Enough! Focus, Penelope! Drive the car!*

"So that answers one of my questions. Now, what about Nick?" I crossed my arms over my chest.

Andrus parked the baby on his hip. "Oh, the gwumpy lady wants to know where dat bastard of your uncle Kinich is," he said again in baby talk to Matty.

"Baaa-ba," she cooed happily and latched onto his black tee with her chubby little hands.

"Yes. Right you are, Matty. It is time for your bottle." He marched off.

"Hey! Now where are you going?" I chased after him.

By the time I caught up in the showroom-like kitchen, he had Matty strapped into a high chair.

He shot a scowl my way. "I don't know where Nick is, but he left you here yesterday. You are in my care until he returns." He glanced at my lower half. "And no. I didn't bathe and dress you, if that's what you're wondering." His stone-cold expression instantly melted into a dopey grin the moment he looked at Matty. "'Cause wittle Matty is the only lady I do that for. Isn't that right, my little cupcake of darkness?"

*Yes, he just called her "cupcake"*—I swallowed—"*of darkness.*"

I hit the reality-denial button—I had been born with one in my brain—and moved on.

His head disappeared inside the extra-large stainless steel fridge. "Helena should be awake in a little while. She'll be able to answer any other questions."

"Okay. And this Helena person, whoever that is, will tell me what attacked me? Or how Nick put me to sleep?"

"Perhaps."

"Is Helena your wife?" I asked.

His head darted out from the fridge, and he gave me a look that could cap a flaming oil well. "No. Helena is Matty's mother. She is *not* mine."

*Ouch! Hit a nerve, did I?*

"Helena is married to Niccolo DiConti. This is their home," he elaborated.

My mind sputtered. "Wait. So you're the nanny?"

He slammed the refrigerator door and popped a bottle of red liquid into the microwave. "I prefer bodyguard and caretaker."

*He's a manny!*

*Or a leather nanny?*

*Hee-hee-hee.*

*Stop that!*

I bit the insides of my cheeks to smother a budding smile.

The microwave beeped. He plucked out the bottle and screwed on a cap before giving it a little shake. The baby held out her hands. He was about to pass it but froze. "If you don't mind, I need to give Matty her bottle."

He didn't want me to see? Jeez. Maybe he wasn't as comfortable with his role as he let on.

"I'll just go use the phone. If that's okay."

"Help yourself." He stared, waiting for me to leave.

I shrugged and returned to the living room, where I found a phone off to the corner on a small table. I held it in my hand, staring at the white-and-black buttons.

What was I going to say to my mother? That I'd been attacked in our apartment by a monster and saved by a man who I may have slept with after being drugged by his lunatic sister who had offered me one million dollars to be the surrogate mother of his child, a child he had no interest in having? And that here comes the giant cherry on my sucky sundae, I might now actually be carrying this man's baby! If we slept together at all, but who knew?

*Aaah yes. Now there's a story every mom wants to post on her Facebook timeline. "Oh! Lookie here what my daughter's been up to!"*

*Like?*

*Click!*

No. She needed to focus her energy on healing. I'd have to pretend everything was okay and save the truth for another day. Perhaps after my death.

I dialed, but her cell was once again busy. Maybe because she was overseas? I'd have to call the clinic in Sweden directly, but I didn't have the number.

I returned to the kitchen, hoping Andrus wouldn't be too offended by the intrusion. Maybe he had to see that I was cool with the whole man-nanny-bodyguard thing.

"Andrus?" I called out.

He sat at the kitchen table holding Matty in his arms, the bottle filled with red liquid in her mouth.

"What's that?" I asked.

"Uhhh, cranberry juice."

I'd done the babysitter gig for a few years in my early

teens and never remembered giving anything other than apple juice, water, or formula to a baby that young. "And she likes to drink it warm?"

"She...um. She loves it. Lots of vitamins 'n' stuff. Is there something I can help you with?"

*All righty then.*

"Is there a computer I could use?"

"In the study," Andrus replied. "Just through the living room. Help yourself. The password is *demilord*."

I thanked him, happy to escape his scathing sneer.

I found the study easily enough. Aside from the breathtaking view, nothing about it stood out: bookshelves, a few family photos on the walls, et cetera. Despite its normalcy, something about this entire home really struck me as, well...off. I couldn't put my finger on it.

I popped open the laptop, typed in the password, and did a quick search, but shockingly found nothing. Had I forgotten the name of the clinic? No. No way. Center for Immune Management and Integrative Lifestyles. Stockholm.

I scratched my head. Why wasn't it coming up?

I tried several versions of the spelling before deciding it would be faster to call my neighbor.

I dialed the number and Mr. Harris, a retired plumber, answered. He said he had no idea where my mom's information was, but that his wife would be home in a few minutes. Oddly enough, when I asked if everything was okay after all the commotion, he had no clue what I was talking about.

"So you're sure? There's nobody weird hanging around the building?"

"No, Penelope. Why? Are you in some sort of trouble?" he asked.

*You bet your plumber's crack I am!* "No. Everything's fine. Just some disgruntled ex-boyfriend," I lied. "Nothing I can't handle."

I looked at the clock on the desk. *Oh no!* I had a karate class to give at seven.

I rubbed my face. I was on the edge of losing my sanity, so keeping what remained of my life intact felt like a necessity. Yes. I would go home, get my gi and other personal items, and stay with a friend until I could figure out what was going on.

*That's right, honey. You take that steering wheel!*

# Thirteen

⌒

"Kinny-Kins! Oh my God!" Dressed in a floral terry cloth robe, Emma threw her arms around Kinich's neck. "What enormous cojones you have showing up here!"

Kinich smiled and gave her a tight squeeze. He always did like Emma; she was lively and brave, a bit reckless, too. Then again, she had to be if she was going to marry his brother Guy.

Despite his views on Payals, he couldn't deny that Emma truly was special. He almost thought of her like a little sister, perhaps because there was a time when Emma had been the gods' only connection to the outside world (a little unfortunate mishap having to do with the Maaskab).

Emma unwrapped her arms and ushered Kinich inside the luxuriously renovated loft mansion built in the 1860s. The six-story engagement gift, complete with indoor swimming pool and basketball court, had set Guy back a mere sixty million dollars. A drop in the bucket for a god who had all the time in the world to accumulate wealth.

Kinich's eyes wandered over the large potted plants, elaborately tiled floors, and rustic furniture. Despite being situated in the heart of New York City, Emma had done a phenomenal job of replicating the interior of Guy's Spanish-style villa located in Italy. "It's lovely, Emma."

She flicked her wrist. "It's nothing. Just wanted Guy to feel at home." She eyeballed Kinich. "You look great by the way. Something's different. Lose some weight?"

Funny woman. The gods did not need to worry about such things. "Must be my new tailor." That man certainly knew how to cut a pair of slacks for the extra-extra-large male.

She shook her head. "Uh-uh. I can't place my finger on it, but it's like you're radiating something new."

Holy saints. Could it have something to do with Penelope?

He quickly changed subjects. "I'm here to see my brother. Is he still angry?" Kinich asked.

"You betcha," she replied.

"And you?" Not only was Emma a Payal, but she wanted children—something he felt should not be allowed. Without question, Guy had already told her this.

She smiled. "Why should I be? You're only doing what you think is right."

He bowed his head. "A very mature attitude. I think we could stand to learn something from you."

"Well, I can't help it if I'm smarter than the gods, you included. I mean, it's totally ridiculous to believe the Payals are throwing the universe out of whack. If anything, it's you gods with your antiquated ways that are messing everything up. I mean, seriously, have you taken a good look at your crew? Total misfits!"

"Well," he said, "I wouldn't call them—"

"With the exception of Guy, no one else has ever lifted a finger to help humanity evolve in a positive direction."

"Well, we've...uhhh. Well, my sister Colel—"

"The Bee Whisperer lady? Really? That's your best example? A goddess who assists in the making of bee vomit?"

Maybe she had a point.

"The way I see it"—she poked his chest—"we're an upgrade to the deity melting pot. Look how far Guy's come along since he met me. He's more civilized—"

"Emma!" Guy bellowed from the other room, "get your hot ass back in here, woman! We have not completed our evening lovemaking."

Emma smiled at Kinich and then whispered, "Except in bed, which is just how I like it." She sighed. "Gods, I love that deity."

Kinich flashed a polite smile. Truth was, he felt uncomfortable being around Emma and Guy when they were together. Perhaps because he'd spent several millennia convincing himself the gods weren't destined for love or relationships. He'd resigned himself to the desolate, unsavory notion of an eternity alone in the romantic sense. Yes. He had his role and humanity to look after. That would have to suffice because any other option was unnatural.

Emma gestured him toward the living room. "Let me tell him you're here. Maybe I can get him to play nice."

"Much appreciated, Emma."

She winked. "Anything for you, sunshine boy."

At that moment, his cell rang. "Yes."

"It's me, Andrus. Your human has taken off."

*Son of a...*

"You were supposed to watch her!"

"Hey, I was feeding the ba— Sharpening my sword. Not my fault."

"Not your *fault*?" he screamed.

"Gotta go, Matty needs me to change her diap— Uhhh—tires. That's right. Tires on her tricycle."

"Get over it, Andrus. We all know you are the nanny."

"I am a lethal assassin!" Andrus argued.

"Keep telling yourself that, especially when you are experiencing my fist pounding into your skull, which is exactly what I will be doing after I find Penelope." He hung up the phone, vowing to make Andrus pay.

He quickly dialed Penelope's cell. To his surprise, she answered on the second ring, but instead of disclosing her location, she ignored his warnings, ranted about some goddamned lost twig, and hung up on him.

*Gods-damned stubborn woman!*

He was about to head out when Guy appeared, wearing nothing but a scowl and a pair of silky, red boxers with white hearts. "Not one word, Kinich. They are a gift from Emma," he said. "Start talking. You have two minutes! Two! But not because I give a shit about you—Emma promised to do that thing with her tongue if I played nice."

With her tongue? Like he'd dreamed of Penelope doing?

He suddenly felt hot underneath his thick, white turtle-neck and black wool pants. "I have to go. Something's come up." He turned to leave but found Guy blocking his way.

"Emma was very specific," Guy said. "I must listen to

you blabber for two minutes about why you are here or no tongue. So don't you even think of fucking going near the front door until you've spoken for one hundred and twenty seconds."

Thinking of Penelope scampering about the city alone, Kinich snarled. "I'm here because I encountered a Maaskab in the city yesterday."

Guy's eyes lit with fury. "Here? In New York? And you waited an entire day to tell anyone?"

"I killed him. I would have told you sooner, but I had some important business to attend to," Kinich explained.

"Must've been pretty damn important if it supersedes this. So what the hell happened?"

"The Maaskab attacked my— A woman," Kinich said. "I'm hoping you can help me find out why."

"Who is the woman?"

Kinich did not wish to disclose the details, but sooner or later, Guy would learn the truth; Cimil had the loosest lips in the universe. "She is a human I slept with. I think."

Guy burst out laughing. "You! You have a girlfriend?"

Kinich felt his face turn bright red, the flames of anger flickering beneath the surface. "No. This is Cimil's doing. She drugged us, hoping I might impregnate the woman and then change my mind about putting the procreation-with-humans issue to a vote. Her plan failed—if we did sleep together, Penelope removed the jade necklace so there will be no offspring."

Gods could only be intimate with a human when they wore the black jade. If conception occurred, the fetus would only survive if the mother continued wearing it. Otherwise, the god's light was too potent for a human body to endure.

Still smiling, Guy narrowed his eyes with suspicion. "And you are here because . . . ?"

"If the Maaskab want Penelope, there must be a reason."

"You think she is like Emma?"

"Possibly. But I do not sense our light inside her. This is why I wish to find out why the Maaskab hunt her. If the attack was random, then I may take a different approach to protecting her. Niccolo advises that you have someone on the inside."

Guy's eyes widened with anger. "Dammit, sunshine," he whispered acerbically. "Shut the fuck up; Emma might hear you." He glanced over his shoulder toward the hallway leading to his bedroom.

Kinich quirked a brow. "You keep secrets from Emma? From us?"

"Yes. We cannot risk the Maaskab getting hold of this information. The fewer people who know, the better."

Kinich's suspicion was roused. "Why hide it from your brethren?"

Guy stepped closer. "After what happened with Tommaso, we cannot be so naive as to assume that he is the only traitor among us."

"Surely the gods can be trusted." Kinich thought of Cimil and a few of his other brethren, idiots with no sense of discretion whatsoever. Then there was Chaam, their brother who had betrayed them all. Who was to say another god might not fall. "Never mind. Good call. Having a spy inside the Maaskab is invaluable. So when might you be able to contact him?"

Guy scratched his chin. "This is the issue. I have not heard from him for several weeks. He keeps a solar-charged satellite phone hidden in the jungle. On his last call, he mentioned that the Maaskab were about to make a big move. Now the phone has been turned off. The satellite does not detect a signal."

"Is it possible that Tommaso recognized your spy?" Tommaso, the evil ex-Uchben bastard of a traitor, was assumed to have fled with Emma's grandmother back to the Maaskab. And since Tommaso had been an Uchben for many years, he knew just about every ally to the gods.

Guy shook his head. "No. This is not a concern. I chose carefully."

Kinich's phone rang. He dug the device from his pocket. The word *Cimil* displayed on the screen.

"You bitch!" he answered. "I'm going to have you disemboweled, stuffed with flesh-eating beetles, chained to a large boulder, and thrown into a volcano!"

"Ha! Been there. Done that! Got the tat. On my bum." Cimil chuckled on the other end of the phone. "And I don't know why you're so bent out of shape; the midget idea wasn't mine. Neither was the whipped cream. The YouTube video was, though! Can you *belieeeve*? One million hits already! You're a superstar, baby!"

"What the fuck are you talking about?" Once again he wished he had the gift of sifting so he could go to her and tear out her throat.

"You know..." Cimil elaborated, "the video we took of you that night when you were with Penelope? I drugged you. There were midgets? Oh, never mind. What's got your man thong in a twist?"

"For the record, I am commando. And you know damn well, Cimil! You crossed the line this time!"

"According to the video and one million viewers, I'd

say you had the time of your life. Personally, I had no idea you were so acrobatic. We should rent you out for parties."

"I'm going to fucking kill you! Kill. Kill. *Kill* you!" He felt the flames rising to the surface of his skin. Unfortunately, though he healed fast, the heat was excruciating when his power was unleashed.

Cimil cackled. "Not if you want me to deliver your precious people-pet, safe and sound."

"*What?* You jest," he snarled.

"Jest? You mean, as in quips, rib-ticklers, bon mots, tomfoolery, shenanigans, or monkeyshines?"

He exhaled a billow of smoke. "Yes."

"Then...no. Not my style. At least not on Tuesdays. Everyone knows that."

"Today. Is. Wednesday," he snarled.

"Really? What year?"

"Cimil! Cut the crap!" Kinich roared.

"Never! Crap is my middle name! Except on Tuesdays. Then it's Biaaaanca."

"I'm hanging up now. And then I will spend every waking hour hunting your bony ass."

"Hunting *me*? Maybe you should focus on your baby momma, lover boy; I spotted Penelope frolicking out and about alone. Not so smart when she's on the Scabby dessert menu."

"I do not believe you," he said.

"Okay. I did *not* just see Penelope coming out of her apartment building toting two large duffel bags. I am *not* following her in my goddess-mobile."

A horn honked in the background.

"Hold that thought, sunshine."

It sounded as though Cimil had dropped the phone.

Next there was screaming in the background. "Shut your pieholes and go the fuck home!" Pause. "What? Did you give me the finger? I'll rip it from your pasty little hand and stick it where the sun don't shine!" More screaming in the background. "Oh yeah? You try it, you little fucker!" Cimil barked at someone.

"Gods dammit, Cimil!" Kinich yelled into the phone.

He heard Cimil grumble, tires screeching, and then clunking and static as Cimil picked up the phone.

"Fucking Cub Scouts," she huffed. "Give them some mistletoe and a few Christmas carols and they think they own the whole fucking holiday!" Pause. "Okay, I am a good goddess. I am a kind goddess, oh, hell. No, I'm not. So! Where were we, Kin?"

Guy must have noticed the flames in Kinich's eyes because he snatched the phone away.

"Cimil? What the devil is going on?" asked Guy. He listened and nodded. "I see. Yes. You know that you will eventually pay for your underhanded ways." Pause. "No. I have not seen the video. Was it good?" Guy laughed. "Really? He did that? With the human and the midgets? Classic. Emma and I will be sure to watch it later."

*I will kill them both.* Kinich lunged for the phone, but Guy stepped aside and then turned his broad back.

"Yes," he said. "I will tell him. Deliver the girl." He hung up the phone.

Kinich's entire body smoldered. "You fucked with the wrong god."

Guy shook his head and laughed. "Calm down, brother. Cimil is guarding your human. For a price, of course."

"Which is?"

"Forgoing any revenge," Guy said casually.

*Gods fucking dammit!*

"Did she say where Penelope is?"

Guy shook his head. "No, she merely said she'd drop her off at Niccolo's later, but she had some cubs to mow down first. Sometimes her humor escapes me—why are baby bears loose in the city?"

Kinich resisted imploding from frustration. "I will go to Niccolo's and wait for them." Kinich turned toward the door.

"And Kinich?" Guy added. "I will keep trying to contact my spy. If I am successful, I will inquire about your girlfr— Human friend. I suggest, in the meantime, you assume she is a Payal and, therefore, wanted by the priests. Perhaps you should take her to your compound in Sedona."

"Guy!" Emma screamed from the other room. "Get your sweet ass in here! My tongue and I are waiting!"

Kinich tried very hard not to think about his erotic dream with Penelope. Instead, he focused on his anger. He had plenty of that.

# *Fourteen*

⌒

Turned out, I'd had no reason to worry; someone, a neighbor perhaps, had locked the front door to my apartment. After getting the spare key and the contact info for my mom from Mrs. Harris, I formulated my plan of attack. I would quickly go inside, grab my karate gear, cell, a change of clothes, and my purse.

Then I'd run like hell.

Later, after giving my class, I'd call one of my friends, Anne or Jess, and crash with them for a few nights or at least until I figured out what to do. Who knew if that monster might come back, which put a serious crimp in my living situation.

*One pickle at a time, Pen.* I pushed the front door open and stepped to the side, listening for any movement.

Nothing.

I slowly peeked through the doorway, shocked to learn

that someone had tidied up. The apartment smelled clean and fresh, like exotic plants and sunshine.

*Kinich.*

Every ounce of anger and confusion inexplicably dissipated as my entire body felt lit up like a Christmas tree. A very, very naughty Christmas tree that wanted to do dirty, dirty things to a very sexy man's candy cane, a man who most certainly wasn't Santa.

*A sex god maybe.* Even in my dreams he knew exactly where and how to touch me. *Exactly like the Orgasm Whisperer I'd read about in* Cosmo*!*

And to make Nick even more irresistible, he had gone and won a huge brownie point for cleaning up my place. To be clear, nothing was hotter than a hot man who enjoyed cleaning. Man-jackpot.

*Yeah…but all the weird things he did and the way he treated you that night and—*

*No! I'm not thinking about this right now.*

I dashed around the apartment, collecting clothes and toiletries, shoving them into a large overnight bag. I slipped my cell in my pocket. *Yikes. Twenty missed calls from Anne and Jess. Nothing from my mother?*

I was almost out the front door when I realized I'd forgotten something.

*The stick!*

I headed for the bathroom.

If I was pregnant, I'd…I'd…I didn't know what I'd do. There was a nagging little tug on my heartstrings when I thought about Kinich. I barely knew the man, yet I couldn't ignore how he made me feel or how he affected me.

*Yes, and how he accused you of being a sperm-napper! Wait. We're not thinking about this. Remember?*

*Yesss. But it's hard not to think about how he rescued me from that monster.*

*Okay, he did say that...that thing didn't actually want to kill you. Was it really a rescue? Maybe it was a misunderstanding. Maybe "it" wanted to borrow your shampoo and deodorant.* The monster clearly had been deprived of badly needed personal hygiene products. *I mean, that would make me angry, too.*

"Oh no!" The stick wasn't on the counter where I'd left it. Kinich must have found it when he'd come to clean up.

He knew! That turkey knew, and I didn't?

My cell suddenly rang. *Caller unknown.* My mom maybe?

"Hello?"

"Damn you, woman! Where the hell are you?" Kinich's voice roared through the speaker.

*Wha...wha...?* "What!? Did you just call me 'woman' and bark at me like a child?"

"Yes," he replied coldly. "And if you don't want to find yourself dead, you'd better tell me where the hell you are!"

"Oh my God! Who do you think you are? I'm a grown woman. I can take care of myself. And for the record, you can't 'find yourself dead.' That's silly."

A low growl came through the phone. *"Where?"*

"I want it back! Where's the stick, Kinich? What did you do with it? What did it say?"

"Stick? You have Maaskab trying to kill you, and you're worried about a twig? Why didn't you stay with Andrus?" He then grumbled something that sounded like "foolish morals." Or did he say "foolish mortals"?

"You said the monster wasn't trying to kill me."

"Yet!" he screamed. "Not yet! But soon! Gods dammit, woman. Tell me where you are so I can come get you."

*Yet? I must've missed that part. Oooh. Not good.* "I'm..." I paused. Something on the floor right next to the vanity caught my eye. The pregnancy test. It must have fallen.

I plucked it off the floor, almost dropping it with my trembling hands. It took only a moment for my eyes to deliver the answer I needed.

My heart dropped to my ankles. "Oooh," I said, followed by a slow breath out. "I'm—uh...uh...Good-bye, Kinich. I'll be fine. Just—just leave me alone. Okay?"

"Penelope!" he screamed before I hit End Call.

With three minutes to spare, I arrived at my class, grateful for the escape of one single, solitary normal activity. I needed a distraction from the emotional hokey-pokey going on inside my head. Take my feelings toward Nick, for example. Was I in? Was I out? Or would I just keep shaking it all about?

*Yikes. What a horrible analogy.*

*Fine. Let's move to hands.*

*What? Now you're an octopus? Because you'll need lots of hands to weigh the pros and cons of this cluster.*

*Ugh! Stop it.*

On the one hand, his arrogance made me want to knee him right in his man-fritters. And yet, I had to admit, a part of me felt slightly terrified because of what I'd seen him do. It wasn't...normal for a man to have those abilities.

Then, on the other hand, I liked him. A lot. He made

me feel things that, frankly, I didn't know one person could feel for another, like earth-shattering, burning, uncontrollable lust. Then there was that connection. It ran deep into my bones, though I didn't know why or care to truly admit it. And finally, I had an irrational desire to make him mine and never let go, which led to my next emotional dance-off between loss and relief. No hokey-pokey for those two. Uh-uh. The pregnancy issue was a definite tango. Maybe even a lambada followed by some hula dancing and a luau. With poi. I shivered. Poi was gross.

In any case, with so much noise inside my head and heart, I needed a healthy distraction, and the kids, ages three to five, were exactly what I needed. Nothing eased my heavy thoughts more than seeing their eager, little faces as they laughed and punched and screamed, "*Haiya!*" I loved children.

In college, I was a karate camp counselor three sum-mers in a row. I supposed I liked it because teaching was something I was good at. I showed the kids respect. They listened. We understood each other. Simple.

Relationships with grown-ups were always so com-plex. Hokey-pokey case in point...Nick.

Well, at least now it was slightly less complex. Not being pregnant was, first and foremost, a huge relief, despite any irrational mixed feelings I might have.

And never, ever, ever—cross my heart and hope to die, stick a champagne roofie in my eye—would I again put myself in that situation. Yes, yes. There were extenuating circumstances like being drugged, but that didn't excuse my stupidity for having gotten mixed up with these people.

*It's in the past so get the hell over it.*

I would. I knew I would. I simply needed time. Lots of time. And to talk to my mom. The good news out of all this was her being off in Sweden getting her treatment, thanks to Cimil who let me keep the money for "showing up to the party."

*Well, I sure as hell showed up. Danced on the frigging table, and put a lampshade on my head, too!*

While I packed up my gear and waved good-bye to my last student, I called Anne, my best friend in the whole world besides Jess. I'd met them both my freshman year at a romance book club slash tapas cooking club called We Take Off Our Tapas. Anyhow, the three of us clicked and were friends ever since. They'd been especially good to me this past year while I'd been dealing with my mother.

"Penelope!" Anne squealed over the phone. "Where the hell have you been?"

I rubbed my forehead. "You would *so* never believe me in a million years. Hey, I need a favor. Can I stay with you for a while?"

"Sure. Is everything okay?" Anne asked.

I noticed a tall blond man dressed in black sweep past the plate glass window. He was larger than your average guy, which was noteworthy in itself, but what caught my attention was the way he moved. He sort of . . .

*Floated?*

"Um. Yeah. I'll be there in a few. Okay?"

"Okay, girlie," she said. "See you pronto."

I hung up the phone, flung my duffel bag over my shoulder, and reached to flip off the lights. Something told me I was an idiot—yes, yes . . . again—for not telling Kinich where I was.

I toggled to Kinich's number and was about to hit Send when the blond man came out of nowhere.

I shrieked and smashed my cell phone into the side of his face. He stumbled to the side and grunted. I didn't look back as I bolted for the door and out onto the street. It was cold and dark, but at least there were people. I rounded the corner as a woman was getting out of a cab. I jumped in and slammed the door shut.

"Drive! Go! Go!" I screamed at the driver through the Plexiglas.

"Well ... sure thing, baby cakes!" she said.

I flashed several glances over my shoulder, thankful not to see the man following.

"So, what are we running from, Penelope?"

*Huh?* I looked at the driver. "Oh my God. It's you!"

"Miss me?" Cimil cackled as we screeched into traffic.

# *Fifteen*

Unable to believe his thousand-year-old Viking eyes, Viktor stared at the woman's cell phone in his hand. There, on the tiny screen, peering out from behind the streaks of blood—*damn, that human hits hard!*—was the image of the blonde female he'd dreamed of for five centuries.

His heart pounded inside his chest, but his body remained immobile. He knew he was supposed to go after the human girl, Penelope, but this was bigger than Niccolo—his best friend for the last millennium who'd sent him to watch over her—this was Fate's handiwork. It had to be. Because only Fate had such a wicked, sadistic sense of humor.

He'd been searching for this golden-haired beauty, now staring at him from the screen, for over five centuries— the same number of years that she'd haunted him day and night. He'd searched the ends of the earth for any clue that might lead to her, prophets, psychics . . . He'd even slept with that despicable creature Cimil once, a scary, scary endeavor that involved pink jelly beans and some very loud music from a group named *fun.*, while Cimil called him by the name Eric. A complete waste of time. After Cimil had her way, she merely said his future was blank.

*What the bloody hell did that mean anyway?*

Did it really matter now? He'd found the woman. He bloody fucking found her! Her smiling image was staring right at him.

*And you're letting the only person on the planet who knows where to find her get away. Plus, the girl is being hunted by Maaskab.*

Viktor's body jerked. *Oh, crap!*

He sifted out the door and followed her scent around the corner in time to see the back of her head through a taxi window, with a very recognizable redhead driving. He blinked and the cab was gone.

"Son of a bitch! Cimil!"

# Sixteen

Kinich burst through Niccolo and Helena's penthouse door and stormed into the wide-open living room, ready to rip the head right off of Andrus's body for having let Penelope leave.

Andrus quickly appeared, armed with a gleaming sword in each hand and a soiled burp cloth over one shoulder.

He caught sight of Kinich and rolled his eyes. "Oh, here we go. Princess Sun Goddess is going to have one of his infamous temperature tantrums. May I remind you, Nick," Andrus said with a sharpness that indicated he was saying "Nick" but really meant "asshole." "That there are children present."

"How could you let her leave? You son of a bitch! I'll kill you." Kinich lunged for Andrus.

A hand whipped out, plucked Kinich from thin air, and deposited him on the other side of the room.

"Back off, Sun God!" Helena snarled. "No one touches Andrus! Not when he's here to protect me and my baby while Niccolo's away training *your*"—she poked him in the chest—"Uchben army. And don't forget Cimil was the one who put Andrus here."

She was right. And he couldn't afford to cause conflict among allies, especially now. But that didn't diminish his anger.

Kinich was about to apologize when Helena cracked a big smile and began laughing. "I thought you said that you didn't like Penelope. But you do. Don't you, Kinny-Kins? Huh . . . ?"

Kinich felt his face turn red-hot. "I happen to care for the woman. This is true. But may I remind you that I care for all humans. Vampires not so mu—"

The front door flew open and a red-faced Penelope scrambled in. "Monsters! Help! Oh my God! Monsters."

She jumped into Kinich's arms, hurling him back several feet. The raging fire inside him instantly cooled.

*Thank the gods she is all right. Oh, hell. Why am I so happy to see her?*

"What happened?" He tried peeling her off him, but her death grip was remarkable. She reminded him of that cat Cimil had once taken swimming in her pool. A long story. He hated Cimil's party games.

Panting, Penelope released her grip, doubled over, and pointed toward the giant floor-to-ceiling windows that were flush with the front of the building. "Monsters . . . they . . . I can't breathe!"

"She's hyperventilating." Helena eased her up, and then lifted her chin and stared into her eyes. "Slow down. Breathe slowly," she said in a calming voice.

Kinich frowned. Helena was glamouring Penelope. He found that irritating. Maybe because he hadn't thought of it first and he wanted to be the one to help her.

Penelope sucked in a lungful of air. "Oh. Wow. Thank you," she said to Helena. "Much better. How'd you do that?"

Helena shrugged. "It's a gift. I do it with the baby sometimes."

"That would be super helpful when I'm teaching. Could you show me how—"

"Penelope!" Kinich barked. He couldn't believe the two ladies were pausing for a little chat.

Penelope blinked and then shook her head as if trying to dislodge something from her ears. "Right. Ummm." Her face turned a ghostly shade of white. "Monsters! Oh my God! Monsters!" She jumped up and down.

"Calm yourself, woman."

"Stop calling me 'woman'! That's so archaic. And annoying! You don't see me calling you 'Minotaur' despite the fact that—"

"Well, that would be ridiculous," Kinich declared. "The Minotaur was a violent, misunderstood creature that should never have existed. Damn Cretans."

Penelope blinked. "I-I was referring to the fact that the Minotaur has a giant bull's head. Or was it a bull's body?" She stomped her foot. "Dammit. It doesn't matter! Stop distracting me. The point is, you're constantly dishing your pompous bull crap!"

Kinich was inches from turning the woman over his knee and giving her a very, very nasty sunburn on her bottom. "Pen. El. Op. E. What happened?"

"Fine. But this conversation isn't over, Minotaur!"

She took a quick breath. "There was a blond man chasing me—he was huge. I mean huge! And I was going to go to my friend Anne's house, but the cab pulled up, and it was her! Your sister. She started yelling, saying that I was doing it all wrong. That I messed up the future, and she couldn't see it anymore!"

Penelope paused and frantically fanned her face with her hand. "I don't know! I don't know what she meant! She said I had to come back here or the world would explode or something. She pulled up to the curb downstairs—oh my God, why is your sister driving a cab? That's crazy. Isn't she rich?—and then I was going to run for it, but one of those monsters came out of nowhere! I screamed. I mean, there was nothing else I could do. Right? When the monster grabbed me, the blond man showed up and tackled him. How'd he get there so fast? Am I in some alternate universe? This isn't right. Then a van pulled up and these three guys in black leather jackets with fangs grabbed me. Cimil jumped out of the cab and tossed them, I mean...*tossed* them across the street. What the hell does that woman eat? I ran inside the building and dove into the elevator!"

Kinich's mind reeled through the frantically delivered story. It was like that time they'd played charades while blindfolded. Underwater. Again, with that poor, poor cat. He'd have to chat with Cimil about her stance on animal rights later.

Unexpectedly, Viktor sifted into the living room, appearing out of thin air directly in front of Penelope.

*Oh, great.* Kinich braced himself.

Penelope screamed at the top of her lungs and passed out. Kinich caught her in his arms and scooped her up.

For one brief second, among the ensuing chaos, Kinich experienced a profound serenity while holding Penelope in his arms. The tiny embers nestled deep inside glowed with euphoric warmth and not the usual hot rage.

Kinich's mind sputtered and stalled like an old engine. *Bloody hell.* He couldn't afford to become attached to this admittedly exquisite, statuesque woman. He had obligations to fulfill.

*Yes, but haven't you spent an eternity taking care of mankind? Fighting for them? Are you not deserving of a life of your own?*

In the early days, watching over humanity was simple. A few pockets of humans existed, scattered across the globe. It was nothing the fourteen gods couldn't handle. Or thirteen, really; Kinich had spent much of those earlier years—during the age referred to by the gods as "pre-calendar" because, well, there were no calendars—living in the human world, wandering. He traveled on foot to every corner of the world. Alone. Thinking. Loathing. It boiled down to one simple matter: his place in the world had been forced upon him with no end in sight.

*Eternity. Eternity. Eternity. Shit.*

Through the dank, musty jungles, through the frigid mountains and scalding-hot deserts, he walked alone, lived alone, slept alone with only the sun on his face and his gnawing, unanswered questions to keep him company.

Where had the gods come from? Was the Creator a real being as Cimil claimed? If yes, then why hadn't he or she spoken to him? Might be nice to know why he, Kinich, existed or if he was truly destined to live for an eternity, caring for humans.

But alas, there would be no answers to these questions, nor would he find any semblance of peace in his soul until the Day of the Penance. That had been nearly five thousand years ago.

While standing on the scorching-hot riverbank of the Nile in Giza, Kinich—known to the Egyptians as Ra, the Sun God—witnessed a great flash of silver light across the sky. Within moments, his life force weakened, and through his otherworldly connection, he determined that his brethren had experienced the same.

Soon, they would discover that Earth housed a new species of transformed humans, six of them to be exact, who drank blood and roamed the night. They would call themselves the Ancient Ones.

Many centuries later, their folklore would state that the diminishment of the gods' powers enabled the birth of the vampires. And that the vampires were the Creator's punishment for the gods becoming complacent and lazy.

But were the vampires truly a punishment?

Kinich thought not.

Shortly after the flash of light, Kinich came upon a pharaoh named Narmer facedown in a pool of mud, too weak to move. Narmer, who would later settle in Spain and take the name Roberto—a very long story involving another of Cimil's scandalous plots—had no recollection of what occurred. When Kinich carried the man to his temple, there was no mistaking the animal-like fangs protruding from his mouth. Later, the man would devour the blood of ten slaves for his supper.

Shocked and intrigued, Kinich remained in Giza to

observe the creature. He would learn what he could before returning to the gods with this startling news. This was when Narmer the Ancient One would become Kinich's greatest teacher.

"Life is not static, Sun God," Narmer would say. "The universe is in a state of constant flux. Energy exchanging, transforming, and evolving from one form to the next. The apple falls from the tree. The worm eats the apple and is eaten by a bird. The bird is eaten by a cat.

"Yes, harmony disguises itself, cloaks itself as a random event. But if one looks closely, the events occur with exquisite balance. Death, life. Struggle, abundance. Love, hate. Think of what would happen if any of these were to dominate or disappear. Even a lacking of sufficient evil might be detrimental. Humankind would grow complacent and lazy. They would cease the quest for enlightenment. Morals and spirituality would become obsolete."

Narmer's words pertaining to the ebb and flow of these various forces were nothing new. But "exquisite balance"? This was the key.

If the gods killed every soul with a blackened heart, then only the virtuous would remain. That would create imbalance. Imbalance would lead to destruction.

This is why he believed the vampires were sent to restore balance, to do the dirty work the gods could not: kill humans indiscriminately, the innocent included. And the gods? Their role was to ensure the universe remained in a constant state of equilibrium.

Sadly, however, balance would not be so easily maintained. Even the six Ancient Ones would face their own breakdown when one of Narmer's brothers split off and created the Obscuros—those vampires who preferred to kill innocents and only innocents. Narmer was eventually forced to proclaim this act, one that he did not initially oppose, forbidden.

Kinich would also face challenges. After returning to his realm, the gods did not rally behind his new philosophy. This was because they had no laws, order, or values. They were a divine, powerful group of children, but he would change that. If he was to be stuck in this...this fucking role as a god for eternity, then, by gods, he would see his sacrifice meant something.

That was then.

Now?

Now his own balance was in jeopardy. His inner demons, his buried pain for having been denied free will, it was catching up, awoken by one night with one human female. Penelope. Yes, after all these years, he once again desired freedom. To be human. To live. To die.

But this was not his path.

*A demon to confront another day.*

Kinich, as he'd been accustomed to doing since precalendar, buried his torment and manned up, as modern humans liked to say.

He glanced at Viktor who'd just made his grand appearance in Helena's living room and nearly given Penelope a heart attack. "What the hell happened?"

Viktor, an ancient Viking warrior and force of his own to be reckoned with, narrowed his cobalt-blue eyes. "I saved your woman from a Maaskab who was about to sift her away. That's what happened."

"She is *not* mine. But the effort is appreciated. And do you happen to know where my sister is?"

Viktor picked a piece of Scab hair from the leather

sleeve of his long coat. "She went after the vamps in the van. Looked damned happy about it, too. Like she was going off to buy another Ginsu knife. How many as-seen-on-TV products does one goddess need, anyway?"

Helena, Andrus, and Kinich exchanged glances before responding with spontaneous, synchronized shrugs.

Viktor tossed the tiny clump in the wastebasket in the corner and shook his head. "Whatever. Point is—and I say this with all the vampire love in my cold, undead Viking heart—what the fuck, people! Did you not hear what I said? Obscuros? Maaskab? Together!"

Kinich's stomach lurched, rolled, burrowed deep underground, and then sprang out of a dark, dark hole.

*Uh-oh...*

He shifted his weight. Penelope was light as a feather cradled in his arms, but he instinctively wanted to hold her even closer. "We will leave for my desert retreat now. It is unsafe here."

"Cimil told us they'd unite," Helena griped. "Maaskab. Obscuros. Someone will have to come up with a whole new name. Do you have any idea how hard that's going to be?"

Kinich raised a brow.

Viktor chimed in. "I vote for *Mocos*. It means 'boogers' in Spanish."

Helena laughed hysterically. "Good one! Oh! Oh! I've got it!" Helena said, raising her hand. "O'Scabbies."

"Perfect. Yes, very good." Viktor regarded her with the affection of a proud father.

Andrus sighed and shook his head.

Helena scoffed. "What? It was funny."

Andrus stared blankly.

"Ugh! You're no fun," she protested. "Let's see if a trip to Sedona with Kinich will wipe that smugness off your face. I know how much you love hanging with vamps and Uchben."

"Sedona?" Andrus said. "If Penelope is being hunted, you and the baby need to be as far away from her as possible. We stay here and let her go with Kinich."

Helena's vampire eyes gleamed with hypnotic intensity. "I want to see Niccolo. We. Are. Going. To. Sedona."

"Like hell you are." Niccolo's large frame hovered in the entrance, his dark camouflage outfit and black hair contrasting with the brilliance of his turquoise eyes—eyes that were once dark, too, but had changed when his vampire days ended and he became a demigod.

Helena's face burst with joy. "Niccolo! Oh my god! I mean, oh my demigod! You're here!"

They shared a long, publicly inappropriate kiss, tongues and hands flying everywhere. Once again, Kinich felt that same gnawing discomfort he'd had when in the presence of Emma and Guy.

"Uh-hum!" Kinich cleared his throat, but the two did not stop for several awkward moments. He glanced at Andrus, whose ego had clearly deflated.

*Poor sap still cares for the woman. You'll never catch me degrading myself by pining for some female.*

When they finally broke their lip-lock, Kinich asked, "How did you arrive?" Being an ex-vampire, Niccolo was no longer able to sift.

"Air Uchben. After your call last evening, I decided to check in on things." Niccolo turned to Helena. "So, you see, you aren't going anywhere, my love." Niccolo cupped both of Helena's cheeks. "I am taking two days off and will spend them making your toes curl, followed by a long nap, yours, of course, during which time I will play with our little Matty and adorn her with kisses until you awaken."

Without so much as a glance in Andrus's direction, he said, "You are on leave now, soldier."

As Andrus marched from the room, he snarled, "You're welcome for my protecting your wife and child, *Niccolo*." And by "Niccolo," he meant "asshole."

*He is very good at doing that,* Kinich noted.

"Well, this has been fun." Kinich bowed his head. "Niccolo, if you are not opposed, I will take the Uchben jet to my sanctuary."

Niccolo glanced at Kinich and then at the dormant Penelope in his arms. "Ah, Kinich. I've always wondered if boring someone to death was possible. I should have known you'd accomplish the task."

"So says the ex-vampire who wept like a baby at my sister's feet, begging her to help him, and then ended up entombed in her piggy bank for three centuries."

"Vampires do not cry! Everyone knows that," Niccolo replied.

"Like a newborn baby, according to Cimil. She claims there are photos." Kinich chuckled.

"So says the Sun God, who has over a million hits on YouTube. The midgets were a nice touch, by the way. Your idea?" Niccolo said sharply.

Dammit! He had no clue what YouTube was, but he'd throttle Cimil when he caught up with her!

"Niccolo. Kinich!" Helena scolded. "Have your pissing match on someone else's time."

"You are right, my little vampire. We must not waste a moment. It feels like there is a kickstand in my pants." Niccolo pulled Helena into his body and began mauling her with his lips again.

One of Kinich's eyes ticked with annoyance. Time to leave.

He turned toward the door still grasping Penelope in his arms, but Viktor prevented his speedy exit. "I'm coming to ensure you arrive safely. It is the least I can do after I failed you both."

Kinich admired Viktor's sense of responsibility. "Very respectable of you, Viktor, but I am sure we will be—"

"I insist." Viktor's eyes simmered with determination.

Kinich gave it a moment's thought. "Thank you," he finally replied. He could not deny that having an extra set of skilled warrior hands would be useful, not to mention provide a distraction from Penelope. Kinich knew, without a doubt, he should not be left alone with the human; something about her was far too tempting.

Was it her curvy, athletic body, the body of a female warrior? Perhaps her perfectly round ass? Those dark green eyes, satin-smooth skin, and sensual, soft lips? No. By far, her most tempting feature was her full, plump breasts with those little pink rosebud nipples. The gods themselves couldn't conceive a more perfect set.

*Dammit. Pure temptation. Every goddamned last inch of her.* Kinich ground his teeth with frustration.

As soon as possible, he would find other arrangements for her safety. The world was teetering on a tumultuous precipice, and this distraction was the last thing he needed.

# Seventeen

⌒

When I woke *this* time—damn, I really needed to stop making this a habit—I was lost. I mean that in both the mental and physical senses of the word.

For starters, I was lying on yet another giant, fluffy bed—*do these people buy bulk and get a discount rate?*—in the center of a spacious, bright room, surrounded by even fluffier burnt-orange pillows. The sandstone-colored walls displayed several headstone-size tablets with hieroglyphics, and on the nightstand, two clay figurines with Mayan headdresses stood back-to-back. Oddly, one resembled Nick, six-pack and all.

At the far end of the room was a large panoramic window overlooking a never-ending stretch of rolling desert with the only green in sight being the impressive saguaro cacti. The gray, angry-looking clouds blanketing the sky were perforated by random beams of sunlight. Something about the way they shined on the desert floor made them seem like spotlights from heaven.

I shook my head from side to side and eased myself from the bed. The clock on the wall said 7:00 a.m. I'd slept through the entire night but noticed I still wore my karate gi.

*Well, that's something. No one's changed my clothes. This day might not turn out so bad.*

*Wait. Your litmus test for a good day is that no one's taken a gander at your privates while you slept?*

*Hey, considering all of the other crap... Cringe.*

Memories, dark and disturbing, jackhammered my mind: a monster appearing out of nowhere, pulling me from Cimil's cab—*WTH, that woman really drove a cab?*—the scummy-looking dudes in leather jackets pulling up in the black van (something was seriously wrong with them, like they'd forgotten their souls at home along with any sense of hygiene). And that man appearing right out of thin air. *And*, I sighed. "Nick..."

"You called?"

The sexiest male specimen I could ever hope to see, in this lifetime or the next, occupied a predominant percentage of the space inside the doorframe. I didn't know what made my girlie bits more peppy; his sizzling smile that could melt my panties right off, or his deeply bronzed, hard chest and ripped abs or his... My eyes traveled toward the south pole.

*Swoon alert! Don't fall over. Don't fall over.*

For heaven's sake, the man wore nothing but a towel; nonetheless, my mind had no issue filling in the blanks. *Or the, uhhh... what's the opposite of* blank? 'Cause his man-treat was a far cry from a word defined as a "void" or a "space." Space shuttle, yes. *With supersized landing gear. And a glorious moon right around the corner: firm, round, and solid as a rock.*

In any case, horny little space analogies aside, my body didn't seem to give a hoot if my memory of that night with Kinich was fictional; as far as it was concerned, he'd rocked my world and it wanted another go.

Stupid body.

I swallowed, my mouth suddenly as barren as the desert outside. "Nick. Mind telling me how I got all the way to . . . ?"

"Sedona." One corner of his mouth curled.

*Oh, that smile.*

"What was I saying?" I asked.

He laughed.

*I amuse you, do I?* That moved the needle from lusty fog to ticked off.

He must have noticed the steam spewing from my ears, because he suddenly offered, "I will tell you everything. First, let me hunt down some breakfast. You'll need your strength for this."

"But I . . ."

He turned and disappeared down the hall before I could protest.

*Well, great. I'm all gross and crusty, and the gorgeous, infuriating man wants to cook for me.*

"I'm taking a shower first!" I called out to an empty space.

I surveyed the room for fresh clothes, surprised to discover my belongings from my overnight bag neatly stowed inside the walk-in closet that happened to be the size of my entire apartment back in New York.

I grabbed a comfy pink tee, jeans, bra, and undies and scampered off to the attached bathroom, where my jaw dropped.

"Holy deviled ham," I whispered. It was exactly like the photos I'd seen in *Cosmo*. Yes, yes. Right next to that article about the Orgasm Whisperer. I wanted to live in this bathroom. I wanted to die in this bathroom. I wanted to *be* this bathroom. Sunken Jacuzzi tub for four surrounded by fresh white candles, clear glass bowls filled with lavender bath salts, and bottles of infused oils; white wicker sitting area with a cappuccino machine and mini-fridge; and a shower big enough to bathe a small nation.

*Saints. Every girl deserves a bathroom like this.*

In two minutes flat the tub was filled—another amazing feature—and I lowered myself into the steaming-hot suds. The tips of my cold toes and the ache in my back melted away. The only thing missing was . . .

*Kinich.*

*I'm hopeless.*

"So. That's where you disappeared to." His cocoa-brown face and shimmering turquoise eyes hovered over me.

I sucked in a fortifying breath to keep from turning into a soggy, little globule of neediness.

Fact: He took my breath away. He created a vacuum in my mental atmosphere.

Fact: I wanted this man. More than my date with five-star Mr. Bubble.

Fact: Something about him wasn't right, and I was about to find out why.

Fiction: I was going to keep my cool.

He observed the sudsy water rippling over my body, masking my bareness.

"Sorry," I said nervously. "I really missed my bathtub. And what a surprise! You have the exact same one as me."

Nick raised one brow.

"Kidding."

"Oh." He nodded. "I wondered how that might be possible. The tub was custom built by a man in Japan who only accepts gold bullion as payment."

I flashed him a questioning frown.

"That was a joke," he said. "Who carries around gold bullion these days?"

"Not me. Bullion is heavy. I prefer gold coins," I said facetiously.

"Exactly. So much easier to transport and hide."

*Ummm... yeah.*

"I was about to get out," I said. "So if you want to talk—"

"Actually"—he raised his hands, encouraging me to stay put—"it might make what I have to say easier if you're relaxed."

"That doesn't sound good." My heart thumped away, doing a lowrider bass beat.

"It is neither good nor bad; it simply is what it is."

Frankly, after all of the weirdness I'd endured, there was no explanation under the sun that could quell me into a state of buying "it simply is what it is." That's the sort of thing you'd say about having a big ass or freckles. You might even say that about a rainy day or ugly painting. But not this. No. Because whatever he was about to say, it had to be big. And weird.

I poked the Jacuzzi button to turn off the jets. "I'm listening."

*I'm freaking out.*

Nick cleared his throat, his piercing eyes vacillating between the deepest shades of green and aquamarine. "I've never had to tell a human this before, so bear with me."

"Hu-human?"

*So glad I peed before I got in the tub.*

Nick scratched his chin. His deep, rich brown stubble, I then noticed, was slightly darker than his golden-streaked hair and thick caramel-colored eyelashes. God, he was gorgeous. It hurt to look at him. Not that it would stop me.

"No easy way to say this, I suppose." His voice lowered one octave. "First, I want it made abundantly clear that I do not know why the Maaskab are after you. But I do intend to find out."

"What's a Miskeeb?"

"Maaskab."

"Fine. Whatever."

"Originally, they were a group of Mayan priests who worshipped the dark arts. They pillaged, murdered, and raped, all in the name of their holy quest to gain power. Eventually, their bloodlust triggered the collapse of the Mayan civilization. Today, they are a thousand times stronger and have their sights set much higher."

*Oh, shit! And they want me? Me! WTF! Why me? There are, like, what? Seven billion people on the planet. So why me?*

I popped out of the water, unable to contain the need to run like a fat little rabbit about to be gobbled down by a hungry wolf. "Please tell me this is a joke!"

Nick's body froze. His eyes wandered leisurely south from my face. "I...I...for gods' sake, woman, you're so *damned* sexy."

I blinked and looked down at the sudsy clumps slinking down my bare skin, racing back to the pool of water below.

"Oh!" I crossed my arms over the strategic parts. "Toss me a towel." It wasn't as if he hadn't seen my naked glory, but that didn't mean he had a season pass.

Nick remained motionless, staring at my breasts.

I dropped back into the water. "Towel?"

"Sure." He pointed to a neatly rolled stack near the sink in a wicker basket.

"Funny. Can you toss one over?"

He glanced at the towels and then back to me. A wicked little smile do-si-doed across his face. "Sorry. Fresh out of tosses."

I huffed in protest. "Fine. Then I'm staying put."

"Did I ever tell you that I have amazing stamina? I only require one or two hours of sleep each night, oh. Wait. Didn't have to tell you. Because you've lived it. That's right."

*What? Smug son of a...*

"Neither of us is certain we 'lived' anything that night. And if we did, who's to say you impressed me with your awesome stamina?"

"Because there is no other possibility."

I made a little hiss. "You are so arrogant—"

"Arrogant?" He winked. "Yes, I suppose it's a gift."

"Nick. Please, either talk and get this over with or leave so I can get a towel. This isn't funny."

The smile melted from his full lips, the full lips I

dreamed about sucking and licking. The full lips that per-haps had done things to my body, in places and in ways no one had ever attempted.

He stood up straight, and I noticed he was wearing a pair of white linen pants and a button-down shirt, the upper half strategically left open so that the hard ripples of his stomach peeked through the opening.

God, he was delicious. Even his smell did it for me.

He sat down on the edge of the tub and began swirling his finger in the water. "The temperature is cold. Let me heat it up for you." Within moments, the water jumped ten degrees.

"How did you do that?"

His eyes focused on his swirling finger. "Another gift. There are fourteen of us, each with a set of unique abilities."

My eyes fixated on his exquisite, flawlessly masculine face. Maybe I hadn't wanted to see it before, but looking closely, I noticed an odd radiance in his light brown skin. Even the golden highlights in his caramel-brown hair seemed to sparkle with flecks of red and gold. And those eyes; when I peered into them, they shimmered with a thousand shades of turquoise, aquamarine, sky blue, and sherbet green.

What was he? Whatever the answer, he couldn't be human. No.

"G-g-go on," I mumbled.

"This world is full of mysteries, Penelope. Life-forms of the most amazing sorts. Miracles of nature, of the uni-verse; I am simply another one of those miracles."

*Miracle?*

A miracle was walking on water or spontaneous healing.

Or the fact *Jersey Shore* hadn't been canceled yet. Or that a Fudgsicle was only five points.

If the word *miracle* was indicative of his species, then...

"Oh my God, you're an angel, aren't you?"

Kinich's head snapped up. "Gods, no! I'm a...a god. The God of the Sun. Angels are disturbingly fanatical with their do-gooding." He made a sour, icky face.

*Did he just say...*

"God? Har-har. Very funny."

He leaned over the edge of the tub, entrancing me with his hypnotic gaze. "Touch your nose."

My hand shot from the water and my index finger made contact with the tip of my nose. "How did you do that?"

"I am a deity. I have gifts," he stated blandly.

"That was some mind trick. Come on, Nick, stop messing around."

"You'd believe I am an angel, but not a god?" He frowned.

"I don't know what to believe. I'm sitting naked in a tub being told there's another species sharing our planet."

"There are others, too," he added. "That man who appeared in Helena and Niccolo's living room, for example, is a vampire, as is Helena."

"Vampire?" I asked.

"Correct," he replied.

"Seriously? Like, as in, people who drink blood, walk around in capes, and turn into bats?"

"Bats, no. Capes are optional. Helena, for example, loves floral prints and Hello Kitty."

*Sweet-pickled demons on a Triscuit. I knew something was off about that family, especially that fangy little...*

"The baby, too?"

"Yes," he replied, "Matty is half-vampire."

Did I want to ask what the other half was? I decided no. With my luck, it would be something over the top, like a hobbit.

*Vampire hobbits? Now, that's just crazy talk, girlfriend!*

"However," he continued, "these vampires are not evil. They are our allies."

I'd need to digest all this later; it was a teensy bit too much. "Peachy. Anything else?"

"The Maaskab have joined up with a faction of evil vampires called Obscuros. They are planning a war against us. All of us. If they win, it will lead to the apocalypse."

*Holy crappity crap.* "End of the world?"

He nodded once.

"You're not joking, are you?"

He shook his head no.

I held up a finger. "Give me a sec."

*Vampires are real. Those evil monsters are really some sort of priests who want to kill everyone. Kinich is a god. The Sun God. I'm sitting naked in the tub. Talking to a god. Of the sun. And I may have slept with him.*

*Oh, God.*

It was all making some sort of sad, sad sense in my mind. Kinich's flash of light had been accompanied by intense heat when the monster had attacked him. And who could forget the heat I felt when I was near him?

*Ohhh, the heat of his body.* I licked my lips. No wonder I couldn't resist him, he was a real live god. He radiated sensuality.

Then an odd question popped into my mind. "You

didn't use that mind control thing to get me to like you? Hey, did you say apocalypse? Dammit. Why can't I think straight when I'm around you? It's your mind control. Isn't it? Oh, crackers. I'm doing it again."

"Mind control? Don't be absurd, woman. I mean, yes. I am gifted with such a skill, but why on earth would I use it in such a situation? Gods are like magnets to mortals. I merely walk into a room, and the females are mine for the taking. I also emit pheromones that interfere with your synapses. Makes you more compliant...But mind control to make females want me? Never."

My mouth fell open. He'd been putting the god-lust whammy on me the whole time? And there I'd been, prancing around like a lovesick moron. He probably got a huge kick out of it.

"You disgusting! Scummy. Pig!" I burst from the tub and slapped him across the cheek.

His eyes flared with silent rage, though he didn't flinch. "What the devil was that for?"

"*That* was for every woman you've ever taken advantage of with your lust whammy! I only wish I could slap you once for each of them, but I bet there are thousands, and I don't want to spend one more minute with you, you...god slut!"

I swiped a towel from the basket and stormed from the bathroom to the walk-in closet. I'd left my clean clothes in the bathroom so I'd have to grab new ones. I closed the door, dressing quickly and shoving the remainder of my belongings into my bag. No way was I going to hang out here. Not with him. Not after what he'd admitted.

Nick knocked loudly. "Penelope, please listen."

"No! I'm not listening to you...you scumbag!"

"I am *not* a scumbag."

I pulled my still-dripping hair into a ponytail and yanked open the door. "Really? Then what would *you* call a being such as yourself who uses his 'gifts' on innocent women?"

He narrowed his eyes, and for a moment, I could swear flames danced across his pupils. "I do not use my powers to seduce women."

"You just admitted it!"

He laughed. "Penelope Trudeau, you are jealous."

*Oh, that— That is such...*

"Bullshit! Why would I be jealous?"

Amused, he crossed his arms. "You must want me. Quite badly judging from your reaction."

*Yes. Yes, I do.* "Nooo. No! You're the one who brought me here. And let's remember, it was your crazy sister who pulled me into this train wreck you call a life!" I slammed the door in his face.

Wait. If he was a god, would that make his crazy sister a...?

I grabbed the door handle and pulled. Nick stood inches from my body, staring down at me with a slow burn.

"Is your crazy sister Cimil a goddess?" *Please, say no. That would be so, so wrong for humanity.*

"Penelope, you need to listen to me. There is more I need to tell you—"

"Answer me!"

"Yes."

*Great! Just great. The crazies are in charge.*

"Andrus, too?"

"No. He was once a Demilord—a vampire taken to

our realm and given the light of the gods. Now he is a demigod—his maker, the vampire queen, died, and therefore, his vampire blood died, too."

Huh? What were these people—um…deities—smoking? God crack?

*Grack?*

"You know that made zero sense. Right?" I pushed past him to grab my boots near the side of the bed. "But you know what? It doesn't matter! You could be leprechauns with pots of gold, wanting to make me your queen. I don't care. I don't want anything to do with you, Nick!"

I bent over to tie my shoes.

"Leprechauns do not have a queen. And you are not leaving," he said bluntly.

"Why the hell not?" I barked.

"Because they are nomads."

*Wha-what?*

"I'm not even going to ask. But I *am* going to leave; the last time I checked, my wagon wasn't hitched to yours, so I can do what I damn well like," I seethed.

"First, you are very upset. Second, it is not safe; the Maaskab want you, and they will not stop until they have you."

"Well," I replied bitterly, "seeing that it's my life, I think I get to make that choice for myself. By the way, big boy, I don't need a mother! I already have one."

Oh no. My mother. I still hadn't spoken with her.

"Well," he said coldly, "how would you like for the next time she sees you to be at your funeral? But there won't be a body. I can guarantee it because the Maaskab won't leave one behind. So you best accept that your wagon *is* hitched to mine."

Damn this man ... deity ...

"Get out! You man whore!" I gave him the George Bush Iraqi salute. (I threw my shoe at him.) "Just get out!"

Nick held up his palms and bowed his head. "As you wish. But for the record," he said as he turned to leave, "you are the only woman I have *perhaps* been with." He closed the bedroom door behind him.

Really? He'd never been with anyone? *Him?*

My anger instantly melted.

Then I gasped.

It was true. I had been jealous. And now that he'd told me I was the only woman he had "perhaps" been with, I wanted him even more. As irrational and childish as it was, I didn't want to share him. I wanted to be the only woman—past, present, or future—in his life.

*I'm so confused.* I burst into tears.

Now, normally, I wasn't a crier or a lame shoe thrower and didn't waste a lot of time feeling sorry for myself, but the pressure valve needed a little workout or I'd flip.

I saw my purse sitting on the dresser and practically dove for it. I dug out my cell and the piece of paper with the number for my mother's clinic. I dialed and it finally rang.

*Oh, thank heavens.*

"Hi, my name is Penelope Trudeau. I'm calling for my mother, Julie?"

The man spoke in clear-as-day English.

"What do you mean, 'wrong number'?" I asked, hiccuping and sniffling.

I repeated the number. I had it right, but there was no one there by my mother's name. To make matters more unsettling, it was some bar named Fugly's—yes, a Swedish bar named Fugly's—not a medical clinic.

The phone slipped from my hand. This couldn't be happening. It couldn't. What was going on? What was I going to do?

*Cry some more. Yeah, that will feel gooood.* I burst into tears once again. And whattaya know? I felt better! For ten whole seconds. Then I realized sobbing wouldn't help me find my mother and that I needed to apologize to Nick—*OMG, a god? Really? And you called him a man whore?*—for acting like the giant ass that I was.

*What are you waiting for, Penelope? Groveling should be treated like a Band-Aid.*

I turned for the door and collided with a black leather wall. It was the enormous blond man, the vamp...the vamp...I couldn't say or think the word.

He studied me with his intense, deep blue eyes as if wondering what I might do so that he could decide what he might do.

"I can save you from having to guess," I stated quietly. "I was about to scream but decided it's useless."

"Good choice." He swooped down, picked up my phone, and held up the screen. "The woman, who is she? I must know."

My mind ricocheted like a pinball. Now that I thought about it, the last time I'd seen my cell was when I'd slammed it into the side of this vamp...man's face.

"You put my phone back in my purse, didn't you?"

He nodded yes. "Who is she?" he asked again.

Had he come all the way to Sedona specifically to give me back my phone and find out who my mother was?

"Why are you asking? Aren't you a..." *Oh my God. Oh my God. I can't say the word. I can't say it.* I wiped the tears from my cheeks with the back of my hand.

"Yes. I am a vampire. My name is Viktor."

*Oh, thank goodness, someone said it.*

"Please," he continued in a deep, lulling voice. "Penelope, I must know. Who. Is. The. Woman? Where can I find her?" Something in his eyes made me want to tell him.

Mind control? These people were so, so not going on my Friends list.

I felt the words involuntarily bubbling up. "She's my mom. And she's sick. Really sick. I don't know where she is. She's supposed to be in a Swedish clinic, but she's not—"

He snatched the piece of paper I still held in my hand. His blue eyes turned the deepest, darkest black I'd ever seen. I stepped back.

"Center for Immune Management and Integrative Lifestyles?" he said with a feral growl. "Fucking hell."

"What?" Why was he using the f-word? That was reserved for the direst of situations.

*Or the sexiest. Like the time when you dreamed that Kinich—*

*Shut it, Pen! Idiot! Now is not the time to think of dirty-deity dancing.*

"Center. Immune. Management. Integrative. Lifestyles," he repeated.

I looked at him.

He looked at me.

I was lost.

He was not.

"C-I-M-I-L," he stated.

*Oh, fuck!* "Cimil? She has my mother?"

Viktor shook his head. "Not anymore."

"I don't understand."

He ran his large hands through the length of his thick blond hair. "Whatever plans Cimil had for your mother have been derailed. This I am sure of."

"I still don't follow. Where is she? What's happened to her? How do you know all this?"

I didn't know Viktor or anything about his people, but I could tell he was in a dark place with bad, bad thoughts, and the fact that my mother had anything to do with those bad, bad thoughts scared the hell out of me.

He turned for the door looking smaller, defeated somehow. "I must speak with Kinich. Immediately."

"Wait! Tell me what the hell is going on!" I tried to follow but he was gone in a blink.

*Christ!* Vampires were definitely not going on the fav list.

I followed the hallway past several vacant bedrooms until it hooked to the right and ended at a set of double oak doors. I was about to turn back, but caught a whiff of exotic flowers, fresh ocean air, sunshine, and fruit.

I pushed open the doors, stepped inside, and inhaled like a junkie getting a fix. *Kinich.*

This had to be his room. Hanging over the headboard was a large sun made from hammered copper, and a free-standing bar stood in one corner next to a sitting area with a cozy, khaki-colored couch.

*Running water?* I turned my head left and noticed a doorway with a glass wall to each side. Sheets of water flowed over the panes, disappearing into a gap in the floor, to create an aquatic privacy screen. Whatever kind of bathroom was on the other side, it had to be something spectacular.

Despite the beautiful decor and pre-Hispanic art

adorning the walls, I became fixated on the nightstand. What did this deity keep in his drawers? Did he moisturize? After all, he was the Sun God—*demon crackers, gods can't be real*—but all that exposure to the sun's power had to leave him chapped. Or maybe he read dirty magazines. What kind of women would he like?

*Definitely tanned women.*

I stepped toward the dresser.

*Penelope! Focus! Mom's missing, remember?*

I gasped, realizing what was happening. His smell was an instant ditz-ifier. God crack!

*Grack!*

I scrambled from his room and backtracked down the brightly lit hallway until I found Kinich and Viktor arguing in the living room.

"I have never in my existence asked the gods for anything," Viktor disputed. "I have served. I have been loyal and obeyed. I have suffered. And now I make this one request, Kinich."

"Going in alone is madness—suicide! What does the book of the Oracle say?" Nick asked.

"Nothing. I've consulted the pages hundreds of times. It never mentions me, and it never will."

"You don't know that for certain. Perhaps you should look again," Kinich argued.

"It is a moot point; Cimil is currently in possession of the text, and she is nowhere to be found."

"Cimil? Why would *she*, of all people, need a book that foretells the future?"

Were they speaking of that thick leather text she kept poring over when I was in her study? And it told the future?

*Devil crisps.*

"I do not know," Viktor stated coldly. "It isn't my concern; however, Penelope's mother is. I must go after her. Even if it means angering Niccolo."

*Oh my God!* They were arguing about rescuing my mother?

"Niccolo will not be angry; he will be furious! He may never speak to either of us again," Kinich grumbled. "Helena's life is bound to yours, you are her goddamned maker! She would perish if anything—"

I pushed myself between the two towers of muscle. "If you don't tell me what the hell is going on, I swear to God...or gods...or—whatever! That I will take you down! Both of you!"

The men regarded me with utter curiosity.

"Talk or I'll stake you or...or lasso you with silver or something you won't like."

Instead of anger, irritation, or any sign of my threat displeasing him, Viktor's eyes filled with...

*Affection?* Wondering why, I stepped back a smidgeon.

"Penelope"—Viktor brushed the loose strands of hair from my face—"I realize you do not know me, but you will. And until then, you will simply need to trust me."

I shook my head. "But I don't..."

Kinich pushed himself between us as if claiming his territory. "Leave now, Viktor. I'll give you two days. If you do not return before then, I will be forced to tell Niccolo. Our relationship with the vampires loyal to him cannot be jeopardized, nor can his focus on preparing for the war."

Before I could speak another word, Viktor was gone.

"Son of a..." I looked at Nick. "Where did he go? What the hell is going on? Where's my mother?"

Nick grabbed me and pulled me into his body. I struggled hard, but he was strong and warm and his scent lulled me into a state of calm.

He stroked the back of my head. "I will tell you, Penelope, but you must trust we will do everything we can."

"Just tell me," I whispered.

"Viktor believes he is destined to save your mother, that it is his life's purpose. He's dreamt of her for five hundred years. And . . ." He paused. "Of her being taken by the Maaskab, snatched away from right under Cimil's nose."

"The monsters have my mom?"

"He believes so, and I concur; the dreams are a premonition."

I began to sob. "Is she going to die?"

"I do not know. There is more to his visions, but he will not say. I can only tell you he has been obsessed with finding your mother for the last five centuries."

*No. No. No!*

My mind swam in a swampy cloud of jumbled thoughts and emotions, but my heart could take no more.

It cracked wide open.

# Eighteen

When life hands you lemons, you take those lemons and shove them right up life's...well, you get the picture. A little crude, I know. But that was my motto. No lemonade for this girl. No, sir. Nevertheless, this situation was something so surreal, so terrifying, so...*surreal—didn't I say that already? I can't think. Why can't I think?*

*You're on grack! That's why. You need to clear your head so you can figure this out.*

*But I like it here. He's so warm and strong. I feel safe wrapped in his big arms, and...yummm, he smells really freaking good.*

"Penelope? Good lord, woman, I've never met a human so susceptible to me." Nick gave me a little shake. "Penelope? You there?" I heard his voice off in a distant corner of my mind, yet I was somewhere else, somewhere completely safe and happy. My own mental tropical island.

"Penelope!"

*What a pest! Can't he see I'm busy?*

"Woman," his deep voice commanded, "you will come back to me now. You will no longer be affected by my energy. You are immune to my scent."

Like being shoved off a cliff into an icy, frigid ocean, I came to. "What happened?" I was sitting on Nick's sandstone-colored leather couch, with said man gripping me by the shoulders, staring deeply into my eyes.

"I believe you are having what people refer to as a nervous breakdown. It looks very unpleasant." His tone was deep and melodic, though something had changed.

"What did you do to me?" I shook my head.

"I have instructed your brain to ignore any impulses it may feel due to my energy. You are immune until I remove it."

*Oh, wow.* I took a deep breath to test it out. He still smelled incredible, but my head felt clearer. "Couldn't you have come up with that little trick any sooner?"

He shrugged. "Hadn't really thought of it until now."

"You're a god. Don't you think of everything?"

The edges of his mouth curled into a delicious little smile that made my heart disco dance. He was still the most gorgeous man I'd ever seen. Apparently I wasn't immune to that.

"We are not perfect nor omnipotent; although we are quite powerful, especially when in our own realm. From there we may observe the human world and influence events or people with surgical precision. However, we cannot see everything at once. It is like having a satellite one can focus on specific areas or people."

"You spy on us!"

"Of course," he replied without any hint of shame. "How else would we do our jobs?"

I gasped. "Do you watch people doing...private things?"

He leaned back into the overstuffed couch, unbuttoned one shirt cuff, and began rolling it up his thick arm. "It is unavoidable. Still, after observing humanity for tens of thousands of years, one becomes desensitized."

I gasped again. "Oh my God, have you ever spied on me?"

"No." He grinned from ear to ear and began working on the other sleeve. "I assure you, now I will."

Great. I'd never be naked again. It's really, really hard to take a good shower if you're not naked. And imagine trying to shave your bikini line. Or your legs.

"You can't do that!"

He made the last roll. "I can do anything I like; I'm a god."

"A rude Peeping Tom god," I grumbled.

"A man has to have his pleasures in life." He paused and stared pensively at my face for several awkward moments before he reached out and brushed his thumb along my lower lip.

Was I one of his "pleasures"?

We stared at each other for a very long moment, and I couldn't resist marveling yet again at that face: full lips; thick, honey-colored eyelashes framing his turquoise eyes; deep, flawlessly bronzed skin; and a hint of a dent in the middle of his stubble-covered chin. And that hair. Every strand was thick and shiny. I wanted to run my fingers through it while he kissed me with reckless abandon and ground his naked, hard, muscular body...

"Are you sure you did your little spell correctly?" I asked.

He cocked his head. "Of course. Why?"

*I'm tingling down there.* "No reason." I stood up and stepped away, massaging my temples. "Maybe I need a minute for your little spell to fully kick in." There was a nagging thought ticking away in the back of my brain. I felt angry about something. And sad. Really, really sad.

"My mom! Those monsters took her. Why?"

"I'm uncertain, Penelope. But I will tell you everything I know. Sit."

"I want to stand." *Being so close to you is too distracting.*

"I want you to sit." Something in his voice tugged on my resolve.

"Hey! I thought you made me immune to you."

"To my scent and energy, yes. Not to my voice. Sit." I felt my willpower melting away. Now I really, really wanted to sit.

*Ugh! He doesn't fight fair.* "Look," I said, "I'm sorry I accused you earlier of being a god slut and man whore— that was wrong of me to say—but that doesn't mean I've forgiven you for using your gifts on me that night or give you permission to keep doing it."

He lifted one delicious brow. "Is that what you believe? That I used my 'man whore' gifts on you?"

I nodded.

"I see." He rubbed his chin. "So you are saying there is no possible way you would ever want me of your own free will."

"That's right." *Oh, that's the biggest load of BS, Penelope. He could be lying in mud, covered in pig poop, and you'd still want him.*

*Would not.*

*Would, too!*

"Okay. Yes! Yes, you're gorgeous. You make my girlie parts melt like butter on a hot sidewalk. But that doesn't give you permission to be a Mr. Bossy Britches or use your voice to get your way."

Another charming, breathtaking smile crept across his face. "Noted. I will refrain from being a...Mr. Bossy Britches." He patted the spot on the couch to his side.

I took a deep breath and sat.

"Let me start from the beginning." Nick began telling a story that could only be described as the most unbelievable, horrific tale ever told. About eighty or so years ago, his brother Chaam, the God of Male Virility, lost his marbles and began plotting to wipe out mankind. And because all of the gods were "hardwired" (as Nick called it) to protect humanity, they didn't know why or how Chaam changed, but they did know he discovered a substance called black jade.

Chaam and his army of evil priests used the jade for all sorts of sinister deeds. Example: They once trapped the gods by poisoning the water inside these pools called cenotes—the gods use them as portals. Then Chaam figured out he could grind the stuff up and inject it into people to make them his evil minions. The sickest of all was that Chaam discovered that if a woman wore this jade, he could sleep with her and make little Chaams. Or Chaamettes. Turned out, though, only the firstborn children carried Chaam's deity genes—including any firstborn children from subsequent generations. Then he started to sleep with lots and lots of women. If the children were male, he gave them to the Maaskab for their army. Females, or Payals, on the other hand, weren't so lucky; once grown, they were slaughtered and used as deity-charged biofuel for his weapons—some sort of black jade pyramids he'd built.

"How sick. How twisted," I said. Then I remembered something. "The necklace I wore the night we were together, was it made from the same stuff?"

He nodded yes.

I cringed. "You made me wear the evil jade?"

"I suppose I did, although I do not recall that night. The jade, however, is not evil by itself. It is merely a substance capable of storing particular kinds of energy, supernatural energy. If it is exposed to good energy, then that's what it will contain. If dark energy, the same. Luckily, only one being knows the secret to releasing the charge, Chaam, and he's not talking."

"Because he's stubborn like you?"

Nick frowned. "He does not speak because he's locked away inside his pyramid under constant surveillance by our human allies, the Uchben."

That didn't seem like a sufficient punishment. He'd purposefully had children only to enslave or murder them. Perhaps a punishment befitting his crime didn't exist.

*Those poor, poor women.*

"Did any of his daughters survive?" I asked.

"Yes. And they lived to have more children. Emma is Chaam's great-granddaughter and is engaged to my brother Guy. We believe there are more Payals scattered across the globe and hundreds imprisoned somewhere by the Maaskab. We've been searching for them for over a year without success. Though Chaam is contained, his Maaskab still roam free, determined to carry out his wishes. We hope to find the women before there are none left." His serious expression changed to dread. "Penelope, I must ask you something. They took your mother, according to Viktor, and are now after you. I assume you are both firstborn females?"

"Yes, but—"

"Do you know anything about your family's history?"

No! He wasn't saying...He couldn't be saying...

"That can't be right. I knew my grandmother. She was a nice, normal person who raised horses on a farm with my grandfather in Indiana. He and my grandmother died when I was little, but I can tell you for sure she wasn't different. Neither is my mother."

"It's possible they never realized it. We don't have much to compare to, but Emma had no clue what she was until—"

"No! This can't be right." My heart thumped.

Nick brushed a stray lock of hair behind my ear. "Perhaps I am mistaken, but all of the signs are pointing to only one explanation."

I stood up and began pacing. *No! No! Not possible.* "Wouldn't I know if that disgusting brother of yours were my great-grandfather? And...Oh no! You and I might have slept together! You're his brother! You've turned me into an incestuous skeez!"

Nick stood and made little waves with his palms. "Slow down. I only call him my brother, just as I call Cimil my sister, but we are not related in such a way. We did not have a mother or father."

I breathed a sigh of relief. "How were you made?"

Nick shrugged. "We do not know. We simply awoke one day, approximately seventy thousand years ago. Aware. Existing.

"Cimil claims the Creator made us to watch over the world, though I have never seen or heard this Creator personally."

I suddenly felt woozy. My brain was going into overload. I stumbled to the side.

Nick reached out and caught me. "You need to eat something."

He gently placed me down on the couch and propped my head up with a cushion. I didn't want to rest. I wanted to fight. I wanted to hunt down those vile creatures and get my mother back. But he was right; I was hungry and fried.

Nick returned several moments later with a tall glass of water and stack of Oreo cookies.

"Cookies?" Had this been that breakfast he'd mentioned earlier? *My kind of chef!*

"My kind does not require food," he explained, "so when I eat, it is for pleasure. My preference is tropical fruit. I keep these around in case my brother Guy stops by. He likes them very much."

Weird, but I supposed it made sense. If they didn't need food for fuel or have to worry about waistlines, then they ate what they liked. Of course, if I were a deity, I'd sign up for the egg roll, mochi ice cream, and sourdough bread diet.

I reached for the tall glass and took a swig. I promptly spit the fiery liquid all over Nick's flagstone coffee table. "What is that?" I hacked.

"Rum. I thought it might help to take the edge off."

*Yeah, for the next three days.* "Thank you, but I'm not scheduled to become an alcoholic until next week."

He looked confused.

"Joking. Why be a drunk when I have grack at my fingertips? That's way more fun."

He stared blankly.

"God crack? Grack?" I said.

He continued staring.

"Just ignore me," I mumbled.

He dipped his head. "I'll bring you that water." He returned with a real glass of water and sat down on the edge of the couch. "I will send one of the Uchben out for groceries while you rest. Then we will finish answering your questions."

"Uchben? Those are your 'human allies,' the ones guarding Chaam, right?"

"Yes. They have a very large army and use my grounds for training, as do our vampire allies. There is an encampment about a half mile from here along with several guesthouses, apartment complexes, a convention center, airstrip, airplane hangar, helicopter pad, underground bunker for fifteen thousand, missile silo, ten-year supply of clean water, fifty self-sustainable greenhouses that double as emergency oxygen generators, a state-of-the-art underground hospital, a library, war room, and satellite control center."

I quirked one brow. "Is that all?"

Contemplating, Nick's eyes shifted to the mural-covered ceiling (it was a replica of the *Sistine Madonna* with the two cherubs). "Oh. And a bar with pool tables and a few hundred board game stations."

"Board games?" Was he serious?

"The men are very competitive, especially the vampires. There's a tournament every year. I believe this year's pick is Hungry Hungry Hippos. Cimil is usually the master of ceremonies."

"Seriously?" I asked.

"Absurd. Is it not?" He shook his head.

"Yeah. Just a tad."

"Barrel of Monkeys is much more challenging. Those little red buggers never stay together."

*Okeydokey.*

"At any rate," Nick continued. "General Niccolo DiConti, who has direct, day-to-day responsibility for the army, stays at the camp along with the Uchben chiefs, assisting with training and preparations for the Great War—the war that will decide the fate of mankind. With so many well-seasoned warriors about, the Maaskab are less likely to attack us here."

"Only *less* likely?" I started to sit up. Where I was going, who knew? But running sounded like a fab idea.

He gently pushed down on my shoulder. "You need to rest." He brushed the hair back from my forehead. "Please. I will watch over you. Nothing will happen."

Although I could take care of myself, it felt oddly pleasant to have a real live deity wanting to protect me. An unexpected giddiness washed over me.

"Why are you smiling?" he asked.

I sighed and closed my eyes. "No reason."

# Nineteen

When my dizziness subsided, I opened my eyes to the heavenly sight of Nick, eyes closed, sitting at the other end of the couch. His large hands rested on top of my legs, which were propped over his lap.

Now that I could think clearly, I saw the truth: I liked this man—deity, whichever—a lot. I loved being near him. I loved having my hair and clothes saturated with his delicious, exotic scent. I loved how he made my cuticles, and other unmentionable parts, tingle with adrenaline.

It didn't matter that I knew next to nothing about his past, his world, or—*gulp*—species. It didn't matter that the timing sucked or that my world was falling apart. My heart knew what it wanted. It knew the moment we'd met.

How did he feel about me?

Pondering the question, I studied his exquisitely masculine face and watched his wide chest rise and fall with the peaceful rhythm of his breath.

*Ask him.*

*I can't.*

*Since when did you become shy? And think of the agony you'll feel not knowing. Ask him!*

*Ugh. Okay.*

"Nick?"

His eyes snapped open.

"Oh, sorry," I said. "Did I wake you?"

"No. I was thinking," he said.

*About what?* I wondered.

He ran his hands through his golden-brown hair and then stretched his arms above his head. He still wore his white linen shirt buttoned just above the navel.

On any other man, the partially exposed chest look would be so "player," but not on him.

"Feeling better?" he asked and gave my legs a little rub that only made me turn warm and gooey inside.

"I think so." I sat up and pulled my legs away; I needed to concentrate. "Can I ask why you're helping me?"

He glanced away. "Because I must."

"Must? Like, gun to head 'must' or compelled by your own emotions?"

He leaned forward and placed the heels of his palms over his eyes. "This is what I've been contemplating; I am compelled to watch over mortals, but with you, it is something entirely different. The two weeks I searched for you, following our night together, were...extremely distressing. I thought of little else besides you."

My brain buzzed with ego-laden joy. It was almost too surreal to think that someone like Nick could have feelings for someone like me. He was a deity, for heaven's sake. And a really, really hot one at that.

"Nice to know I wasn't alone," I mumbled.

He threaded his fingers through his hair. "I have yet to find a reason or to come to terms with it, but the need to be with you, to be physical, is extremely"—he peered into my eyes—"potent."

"Potent?" I gulped.

His fierce gaze burrowed into me as he nodded slowly.

If we hadn't slept together yet, then I sure as heck wanted to now. If we had, then I wanted him again. *And again and again and again.* I wanted to feel his hard flesh buried deep inside my body. I wanted to feel the friction of his sculpted chest against my breasts.

"Wow. Is it getting really hot in here?" I fanned my face with my hand.

Without breaking his hungry gaze, he replied, "Yes, very, very...hot."

I was about to lean forward and show him exactly what *I* meant by "hot," but then he turned away and said, "We can never be together. We are not of the same ilk, Penelope."

Ilk? Was he trying to say I wasn't good enough for him? That I was from some lower class not worthy of his greatness?

"What does that have to do with anything?" I asked in a not-so-happy tone.

"There is no future for two beings as ourselves. We live in different worlds, and I am forever bound to my role—its very nature precludes having a life with a human woman, or any woman."

"Oh." That was a better response than I'd expected. At

least he wasn't shunning me for being human. But still, I didn't know how to respond without sounding needy or pathetic. Because what I really wanted to say was, "Are you out of your frigging mind? You can't throw up your hands! You giant, stubborn ass!"

He continued, "I struggled with the limitations of my existence for thousands of years, but eventually, I grew to accept the truth: my plight is eternal. It does little good to fantasize about it changing."

Once again, he turned his gaze on me, and I thought I might turn into a pathetic little puddle of nothingness. The sting of rejection bit hard.

"Believe me, Penelope," he said with a gravelly voice, "after the things I've dreamt of doing to you, it would break a mortal man's soul in half to walk away. I have no other choice."

How could he simply accept there was no hope for change in his life, no hope for us? As petty as it might be, I suddenly felt angry. "Funny how your brother seems to disagree. Didn't you say he's marrying a Payal?"

Nick sprung from the couch. "Because he is a self-ish fool. It's only a matter of time before he is forced to choose his duties over Emma. He will hurt her."

I didn't know what to say. His resolve, his belief was ironclad. So if he didn't think love was worth fighting for, then maybe he wasn't the man I thought.

*Maybe he just doesn't think you're worth fighting for.*

*Ouch. Thank you, self-deprecating thoughts. Your timing is impeccable. Shoo!*

"I will see you through this ordeal, Penelope. And then we will go our separate ways." He moved toward the doorway that led to the bedroom wing of the house.

"Are you sure about your destiny?" I asked.

He stopped, but did not bother to turn around. "I am a god. I am always sure."

Who knew a man filled with so much heat could be so cold?

# Twenty

I paced the length of my room for about twenty minutes before deciding I wasn't buying his "I'm a god, so don't argue with me" garbage. At a minimum, he owed me an explanation about our plans to save my mom if Viktor didn't return. How could she possibly be a Payal and not know? How could *I* be a Payal and not know? If we were Payals, what exactly did it mean? Was I inherently evil?

I wanted my answers. This was my life! Mine. And nobody would take away my right to drive the Penelope-mobile.

*Go take that man his lemons, Penelope!*

I searched the living room and kitchen—a very nice stainless steel and granite-everything kitchen—but saw no signs of Nick. I found it hard to believe he would go far when monsters had my name on their hit list.

Then I went to Nick's room but didn't see him there, either. (Again, I resisted looking at what was in his nightstand, which almost killed me.) When I turned to leave, a movement outside the large French-style glass doors caught my attention.

*Nick.*

He was soaking in the swimming pool, his bronzed face tilted toward the hot sun and powder-blue sky. His muscular arms stretched along the edge of the pool, and the swells of his insanely powerful biceps sparked a wave of tension deep in my belly, reminding me that when all was said and done, humans were still animals.

*Grunt, grunt. Me want big, strong, stubborn man. Me like. Grunt, grunt.*

Yes, he spoke to my inner cave girl in a way I'd never comprehend. How incredibly frustrating, given how he'd flat out rejected me.

I swallowed hard, slid open the door, and stepped onto the sprawling flagstone patio. I sucked in a lungful of the fresh desert air from the gentle breeze.

*Breathtaking.*

The area surrounding his estate was a tropical oasis of palm trees, lush green plants, and bright tropical flowers—oranges, yellows, and reds—that contrasted with the monochromatic starkness of the surrounding desert. On one side of the yard was a fifteen-foot wall made up of stacked boulders. A waterfall ran down their smooth, rounded faces and flowed into a pebble-lined trough that trickled into the swimming pool. Opposite the waterfall stood an enormous adobe chiminea surrounded by overstuffed chairs.

This was the perfect place to lie in the sun, sip a piña colada, and relax with a good book.

*Or make out. With Nick.*

*Ugh! Stop that!*

I marched over to the pool and hovered above him. "Hi."

He remained perfectly still, his face tilted toward the afternoon sun.

"Nick, we need to talk."

No movement.

"Oh, the silent treatment. I get it. Big bad Sun God is going to ignore the pesky little human. Well, I have news for you; we're not done yet, and I'm not going to scurry away like some timid little monkey"—*I'd much more like to dry hump you like a dirty little monkey*—"even if you are a god."

No response.

"Okay. Fine." I pulled off my shirt and jeans, leaving on my black bra and underwear, and slipped into the shallow water right beside him.

"I'm not leaving until we talk. Now that I have your undivided, divine attention, I'd like to say that I'm extremely disappointed. I mean, I get let in on the big news—there are actual, real live gods living on the planet—but instead of it being a nirvana-like experience where I feel enlightened and inspired, I just feel sad. Wanna know why?"

I paused for a moment, but he still didn't respond.

"Was that a yes? Good, because I'm going to tell you. You're more lost than any human I know. Really, who's going to feel wowed by a being of a *higher* form who doesn't fight for what he wants. In fact, he sounds more like a dog who's been kicked and beaten down. Defeated. Don't get me wrong. I think you're sexy as hell, and I want you in the worst kind of way, but you come up pretty darn short in the inspiration department, bub."

Slowly, Nick turned and rose up, towering over me as he gazed down.

I instantly felt like an ant about to be squashed. Not that I'd ever let him know that.

"Are you finished yet?" His nearly translucent eyes bore into me.

I stepped forward, away from the pool's edge at my back, and balanced on my tiptoes, meeting his scowl with a snarl. "Um. Let me think...Nope." I poked his bare chest. "Just warming the hell up, big boy."

"Enough! You are twenty-five and mortal. You have no understanding of the universe. I, however, have existed for seventy thousand years. This is how I know not to waste my time weeping and whining over that which cannot be changed. This is not defeat. This is wisdom!"

I huffed and gave him another poke. "Really now? You've already admitted you don't know everything, so how do you know your life—existence, whichever— won't change? Personally, I think you're afraid, afraid to try. Maybe even afraid to fail because your enormous ego can't handle it."

"Are you speaking of my place in the universe or of us?" he fumed.

I gave his question a moment to process. Then I noticed how our bodies were lightly pressed together. Tiny sparks fluttered throughout my body.

"Y-y-yesss. Matter of fact, I am speaking about us," I replied with a raspy voice.

"Did I mention it is very likely that the existence of Payals is accelerating our path toward extinction? That's right. The gods derive our energy from the life force of the universe, and the further away we all become from its natural state, the more likely my kind will become sick like Chaam. And if that were to occur, humankind wouldn't stand a chance. No. I supposed you didn't think about that, did you, twenty-five-year-old Penelope Trudeau?" His eyes narrowed. "Never confuse ego for wisdom."

"You think my existence is going to destroy the world?"

He looked away and took a small step back. "We are not certain you are a Payal, but yes. They are not meant to exist because gods and humans are not meant to procreate; it is...unnatural."

"Then why was Cimil trying to get us to...you know?" I questioned.

He flashed a cold look in my direction. "She holds different beliefs."

*Lightbulb!* "So, Cimil was using me to make a point?"

"Yes. She failed. At the end of the day, her beliefs won't change reality," he said.

Now I had a whole head full of flickering lightbulbs; perhaps Cimil wasn't so crazy after all. Okay, that was a stretch; she was off her rocker. But the point was, she and Kinich were clearly divided on this topic, and even if Kinich wanted me, he wouldn't back down. His ego would never let him.

*Well, there is only one part of a man stronger than his ego.*

His smoldering gaze didn't waver as I leaned into him and pressed my breasts against his torso. "But what if she's right?" I whispered. "What if *your* brother is right, too?" I planted a tiny, lingering kiss on his shoulder. "Maybe I'm the change you've been waiting for."

"Gods and—and hu-humans," he fumbled with his words, "are not compatible."

I brushed my lips over the swell of his smooth pectoral, just above his slightly puckered nipple. "Then why are you in love with me?"

Nick unexpectedly grabbed both my shoulders and leaned down, putting us nose to nose, our lips one inch apart.

"Who said I'm in love with you?" he snarled.

I winked. "Wisdom, baby."

Before I could utter another word, Kinich was on me hard and fast, his lips pressed forcefully against mine, his hot, strong hands cupping both sides of my face. His tongue slipped past my teeth, and his taste ignited every R-rated dream I'd had of our mystery night together.

Unlike those dreams, I *knew* this was reality. And in this reality, I needed him. I needed to feel his skin against mine. I needed to feel him move deep inside me to release that excruciatingly delicious tension relentlessly building.

"Gods, woman, you drive me crazy," he said with a gruff voice between breaths.

I flung my arms around his neck and wrapped my legs around his waist.

He backed me against the smooth tile wall of the pool and cupped my ass as I savaged his mouth with mine. Wisps of steam snaked from his breath as he thrust himself against my juncture with only the thin fabric of my panties and his shorts between us.

I inhaled sharply. I wanted to touch him, to feel the thickness of him in my hand. Was he as large as I dreamed?

I reached into the waist-high water between us and

wrapped my fingers around the top of his hard flesh through the fabric of his wet shorts.

*No. He's larger.* I couldn't even close my hand and it turned me on.

My mind recalled all of the things I'd dreamed of doing to that enormous part of his anatomy: laving every thick inch of him with my tongue, rubbing the velvety tip of it over my lips, and reveling in his sexually primal groans. These were things I'd never wanted with any man, any man but him.

And it shocked the heck out of me.

*Not us. We like him! We like him! We like.*

Oh no. The eggs were back.

*Shush, you little troublemakers!*

His hands slid the bra straps from my shoulders and then tugged the wet fabric down to expose my chest. With his chest rapidly rising and falling, he gaped at my breasts, pausing to cup each one and leisurely run his rough thumbs over each hardened nipple.

A rumbling groan escaped his lips, and I sucked in a breath when the sensation of his fiery touch released waves of warmth between my legs.

Did he truly believe we weren't meant to do *this*? Because it felt pretty damn perfect to me—his hot, wet skin against mine; his luscious mouth moving frantically down my neck; the heat of his tongue massaging my aching nipple; and the unbearably hot tension building deep inside.

*Crazy, gorgeous man.*

Suddenly, I was unsure if the water was boiling or preventing me from burning up, but every part of my body felt like it was on fire.

Nick suddenly pulled away. "Penelope, I must—"

"No"—I planted frantic kisses over his mouth and continued massaging his deliciously large erection—"don't you dare stop."

He kissed me for a moment longer, thrusting himself against me. "I must go"—he gave me another long, wet kiss—"get the necklace"—he kissed me again—"or we cannot..."

*Oh, the necklace.*

Then a stupid question popped into my mind. "Are you sure about this?" It was a stupid question because my fingers were wrapped tightly around the evidence of his resolve. But nevertheless, a tiny voice in the back of my mind reminded me how he'd just boldly declared that "we" would never happen.

To be clear, I'd realized how badly I wanted "we" to happen.

He froze and stared deeply into my eyes. "I can think of nothing but bedding you," he whispered.

*Works for me.* "Hurry. Get the necklace."

Nick was about to lift himself from the pool when I grabbed his arm. "Wait. Five more seconds."

He sank back into the water and hurriedly complied with another hard kiss. His stubble rasped the fragile skin around my lips.

Once again, I wrapped my arms around his neck. It was getting unbearably hot, but I couldn't stop. Not even if my life depended on it, which I'm pretty sure it did because he abruptly pushed me away.

"I'm about to lose control of my energy, and I do not want to cook you." He flashed a glance toward the sliding glass door across the patio leading to his room. "It's right there next to my bed."

*Oh. So that's what Sun God keeps in his nightstand.*

"Okay. Okay, just hurry. Before..." I panted.

"Before?"

"Before I spontaneously orgasm from wanting you so badly."

The look in his eyes went from raw lust to savage hunger to...

*Huh?*

His face turned bright red; flames licked from his eye sockets.

I winced as his heat singed the drops of water from my wet skin.

*Holy crap! What's happening?*

He clenched his eyes shut and groaned in agony.

I wanted to reach for him, to help him, but his skin glowed like a smoldering campfire.

Then...I glanced up.

Standing above him at the edge of the pool was a Maaskab. Its eyes were bloodred pools with dark, empty holes in the center. His long black ropes of hair were caked with a brownish-red paste—*holy shit! Are those teeth hanging from the ends of those nappy dreads?* His body was smeared with black soot, and his loincloth was made of some sort of animal hide—*holy shit! Is that human skin?* I didn't know of many animals that had heart-shaped tattoos with the word *Bob* in the middle.

Then the smell hit me. Eau de festering wound mixed with Porta-Potty.

I pointed and screamed at the top of my lungs.

The Maaskab raised his arms and tossed a black jar in the water. At that exact moment, time moved in slow motion.

Nick's eyes, glowing and red, locked on my face while his hand reached behind and latched onto the Maaskab's ankle. *"In halach puczical, in uchucil, ca kaxah yokol-cab ichi pixan,"* Nick whispered.

It felt like I'd been struck by a bolt of lightning. Then I saw him. Kinich. Not the image perceived with my eyes, but his essence, his light. It branded itself on my very soul.

Before I knew it, the Maaskab's body turned to ash and landed in a pile on the ground. Kinich slumped over in the water.

"Oh my God! Kinich? Kinich!" I pulled his face from the water and slapped his pale cheeks. He didn't respond. "Help!" I screamed.

I hooked him under the arms and maneuvered his large body over to the pool's steps. I heaved and pulled and blubbered hysterically, but none of that, especially the blubbering, made a difference; he was so damned heavy all I could do was inch him halfway out of the water.

"Did ya actually have tae go and break the man, lass?"

A rather tall, burly man with long red hair, and wearing a kilt, stared down with amusement.

I didn't know who he was, but he wasn't a Maaskab, and that was good enough for me.

"Oh my God. Help! I think he's dead!"

He gave a hearty chuckle. "Oh, now, lass, they cannae die. Those immortal buggers are like roaches—cannot get rid o' them. And believe me, I've tried."

"No! I'm serious. One of those Maaskab showed up and threw something in the water."

The man squinted at the bobbing black jar. "Ah. So he has." He scratched his chin. "Well, now, not to worry; we'll get him out o' there and he'll be like new."

The man latched onto Kinich's wrist and plucked him from the water like a wet noodle.

When I pulled myself out, I noticed my skin was covered with tiny blisters.

"Looks like ya got a little Sun God burn there. Did ya, lass?" He chuckled again.

I'd worry about the burn later, but why was this crazy Scotsman so damned happy?

I kneeled beside Kinich, who now appeared even paler. "He's not waking up."

"Hmm. 'Tis a bit odd." He kneeled over and slapped Kinich's face. "Wake up, you ol' bastard."

"Hey, do you mind? Name-calling isn't going to help." I winced. My skin was scalding hot.

"I'll take him tae his room and call the doctor. Looks like you'll be needin' his help, too, lass. That's some sunburn ya got there."

# Twenty-One

Almost thirty hours after the incident with the Maaskab, I was having an epic breakdown. Kinich still lay in his bed, limp, pale, and lifeless.

The Uchben doctor, a youngish-looking man with brown hair and glasses, had made at least a dozen visits, each time taking blood samples, listening to Kinich's heart and lungs, offering zero useful information other than Kinich was still alive.

Regardless, I couldn't help but hold my breath and dig my nails into my palms as the doctor examined Kinich for the thirteenth time.

"And if he dies?" I asked.

The doctor made a nondescript gesture with his hands. "His light would be sent to a cenote, and he'd get a new body."

Kinich had mentioned the cenotes—ancient Mayan pools the gods used as portals between worlds—but I wasn't aware they could simply check in and get a new set of human wheels every time they crashed the car, so to speak.

The doctor gathered up his vials of blood and instruments. "Ms. Trudeau, a word of advice, if I may?"

How did he know I so badly needed some? Was it the terror plastered on my crispy, red face?

"You need to heal. Perhaps you might benefit from a few hours of relaxation." His eyes glanced at the wall of running water that separated the bedroom from the bath. And yes, it was a bathroom fit for a god: twice the size of the one attached to my room with a private meditation suite.

*Sure. Just what I need. A bubble bath. Then maybe after, I'll write some colorful poetry about a fluffy cloud and go frolicking gaily in the meadow with the baby animals. Happy fucking times!*

Was I the only person taking this situation seriously? Something was very, very wrong with Kinich, and I knew it in the pit of my stomach.

I turned to the crazy Scot who I learned was Gabrán, the highest-ranking Uchben chief and a very close friend to Kinich and his brother Guy. He'd explained that they had encountered these black jade jars once before—the Maaskab had used them to hex the gods' cenotes—but once the jars were removed from the pools, everything, including any trapped gods, returned to normal, for the most part.

This situation was clearly different. Wasn't it time to panic? Panic sounded reasonable and appropriate.

"Isn't there anything we can do?" I asked.

"We wait," Gabrán responded. "Wait and pray."

"That's what I've been doing." And it had been about as useful as a bacon breath mint.

Gabrán scratched his head. "Whatcha be needing, lass, is tae follow the good doctor's advice and rest."

I sighed. He was right; I was a mess. My skin, though beginning to heal, had burns and blisters on every square inch. I resembled a charred tomato. Whatever had happened to Kinich—*hey, you're calling him Kinich now. What does that mean?*—I was certain I'd come within an inch of being cooked alive.

But that was on the outside. On the inside, well, I was already toast. Viktor had been gone more than a day, and though Kinich promised to give him two days before telling anyone, I felt the burning need to say something. What if Kinich's state was somehow connected to all this? However, if I told Gabrán, would that derail Viktor's chances of rescuing my mother?

Pacing alongside Kinich's seemingly lifeless body, I agonized over what to do.

What would *he* want me to do?

I fell to my knees beside the bed for the twentieth time. "Kinich, oh, God. Please wake up. Please." I brushed his forehead, planting gentle, coaxing kisses on his pale, stubble-covered cheeks. And when that didn't work, I reverted to shaking him. "Please, Kinich. Wake up. I don't know what to do. You have to wake up." I choked. "I'm sorry I said you were a coward. And a man whore. And a god slut. And an arrogant mantard. Okay, I never said that last one to your face, but I said it! And I'm sorry! I'll do anything if you wake up. I'll even admit you were right about us not having a chance, even though you're wrong, because it's completely stupid to think you're never meant to love. Idiot! How can you believe that? Really? But I'll say it. I will! If you want, I'll leave you alone forever. Just . . . just come back. Tell me what to do," I blubbered shamelessly.

"Oh, lass."

I looked up to find Gabrán staring at me with his large green eyes, a trait many seemed to have in these parts.

"I thought you left." I plunked my head down on Kinich's chest, fisting the white T-shirt he now wore.

"With all the caterwauling, I was certain the Scabs had returned. Or a rabid coyote had gotten intae the room." He shook his head. "Your tears won't be savin' him, ya know."

I grabbed a wad of tissues from the box on the nightstand and wiped my nose. "I don't understand why he won't wake up."

Gabrán shook his head. "Nor do we, lass. 'Tis perplexing tae say the least. But ya must not give up hope."

I had to tell him. I had to. There was no way I could hold this in any longer.

I took a deep breath. "I have to say something, and I can only hope you'll do right with this information."

He nodded. "Go on."

"My mother was taken by the Maaskab, and Viktor went after her."

Gabrán rubbed his chin. "Is that so?"

"Yes. He said something to Kinich about having visions of her for five hundred years. He begged Kinich to give him two days to find her and bring her back before alerting the other gods."

A long silence followed; then he said, "We ought to tell the general and Votan."

"You mean Niccolo and Guy?" I couldn't keep all of these names straight.

"Ay. But first, did he tell you anything else? Anything that might prove helpful tae me and my men?"

"He thinks my mother was a Payal."

He raised his brows and puckered his lips. "That would explain why the Scabs might be after ya mother and you. But nae what they've done to our here Sun God."

"We have to help him!" I pleaded.

"Ay," Gabrán replied sympathetically. "I have a sneakin' suspicion that only those nasty priests are knowin' the cure."

I felt my blood boil. *The Maaskab.* Who knew I'd ever be capable of such profound hate. Yet there it was. I hated them. Profoundly.

I felt my face turn an even brighter red and my body heat up like a lobster in a pot. Smoke rose from my shoulders.

I jumped. "Ouch! Son of a bitch!" I swatted the smoldering fabric of my clothes. "What the hell?"

Gabrán watched me with pure amazement. "Did ya just catch yerself on fire, lass?"

I stood there panting. "Yep. I guess I did."

Then I passed out.

# Twenty-Two

"Penelope. My name is Emma Keane. Can you hear me?"
I felt a gentle pat on my arm. "I think she's waking up,"
the female voice whispered.

When my eyes cracked open, they encountered a red-
headed woman about my age, standing next to Gabrán.

Then, one of the largest men I'd ever seen in my life,
dressed in dark gray cargo pants and a snug black T-shirt,
stormed into the room. His midnight-black hair, streaked
with indigo blue, hung past his broad shoulders. His angry
eyes, a fierce, iridescent turquoise green very similar to
Kinich's, were nothing shy of scary. He even smelled
scary, like smoke. Maybe he could give me deodorant tips
since I was now spontaneously catching on fire.

"Tell me what happened," he ordered.

The young woman elbowed him. "Let's help her off the
floor and explain who we are before barking commands,
honey."

He grunted and shot a look at Gabrán, who then helped me onto the couch in the corner of the room.

"I am Guy Santiago, Kinich's brother. This is my fiancée, Emma."

I nodded, knowing exactly who they were. This was the god who was going to marry the Payal.

I made a sad, little wavelike gesture. "Penelope."

Gabrán spoke up immediately and began retelling the story of the Maaskab and Kinich, leaving the part about my spontaneous combustion until the end.

Emma turned to me. "What were you thinking about the moment it happened?"

I blinked.

Okay, maybe this was like being at the doctor. As embarrassing as it might feel, I had to answer the question openly and hope the experts would know what to do with the information. "If you must know, I'd been thinking about how badly I wanted to sleep with Kinich."

There was a low, stifled chuckle from Guy and Gabrán.

"He's a total hottie, that's for sure." Emma cracked a smile.

"What?" Guy said. "You have desires for my brother?"

Emma patted him on the cheek. "Baby, that was a little joke. Get it, 'hottie'? He's the Sun God?" Guy kept glaring. "Oh, you're so cute when you're jealous," she said. "Or is it scary? I'm not sure. In any case, you know that no one stacks up to you."

Her exaggerated reassurance seemed to placate the beast of a man.

"Sorry, Penelope," Emma said, "I meant, what were you thinking about the moment you felt your body heat up?"

*Oh. That.* "About the monsters who took my mother and attacked Kinich. Can we talk about that later?" I was not ready to face the truth about what was going on with me personally. There were much, much bigger issues at play.

And yes. Denying reality was a gift. So sue me.

I glanced at Kinich's immobile body. "Do you know what's wrong with him? How to help him?"

Guy ignored my questions. "Bastards. I'll kill every last one of them."

"Stop," Emma warned. "Let's leave the revenge until later."

"I can't help myself." Guy began pacing. "The Maaskab have obviously been honing their weapons against us. Look at him. Kinich is completely useless to us like this."

Then they both stared at me as if they expected me to say or do something.

"What? Aren't you going to help him?" I asked.

"The thing is," Emma explained, "we don't know what to do. The Uchben have already searched their databases, and we've checked with the other gods—"

"Except Cimil," Guy interrupted.

"Yes. Except Cimil, who's MIA," Emma added.

"Has something happened to her?" I asked. Half of me hoped the answer was yes. I knew revenge was a four-letter word, and I should rise above the desire to see her suffer, but... come on! The woman so deserved a little pain. Like being thrown into a pit of angry vipers. Or perhaps shoved in a rocket filled with vile, tiny, green men who had horrible flatulence, then shot off into space, where she would be forced to watch them pick their noses and scratch themselves all day long.

On second thought, Cimil might enjoy that.

"Cimil has a nasty habit of disappearing when she's needed most," Guy stated coldly.

Emma nodded. "I'm sure she's fine. But Kinich—" She regarded him with sadness. "The only idea we've come up with is to...um..."

The three exchanged glances. "What?" I asked.

Guy spoke up. "Kill him. So his light is returned to the cenote."

"Are you people, deities or...partial deities—whatever—crazy? You can't do that," I argued.

"Exactly," Guy said. "We are immortal. He cannot be killed."

I moved between Guy and Kinich. "You said you have no idea what's the matter with him. What if you're wrong?"

Gabrán chimed in. "The girl has a point."

Without warning, Emma, who stood near the foot of the bed, whipped out a large Buck knife from the waist-band of her pink yoga pants—*Christ!*—and made a small cut across the top of Kinich's exposed foot.

I shrieked at the sight of blood pooling in the gash. "Why did you do that?"

She ignored my question and stared at Kinich's wound. After a moment, the blood dribbled to the tile floor. She shook her head.

"'Tis nae healing," Gabrán declared. "The girl is right. Whatever the Maaskab have done to the man may have changed the rules."

"You keep assuming I'm part of your club and get what the hell you're talking about." I felt seriously panicked and was not giving a crappity crap if I offended anyone at this point.

"A god would heal in seconds from a cut that size," Gabrán explained. "'Tis possible he's been changed somehow."

"Which means?" I asked.

Guy answered, "We will have to keep searching for a way to undo this dark magic."

"How long will that take?"

"Anywhere from a few weeks to a few decades, if we are lucky."

After everyone left Kinich's room in a heated debate, I slumped down on the bed next to him.

"Dammit, Kinich." I brushed his caramel locks back from his forehead. "What's happened to you? What's happened to me?" He was freezing, and I was boiling like a lobster.

I plopped my head down on his chest. "Where are you?"

"Right here. Why are you crying?" Kinich suddenly sat up as if he'd had the most refreshing nap ever.

His surreal, turquoise eyes stared back at me with a twinkle, and his lips were pursed with a sneaky little grin.

"Kinich!" I yelped and threw myself on him. "You're awake! Oh my God!" I couldn't help but cry again, this time with the utmost relief.

I buried my face in his chest. It was warm again. Oh, so warm.

His hand stroked the back of my head, following the length of my hair. "Shhh. Shhh. Do not cry, Penelope. Everything is fine." He peeled me off his chest. "No more crying. Please." He wiped the tears from beneath my eyes.

I sniffled and gave him a nod. "What happened to you?" I mumbled.

He shrugged casually. "Nothing. I feel great."

"You've been in a coma for over a day. I thought you were dead."

His brows pulled together. "Dead? I am a god. We can't die as much as I wish otherwise."

I cupped my hand over his mouth. "Don't ever say that. I thought I'd lost you . . . I thought . . ."

Wow. Was I really going to let that tiny door inside my heart open up and allow those buried emotions to be said out loud?

My inner voice chimed in. *Activate reality-denial button?*

No. Not this time.

Kinich stared at me, his eyes filled with intense emotion. "Yes? You thought you'd lost me, and what?"

I couldn't say the words just yet, but I could show him how I felt. *I need you. I want you. I might break into a million pieces if you don't feel the same.*

I leaned forward and kissed him.

His reaction was immediate. It was raw. It was what I'd hoped for.

He flipped me on my back, pinning me beneath him, kissing me hard, kissing me like he meant to fill me with his own avalanche of emotions.

His heavy frame instantly shifted, shaping to my hungry body. His knees slid between mine and parted my thighs. I exhaled sharply when I felt his hardness prodding me in just the right spot.

A groan left his lips while his tongue slid in and out of my mouth with an erotic pumping rhythm.

My fingertips moved through his silky strands of hair and then traveled down the sides of his face to his neck and arms, savoring every muscle packed with heat, power, and steely hardness. His body turned into hot, twisting barbs of steel, intent on caging me. His erection thrust against me, and the heat of him on my most sensitive skin almost sent me over the edge.

"Oh, God. Yes. Yes," I panted.

His hot tongue and velvety, plump lips moved down my neck, their sensuous texture deliciously followed by the roughness of his unshaven jaw.

Kinich pulled up my T-shirt and palmed my breast before he placed his mouth over my sensitive nipple and began sucking. Gentle at first, then hard.

"I love your breasts," he said with a breath, talking directly to my puckered, and now red, pebble. "I want to do very dirty things to them."

*Oh. Sun God is a breast man!*

"But not before I do this." He flipped me over like a hotcake on a griddle and straddled me below my backside. I felt his large hands cupping both fleshy mounds. "These, I have missed. Your ass should have a pyramid built in its honor."

*Could he arrange that?*

"Shouldn't I get two? One for each side?"

He tugged down my jeans, leaving my thong panties in place.

"Yes. They are gorgeous," he said with a gravelly voice and began lavishing a long, hot, wet kiss on my right cheek.

His sizzling tongue felt so silky, like warm chocolate being drizzled over my skin.

He suddenly flipped me once again, startling my breath away.

Like a man on a mission, he made no production out of removing my panties or tearing off his own T-shirt and drawstring pants.

He crawled up the bed and lay over me, briskly separating my legs. "I want you, Penelope. I want to be inside you and hear you moan my name like I've dreamt about."

I loved that he'd had those dreams, too. I loved that I was the only woman he'd "perhaps" ever been with.

I responded to him with a hard kiss and felt him slide his hand between us, positioning his thick shaft at my entrance.

He wrapped my leg around him and began pushing into me.

"Wait! The necklace. Don't I need the . . . ?" A searing heat pulsed through me.

I exhaled sharply and looked up to discover Emma swatting me with a towel. "Christ, Penelope! You're on fire!"

I sprang from the bed, peeled my smoldering shirt from my body, and whipped it to the tile floor. I stomped out the flame.

"Wow," Emma said. "That must've been one smokin' dream you were having." She laughed.

*Dream?*

My mind spun in dizzying circles. I swiveled my head toward Kinich, only to find him lying there like a lifeless sack of dirt.

*Shit. Another goddamn dream.*

My heart sank and tears of disappointment welled in

my eyes. I was never a crier, but I'd let 'em rip more times in two days than I had in my entire life.

"Oh no! Penelope. Don't cry." Emma's bright green eyes filled with worry. She leaned over and grabbed my hand, pulling me up from the bed.

"I know what you need."

"A cold shower?" I asked.

"Better."

# *Twenty-Three*

⌒

"Where are we going?" I asked.

Emma led me by the hand down the hallway through the living room. Her springy red curls bounced as she trotted eagerly to our destination. Although she was several inches shorter than me, and wearing a girlie floral blouse and capri jeans, I felt somewhat intimidated. Her petite size felt like an illusion that masked something dangerous and powerful.

"So. Kinich told me you're a...Payal?" I asked hesitantly.

Emma smirked and flashed a smile over her shoulder, but didn't answer. She led me through the enormous modern kitchen out to the garage, a garage unlike any I'd ever seen. It was a madman's luxury car showroom, complete with a bar—*how many bars does one home need?*—living room, polished cement floors, recessed lighting that lovingly bathed each vehicle (six NASCAR-worthy convertibles, one silver hardtop, and a rather large-looking red Jeep with extra-large tires), and a variety of pristine cupboards and racks to house tools.

Emma released my hand. "Hmmm. Eenie, meenie, that one!" She pointed to the silver hardtop.

"Where are you proposing to take me?" I didn't want to leave Kinich.

"For a drive."

*No derrrr.* "I should go back to Kin—"

"Come on. One quick drive. The night air will clear your head."

She was right; I needed to get out of the house, but ...

"Is it safe? I mean, those Maaskab pop out of nowhere."

She laughed. "Safety is an illusion. There's nowhere on this entire planet that a Scab can't get to you. Being with me is about as safe as it gets. I now hold the kill record." She flicked her hand. "It's all in the wrist."

She plucked a key from a hook on the wall, marched over to the car, and slid in. "Aston Martin One-77. I've been dying to drive this baby ever since he got it."

The sleek, modern lines said one thing. "Expensive," I mumbled.

Emma grinned from ear to ear as I slid into the black leather passenger seat.

She slowly ran her hands over the top of the steering wheel. "Oooh, you have no idea. Kinich would never let me drive this car, but since he's in a coma..."

These were quite possibly some of the most insensitive people, or beings, I'd ever met. Either that, or they were all too crazy to be worried about anything.

"If you've ever heard the phrase *boys and their toys*, the gods put a whole new spin on it." She revved the engine and pushed the garage door opener. "Let's roll!" The screeching tires left behind two plumes of smoke.

I instantly gripped the sides of my seat. Clearly, Emma was a little wild. "Where are we going on this 'drive'?" I asked over the rev of the accelerating engine.

"Woo-hoo!" Emma screamed. "This baby can fly!" The car didn't fly, it rocketed down the dark dirt road that eerily seemed to have no end, but could, at any moment, turn into a nocturnal version of the cliff-diving scene from *Thelma & Louise.*

"Emma, you really should slow—"

I unexpectedly heard the unmistakable chime of the *Woody Woodpecker Show*?

"Hold the wheel, Pen." Emma began digging in her pocket.

*Sweet-and-sour demons!* I leaned hard and gripped the wheel with my left hand. "Could you slow—"

"Hey, baby. One sec." She turned to me and whispered, "It's Guy. He's so pissed." She giggled and turned her attention back to the phone.

"Emma, could you, please slo—"

"No," she said to Guy, "I didn't tell you because we're just hopping over to Camp Uchi."

*We are?*

"We'll be fine," she continued. "There are plenty of swarthy warriors who've been trained by the most fearless, sexy god known to creation."

She must've meant *him.* I guessed the gods responded to buttering up, like any guy.

"Well," she continued, "if I see a giant Scab, then I'll crack his crusty ass in half." Pause. "Nope. I will not 'return this instant.' And haven't you learned by now that threatening to spank me only gets me hot?" Pause. "So does that." Pause. "And definitely that." Pause. "Nooo. I'll come back when I'm good and ready. Love you. Bye." She disconnected the call and shook her head. "Gods. They think they're so high and mighty."

*Um. Okay.*

She took the wheel but kept the pedal to the metal. The car soared over the bumpy desert road.

"Could you please slow down before we hit something? And what's Camp Uchi?" I asked.

"It's where the Uchben on this side of the globe train and live. There's another in Italy."

I remembered Kinich speaking about it. The place sounded enormous. "Do the Uchben have a lot of soldiers?"

"About five thousand are visiting this week, but they're over a million strong, if you include everyone: soldiers, regulars, and spies. They've also got a killer medical plan; own a few oil-producing countries, the nice ones; and have about ten kick-ass universities, too. You can study anything you want for free. I'm studying to be a doctor—ob-gyn."

"Really?" Couldn't imagine Speed Racer delivering a baby. Then again, might be kind of nice to have some- one like Emma; she'd make sure the whole delivery expe- rience was like going to the drive-through window. No twenty-hour labor if you were her patient.

"Oh yeah," she replied. "Guy and I were trying to have a baby for a few months, and when nothing happened, I thought something was wrong with me. I mean, look at him; he's the kind of male that can knock up a woman just by looking at her. Of course, I'd kill him if he ever looked at another woman but you get the picture."

"Sure." I felt the same darn way about Kinich, and he wasn't even mine.

"So," she said, "I saw my Uchben doctor and learned none of them had experience with fertility. And since I'm...special and can't go to a regular doctor, I realized someone had to step up to fill the role. Who better than me? Both my parents are doctors, and I love kids. If for some reason I never get to have my own, maybe I can end up helping others. Especially my sister Payals." Her eyes flashed my way. "Like you."

I didn't want her to feel insulted, because there was nothing wrong with the way she was, but that didn't mean I wanted to belong to the Descendants of A-hole Chaam Club. "How do you know I'm like...you?"

She made a little shrug. "I just do. You don't have to take my word."

"Is that why we're going to Camp Uchi?"

"Ah!" Her index finger shot up. "Now, that is an excellent question. Sadly, you'll need to remain in suspense for another ten minutes."

Although it was a moonless night, I could see that Camp Uchi was no military base. It was an enormous five-star desert retreat. Tuscan-style fountains with colorful lights, elaborate cactus gardens with exotic flowers, and Southwestern-style adobe casitas were scattered around the grounds. Tiki torches lit the way to large clearings with inviting fires that glowed under the star-covered Arizona night sky. "This isn't what I imagined."

"Nothing about their world ever is," Emma spouted while I trailed behind her. It appeared we were heading toward a large domed structure. "Tomorrow I'll show you the underground mall. They have Manolo *and* Jimmy Choo, friends of the family."

She then stopped and eyed my clunky boots, which were all I'd brought. "And a few stores for the wildly unfeminine, if that's your thing, which I'm hoping it's not. 'Cause I could use a really good shopping buddy and Army Surplus isn't really my style. Have you ever had a fashion makeover, Penelope? I'm really great with hair and makeup. Don't get me wrong. The natural look is so... natural, but I could do wonders with that face of yours. You have great bone structure. I bet you're hiding a rockin' body under those jeans and T-shirt."

"I-I... well, I..." She really wanted to talk about dressing me up and making me over? I didn't know if I wanted to laugh or poke her in the eye. "Not to be rude, but could we..." I glanced at the door.

"Right. Okay. No thinking about Kinich or your problems. Just keep an open mind. I promise this will change your life."

Wow. Exactly what I needed, more life-changing events.

"Afterward," she added, "you'll be in a much better position to deal with"—she waved toward the night sky—"your new world."

"I don't want a new world; my old one was great, and I'd really like to get it back. Why doesn't anyone seem to get that or give a damn, for that matter?"

She gave my hand a comforting squeeze. "Of course we give a damn. More than you know. In fact, there are already plans in motion to rescue your mom and Viktor. The finest, most-skilled warriors on the planet are preparing as we speak. Even Guy and I are going on the mission. Absolutely everything will be done to bring her back safely. So please, Penelope, give me ten minutes. After that, I'll take you back to Kinich."

"You really believe I'm like you?"

"Your power is so strong, we could light up a small city with it."

Me? Power? I guess Emma was also smoking grack. Well, clearly she wasn't going to take me back until she had her grackhead way. "Fine. Ten minutes. Then we're going back to Kinich. By the way, what did you mean by cracking Scabs?"

Emma laughed. "You are so going to love being a Payal, Penelope."

# Twenty-Four

Emma yanked open the double doors of the cavernous, well-lit auditorium filled with several hundred men—large, shirtless, ripped, sweaty men sparring with swords, poles, and other weapons. When all eyes fell on us, the room became silent and the men motionless, except for their meaty, pumping chests.

Were we crashing their hunky dude party? Whatever was going on, it didn't appear we were welcome.

"Emma? What is this?"

She pulled me into the sea of burly men. "There's a special training room I want to show you."

"Are you sure we're supposed to be here?" I scanned the silent, shirtless mob of towering soldiers who made way for us.

Unexpectedly, a colossal man with cropped, dark brown hair emerged from the crowd to block our path. He crossed his thick, bare arms over his immense chest.

"Brutus. Good to see you," Emma said. "Now move."

He grunted but did not speak.

"Don't you start with me, too." Emma wagged a finger in his face.

He stepped forward, pushing Emma back.

*What an ass!* He was a good twelve inches taller and outweighed her by a ton.

He narrowed his eyes and jimmied her back another notch.

My blood began to boil. I didn't know what was going on between these two, but there was no excuse for a man, especially of his size, to strong-arm a girl.

"What's the price this time?" she sidled up to him defiantly. "Did Guy promise you that Barbie you've had your eye on if you dragged me back to Kinich's house?"

Barbie? She had to be joking. This guy looked like he ate baby chipmunks for breakfast.

The room erupted with laughter and the brawny man's face turned bright red. Before I could say, "Yowza," his arms extended and she flew several yards back, landing on an exercise mat.

*What the...?* My arms shot out, landing a blow in the center of his chest. Fire burst from his pecs, and he flew a good twenty feet. "Touch her again, and the next time it'll be your balls!" I screamed.

The room fell into a steady stream of sidebar whispers. The sound of laughter came next.

I swiveled on my heel.

Emma rolled onto her back, roaring, gripping her stomach. "Yes! That's the stuff!"

The brawny man laughed, too.

"What the hell is going on?" I parked my hands on my hips.

Emma flipped onto her stomach and began crawling toward me, still chuckling. "Woo-hoo! Payal power!"

*What just happened?* I was about to ask, but I didn't want to believe what I'd seen, what I'd done.

*Denial button activated!*

I took a deep breath and headed for the door. "Take me back to Kinich. Your ten minutes are up."

During the drive back, Emma didn't attempt to discuss the incident. Maybe the tiny plumes of smoke snaking from my ears or the licks of flames flickering from my fingertips were an obvious sign that I was pissed.

As soon as she pulled into the garage, I stormed from the car, which, by the way, was scorched on the passenger side where I'd been sitting, and marched through the house. I ignored Guy, Gabrán, and a few other unknown faces who stood in the kitchen.

Yet the moment I laid eyes on Kinich in his bed, my anger dissipated into worry. What if he never woke up? What if my mother didn't come back? What was happening to me?

I shook my head. This was not a good place to be. I felt helpless and lost. I needed Kinich to get better. I needed his help.

*Really now, Penelope, are you sure about that?*

*He thinks your kind is a mistake!*

*"Your kind"? I thought we hit the denial button on that one, Pen.*

Shit! I couldn't play the denial game. That only worked

for mundane crap like when your jeans are too tight: you hit the denial button, and magically, the reason isn't because you splurged on cookies and drank too much wine with the girls, but because you must've dried them on the high setting.

Fire coming from your fingertips required a much larger denial tool, as did my entire situation.

*Tequila?*

*Oh yeah.*

I made a beeline for the bar in Kinich's room and found my poison. Boy, these gods sure loved to drink.

I plopped down next to Kinich and pulled out the cork. "Cheers, Sun God!"

I took a large swig and began eyeing his nightstand drawer. Up until then I'd resisted taking a peek because it felt pretty low to snoop on a helpless man. But a brand-new world called for brand-new lines of decency.

I slid it open. "A copy of the *Popol Vuh*?" Autographed by the other gods. Weird.

Several Icy Hot patches. Odd.

And a thick three-ring binder.

I flipped it open. Each page had a photo of a child with notes, tiny mementos, or letters written in crayon. Page after page. One little girl, whose name was Jenny, had pink ribbons in her blonde hair and a toothy smile. Below it was a drawing of two smiling stick figures. "Nick and me" was written on the paper. Of course, Kinich was portrayed with a giant sun over his head.

Then I noticed handwritten notes in the margins.

"Oh my God. These are children from—"

"Orphanages." Emma stood in the doorway. "Kinich loves kids. He spends his extra time with them: coaching Little League, organizing trips to Disneyland, he even started ballet schools in ten cities. All for needy kids. He thinks we don't know. I guess he's afraid the other gods will think he's a softy—maybe they do. But I think it's sweet."

"Why? Why does he do it?"

She walked to the other side of Kinich's bed and took a seat on the edge. "I think because he never had a choice. None of the gods did. They got stuck with their lives, and maybe to the everyday person, it sounds like the coolest gig ever, but immortality and being responsible for the entire human race isn't an easy cross to bear. I think this is his way of coping. He gives these children hope and a choice."

*Oh. I-I...*

"That's the saddest and sweetest thing I've ever heard." I stroked Kinich's ice-cold cheek. "You're so full of surprises, Sun God," I whispered.

"So," Emma asked, "are you going to keep wallowing, or are you going to disembark from the SS *Pity*?"

"Sorry?"

"What's *your* move?" she asked.

"Are you saying I get a choice?"

She nodded.

"But I didn't choose this," I pointed out sadly.

She shook her head. "No. You didn't. But now you get to choose what you make of it."

"What can *I* do?"

"Step one," she replied. "Stop being afraid, and accept what you are. We need every able body we can get to face what's coming. After we've trained you, you'll make us that much stronger."

"This is too much. I'm not ready for all this."

Emma's green eyes glowed with warmth. "You are my sister now, and I'll be here to make sure you never stumble."

"Sister?" My eyes filled with tears—*yes, yes. More crying.*

It was one thing to grow up without a father, but not having any siblings was hard. It seemed all my friends had sisters and brothers to play with or watch over them, everyone except me. That's why when I was little I worried to death about who would be there for me after my mother was gone. Would I die alone without any family there to love me?

When I got older, however, I became tired of feeling helpless, so I turned to martial arts. Somehow knowing I could defend myself didn't make being alone so scary. Truth be told, it made me feel confident, strong, independent, like I could handle anything that came my way.

But nonetheless, the absence of a sister or brother, a best friend who shared my blood, stayed with me.

"You and I are Payals, Penelope. I don't know why life turned out this way for us, why the people we love have been taken, but there's a reason for all this. I can feel it in my bones. I have to believe that."

"Who? Who was taken from you?" I asked.

Emma's eyes reflected her dreary thoughts. "My grandmother was taken by the Maaskab a few years ago. I thought it was the worst day of my life. But it wasn't. That day was when she showed up on our doorstep in Italy, leading her own army of Scabs; I almost killed her. She was crazed from the black jade they'd injected her with." Emma whisked away a tear. "I don't know how, but

I managed to hit her with just enough energy to knock her out instead of killing her. After everything was over, I'd planned to have Guy take my sedated grandma back to Mexico, to the cenote so he could take her to his world."

"Why?"

"So the gods would make her immortal and cure her with their light." Emma took a deep breath and blew it out. "I never got the chance, though. A man named Tommaso, a man I thought was my friend, released her and fled."

"Emma, I'm so sorry." I didn't know what else to say; her story was so sad. "Why did he do it?"

She shrugged, her expression bleak. "Because he was born evil, and there's no cure for that." She paused. "Doesn't matter now. Because I'm going to get her back, and then I'm going to kill him."

Wow. That was one hairy ax to grind.

"We leave the day after next."

"What if it doesn't work?" I asked. "What if you find her and can't cure her? What then?" Did I have any business asking her this?

Emma explained that the gods' light made a person immortal, not indestructible; the cenote wouldn't build them a new body if theirs was destroyed.

"If we can't cure her," Emma said with a frigid tone, "then I'll do the right thing."

What a horrible thought. I couldn't imagine what Emma was going through.

"As for you, we'll face whatever comes together," she said, changing the subject quickly. "All you need to do is decide. Are you going to stand up and fight for the people we love? Or are you going to crawl in a hole and hide?"

She stared directly at Kinich, and then so did I, which made me think: if someone so powerful could be brought down by the Maaskab, then what chance did I have?

"I need time. A lot's happened."

Emma reached over Kinich and rubbed my arm. "Don't worry. We're not going anywhere. We'll be here when you're ready."

"So will we." Guy, Gabrán, and that man I'd walloped in the training center stood with fierce, determined expressions just outside the doorway.

"We're the good guys, Penelope. We've got to stick together." Guy flashed a cool smile in my direction.

I felt it then. Their power. Their determination. Their loyalty toward one another. I didn't know them, but I got it now. Like Kinich, they'd all been dealt their cards. They could've run away or tried to deny it. Instead, they'd chosen to fight. To do good. To not hit the denial button.

I stood and smoothed down the front of my wrinkled, charred jeans. *No. No lemonade for this girl. Stick those lemons where the sun don't shine!* "Okay. I'll fight. I want to go on the rescue mission."

Guy stepped next to Emma, hovering over the dormant Kinich. "You told her about the mission?"

"Of course. She needs to know we're doing everything to get her mother back from the Maaskab. That said"—she looked at me with a sour face—"are you crazy, girl?"

"What?" I asked defensively.

"Penelope." Guy's tone was flat and firm. "You're not combat trained."

I huffed. "I've got a black belt in karate, the ability to throw fireballs with my hands, and I can light the interior of extremely expensive sports cars on fire with my ass. I can handle myself."

Emma and Guy exchanged glances with Gabrán, who was smiling.

"Not a word out of you!" Guy pointed to Gabrán and then turned his irate gaze on me. "No. You will be a liability to my men. We cannot risk—"

"Honey," Emma chimed in. "I think you should consider her wish. It's her mother; she should have the right to put her life on the line if she wants to."

"No! I've already gone head-to-head with Niccolo on this matter because he insists on saving Viktor himself, which I refused on the grounds of Niccolo's strategic military value. He would consider it an insult if I let her go on the mission, but not him."

"Honey," she argued. "This is different. Cimil has prophesied that we can't win the Great War if Niccolo isn't leading the army. If he dies, it would mean an apocalypse." She turned toward me. "No offense, Penelope, but the world wouldn't end if you met yours—not that I want that to happen."

Morbid, but true. "No worries." I flashed a quick smile. "I understand."

Guy growled. Like any man, he likely didn't appreciate being cornered. "She's never been in a battle, and we do not have time to train her."

"I will train her," Brutus said in a deep, scratchy voice.

Guy's mouth fell open. So did Gabrán's. Now, as for Emma...

"Oh, fine!" she griped. "You'll speak to help out Penelope, but you won't even give me the courtesy of one lousy 'hi.' It's one syllable, Brutus! One!"

One corner of his mouth curved upward.

These people were truly bizarre. Sweet and powerful, but bizarre.

"Thank you, Brutus. When do we start?" I said.

He stared at me without so much as an acknowledgment of my question.

"Okeydokey, then. I don't know how this silent training thing works, but I'm an open-minded gal. Let's start now."

Guy, obviously not aligned to my involvement and knowing he'd lost the argument, turned to leave, grumbling, "You have one day, Karate Kid."

Hey. That name sounded kind of cool, but wouldn't something snazzier make me feel tougher? Something like Fireballs or Smoky Pants?

*Hmmm…maybe not.* I'd need to work on a handle. Maybe get myself some red tights and a blue, waist-high half leotard.

*Pen! You're not a superhero. You're just crazy. And apparently contaminated with the DNA of a supernatural serial killer.*

*Lucky me.*

"Hey, Guy! Wait up." I ran down the hallway after him, and when I caught up, I couldn't help but shiver in my smoky pants. He was so damned huge. "About this mission…"

He crossed his mammoth arms. "Let me guess, you want to right the wrongs for all who have suffered. You wish to make the Maaskab pay for every evil they've committed. You want to wring their necks one by one and watch them choke on their own sick, but not before you've extracted their fingernails with a pair of rusty tweezers and removed their eyes from their sockets with a hot poker."

*Oh my God!! Yes! That's exactly it! If I were a sick, depraved, revenge monger hung up on violence and acts of meaningless retaliation.*

What the hell was wrong with these people?

"Um. Not exactly. Though that is an excellent suggestion. By the way, you're the god of what, exactly?"

"Death and war."

That explained it.

I smiled stiffly. "I am getting the impression that your policy is to exterminate any priests you come in contact with, but they're the only ones who know what's wrong with Kinich."

"Ah. I see. You want us to take prisoners for interrogation."

"Yes," I replied.

"This is very challenging; we must kill them quickly or knock them unconscious before they sift away. We typically choose killing."

"Sift?" I asked. Wasn't that something you did to flour?

"Teleport. Although they travel only short distances, they are difficult to contain."

Oh. Well, that explained how that Maaskab who'd attacked me at my apartment kept popping up on the street.

Then I remembered how Viktor appeared out of thin air. "It's pretty weird that the priests have the same abilities as vampires."

"At first we thought so, too. But then we discovered they had aligned with the Obscuros; we imagine they've been learning from each other."

An idea hit me. "Can we use that black jade stuff somehow? I hear it has some magic juju something or other to absorb power."

He scratched his chin. "Perhaps. I will consult my chiefs and give it consideration." Guy peered over my head in the direction of Kinich's room. "Emma! What are you waiting for, woman? It is time for our evening lovemaking!"

*Classy.*

Emma came skipping out of Kinich's room and made a little wave as she passed by and disappeared into one of the guest rooms.

Well, at least I wasn't the only one who had a bizarre relationship with a deity, punctuated by the word *woman*.

# Twenty-Five

I wrapped my favorite blue scarf around Kinich's neck and kissed his icy forehead, wishing he knew I would do everything possible to help him. It killed me to see this magnificent male reduced to a lifeless-looking shell, so pale, so vulnerable. This is why I'd made the insane decision to go on the mission. I couldn't bear to sit one more day at his side, hoping a miracle might wake him up. I couldn't go another moment wondering what those vile cretins were doing to my mother. And bottom line, Emma was right: I had to step up and fight for what I loved. I only prayed it wasn't too late.

I pushed away the dark thoughts, trying to remain positive because if they had harmed a hair on my mother's beautiful, already fragile body, I would jump on Guy's strangulation, rusty tweezers, hot-poker bandwagon so fast they'd piss their... Well, they didn't wear pants. No. They wore the icky, leathery-looking bikinis made from human skin.

*Psychos.*

"They'll piss their icky, psycho mankinis and wish they were never born." I closed my eyes and sighed. What a turn my life had taken. Only a few short weeks ago I'd been worrying about money for my mom's treatment, thinking about how I'd make ends meet for Christmas.

*Holiday crackers! Less than a week until Christmas.*

No one had mentioned a thing, but then again, it would be a little strange for the gods—except Cimil, obviously, because she was just weird—to observe a human holiday. I'd have to find out what they did celebrate. Probably some weird crap like Hot Poker in the Eye Day.

Well, it didn't matter that I was missing Christmas; I was in no mood to celebrate. I was in the mood to fight, win, and then pick up the pieces of my life.

"And when you're all better," I said to Kinich, "we're going to finish what we started." I rubbed my nose against his. It was cold. I winced and resisted letting the sadness back in.

No. No more.

"It is time," a deep, raspy voice said from behind.

I practically jumped from my skin. "Brutus! You scared the hell out of me!"

Brutus was dressed in his combat gear: black from head to toe, a gun holstered to each side, electronic equipment wired to his head.

He held out a large pack.

"Parachute?" I asked.

He nodded once.

"I love parachuting." I'd dropped five times, but it had been for fun. This was different. This was war. Life or death. But I was ready. Brutus had spent the last twenty-four hours making sure of that.

"Okeydokey. Let's go get my mom."

This was it.

Five hours later I'd successfully herded the scaredy-cats scrambling around inside my head and locked them in a cage. Brutus had explained, in exactly ten words, that the key to winning any battle was having a clear head and calm nerves. He and his men meditated for a minimum of two hours before every mission.

I bet he wished Emma had followed the regimen, not to mention learned to skydive. He did not seem happy suiting up for their tandem jump.

"Dammit! Stop wiggling!" Emma barked over her shoulder. "And that had better be your flashlight!"

I tried not to laugh but couldn't resist.

"Ma'am?" One of Brutus's men, sitting to my side on the long bench at the tail of the plane, helped me with my parachute.

My scaredy-cats began getting restless in their cage, chucking hair balls. This was it.

Dressed in a black jumpsuit, I strapped on the pack and got into formation behind Guy and Emma, who were deep in conversation, and Brutus. Over the roar of the engines, I couldn't hear what they were talking about, but I saw their faces and couldn't help but be envious. The way Guy regarded Emma was nothing short of worship.

Then Emma elbowed Brutus and spouted, "Okay. I'm ready. Let's kill some Scabs and get my granny!"

*Let's go get my mother and capture at least one Scab?* Those bastards would pay, but not before telling me how to cure Kinich.

She glanced over her other shoulder toward me. "Ready?"

"You better believe it," I replied. "These clowns picked the wrong girl to mess with."

I thought I knew what terror was—finding a giant fuzzy spider staring you down in the shower or discovering a mysterious curly hair in your salad after you've eaten the entire thing, for example—but nothing in my life compared to the moment I found myself hurtling through a black void on a moonless night toward Earth, scared out of my frigging mind, hoping my altimeter didn't fail.

"Penelope? Are you there?"

*Voices. I'm hearing voices. Oh perfect.* Dammit. This was no time to lose my marbles. Go figure.

"Penelope, please respond."

The voice sounded like Emma.

*Headset! Headset.* I sighed with relief. I pressed the transmission button on my neck. "I'm here."

"Don't forget Guy's instructions: wait for Brutus to signal you."

I remembered every word. Once everyone was on the ground and in position, the Uchben would go in first. I'd stay behind until given the word—or a poke, since he didn't really talk—from Brutus.

"Got it," I replied.

The alarm on my altimeter beeped. Time to pull the cord and pray: *dear Lord, or universe, or anyone out there powerful enough to save my unworthy, stupid ass, please don't let me land on a power line, something sharp, or a really tall tree.*

I was surprised the dear Lord, universe, or other being powerful enough had listened. I landed with a soft thump in a soggy, grass-covered clearing along with three other Uchben I didn't know. One came over and helped me out of my harness, then pointed to a tall patch of grass several yards away. I scurried over and crouched.

It was the dead of winter, but the tropical air of southern Mexico was moist and heavy. The dank, earthy smell of the jungle instantly penetrated my nose.

Now, I know any normal person would wet themselves at the thought of jumping headfirst into this situation, though, perhaps as a testament to my "exotic DNA," my body buzzed with anticipation. Now that I'd decided not to take my situation lying down, I felt like I had been born for this moment, to serve justice to these horrible beings who'd harmed the people I loved.

*"People" you...love?*

I loved my mother. That was a given. But did I love Kinich, too? We barely knew each other, frankly. Yet there I was, ready to put my life on the line for him. Yes, if my mom weren't a part of this, I'd still be here.

It was a startling revelation, really. How had I gone from infatuation to soul-clenching lust to...love?

*True love defies logic. That's its signature trait.*

Funny, people always said love was something that grew in both intensity and depth as you got to know a person, but I was never sure about that. Maybe the love is already there, dormant inside your heart, waiting for "the one" to unlock it. That would certainly explain how I felt; I loved him. I felt like I always had and I always would.

"Great. I'm in love with a comatose deity who has

mixed feelings for me," I whispered to myself. Could my life possibly get any more complicated?

"Penelope," I heard Emma call out on my headset.

"Yes?" I whispered back.

"Um, don't freak, okay?" Emma's voice crackled over the tiny speaker in my ear.

"Well, since you put it *that* way, I'll be sure not to," I hissed.

"Point taken. Listen, Brutus is coming to get you."

"Where are you?" I asked.

"I'm standing in the middle of the Maaskab village."

"Are you okay?"

"Yeah. Everything's fine," she replied with a melancholy tone. "See you in a few."

Wait. This so didn't make any sense. They couldn't have taken down the Maaskab that quickly. Was it a trap?

*Oh my gods. Oh my gods.*

The unmistakable, hulking shadow of Brutus emerged from the nocturnal shadows. He signaled for me to follow.

I scrambled over. "What's going on?"

Of course, he didn't answer.

"Nice time to pull the mute card, Brutus. I'm beginning to see why Emma has it in for you."

I thought I heard him chuckle, but couldn't be certain.

Brutus whipped out a machete and hacked away at the small branches while we slogged forward. With my night vision goggles everything resembled a leafy version of *Tron*. "Brutus, you have to tell me. Please?" I begged.

He marched ahead at a steady clip until we arrived at another clearing. A group of twenty men, Emma, and Guy congregated near a small hut. Several men gripped flashlights and everyone frantically debated.

This didn't look good at all. "What's going on?"

Emma turned toward me. "Oh, Penelope. Listen—"

"Where's my mom?"

Guy stepped forward. "She is not here."

My heart trembled. "What do you mean 'not here'?"

Emma gently squeezed my arm. "The village is empty."

*No. No. No!* "Where'd they all go?"

"We do not know," Guy answered. "Our satellites show this camp is occupied. Our people back in the control room also confirm they still see it as such."

I flipped off my visor and looked around. "I don't understand. How can they see Maaskab on the satellite when there's no one here? Have they hacked into your system?"

Guy shook his head. "Not likely. The Maaskab are not technologically savvy."

Apparently not. This village reminded me of a pre-Hispanic version of the Renaissance fair but without the ale, hippies, or ouds.

"It is an illusion," Guy said. "They are becoming more powerful with their dark arts by the day."

That sounded bad. Really bad. "So what do we do? Are there other villages or places they could hide her?"

"I must return to my realm," Guy stated acrimoniously. "I have a much better chance of spotting traces of them from there. I will also look for that goddamned sister of mine."

"Cimil?" I asked.

"Yes."

"If you find her, tell her I have a few bones to pick," I griped.

"Get in line," he responded.

"Do you have to leave?" Emma sounded on the verge of tears.

Guy cupped her cheek and kissed her deeply. She pulled back and whisked away a tear with her camouflage sleeve. "I'm sorry. I know the fiancée of the mighty God of Death and War shouldn't cry."

"I love you, Emma. Tears and all. I will see you back in Sedona, and we will spend the entire day making love."

"That would be nice," she said in a melancholy voice.

This was my cue to leave. I was in no mood to listen to their horny little plans, but then Guy turned to leave. I guessed he was heading to find a portal cenote thingy.

"Hey!" Emma called out. "Aren't you forgetting something?"

*Oh, great. Are they going to have a quickie before he goes?*

Guy stopped in his tracks, his back to us. Did he groan?

"Please?" she begged. "It will grow back."

*Grow back? Yikes. I so don't want to know.*

He turned slowly, his eyes glowing in the night. "Yes, my love. Of course." He reached around to the small of his back and whipped out a large knife.

What the *hell* was he going to do with that?

He spun Emma and swiped the blade across her braid near the nape of her neck and then promptly cut off his own ponytail.

He held the hair to his chest and chanted toward the starlit sky, "*In halach puczical, in uchucil, ca kaxah yokolcab ichi pixan.*"

The air kicked up around us, and as it did, my memory flashed to when Kinich last spoke to me.

My blood pressure plummeted when I realized he'd recited those exact words the moment he incinerated the Scab.

Guy quickly kissed Emma's nose. "I suggest you don't break the bond this time, my love."

She lovingly brushed his stubble-covered cheek. "Never."

He crouched down, placed the locks of hair in the dirt, and ignited the pile of strands. Brutus and the other men stood quietly behind him, staring in awe as the hair quickly dissolved into nothing.

My mind raced. What did it mean?

"Good-bye, my sweet." Before you could say "flaming hair ball," Guy disappeared into the jungle.

"Well. Time to go back to Sedona, I guess." She wiped away another tear and began walking.

"Emma?" I trailed behind her like an eager puppy. "What did it mean? That phrase and burning your hair?"

Quietly, with an unmistakable sadness in her voice, she said, "My heart, my power, we unite in this world inside my soul—it's a prayer, the Prayer of Loyalty and Protection."

What a beautiful phrase. "And the hair?"

"It completes the ritual; it creates a bond between two souls. I guess you could burn another part of your body if you wanted, but hair is the least painless thing to lose."

"I'm sorry, but I don't understand. What do you mean by 'bond'?"

"It creates a connection that enables the gods to keep track of you more easily. It's like being tethered to their life force. With Guy, it allowed him to speak to me when he—well, his soul was trapped in the cenote by the Maas-kab and..."

Emma continued to speak, but my mind detached from present time. It spiraled and swirled as it computed and calculated and put the pieces together.

*Oh my gods! Kinich.*

# *Twenty-Six*

The long flight back on Air Uchben was the worst, most depressing wait of my existence. No one spoke a word. But what was there to say? The bad guys had outsmarted us, and everything we loved and cared about was on the line.

Strangely enough, I sensed that my mother remained alive, though I had no clue in what condition. But a hopeful little voice inside my head told me she hadn't left this world yet and we still had time to save her. I clung to that thought like a lifeboat.

As for Kinich, well, that was a whole other enchilada in the oven. My heart and stomach were vacillating between elation (Kinich tried to bind himself to me) and terror (I didn't know what would happen when I completed the ritual).

When I arrived at Kinich's home, I immediately went to the kitchen, found a pair of scissors and some matches, and then headed for his room.

No surprise, Kinich was in his bed, right where I'd left him. The doctor, that same young-looking man with short, brown hair, leaned over him, checking his vitals.

"Any change?"

"I'm sorry. I'll come back this afternoon."

I shut the door behind him and stared down at Kinich's large form, peacefully resting on the bed. His bronzed skin had turned to a pale taupe. I sighed and dropped to my knees, placing a kiss on the top of his hand.

"Please, work. Please?" I looked up at the ceiling, fending off the tears.

I gently turned his head to the side and cut off his silky caramel strands. I rubbed the thick, soft hair over my cheek, then placed it on his chest as I cut off my own ponytail.

My hair had never been my obsession, although my mom had always fussed over it and said it shined like obsidian. I think I kept it long only to make her happy.

*It will grow back, Pen. It's just hair.*

I pushed my now chin-length hair out of my eyes and headed out to the patio. The first rays of sunlight tinted the night sky with an orange hue to the east. The surrounding desert was unnervingly quiet, as if the universe herself was holding her breath.

I looked to the sky and said a little prayer, to whom, I didn't know, and placed the hair on the ground. I ignited the two bundles and watched them burn, knowing I'd break into a million pieces if this didn't work.

The tiny fire fizzled out quickly.

*Here goes.*

"Kinich? Can you hear me? Kinich?"

I waited, my heart thumping in overtime. "Kinich," I whispered, "please, please, answer me."

He did not.

*Oh gods, no. It didn't work. It didn't work.*

I felt like I'd lost Kinich all over again.

Exhausted from being up all night and the endless disappointments, I staggered inside and curled up against his cold frame.

# Twenty-Seven

⌒

"Penelope, you look ravishing today," Kinich whispered in my ear.

I snuggled against his warmth and wrapped one arm tightly around his waist. "I've missed you."

"Not nearly as much as I missed you." His body shifted on top of me. "We have some unfinished business."

My eyes popped open and our eyes met. The frisky grin on his face told me what he wanted, but I asked anyway. I wanted to hear him say it.

"What sort of business?" I whispered.

His lips were quickly on mine. The heat of his mouth shot straight into my stomach and made my girlie parts perk up instantly.

I sighed with contentment. This was how I wanted my life to be. Him. Me. Our bodies touching.

Kinich unexpectedly stopped. He was now frowning.

"What's wrong?" I asked.

*"You're wasting time. I need you here with me. Now. Do you have any clue how worried I was about you?"*

"Huh? But I am here," I replied, utterly confused.

*"Penelope,"* he growled.

"What?"

*"Penelope! Wake the hell up,"* he screamed.

My eyes snapped open. "No!" I covered my face. "Goddammit! Not again!"

Kinich was still in his bed. Motionless. Cold. Frozen in time like Sleeping Beauty.

I slipped from the bed and staggered to the bathroom. The reflection staring back in the mirror was a sad and worn version of me. That's because that is what I was. I couldn't do it anymore. I didn't have any strength left in my arms to keep throwing back the lemons.

How ironic, I thought. I finally understood why Kinich stopped believing his life would ever change and why he'd opted to survive, but not thrive. Exist, but not live. Everyone had their breaking points. Everyone. Even a powerful god.

"I'm sorry I judged you, Kinich." I hung my head over the sink.

*"I forgive you, now that you're awake. Did I mention you snore like a lumberjack with a sinus infection? It's quite disturbing."*

My eyes popped out of my head. "Kinich?" I looked over my shoulder, right and left, but I was alone in the private world-class spa with mini-waterfall.

*"Yes?"* he answered.

*Holy devil's food cake.* I looked up and down, side to side. No one there.

"Oh, goody. 'Cause dreaming about him every single night just isn't enough."

*"Every night? How intriguing. Are we naked?"*

There it was again. I held my breath. "K-Kinich? Is that you?"

*"I think I will ban everyone else from using my Mayan name ever again. I only want to hear you speak it. Just you with that sweet voice."*

I couldn't breathe. "Is it...really...you? Or am I dreaming?"

*"It is I. What took so long to complete the ritual?"*

I leaned over to catch my breath. "I had no idea that's what it was. Holy crap! Is it really you?"

*"Did you not tell everyone of the incident?"*

"Yeah, but I sorta forgot about the part when you said that weird phrase." I couldn't believe this. I staggered into the bedroom and stared down at Kinich's body. "You're on the bed. I'm looking right at you. Where are you...um"— *what is the right way to say this?*—"calling me from?"

*"Apparently, the universe still holds some surprises. Even for an old deity."*

"Sorry?" I asked.

*"I am right here. With you."*

"Again. Sorry?"

*"I am...inside you."*

When Kinich attempted to open his eyes and failed, he instantly knew something was amiss. Slowly, he explored the physical sensations around him. Toes, fingers, lungs, he could feel them all, yet was unable to take command of his movements.

Was he paralyzed? Dead?

The last thing he recalled was being in the swimming

pool with Penelope, of touching her plump, firm breasts, and of being on the verge of spilling himself in her eagerly pumping hand. The desire for her had been so potent that his body literally ignited. Then, as he had been about to contain the flames, terror swept across Penelope's lovely face.

He couldn't see the Maaskab, but the rank smell wafting in the air was unmistakable. The Scab stood behind him, and whatever it was about to do wouldn't be good. Likely a bit painful, too.

Yet only one solitary thought occupied his mind: he wanted to protect Penelope and couldn't. *Not again. Not fucking again.*

With that moment of utter helplessness came a startling transformation deep inside his immortal soul.

Like a hard blow to the gut, he realized that if given the choice, he would let mankind perish, sacrifice his very soul, if it meant saving her.

*Impossible.*

How, when the gods were hardwired to protect humanity, could he feel this way? He did not know. But he did. The invisible chains had snapped, his soul free to choose which lives he valued more. Free to live, to love, to wish for a different life and possibly obtain it. And at that very moment, he wished to never be separated from Penelope ever again.

Surely the Maaskab was about to kill him. And surely the priest had come to take her away.

There was only one solution: the Prayer of Loyalty and Protection.

With his light tethered to hers, he stood a chance of tracking her down once the cenote rebuilt his form.

He spoke the words and prayed the Maaskab behind him was close enough to touch...to kill. At the very least, he would buy Penelope some time before more showed up.

He reached behind and felt solid flesh and bone.

Contact.

Then there was darkness. Nothing but darkness. Until the sound of Penelope's sweet voice came crashing through the abyss, sighing his name in her sleep.

*"Penelope, wake up. Can you hear me?"*

There was no reply for several moments. Perhaps his light was in limbo. Yet when he felt his body move of its own accord, his eyes unable to see a damn thing, he realized he was hitchhiking inside another body. Indeed, the universe had a sick, sick sense of humor; he was inside Penelope.

*"Be careful what you wish for,"* he mumbled.

"Huh?" she asked, her voice frantic.

*"My last memory, before the Maaskab appeared, was wishing to be inside you."*

"How's it even possible?"

*"It's quite easy to wish to be inside you—"*

He noticed the sensation of heat spread across his own cheeks. She was blushing.

Amazing. He could sense her body?

Yes. Heat on her face, cold in her feet, and...hunger? He'd never felt hunger, but it was a sensation deep within her belly that radiated out through every cell of her body. She was famished. Starving.

He instantly angered. There was no reason on earth for her to go without, to deprive her body of nourishment.

*"When was the last time you ate?"* he asked.

"I had a grilled cheese and ice cream a few hours ago.

Couldn't sleep. Is it really you?" Her voice quivered as though she were on the brink of tears.

A few hours? Were human bodies always so needy?

*"Yes. It is truly I."*

"Are you sure? Because I dream about you all the time. Can you prove it?"

He couldn't help but wonder what her dreams might be like. Were they similar to his? So tantalizing, so graphic, the details so remarkable that he tasted her on his tongue. Even now, with little effort, he could visualize every sensual, feminine curve of her body: her soft inner thighs, the gentle slope of her back that flowed into the most deliciously round, firm ass he'd ever seen. He could recall the color and exact shape of her pink nipples, of her heat as he filled her repeatedly and came inside her. *Dammit, man! Stop that. Think of something godly and boring like picking lottery winners.*

*Not working . . . dammit!* His mind pulsed with lust.

Despite his unrelenting desire and shocking, inexplicable transformation, the irony and bitterness of his situation lurked menacingly in the shadows of his mind.

He could not be with her, even if he wanted her with every molecule of divine energy in his soul. Because two simple facts had not changed: One, the apocalypse was coming. And if he, his brethren, and their allies failed to stop it, life would cease to exist, Penelope's life included.

Two, he was a god. Simply put, he lacked the ability to give a human heart, Penelope's heart, what it needed to thrive. They were two different elements existing in two different realities of the same world. Fire and ice. Reason and passion. Responsibility and desire. Opposite ends of the spectrum. If he acted upon his feelings for her or attempted any sort of relationship, he might end up destroying the very thing that he admired: her spirit. She would always be left wanting emotionally.

*You* will *overcome this irrational urge to be with her. Do your hear me? You will, gods dammit. You cannot afford any distractions.*

"Well?" she said. "I'm waiting."

*"Woman! Stop your foolishness. It is I."*

"Woman? Oh my God! Minotaur, it is you!" she began to squeal.

He felt the weight of her body slam into her heels as she jumped and clapped. He felt the heaviness of her bust jiggle with her movements. His...well, not his body, but his soul tensed up. If he had a penis, it would be harder than a rock right now.

*"This is going to be very challenging."*

"What?"

*"Nothing. Keep jumping."*

# Twenty-Eight

—

I bolted down the hallway, unable to believe he'd been hanging out inside my body the entire time. Now it all made sense... my smoldering rear end, the blast I'd given Brutus. Did this mean that I wasn't a Payal? And if not, then why would the Maaskab even want me or have taken my mother?

Mistaken identity?

I'd have to ask as soon as I delivered the exciting news about Kinich to the gods. Would they believe me? It was a little... strange.

*Come on. Look who you're talking about. The gods invented weird.* They probably had Weird Olympics complete with crazy crab-crawl relay race, garbage can chariot racing, and potato sack hop with the potatoes still in them. While eating potatoes. These folks were the official sponsors of the bizarre and unusual.

*Damn. You fit right in.*

Then, without pomp or warning, the magnitude of the situation struck home like a bad burrito.

*Crap! Inside my body?* He could feel what I felt? Hear my thoughts?

*Testing, testing. You are the sexiest man alive. I want to make you my hunky love slave and hereby decree you call me, "Princess Penelope, Your Eternal Jewel."*

No response.

*Minotaur? Can you hear me?*

No response.

*Well, that's a relief.*

I rounded the corner into the living room to find Emma, Gabrán, and Brutus speaking quietly.

"I found Kinich," I exclaimed.

Emma shifted the gaze of her bloodshot eyes from the floor.

I jumped up and down and pointed to my chest. "He's here!"

Gabrán leaned toward Brutus. "The lass has finally cracked."

Brutus nodded in agreement.

"No. Really!"

I blabbed a million miles an hour, telling them all about how Kinich had said the prayer, but that I'd forgotten until I'd heard the words spoken by Guy.

"Isn't it great!" I said, clapping.

*"Penelope,"* Kinich mumbled. *"You haven't won a new car. In fact, we have a very big problem."*

I turned my head toward the ceiling. Then floor. Then...

"I don't know where to look when I talk to you, so I'll just say this to my shoes." They were snow boots actually.

That's all I had with me. "Up until five minutes ago, I'd thought I lost you forever. So trust me. This is way better."

*"The same could be said about a tuna sandwich,"* Kinich grumbled.

"Wow. Has anyone ever told you that you're a downer?"

*"Yes. Frequently. I believe Cimil refers to me as a Donna Downer, some acquaintance of hers, I suppose."*

"It's Debbie."

*"Ah yes. Debbie is correct. How is it that you also know her?"*

He clearly had no clue who Debbie was. "You don't watch television, do you?"

*"Not this decade, but I understand the MeTube is quite popular. I intend to watch my video—"*

"Eh-hem!" Emma chimed in. "Sorry to interrupt the conversation...with...yourself—sounds pretty interesting, by the way—but could you explain that little part about Kinich again?"

"Oh. Sorry." I jumped up and down. "Kinich's soul, or...light...whatever you people call it, parked itself inside my body."

I explained once again all about the ritual and how I'd completed it.

"You're frigging kidding me," Emma said. "That's almost as weird as what happened to me."

Before I could say another word, Guy appeared in the room.

"Did I miss much?" he said with a cocked brow and arrogance in his voice only a god could pull off.

Emma squealed and ran across the room, launching herself at him. He easily caught her petite frame.

"What happened? Did you find anything?" I asked.

Emma smothered his face in kisses.

"Hold on, honey." He pecked Emma's lips, then set her down. A gloomy frown occupied his face. "I was unable to find your mother. However, I have found a few clues that might lead to the Maaskab. I've called an emergency summit for tomorrow to discuss it." His eyes dropped. "I am sorry, Penelope, not to bring you better news."

"It's still something." *I am not going to cry, I am not going to cry.*

Gabrán then jumped in and informed Guy about Kinich. Surprisingly, Guy didn't seem at all worried. In fact, he looked downright amused.

*See, ambassadors of weird.*

"Well, Kinich," Guy said with a grin. "Seems Fate's having a little fun with you."

*"Fuck off,"* I heard Kinich say. Obviously, Kinich could hear anything I heard, but no one could hear him back. So I said, "He says you've always been his favorite brother."

Guy quirked a brow before turning toward Gabrán, still clutching Emma in his arms. "The others are right behind me; please make sure their needs are taken care of and that they do not destroy Kinich's house this time."

Kinich grumbled his appreciation, but I didn't share because Guy wasted no time relocking lips with Emma right in the foyer. It didn't appear they had any plans to detach this century. In fact, they reminded me of a barnacle and a tanker.

I was about to comment that I wasn't in the mood to watch the prelude to their "lovemaking"—damn, I was jealous—but that's when I saw them.

"Oh my . . . gods . . ."

One by one, they streamed into the living room.

They glowed. They radiated. They exuded the sort of power humans dreamed of. Words could not do justice, so I simply said, "Wow," and let my jaw hang open.

*"Wow, what?"* Kinich asked.

"The other gods," I whispered. "They're here."

*"Ah yes. Stand your guard, woman."*

Um...okay. Was there something to be afraid of? Because I didn't feel afraid. I felt like running to get a camera.

*And would he ever stop calling me "woman"?*

"Sure thing, Minotaur," I sighed.

First, a man with golden skin and ankle-length black hair streaked with silver floated in. He wore a royal-blue toga and an ostentatious, foot-high jade headdress. His turquoise eyes were filled with irreverence as he surveyed the room.

Next came a tall, slender woman with golden waves of hair, wearing a bow and arrow and a short white dress belted at the waist with leather cord—*She-Ra? Princess of Power? Is that you?*—followed by a rather statuesque woman wearing what looked to be a hat shaped like Winnie the Pooh's beehive.

One by one, some with black hair and dark skin, some with white hair and light golden skin, some dressed semi-normal, and others barely dressed at all, the ten beings lined up in front of me while I stood there gawking.

"Hi, I'm Penelo—"

Before I finished, all ten kneeled down and set objects on the hardwood floor.

I glanced at Guy and Emma for help, but they were still engaged in their heavy petting near the front door. Gabrán and a few of his men stood motionless at attention.

"Kinich," I whispered. "What's going on?"

*"What are they doing?"* he asked.

I covered my mouth to stifle the noise. "They're kneeling on the ground. They put stuff on the floor."

One had set out a smallish wooden box; the lady with the white dress, a set of horns from an elk or something. Another, a leather bota. There was also a jar of honey and some other bric-a-brac. It seemed they'd all gone to Cost Plus and shopped in the third world knickknack section.

Then my eyes shifted to the far end of the line to my right.

The woman wore a flowing black dress and lace veil. And though I could scarcely see her iridescent eyes through the cloth, her stare gave me the heebie-jeebies. Then I noticed her little prize.

*Ewww. A dead rat?*

*"They are honoring you. Do not be nervous,"* Kinich instructed.

*Oh, hardy-har-har-har. Suuure. Nothing to be nervous about. The most powerful beings in the world are kneeling in front of me, offering dead things and other assorted sundries.*

"Why are they doing this?" I asked Kinich.

*"Simply thank them,"* he replied.

I was about to when my guilty manners kicked in.

*Oh no!* I hadn't got them anything. My mind scrambled. I had some Tic Tacs in my purse, but they were almost gone. Well, hopefully they were fans of the "it's the thought that counts" rule because they would have to share.

I cleared my throat. "Um. Are these for me? You really shouldn't have."

The man in the middle, whom I'd not had a good look at yet, rose with his right arm crossed over his broad chest, his hand fisted over his heart. He wore a black tee and well-fitted black leather pants, which seemed like the standard-issue uniform for the men in this social circle—and like the other males in the family, he had to be pushing seven feet in height. His thick, loose waves of black hair hung well past his shoulders, and his arctic-blue eyes were an icy contrast to his milk-chocolate skin.

*Really? Seriously? Can these deities possibly be any better looking?* It seemed unfair given they also had preternatural powers and immortality.

"I am Zac Cimi, Bacab of the North. As our tradition dictates, we honor you with gifts, Sun Goddess."

I sighed like a thirteen-year-old meeting her favorite teen idol. Regardless of where my heart was committed, my inner horndog was captivated.

*Pen! Snap out of it. He just called you "Sun Goddess."*
*Right. I'm on it!*

"This is for Kinich," I said. "Phew! I thought you'd all gone on some grack bender and were kneeling for me."

Zac's eyes shifted side to side. His handsome face, with uncharacteristically exquisite cheekbones and thick, black lashes, looked troubled. "No. You now hold Kinich's power. Therefore, you are the ruler of the House of the Gods."

"Sorry?" My eyes bulged from my head. "House of what?" I looked at my boots. "Kinich, this has to be some mistake. Please tell me what to say."

He grumbled, *"Penelope. Just accept graciously."*

"But—"

*"I have been the ruler of the House of the Gods for over half my existence. It is only because the sun is the source of all life. You now house me; ergo, you now rule the gods until we are separated."*

"Uh-uh. No. *Nein.* Nix. Nyet. Not gonna happen."

Kinich snarled a warning. *"Penelopeeee."*

"What about water and oxygen? Aren't those equally important to life? Or…chocolate? Chocolate is powerful, especially dark chocolate. It has antioxidants. Isn't there a god for that?"

*"No, Penelope. It doesn't work that way."*

Oh no. I wasn't going for this. Not at all.

I pointed to the woman in the black veil. "What does she do? Can't she take over?"

She shot daggers with her eyes, at least I thought she did; it was hard to tell with the veil over her face.

"Okay, maybe not her." I pointed to the lady in the short white dress who'd presented me with antlers. "How about She-Ra there? At least she's got fun taste in clothes."

The veiled woman in black sprung from her knees and stepped forward. "Oh, for heaven's sake. Not this same old crap! I am the Goddess of Suicide. What do you expect me to wear? A hula skirt and beer helmet?"

*Goddess of Suicide? Yikes. And I'd thought waiting tables sucked. Her job is way worse.*

A pudgy god, the one who presented the bota and wore several—*six?*—himself, with unkempt, plain brown hair, wearing a green Puma running suit, chimed in. "Yaaaa. Gooood one. I like hulas and beer helmets," he slurred.

Was he drunk?

The suicide lady rolled her eyes. "Shut it, Belch." Her

veiled eyes swept the room. "Why must we go through this every summit? Anyone else want to take a shot at the sad, sad, depressing lady?" She held out her arms and pivoted back and forth, looking at the others.

Everyone ignored her.

"Just kill me now. Please?" she whispered acerbically to no one in particular.

"I'm really sorry," I blurted. "I didn't mean it. Your goth look is a classic." I did a little pump with my fist in the air. "Go, Bela," I said quietly. "I meant Lugosi. Not the *Twilight* Bella."

The gods regarded me with blank expressions.

This was not going well.

"Look, everyone." Half of the gods still knelt. "Please, get up. This is so wrong." I looked over at the door and was about to call Emma and Guy to my aid, but they were gone. "Oh. Come on! Can't you two keep your hands off each other for two seconds?" I called out.

The gods looked at each other with confusion before casting their glances at me.

"I'm leaving now," I said. "I can't accept your lovely, and such..." *Don't look at the dead rat, don't look at the dead rat.* "...inspirational gifts." I began to back away. "Just..." I made little waves with my hands. "Pick a new interim leader. Okay?"

I turned to leave, but She-Ra, the one in the white dress with the bow and arrow, latched onto my hand, sending waves of painful tingles through my arm. "No, Penelope. You will lead the summit tomorrow. It must be you."

I snapped my arm away. "Thank you. I really appreciate the offer. But I'm not—"

I drew a blank as my eyes met with hers. Like Zac, her

eyes were nearly translucent with a splash of sky blue. I was instantly mesmerized.

*"Penelope? What's going on?"* asked Kinich.

"Umm...I..."

*"Dammit. Your human form is still susceptible. Penelope, listen to my voice. Listen hard. Listen only to me."*

*I'm listening, I'm listening,* I wanted to say, but couldn't.

He continued, *"You are immune to the powers of the gods: their scents, their commands, and the influences of their energies. You will listen to only me."*

I shut my eyes and noticed my head had cleared. When I reopened them, the She-Ra woman with flowing golden hair still stared.

She smiled. "I do not care what Kinich is telling you, I have spoken on this matter."

"Who are you?"

She dipped her head. "I am Camaxtli, Goddess of the Hunt."

Well, that explained the antler gift and the Outback Steakhouse-meets-J.Lo outfit.

"I am also known as Irsirra, Legba Fon, Dola, and many others. You may call me Fate." She smiled and walked away.

*Irsalegafondola what?* Her name sounded like a hippie love child gone wrong. "Kudos on the smorga-horror of names, lady, but I'm not doing it."

The other gods gasped at my insult. Except for the suicide lady. She snickered.

*"Penelope,"* Kinich scolded. *"Go back to my room. We will discuss this in private."*

"Wait," I said. "You're not agreeing with her? I can't lead your summit."

*"Penelope. I do not have time to explain all of our laws. But Fate has spoken, and you will simply have to trust me; no one, not even I, tempts Fate. We all learned that lesson long, long ago."*

*Um...okay.* Wasn't that whole "tempting fate" thing supposed to be meant figuratively? In any case, I was so, so out of my league arguing with this bunch, and I knew it.

"Fine, goddammit. I'll do it."

"Knew ya would," I heard Fate snort as I stomped away, accepting defeat with about as much grace as a two-legged pit bull.

When I reached Kinich's room, a few of the gods—I wasn't sure how they'd gotten there so fast—were already outside in the pool, guzzling wine and doing cannonballs. Of course, they were completely naked. Except for the god they called Belch, the already drunk one. He wore a leopard bikini that accentuated his beer belly. Ironically, though, he was still pretty good-looking. Must be a god thing.

I shook my head and drew the curtains. Could this situation possibly get any weirder?

The answer to my question, I'd soon discover, was yes. Absolutely.

# Twenty-Nine

⌒

Step by step, Kinich walked me through each god—names, personality quirks, relative rank, and powers. Each deity was known for something special, a unique gift, but had a variety of abilities. Now, why a god would need the gift of balancing a spoon on his nose (Belch); producing a yodel that could be heard for fifty miles (Fate); or sniffing out the best price on anything, at any time, in any hemisphere (Cimil) was beyond me. It did, however, account for why many civilizations believed in a multitude of deities when in actuality there were fourteen.

Thank goodness for that. As it was, I would never keep their names straight. Aside from Cimil, Guy, Kinich, Chaam (the evil brother now locked inside a pyramid), Zac (the hunky god in black I'd just met), Camaxtli (Fate), and Acan, the God of Wine and Intoxication (aka Belch), there was Ixtab, the Goddess of Suicide (aka dead rat lady); Akna, Goddess of Fertility (going to stay far,

far away from her); Ah-Ciliz, the God of Eclipses; and Colel Cab, Mistress of Bees (that explained why she gave me honey and had a hive on her head). And last but not least...K'ak. Apparently his full name meant "Smoking Squirrel." And aside from being able to summon bolts of lightning, no one really knew what he did, though his name seemed like a gift all its own, as did his fashion sense. (He was the one with the ankle-length hair and the giant headdress.)

Those were merely the gods I could remember, but there were several more, including the Goddess of Forgetfulness (who Kinich said I'd never remember because no one did).

Next, Kinich tackled the topic of summit protocol. The agenda had to be set at the beginning of the meeting. This was law. Otherwise, keeping order was like herding cats on crack—not grack—with itchy dermatitis.

Other than that, discussion items could be nominated by any deity but added only with a majority vote. Once a vote was taken, they were recorded, carved into stone. Literally.

"So, what about finding my mother? Where does she fit in the agenda?"

*"Guy will ask to have his recent findings added to the agenda; I am certain everyone will agree to this. After he imparts the information, you will move for Call to Action."*

"If they turn me down?"

*"Not likely, we are gods. Our sole purpose is to care for humans."*

"What about you? We have to find a way to save you."

Kinich became quiet for several moments. *"I am*

*certain my... situation will not go without discussion. I assure you, I am not suffering. Being here is not so dissimilar from my disembodied natural state."*

"You mean, when you're back home?"

*"Yes."*

That statement gave me a jolt. When I thought of Kinich, I thought of a man. One I desired with every girlie part of my girlie body. Lean, tightly packed muscles, broad shoulders, and ripped abs. So, to imagine this fine specimen of sexual prowess without his physical form perturbed me.

"What do you look like when you're 'home'?"

*"I am without form. In my realm, I simply exist. Reduced to thoughts, but able to see anything I wish with my mind and still able to manipulate the energy in the physical world."*

"Really? So you can make the sun shine or do that voice thing to people from there?"

*"Yes. In fact, my powers are far easier to use when I'm home. Here, we are limited by our bodies. They contain us. They require massive amounts of energy to control and move.*

*"There, at home, we feel no physical sensations, no heat, cold, or pain. One doesn't need to breathe or sleep."*

What an odd existence. No eating to worry about. No jeans to squeeze into. No watching your body grow old or having to stop each day to sleep. "Sounds good to me."

*"It is neither good nor bad. It is simply... different."* He paused for several moments. *"Penelope, there is something I wish to tell you."*

I swallowed. "Please, don't let it be bad news." I suddenly felt tired again. I needed to lie down.

I stretched across Kinich's large bed next to his—*okay, this is getting really creepy*—body. "Are you sure your physical form is still alive?"

*"Yes. It has not been damaged, it simply lacks my soul or any of my divine light."*

Good. Because that body, even in its slumbering state, was phenomenal. I had lots of unfinished business to conduct with it.

*Do you love him for his body, Pen? Come on.*

*No, I love ... him.*

"So if it were to die, you would be fine?" I asked.

*"I believe so, yes."*

"And if I died?" I asked. "What would happen to you? Would you go back to that cenote thing?"

*"This is, in fact, what I wish to discuss with you."*

"What?" I asked.

*"Given our current situation, I would like to petition for your immortality tomorrow."*

*Huh?* "Huh?"

*"Penelope, I-I ..."*

There was a long, awkward pause. *"My feelings for you remain ... complicated. I desire you. I have never desired anything in my seventy thousand years of existence, apart from my freedom, but I want there to be no confusion around the topic. I propose this solution because I fear for you. I wish for you to be safe, and in your current form, it will not be easy. Not when you have Maaskab after you."*

*Complicated? His feelings are ... complicated?* My brain was stuck in the mud, my wheels spinning without traction. *Complicated! Complicated?* "So, it's about protecting me. That's all?"

Silence.

"Fine," I whispered, fending off the hurt. "I'll think about it. If I go on another Maaskab mission, at least immortality ups my chances of surviving."

*"What?"* he screamed. *"You went on a mission?"*

I stared at his immobile face, but it felt silly to berate a comatose body, so I looked at my boots again. "Yes! I did!"

*"He let you go. Didn't he? I'll kill him! Guy has crossed the line! And you! Foolish woman! What in the name of the gods were you thinking?"*

"Hold on a second, your holiness!" Gods, I felt silly yelling at him while he was inside me. "I'm a grown woman, and if I want to risk my neck for my mother or the man I love, then that's my choice! Mine!"

*"Did you say you...love me?"*

"I...well, yes. I guess I did! And clearly, I'm crazy! 'Cause you're the last man—deity—bodiless being... Oh! Crappity crap! Whatever!" I huffed. "Dude. You're the last *dude* on earth I should love."

Silence.

"Hello?"

Silence.

"Fine! I'm taking a shower and then a long, long nap. So...just stay that way! Not a peep, Minotaur!"

I stomped to the bathroom and turned on the shower. It was a large stall with beautiful natural stone tiles and several massage heads on each wall. I grumbled as I stripped off my clothes and stepped in. The first few seconds felt wonderful, but then the pang of rejection hit hard. For a brief moment, I considered crying, then realized that was not the answer.

*You're done crying. New chapter.*

Now what? He didn't love me back. I could deal. Maybe. Okay. It hurt.

*Ouch, ouch, ouch!*

⌒

*"I'm sorry,"* he finally said twenty minutes into my shower. *"I assume you went on the mission to find your mother and the answer to what happened to me."*

"Yes."

*"I cannot recall anyone ever risking a life for me. Thank you."*

I stood there nude with a bar of soap in my hands, hanging on every word.

*"Why should I be surprised? Your bravery is what I admire most about you, Penelope. Nothing seems to faze you. Not even my harsh treatment. You"*—he paused for several moments—*"humble me at every turn. And if I were another man...or were a man...I would want you for my own. Still, you must trust in me, Penelope. You must believe that there is nothing more important right now than my duties. Not even you can afford my distraction."*

Frankly, I wasn't able to "trust" him on this because I thoroughly believed he was messed in the head on this relationship topic. Sure, there were other things going on—important things such as an impending apocalypse, him being trapped inside my body, yada yada—but I knew we'd be stronger together. How did I know that when he didn't?

"Let's pretend for a moment that your duty wasn't a concern. Then what?"

*"Then I would tell you that none of the gods are capable of making a human heart content, that we are unable to give a relationship what it needs to thrive."*

"Which is?"

*"Commitment and dedication. Or a normal life full of daily routines and the observance of unspoken rules humans demand from one another. Understand, a god's life is not dictated by social norms. We are not expected to call if we'll be late for dinner; we do not eat. Or bring flowers because the calendar says it is a particular day in the month of February. Our lives are driven by duty and the fact that time is abundant. We go where we are needed, when we are needed, for as long as we must. I can pass decades in my realm before returning to your world, yet, to me, it is only a moment in time."*

"I get the point. Our worlds are different. But I still haven't heard any showstoppers. These are all things a god could work through."

*"Why would I want this? When at the very best, the outcome would be a relationship still considered dysfunctional. By your human definition, I am a male who, on a good day, would be defined as heartless, selfish, stubborn, arrogant, and inconsiderate."*

"When you put it that way, you do sound like quite the catch."

*"Penelope, I would destroy you. My existence is far too cold a place to share with anyone. I am far too cold."*

Cold? This was not a word I would use to describe this being who secretly spent his time and money helping needy children or trying to rescue stubborn-as-a-mule humans—that's me—or . . . who kissed with so much passion and vigor that I only needed one taste to become permanently addicted. No one in this world had more passion than Kinich.

No one.

So what it all really boiled down to was that he didn't believe he could make me happy.

I, on the other hand, had complete faith it would all work out if we were meant to be together.

Were we meant to be? My heart and body said yes. And I believed his did, too. The intensity between us was...epic.

Now I just needed him to realize it.

"Did you mean what you said earlier?" I asked.

*"You'll have to be more specific."*

*Could I say it? Could I?*

*Yes.*

"That your last wish before the Maaskab showed up was to be inside me?"

I heard a low groan. *"I can think of nothing else."*

Me neither. I was obsessed. "Because you should know, I dream about you all the time, Kinich. Of how you taste. Of our bodies molding together. I don't know what really happened that night between us, but my body is addicted to you."

Erotic warmth swirled and pooled around my nipples and deep inside my core.

*"I feel you. I feel your body firing up. It is the most erotic sensation I've ever encountered."* He groaned once again.

If he could feel my body's sensations, then could its reaction make him realize how potent we were together? Or how full of fire his heart truly was? "It's for you. *You* do this to me. I only have to think about you and this is what happens."

*"Touch yourself,"* he unexpectedly commanded. *"I want to feel you come."*

"What? No." I couldn't.

*"Do it."* His voice had transformed from man to god. The kind who expected to be obeyed.

I shuddered, realizing I suddenly wanted to do what he was asking.

"Are you using your voice on me?"

*"No, but I will if you do not obey."*

"You wouldn't." Part of me was shocked, but another part was turned on, a reaction that startled me.

*"I'm a greedy god, Penelope, with little pleasures in life. When I want something, I get it. Right now, I want to experience what your body feels when it comes, thinking of me."*

I'm human, so I couldn't claim I'd never done...*that.* But this felt very awkward. "I-I can't. It's too—"

*"I can feel the deep, gnawing tension between your legs. The moist heat. Your body preparing to take me inside. Give your body what it wants, Penelope. Give me what I want."*

I did want it. But I wanted it with him. I wanted to feel his weight on top of me and his thick shaft stroking me deep inside.

To touch myself like this? With him witnessing? Feeling?

*Do it, Pen. Think of it like phone sex without the phone.*

*Ugh! I can't, it's too weird.*

"I'm going to finish my shower."

*"Yes,"* he whispered. *"That is an excellent idea. Start by washing your breasts. Slowly."*

I could scarcely hear him, but if we'd been face-to-face, I would have guessed he was on the brink of erupting. Each note in his voice was loaded with tension. Hard. Raw. Primal.

Knowing I could do that to him was quite possibly the biggest turn-on I'd ever experienced.

The blood rushed to sensitive flesh between my thighs and deep inside. My hand trembled.

*Then again, what's one more weird thing to add to the list of recent activities and events?*

"I need to pretend you're with me," I said, my voice barely above a whisper.

*"Oh, but I am. There is no pretending. I can feel everything you feel. Everything you touch feels as though I were touching it myself. Now cup your breasts."*

I couldn't believe I was doing this. I closed my eyes and imagined my hands were his.

*"Yes,"* he groaned. *"Your breasts are so firm and luscious. Pinch your nipples."*

"Uh—"

*"Do it."*

I let out a breath and then obeyed. What if this was all we'd ever have. Me and...me? With him as the tactile voyeur?

*Don't think about that now.*

I pictured his rough, large hands cradling my breasts, massaging and pinching my aching, hard nipples. It felt incredible.

Yes. He'd been right. My body needed this. Knowing he felt my pleasure was...

A tiny moan left my mouth.

*"The things I will do to you once I am whole again."*

"Tell me," I whispered.

His voice slow and rough, he began whispering as if we were in a crowded, dimly lit bar, his intimate words for my ears only. *"First, my sweet woman, I will intimately explore your body with my lips and hands while I strip away your clothing. Not a single inch of your silky skin will go untouched. I will worship you. I will savor you. I will leisurely stroke your heat and prepare your body to receive me. And once you are fully aroused, slick around my fingers and nearly at the point of coming, I will thrust your legs apart and lay myself over you. I will gaze into your eyes and watch with pleasure as I plunge my hard cock deep inside."*

A sharp hiss of air left my lungs. I could practically feel his breath on my ear as he whispered every intimate word.

*"I will push you to the brink of pain and pleasure, to a point so intense that nothing in this world will exist apart from the act of me taking you, of my hard flesh pumping and stroking you intimately. And just when you're about to fall over the edge, your body a coiled mass of tension on the cusp of finding euphoria, I will pull out. Slowly. I will make you wait. I will make you beg for my cock to complete you."*

"Like I imagined it in my dreams," I said quietly. He would relentlessly work his shaft in and out like a man who had all the time in the world, yet with an insatiable, sexual thirst. Again and again he would drive me so close, my body sweaty and tense as his hard rippling abs glided over me, his thick arms wrapped possessively around my torso to lift and hold me in place as he pounded until I was ready to explode. Suddenly, in this dream, he would pull out, leaving me panting and needy. Then he'd say, "Tell me what you want, Penelope."

"You," I replied.

"Tell me what you really want." He'd grip his large, velvety hard cock and slide it between my slick, hot folds, slowly moving back and forth, teasing me with every thick inch.

"I want you inside me. To make me come," I'd finally beg.

"Tell me how," he'd say and then nudge his tip inside just an inch. Just enough so that I could feel his heat and thickness, but not receive the sweet, exquisite pleasure and pain of his enormous shaft filling me.

"Hard," I'd answer.

And with those words he'd slam into me and plunge deep inside one last time. He would roar my name as he exploded.

The heat...although it was a dream, I shivered every time I thought about it. His liquid heat was like a drug. Every time he thrust and poured himself into me with hot eruptions, I orgasmed. Again and again. Until my body felt as though it would burst into flames.

Just when I could take no more, he would flip me over and begin the dance again, starting with a trail of kisses down the column of my spine, over my ass and hips. By the time he'd lave every square inch of my body, I was so worked up that all I could think of was getting him inside me once again.

Just like now.

Eyes clenched tightly, the pulsating jets hammered away on my back, I swallowed hard.

*"I can feel it,"* he said. *"You're so close. Think of me bending you over and sliding my cock deep inside you."*

"Yes," I panted.

*"And I will, my sweet Penelope. Soon. I will make your body shudder beneath mine. I will keep you wet and quivering for a solid week. You know I can."* His breathing was heavy and rhythmic, matching mine.

"Yes. I know," I panted.

*"Do it. Touch yourself. See me inside you."*

Thinking of him, I was so close that a feather could brush against my swollen bud and I'd orgasm. This felt so wrong. So good. So erotic.

As the hot water pounded my skin, my hand slid down and my finger pressed. But it wasn't me, it was his pulsing hot erection. It was Kinich teasing and pushing my most intimate spot, asking me to beg for his final thrust.

*"Oh, gods, Penelope. You are so close. I feel it. Your body tensing. It feels so good. Yes, Penelope. Do not stop. Yes,"* he panted in time with the strokes of my finger.

My body ignited. Kinich called out and screamed my name.

I braced myself against the wall.

A few moments passed and my body fell back to earth. Aside from the night I may or may not have spent with Kinich, this had been the most erotic experience of my life.

I turned my face into the warm water. *Oh, God. That felt so...*

*"That. Was. Amazing,"* Kinich said.

I nodded, knowing he couldn't see me but I was unable to speak.

*"Baby. You okay?"*

*Baby?* I sighed. *He called me 'baby.'* Like a real man with a real woman. There was hope for this deity yet.

I shut off the shower. "Sure. I'm really relaxed." I felt like taking a long nap.

I toweled off, threw on some sweats, and trudged over to the bed. I looked down at the sad shell of a body.

"Will things ever go back to the way they were?" I asked.

*"I do not know, Penelope. Please know I am not suffering. My entire existence I've wished to be human, to be mortal. So to experience your body, to feel the world through you, has been extraordinary. It is unlike anything I've experienced in my seventy thousand years of existence."*

Had my plan actually worked? Could he see who he truly was?

"There isn't anything I wouldn't do for you, Kinich. I can't explain it. I hardly know you, but I think I've loved you since the first moment I saw you. And I know it doesn't have anything to do with your pheromones or... species. It's you. Your soul."

I waited for him to say something this time, but there was only silence. That was not the answer I'd expected to receive yet again. But that was the one I got.

"Kinich. Say something—anything."

*"I-I...Sleep, Penelope. You will need your strength for tomorrow."*

*Ouch, ouch, ouch.*

# Thirty

———

Kinich and I spoke only a few words while I got ready the next morning. Really, though, what was there to say? I loved him. He lusted after me and was enjoying the ride inside my mortal body.

*Could be worse, I suppose.*

At least I knew he cared even though he seemed to have made up his mind and refused to consider any other possibilities. We weren't meant to be together, according to him. Period.

The irony was that we felt so right. How could he not see that?

*And he wants to make you immortal.* What did that mean? Talk about confusing.

*He said it himself; he feels the need to protect you. It's "hardwired."*

*Stop, Pen! Stop acting like a victim. Remember, you*

*can't control the lemons, but you choose what to do with them. You choose how to deal. So...deal.*

Okay. What would be my move, then?

*He doesn't love you. You need to move on.*

*Easier said than done.*

I went in the bathroom to fix my hair. My dark green eyes looked much lighter now. Was it because my whites were so red? Or was Kinich's energy doing something to me? I pulled back my now chin-length hair with a red bandanna I'd rolled into a headband. With my hair out of the way, I noticed that even my face looked different: tired, but my cheeks rosier.

*Must be a sun god thing.*

I threw on my last clean outfit, a pink T-shirt and jeans. I hoped the gods didn't expect me to come in some deity getup like She-Ra or K'ak.

When I left Kinich's room, I found Gabrán and Brutus waiting for me. Gabrán wore a blue-and-green kilt with a white dress shirt and had his red hair pulled back into a neat braid. His expression was stone-cold serious.

"Why do I get the feeling that these summits are scarier than everyone is letting on?"

*"Everything will be fine, Penelope,"* Kinich assured me.

I refrained from saying anything snarky or bitter—my wounded ego didn't welcome any comfort from him.

Gabrán turned down the hall with Brutus trailing behind us. I knew we were going to the large meeting room on the west side of Kinich's estate. He'd told me this was where they met.

"The last time these marauders got in tae the same room, they burnt down Sun God's house. 'Twas not the worst of it, tho, lass. Four dinna walk out. K'ak has nae forgiven Acan for twisting off his head."

I cringed. "That's awful. What started the fight?"

"Pretzels."

Kinich groaned. *"Must we relive this?"*

"Pretzels?" I asked.

"Ay. K'ak asked for the pretzels. Acan, God of Wine—"

"You mean, Belch?" I asked.

"Ay. Belch was drunk as usual and had eaten them all."

*Okeydokey.*

"Colel got up to go find more before a fight broke out, but she accidentally closed the door behind her."

Umm. Why did I have the feeling this story was going to a very weird, disturbing place?

Oh! Because it was.

"Ay. Colel is the Mistress of Bees. And where she goes, her bees go. The tiny buggers get verra upset when they are separated, so they began to attack A.C."

"A.C.?" I asked, unsure who that was.

"Ah-Ciliz, the God of Eclipses." Gabrán shook his head. "An lemme tell ya, lass. The bloke does nae have a sense o' humor. He's a verra dark SOB."

*No, reallllly? God of Eclipses, dark? Who would've thunk it?*

"The rest is history," Gabrán continued. "K'ak and Acan started tearing at each other's heads. Kinich jumped in to stop them but got tangled up with A.C. and the bees. O' course, Kinich then accidentally released a spark and caught the furniture on fire. The entire estate went up in flames in twenty minutes." Gabrán chuckled. "Kinich was madder than a naked leprechaun."

*Oh, gods. No. Please don't tell me.* "Leprechauns? They aren't real, too, are they?"

"Ay," Gabrán replied.

*Sure. Why not? Gods and vampires and various combos in between. Just add tiny men dressed in green with pots of gold. Christ, while we're at it, how about the chupacabra? Why the hell not?* "Annnd do I want to know why naked leprechauns are angry?"

Gabrán flashed a smile over his shoulder as we followed him along a long hallway that I'd never been down. He then held up his pinkie.

"Oh." Made sense.

"In any case, be on your guard today, lass. The gods are an unruly bunch."

He stopped in front of two heavy double doors made of blond unfinished wood. The Mayan calendar was carved on one side and the Mayan sun on the other.

He reached for the handle, and then paused. "Any last-minute questions, lass?"

"Did someone make sure there are plenty of pretzels on the table?"

He laughed. "Ay. That we did."

"And a fire extinguisher?"

He nodded yes.

"How about a beekeeper suit?"

Again he nodded.

Kinich finally spoke up. *"Penelope, please stop wasting time. The world's fate lies in our hands."*

"Oh. Right." I took a deep breath. "All righty, then. Let's summit."

The doors opened and Gabrán stepped to one side.

# *Thirty-One*

⌒

Unlike the rest of Kinich's ostentatious Southwestern-style estate, this room could have been a chamber located in the bowels of Chichén Itzá during its heyday when Mayan kings roamed the Yucatán and built massive pyramids in honor of the gods. The walls and high ceilings were pale, with every square inch covered in hieroglyphics of animals, men, suns, moons, and stalks of wheat and corn.

*Is that... ?* I pointed to the wall at my right and looked at Gabrán. "A glyph of Kathy Griffin?" It was an image about the size of a dinner plate, but the resemblance was uncanny.

"Ay. Cimil is a big fan. She insisted we pay homage."

*Sure. Why the hell not?*

My eyes continued wandering over the windowless room. Recessed lighting illuminated the chamber, giving it an eerie glow. In the center was a large, smooth limestone table with six throne-like chairs on each side and one at each end. The fourteen thrones were carved with different symbols: dragons, flowers, and...

"Penises?" I pointed to the throne toward the middle on the left side.

"Ay, lass," Gabrán said in a melancholy tone, "'twas Chaam's."

Nice. This was where the fate of humankind was decided? Upon thrones adorned with critters and man-goodies?

*Suuure, why not?*

"Very impressive. Who's your decorator?" I said.

*"Ah. I hear the judgmental tone. This was far better than the country-western barn theme that Cimil wanted, complete with goats and bales of hay for seats. At least this is fireproof and produces no manure."*

"Good choice."

I pivoted on my heel to inspect the rest of the room. At the far end was another doorway leading to a small chamber with wall-to-wall texts. There was also an enormous flat-screen TV mounted on the wall to my left.

"What's that for?"

"Movie night," Gabrán responded. "The room has built-in surround sound, and if ya press this"—he pointed to a giant, red button on the wall—"the table and thrones flip over an' turn into theater seats. Verra modern, 'tis it not?"

"Oh, definitely." Not to mention so very, very weird. I could only guess what sort of movies they watched—*The Gods Must Be Crazy*. Definitely.

A quiet shuffling caught my attention. Fierce-looking Uchben soldiers filed inside the chamber, lining up against the perimeter of the room. Like Brutus, they wore black tees, cargos, and boots. This must've been Gabrán's elite team I'd heard him mention a few times. Brutus was one, I think.

"Lass, time for you to take your seat." Gabrán pointed to the throne at the head of the table. The back had a large sun chiseled into it. Set out, directly in front of my seat, was the stone tablet and silver stylus Kinich had told me about. They were used to record the agenda and any decisions.

I slipped into the seat and tried to steady my nerves. *Be the honey badger. Be the honey badger. I am the honey badger.*

The way Kinich explained it, there was nothing to be afraid of, but keeping order was difficult. The gods tended to behave like petulant siblings looking to outdo one another. Fights often broke out, which was bad because decisions didn't get made. Therefore, keeping everyone to the protocols and rules was Kinich's, and now my, main function.

The room began to hum and vibrate. I froze.

Kinich spoke in a low, calming voice. *"It's all right, Penelope. Just relax. They are coming."*

"What's happening?" I asked.

*"They are releasing a little energy. It's for show. Simply stay calm and don't allow them to distract you with their theatrics."*

The first to enter was K'ak—*don't laugh, don't laugh*—and, like the evening before, he wore a blue toga. His silver-streaked hair hung to his ankles, and his jade headdress made him an ergonomic accident waiting to happen.

"That looks really heavy. Do you do neck exercises?" I couldn't help asking.

"Among other parts of my body. Would you care to see?" He reached for the hem of his toga and began lifting.

"Oh no. I'll take your word for it."

He shrugged, dropped the fabric, and set a small onyx turtle in front of me. "You forgot to take your offerings yesterday."

Oh no. Not this again.

I pasted a smile on my face. "Thanks."

The room rumbled loudly, like a passing train, as they entered the room one by one, left their "gifts," and then took their seats.

I held back a gasp as suicide lady, again dressed in a veil and head-to-toe black, plopped her dead rat on top of the pile of goodies. "Wow. Thank you. And it's a day older now, too." *So, so special. Yes.*

Finally, Zac sauntered in. Like the day before, he looked exquisite and undeniably masculine. No, I wasn't in the market, but I couldn't help but appreciate his large, well-built body donning leather pants that hugged his powerful thighs.

I blinked and then snapped my gaping mouth shut.

"Your box." Smiling, he held it out for me to see.

I looked at it, then at him. I had no idea what I was supposed to do.

"Wow. That's a...really, really nice...empty box," I said loudly, hoping Kinich would sense my discomfort and throw me a bone.

*"It is for the rat, Penelope,"* Kinich advised.

"Oh! How thoughtful. Thank you." I plucked the rat up

by the tippy tip of its tail and dropped it inside, closing the lid quickly.

With a smile and a dip of the head, Zac's thick waves of black hair slid over his icy aquamarine eyes. "My pleasure."

My entire body broke out in goose bumps. Wow. I didn't know what he was the god of; however, I voted that Zac be the new God of Male Virility. He looked like a hunky, fallen dark angel that had taken up modeling bad-boy clothing. I know, weird, right? Still, that's what he reminded me of, and he wore the look well.

Zac took his seat next to me and continued grinning with what had to be the most blatant, flirtatious smile ever to walk the face of the planet—if smiles could walk, that is. In any case, my inner girlie-girl couldn't help but be flattered.

*"Penelope,"* Kinich warned, *"tell whichever of my brothers is turning on the charm to can it. You are taken."*

*Taken? I am?* My heart did a victory lap. He was jealous. *Oh yeah!*

"Really now? That's not what you said last night," I mumbled quietly into my hand.

*"I said nothing last night,"* he growled.

"Exactly."

Again he growled. *"We will discuss this later, woman."*

"Maybe. Maybe not." Okay. I was being a little petty. Dammit. He so deserved it.

*"Yes, we will. Because my brothers are off-limits."*

"Eternity is a long time to spend alone, Minotaur. So why don't you make up your mind."

Someone cleared their throat. "Uh-hum."

I looked up and found the other gods glaring. Except for Zac. He was still smiling.

"Sorry." I rose from the seat as Kinich had instructed. "I call this summit of the House of the Gods to order on this day of..."

Gabrán quickly chimed in. "December twenty-first."

*Why do I know that date?*

*My mother's birthday?*

*No.*

*Jess's or Anne's? No. Their b-days were in the summer.*

*BOGO day at Macy's shoe department?*

*Nope.*

"It is the day of the Mayan apo...blah, blah, blah..." Kinich's voice faded to nothing.

"Sorry? Did you say apocalypse?"

*"Yes. The Maya prophesied that the end of the world would start today."*

*Holy shit!* "Apocalypse! Today? Well, hell. You could've told me, Kinich!"

I felt a firm grasp on my hand. "It is nothing to worry about, Penelope. They were a superstitious people." Zac's smoldering, hypnotic gaze was relentless.

"Sorry, but," I asked, "what are you the god of? Can't recall."

He smiled brightly. "When I figure that out, you'll be the first to know." He lifted my hand and planted a lingering kiss.

*"Fucking saints! Off. Limits. Penelope,"* Kinich barked.

My entire body tensed up. "What? I didn't do anything."

*"I feel every goddamned sensation in your body. And right now you're reacting to something."*

Hmmm. Was I? Okay, maybe a little. Zac was hot. Who couldn't help but be a teensy bit flattered? In any case, it was an innocent appreciation of an astoundingly handsome male, but it didn't run within a spit's distance of what I felt for Kinich.

Regardless...

"Afraid of a little competition?" I prodded.

"*Grrrr*" was all I heard in response.

A satisfied grin swept across my face.

"All righty. I hereby call to order the summit of the gods. Who among you wishes to nominate a topic for the agenda?"

Instantly, four hands shot into the air.

"Kinich? I can't remember. Do I go counterclockwise or clockwise?" I whispered.

"*Clockwise. The gods are seated around the table according to their rank and power. Except for the Bacabs, who sit in accordance with North, South, East, and West.*"

"What's a Bacab?" I whispered.

"*They are the eldest four and therefore slightly more powerful than the rest, except for those of us whose gifts are based on physical powers.*"

I made a mental note to forget that bit of foolishness as soon as possible.

The first topic, as expected, was nominated by Guy and received unanimous consent to be added to the agenda. Suicide lady asked to discuss a rotation of powers. Apparently she nominated this topic every summit, but everyone voted her down because nobody wanted to risk inheriting her position.

Poor, poor lady.

Next came the topic of what to do about Kinich's and my predicament. Also unanimous. Finally, the Mistress of Bees, who wore a bright yellow, formfitting satin jumpsuit and very large beehive on her head, nominated to address the recent surge in pirated e-books, but no one seemed to know what an e-reader was, so they declined.

"Okay, then." I clapped my hands together. "I hereby close the nominations for—"

*"I have a topic, Penelope,"* Kinich chimed in. *"Two, actually."*

"Oh, sorry. Didn't see your hand." I looked around the table. "Kinich has two topics," I informed everyone since they couldn't hear him.

*"I request that the House of the Gods discuss and call to a vote the banning of deity procreation."*

I gulped. "You mean…"

*"Yes, the banning of the making of Payals."*

He wanted to make me, well, more of me, illegal?

*"Penelope, humans and gods were not meant to bear children. It goes against the natural order of the universe and there are consequences when we take such action."*

Kinich sighed. Obviously, he could sense my shock and despair. Even my hair follicles were sad.

*"Penelope, you must understand. It is my duty to protect humanity. I cannot look the other way simply because I have feelings for you."*

Did he truly believe my life was a mistake? An abomination that would destroy mankind? Me? I couldn't even cook, so attributing the destruction of civilization to me was a pretty far stretch.

It wasn't my fault where I came from or who my ancestors were any more than the fact that I had a deity stuck inside my body.

*Well…well…fine!* He'd made his feelings known. What could I do aside from pretend he hadn't mortally wounded me?

I squared my shoulders and looked up, realizing that the entire room waited with baited breath. "Um...he wants to put the banning of making more Payals to a vote."

There was a communal nod but no reactions. Seemed everyone had been expecting this.

I counted the raised hands around the table. There were five: Belch, She-Ra, Suicide, Bees, and Eclipses.

Bees gave me a sympathetic glance while waving her hand in front of her face to see through the swarm of bees circling her head. "I'm sorry, Penelope; I think we should at least hear what Kinich has to say."

Guy suddenly stood up and pounded his hands on the table. "You are all fools! Fools! And I'm warning you now, if you side with Kinich, I will not obey."

Bees' tiny yellow subjects began circling faster. "Then you will be banished permanently."

Zac chimed in. "We have not agreed to discuss the matter. There must be a majority vote. Only five hands have been raised."

All heads turned toward me.

"How do you vote, Kinich?" Zac asked.

My heart thumped like a bongo. "Please don't, Kinich. Please don't do this," I whispered.

"*I am sorry*," he said, his voice filled with only a hint of remorse. "*I vote yes.*"

"Well, I don't!" I barked. "I'm not going to help you officially declare my life a sin, or mistake, or act against nature, or whatever! My answer is no!"

Bees stood from her throne. Her angry swarm began circling above the table. "That is ridiculous, you do not get a vote."

"Why not?" Zac argued. "She houses the power of the sun, and it is our law that whoever holds this gift will be our leader. Only a unanimous vote from all fourteen can change this, and we will never have one because Chaam is locked away."

Bees huffed, which caused her tiny black-and-yellow soldiers to kamikaze Zac. "Semantics! She is not the Sun God," she blasted.

Zac didn't flinch. "Put them away, Colel," he growled.

She plunked her fist on her hip. "Or what? You have no powers."

"I am a Bacab," he warned. "I may not have gifts, but I am still physically stronger than you, which means I can tear your head clean off without breaking a sweat."

The bees crawled on Zac's arms and face, stinging him and falling to the floor, but he simply stared Colel down, not acknowledging their presence.

"Enough!" I commanded. "Put them away, or I'll turn them into bee fritters."

I hated that idea. Her bees were really cute. Kind of like tiny yellow assassins with a sweet tooth.

She rolled her eyes and snapped her fingers. The bees promptly flew back inside the hive on her head.

"Thank you, Bees—I mean, Colel." I closed my eyes for a moment to enjoy a calming breath. "Right. Where were we?"

Zac straightened his shoulders and looked at each of the gods. "I was attempting to say that Penelope has publicly demonstrated her command of the sun's power. Until she is separated from this power, she is the Goddess of the Sun. It's no different if we decide to do another rotation of duties"—he pointed to Suicide who was about to speak—"but we will not!" He turned back to Bees. "My point is, if we do, then whoever houses the particular gift inherits the title."

"I wanna be Fate next time," Belch slurred and scratched his protruding belly that had escaped from the bottom of his green nylon jacket. "I'm tired of being the life of the party. People respect Fate; they just get knocked up or vomit when I'm around."

Bees sat down and crossed her arms like the cantankerous deity that she was. "Fine. We all know this issue isn't going away. Kinich will be restored to his usual arrogant self by the next summit, and we will vote again. The topic will be addressed."

Guy leaned back in his chair with a smug smile across his face. "Not if you want to win the Great War, which you will not without me."

Belch leaned forward and pointed at Guy. "Or can I be him? I'm tough and strooong." He flexed his biceps and squeezed the flabby-looking muscle.

"Shut it, Belch," said Fate, brushing back her blonde locks. She turned to me, "Let's move on. Penelope is our stand-in Sun God, and she has spoken."

Kinich growled, *"Looks as though Cimil's plan was successful, Penelope."*

"Huh?"

*"All along we assumed she wanted you to be the surrogate mother of my child, when in fact, she was plotting for this. You, the surrogate Sun God. My proxy. A Payal who just successfully turned the tides away from a vote on this matter."*

I gasped internally. Could that be? This entire situation had been orchestrated by Cimil? Holy demon bundt cakes. These people played a pretty mean game of chess. And Christ, I'd followed along with Cimil's plot like a mindless, naive little lamb playing hopscotch with a pack of wolves. With superpowers. And weird tastes in gifts.

Regardless of all that, I couldn't help but feel wounded by Kinich's views on Payals. He was wrong. Flat out wrong. Somehow, I'd prove it to him.

"Kinich, I'm sorry. Despite Cimil's hand in all this, I did what I thought was right. Just like you—"

*"I have another topic."*

"Kinich, I—"

He interrupted, *"I wish to vote for your immortality."*

Trying not to sound whiny, I said, "Oh, for Pete's sake! Would you make up your mind? Payals are evil. Now you want to make me immortal. You don't love me, but you don't want anyone else to look at me. Pick a story and stick to it!"

The gods stared with interest.

"Oh. I love a good fight. Do share what our brother is saying, Penelope," Suicide requested cheerfully.

*"Penelope, raise the topic. We will resolve our differences later. Here is not the place."*

"I don't want immortality. In fact, when this is over, I don't want anything to do with you."

*"Penelope, I—"*

I moved to close the nominations for agenda items.

*"Stubborn woman, this is not over."*

Like he'd instructed, I recorded the topics on the stone, a weird caveman-like iPad of sorts that turned black wherever I touched it with the silver stylus.

I then called for the discussion of the first topic.

Guy rose from his seat and cleared his throat. "I seek

the counsel and wisdom of my brethren regarding my most recent discovery. It seems that the absence of Chaam has not impeded the Maaskab's advancement in the area of manipulating dark energy. They have evolved from astute apprentices to masters."

I noticed his hands, which were firmly planted on the table. I imagined he could crack a man's skull with hands that big.

"Upon returning to our realm," he continued, "I sought to understand why the Uchben were able to detect the Maaskab's presence on the satellite. I found no evidence of them in the physical world, but I witnessed several dozen Maaskab sifting in and out of their phantom encampment. My belief is that they've somehow learned to occupy another dimension, the dimension used by the vampires to sift."

The gods made a collective gasp.

"What leads you to believe this?" Zac's voice rang out among the rumblings of the others.

"I watched as they stepped through the temporary portals they created. The color of their energy signatures shifted frequency as they did this."

I was a bit rusty on my sci-fi lingo. Space-time continuum, tachyons, set phasers to stun—those were concepts I grasped. But this?

"I have witnessed the same fluctuations when observing vampires sift," he continued. "And I can tell you from sifting myself—"

"When? When have you sifted?" asked Bees.

"When we were battling the Maaskab the night I captured Chaam. The black jade pyramid functions as an amplifier of sorts. I merely had to think of moving and my body followed."

I really didn't understand what they were getting at. "So they're hiding in some other dimension?"

Guy nodded. "Everything in the universe is made up of atoms, which are merely tiny particles of energy held together by their positive and negative charges. They form a bond. Similar to how gravity holds the moon to Earth, but on a much, much smaller scale.

"However, between each particle is space. In fact, the entire universe is mostly space. When vampires sift, they slip between these cracks. But they cannot remain there. It is these bonds, these charges that bind the atoms together, that propel the vampires as they are pushed out of the atoms' spaces like a foreign contaminant. It creates enormous momentum and speed."

*All righty then, it's official. Life is stranger than fiction.*

"That is not all," Guy stated. "I returned to their encampment and found another mine. There is a large vein of black jade underneath the location. And I believe," continued Guy, "that they've somehow used its power to create enough of a force to allow them to remain inside the spaces."

The gods held a frantic sidebar for several moments.

God of Eclipses spoke up. "It explains why they've joined forces with the Obscuros; they needed the vampires to teach them how to sift."

I shivered. For some odd reason, an image of a Reese's Peanut Butter Cup flashed through my mind. The Maaskab were the sinister chocolate and the Obscuros were the malevolent peanut filling. Put them together, and you got a whole new treat. Except they weren't really treats. More like festering sores on the ass of humanity. Okay. Maybe the peanut butter cup was a stupid analogy.

I remembered this was where I was supposed to propose a Call to Action that would include rescuing my mother.

I made the motion. Verbal fights about what to do next quickly broke out among the gods...

"We attack! Head on."

"No, we wait until we learn more."

"Where the hell is Cimil? She's never present when we truly need her."

Gabrán gently gripped my shoulder. "Lass, it is time for you to use that power inside o' ya to rein them in."

I cleared my throat. "Ehh-hem!"

No one paid any attention to me.

"Ehh-hem!" I said a little louder. They still ignored me.

*"Penelope, you will need to tap into your strength. Make them respect you. Zac was right when he said that you control my power. You can do this."*

I didn't want to hear any pep talks from Kinich. I just wanted to make this nightmare end and rescue my mother.

I stood up and closed my eyes, taking a deep breath before I slammed both fists on the table, releasing two enormous flames. "Enough! Stop fighting like children! Because if we don't figure this out, there'll be nothing left to fight about!"

The gods stared with looks of astonishment. Zac smiled and tilted his head. "My apologies, Sun Goddess, it will not happen again."

I was really starting to like Zac.

"I call an Order to Action. I start with addressing how we will rescue my mother."

Then it hit me. "Didn't Emma say there were more Payals, but you couldn't find them?"

Everyone quickly came to the same conclusion; the Maaskab had to be hiding them inside this other dimension.

"How do we get in?" I asked.

The gods looked at each other; then Fate spoke up. "Our vampires will enter. It is why our army is meant to be led by Niccolo. It is..."

*Let me guess, Fate?*

"...Fate," she said.

Hey, these gods were actually pretty predictable.

Then Fate added, "If the vein of black jade enables the Maaskab to stabilize inside that dimension, then we can assume the same for the vampires."

"Why can't the gods go in?" I asked.

"Under normal circumstances, our energy is far too dense to pass through the spaces," Guy replied.

"But you said you did it before?" I argued.

"Yes," Guy replied, "and given there is a high concentration of jade, I hope I might do so again. This is why I will go inside with Niccolo if possible. We will use the vampire army to extract any prisoners and flush out the Maaskab. The Uchben will be waiting with the other gods outside of the zones where they frequently create portals."

Well, dang. That sounded like a pretty great plan to me! "I'm going, too."

*"No. You will not,"* Kinich objected.

"With all due respect, I didn't ask you."

*"When the meeting is over, you and I will settle this argument."*

I held my breath and then released it.

I turned toward Gabrán. "Can I do the wrap-up? Sounds like we have an alignment to attack."

"There is still one more topic to address." Fate spoke loudly to overcome the noise in the room.

I looked down at the agenda on my deity Etch A Sketch. "Oh. Yeah. Kinich." We were to discuss his and my predicament.

Fate stood up, and I noticed how the gold trim along her neckline and the golden laces on her knee-high, white moccasins matched the color of her hair.

*Snazzy.*

"Penelope," she said, "you and Kinich have performed the Prayer of Loyalty and Protection."

Where was she going with this? "Yeah."

"Have you yet attempted to break the bond?" she asked.

"Break the bond?" I questioned. "No. Why?"

"I believe that when the Maaskab released the jar into the pool, a jar meant to immobilize him so they could get to you, Kinich's light separated from his humanlike body, leaving behind a mortal shell. Unfortunately, his immortal essence did not return to the cenote, as one might expect. Instead, it was drawn into you. Perhaps because he recited the prayer at the exact moment his light abandoned his body. Perhaps because the Maaskab bespelled the jar in some way. Who knows? Nevertheless, the solution is clear. You must sever the bond."

Why did I think this absolutely made sense and was so darn simple that someone, even I, should have come up with this answer before?

She added, "This will free his immortal essence and divine light to travel on to his humanlike body. Or maybe to the cenote."

Guy glared at Fate. "And if you are wrong? We know

nothing of the Maaskab's magic that created this mess. Dark energy is erratic; it has a mind of its own."

She shrugged. "I am Fate. I'm never wrong. If I am, it is meant to be. Ergo, not wrong."

*Resist rolling eyes. Resist rolling eyes.*

"Hey, here's a question," I said dryly. "Why not mention this earlier?"

Again she shrugged. "Because Fate was not ready to speak."

*Going to smack her. Going to smack her.*

"Kinich, what do you think? I mean, breaking the bond sounds dangerous," I said.

Several moments passed. *"Yes. Whatever the Maaskab did to me and to my human form is a magic unlike any other. But I have no choice. We cannot exist like this, as two souls in one body. I am prepared to accept whatever the outcome is. You will break the bond."*

# Thirty-Two

An hour after the meeting, unable to make the jagged pieces of my emotional puzzle fit together, I found myself staring at Kinich's sleeping form. I stroked the tendrils of his golden-brown locks. They seemed to glow, as if soaking up the midday sun pouring through the window.

I was furious for what he'd said about Payals, but I was heartbroken that he'd chosen his role over my feelings. The fact that he'd said he couldn't help it did nothing for me. It still hurt. I guess a part of me had erroneously believed his feelings for me, whatever those were, would be stronger than his divine instincts or his seventy thousand years of deity baggage, which included the belief that he and I could never work out.

But his feelings for me weren't enough. I wasn't... enough. In fact, he wanted to risk it all simply to separate himself from me. The truth was, I felt terrified I'd end up alone again. I wasn't strong enough to survive in this new world I'd been dragged into.

I slipped off my red headband and ran my hands through my now shorter hair. Oddly enough, I missed it. I missed my mother, my life, and my stupid hair. And now I would miss Kinich being so close; he was part of me and I liked it. Way too much.

My eyes gravitated toward the large glass doors with a view of the patio and never-ending stretch of desert beyond. "You must really hate being stuck inside a lowly Payal," I mumbled under my breath.

*"No, Penelope. How can you say such a thing after all that has passed between us?"*

"How can I not?" I whispered.

*"I've told you before, my feelings for you are... complicated."*

"Ugh! What does that even mean, Kinich?"

*"It is as I've said before; I am incapable of the commitment you deserve and need because my personal desires will always play second to protecting the human race, a race that includes you."*

For some reason, an image of the orphans from his album flashed in my mind. We'd never spoken about them. After all, I'd been snooping through his things (*oopsies*), but a person didn't devote himself to such acts of kindness unless he held a deep sense of commitment, a commitment he claimed he was incapable of giving.

No, there was no one in this world more committed than Kinich. So what was the real problem?

"Exactly what kind of commitment do you think I need?"

*"The kind a man gives a woman. The kind where he promises to love her above all others."*

I didn't need that, did I?

Okay. Christ. Maybe I did. Or maybe I just needed to know he loved me and that would be good enough. I really didn't know anymore.

I sighed. We both kept moving in impossible circles. "Well, then, let's get you on your way."

*"Penelope, I want you to know,"* he paused, *"being so close to you has been a gift. It has allowed me to see into your heart and discover what a beautiful creature you truly are. You have a sense of purpose much greater than my own, which humbles me. But understand, I have a destiny to fulfill, as do you."*

"Destiny? Me?" The only thing in my destiny was finding my mother, then having a long, hot bath, eating a box of doughnut holes, and having a chick flick marathon.

*"Yes. You. Nothing else matters."*

"Sounds pretty heavy. Mind sharing what this mysterious destiny of mine is?"

*"I do not know."*

*Great.* "Do you at least know yours?"

Several moments passed before he answered. *"I believe so."*

"You're not going to tell me, are you?"

*"No."*

Shocker.

"Do we have to break the bond? It feels so risky." What if he didn't come out of this alive?

*"I'm afraid so."*

"Maybe they'll capture a Maaskab and we can find out how to undo this"—*oh, heck, what do I call it without*

*sounding like a cornball? Hex? Spell?*—"thingamabob"—
*Jeez. Nice one, Pen*—"they've done to us."

*"We cannot wait. If there's a chance I will gain back
my form, I must take it. I suspect the Great War is coming sooner than anyone anticipates and my help will be
needed to win. And win we must. I could not bear to watch
the world fall into its descent and you along with it."* He
paused for a moment. *"I cannot stomach the thought of
anything happening to you."*

The walls crumbled just then. His confession only
deepened my love for him.

*Well, dammit! Dammit, dammit, dammit, dammit!*
"You had to go and say that, didn't you? Right when I was
getting ready to hate you forever."

He chuckled. *"Ahhh. There she is. My sweet Penelope.
Ready to create levity in the face of any situation, even
something as difficult as this."*

"That's how I roll."

Yes, I was making light, but only because I felt terrified and didn't want him to know. Then I realized something: I needed to put my faith in this love, regardless of
how complicated, bizarre, or irrational it seemed, and I
had to put my faith in him.

With time, maybe we'd find the answers to the real
reason I walked this earth. Perhaps that reason would
resolve his inner conflict. In any case, there was no other
choice for us but to move forward. To follow our destinies.
Doughnut holes included.

*"Say it, Penelope. Say it before we lose our nerve."*

I balled my fists. *You can do this. Don't be afraid.
Have faith. Have faith. Have...*

"Are you sure?"

*"You must,"* he replied.

"I know," I whispered and then wiped the tears from my eyes. "I love you." I knew he wouldn't say it back, but that didn't seem to matter.

I kissed his cold lips, rested my head on his chest, and then recited the phrase Fate had written down for me right after the meeting. *"Catcha lum tumben caah."*

As the room seemed to suddenly turn into a vacuum, devoid of all light and sound, the air exited from my lungs. My head swirled and my body shook violently.

Then I shut my eyes.

It was over.

Had it worked?

Terrified, I held my breath and covered my face with both hands. What if I opened my eyes and found Kinich's cold body lying there dead?

*Well, then he* could *already be back at the cenote getting a new body.*

It could take days to find out if that had happened.

I felt like my entire world balanced on the fine tip of an enormous stickpin, where standing still was just as painful as falling off.

I peeked through a tiny crack between my fingers. Slowly my eyes focused on the form in front of me. "Yes! Yes!" I jumped up and started screaming. His chest was heaving and his color was back. It had worked!

I leaned over him and kissed his full lips. They were warm! "Kinich! Can you hear me? Oh my God. It worked. Kinich!"

Nothing happened. I froze.

"Kinich?" I shook him by the shoulders.

Nothing.

*Oh no. Oh no. Oh no!* Something was wrong, terribly wrong. His appearance was normal: incredibly gorgeous, and strong, and irresistibly gorgeous, and really, really gorg— *Stop ogling him, you idiot!* But he wasn't waking.

I needed to get help. *Yes, help!* The other gods might know what happened.

I sprang from the bed and rushed for the door.

"Penelope?"

I froze.

"Where are you going?" the deep voice said clear as day.

I swiveled on my heel, and to my heart's utter delight found a set of the most breathtakingly gorgeous aquamarine eyes staring back at me. "Kinich! It worked! You're back inside your body!!"

I ran so fast that I tripped and flew right on top of him.

"Hmm. I think you're very happy to see me again," he said, his voice low and gravelly.

His warm body underneath mine felt amazing. Better than amazing. Like being whole again. I pressed my lips to his, channeling every ounce of my emotions into the kiss.

He briskly rolled me over and planted himself firmly between my thighs. "Gods, you feel delicious, Penelope," he whispered, staring into my eyes.

"That's because I am," I said jokingly.

"I couldn't agree more."

The door burst open. Emma and Guy stared at us.

"Oh, crap! Sorry!" Emma turned away.

Guy, on the other hand, lifted a brow and smiled. "Nice to see you're...*up*, brother."

Kinich growled. "Out!"

Emma tugged Guy out the door and slammed it shut. Her screaming voice trailed off in the distance.

Kinich lifted himself off my body and stood at the foot of the bed, wildly stripping away his T-shirt. His expression was nothing short of fierce and determined.

"Are you doing what I hope?" I asked, unable to keep my body from heating up in all the right places.

He flashed a smile that made me melt on the spot.

I sighed. *Those lips...*

"No more fantasies," he said in a deep, stark voice, "no more dreaming. It is time for you and me to be together and know for certain that it happened."

"What do you have in mind?" I whispered.

Without breaking eye contact, he slipped off his white linen pajama bottoms and stood before me nude.

My eyes drank him in. In my dreams, he was perfect. But in real life, he was magnificent, every inch, starting with his freshly cut, sun-streaked hair to his well-formed biceps bulging with powerful muscles. His chiseled chest and washboard stomach were hard and tanned, as were his muscular thighs. And his man-goodies... wow. What could I say? His erection was impressively large, jutting out like a heat-seeking missile over his heavy sack.

"I'm pretty sure we didn't sleep together that night," I said, my voice barely above a murmur, "because if we had, I wouldn't have been able to walk the next day."

The corner of his delicious lips curled. "We're going to test that theory." He leaned down and yanked me up from the bed. He pulled me to his body, his erection prodding me in the stomach.

"I want you to know," he whispered in my ear, "that after

I've shown you every one of my fantasies, you and I are going to have a very long talk about a few things, starting with what it does to me when you flirt with my brothers."

My head spun in dizzying spirals of conflicting emotions and thoughts. He absolutely refused to believe we had a future, yet it was clear he didn't want to share me. It was also clear he was unable to resist the mind-bending attraction we felt.

We were so... complicated.

"Sounds"—my words stuck in my throat—"like a n-n-ice plan."

He released me and grabbed the hem of my T-shirt. Before I knew it, my bra was on the floor right beside it.

He stared at my breasts while he slowly slid his warm, strong hands up the sides of my body, letting them float over my hips, waist, and rib cage until they reached my hardened nipples. The hungry gaze of his eyes reminded me of a wild animal stalking its prey.

He licked his lips, and for a moment, I thought he would taste my nipples. God, how I'd fantasized about that. Fantasized about his hot, wet mouth massaging my two hard pebbles. Instead, he simply touched and stroked and watched with fascination.

"I like how you respond to me." He sank slowly to his knees and gripped my hips.

When he pulled me to his mouth and planted gentle kisses on my lower stomach, a sharp breath left my lungs. His large hands slid to the waistband of my jeans and pulled down, leaving me completely bare.

A small, primal sound escaped his mouth before he trailed his lips over my belly button, then down my hip bone, over to the crease of my bikini line.

The anticipation of where he might go, what he might do, made me quiver. But he refrained from diving straight for the sensitive, heated flesh between my legs. The throbbing tension was almost unbearable.

His hands cupped my ass, and he planted a small, lingering kiss just above my pulsing, sensitive bud.

I trembled.

Wishing and wanting him to do more, to go deeper, I ran my hands through his thick hair and pulled him into me. Oh, God, the anticipation was killing me. He'd done everything to create the heat, but nothing to extinguish it. Now I was panting and ready. Every intimate spot of my body tingled.

He slowly rose from his knees, and the smoldering look in his eyes promised me one thing: Before the night was through, there'd be nothing left. He planned to devour me. He planned to take me again and again and make me orgasm until I was limp and weak.

I loved, loved, loved that plan.

He rose to his full height, and I became all too aware of both our bodies. Naked. Pressed together.

This felt so right. So delicious. This was heaven.

He abruptly turned away and padded toward the bathroom, taking his hard man-goodies with him. "Hey! Where are you going?"

He disappeared into the bathroom. "Shower. We have some unfinished business to attend to."

Remembering how we'd had hot, kinky mind sex in the shower, a whoosh of air pushed from my lips. "B-b-be right there."

I needed to cool down or I wouldn't last one more second.

I shook my head.

This man would be my undoing. It seemed I could cope with everything—loss, finding out I was possibly the descendant of a psychopathic god, fighting creepy spawn-of-Satan Mayan priests with superhuman powers—but this man was my Achilles' heel. I could deny him nothing. I would give my life just to hear him laugh, sacrifice everything to know he was safe, happy, and content. Even after he said we couldn't be together.

He was my personal conundrum. Meant to test my will and faith.

I was *so* going to win.

"You coming, woman?" he called out from the bathroom.

A smile so powerful that it tugged at my very soul swept across my face. "You betcha."

"Don't forget to put on the necklace!" he reminded me.

*Right. The black jade necklace.* Without it a god couldn't be intimate with a human.

Did they ever wear out or go stale? I wondered.

"I'll be needing you to make a twelve-pack of those!" I called out.

# *Thirty-Three*

Kinich's masculine silhouette was prominent against the shower stall glass when I entered the bathroom.

"The necklace, did you put it on?" he asked.

*Oh yeah.* Surprisingly, the black amulet felt weightless. "Done."

"Good, then get your sweet ass in here," he commanded.

"And if I don't?"

"Then I will come and get you. But I will not be held responsible for my actions."

Hmmm. I liked the sound of that.

"Really, now. What actions might those be?" Naked, I leaned against the sink and gripped the edge of the granite counter, feeling hotter than a bag of fresh kettle corn.

His head popped out from the frosted glass door, his hair dripping down his sleek, hard shoulders and perfectly sculpted chest. "Was that a challenge?"

I felt the urge to nibble my thumb, so I did. "Maybe?"

He burst from the shower stall, wet, hot, hard . . .

I gulped as he stared me down with his fierce aquamarine eyes.

Without warning, he turned my body and bent me over the cool sink.

I inhaled sharply as one strong hand pushed down on the small of my back and the other pushed my legs apart.

"Before I am done with you, Penelope, you most certainly won't be able to walk."

In less than a breath, his hard flesh was positioned at my entrance, pushing with just enough force that I felt the delicious sting of my body stretching around him.

My mind instantly devolved into a steamy, syrupy pool of lust with only one thought. "Take me."

Instead, he backed out. He took the tip of his hard shaft and ran it over my slick, hot folds, igniting every last swollen nerve ending. One more second and I would explode.

"Please," I panted, unable to wish for anything but his hard cock to cease teasing me and fill me instead.

"Mmm," he groaned in a husky, carnal voice. "Not yet. I've waited far too long for this moment. I want to savor every sensation."

Oh no. I didn't like that plan at all. No slow boat to O-ville for me. Like him, I'd waited way too long for this moment, and one second more would be torture. A woman can only spend so many nights obsessing, fantasizing, and wondering what it would be like to be taken by a man that sexy, that large.

What he needed was a little push.

I turned around and dropped to my knees, flashing a wicked little smile as I peered up at him and gripped his thick shaft. So many times I'd thought of tasting him, of sucking him, only him.

"What are you doing, woman?" he said, eyes half-closed.

Oh, he knew exactly what I was doing.

Not breaking my fiendish smile, I ran his velvety tip over my lips. He instantly groaned, which only encouraged me to take the next step. I slid his large head between my lips and swirled my tongue over the smooth, tight skin.

Kinich made a gruff, primal sound. "Your mouth is so hot. I never imagined...it could feel..." He groaned again. "So good."

I languidly sucked him in, taking him as deeply as I could while lazily stroking the base of his shaft with my two hands. I'd never, ever dreamed I would savor such a salacious act, but every stroke with my tongue and lips, wantonly worshipping him with my mouth, was a sensual and erotic experience.

I slowly pumped my mouth over him. One. Two. Three times.

Then I stopped.

He looked down at me, chest heaving. "Gods, woman, why did you stop? That was amazing."

I smiled and stood up. "No more savoring. Shower. Now."

I marched into the still running shower filled with hot steam. Kinich followed behind me like an eager puppy vying for a delicious treat.

Before I could say another word, he gripped my shoulders, spun me around again, and pinned me to the warm tile, lifting me in one smooth motion.

I wrapped my legs and arms around his frame and

kissed him so hard our teeth scraped. I snaked one arm between our bodies and positioned him just right.

"Don't hold back," I whispered.

He leaned his hard body into me as he thrust forward.

Unable to stop myself from reacting, my body exploded from the exquisite release of tension. The euphoria hit me like a hard wave that easily overcame the sharp pain of his solid girth sliding inside me.

He screamed my name as he came violently. But all too soon, his groan evolved into a cry of agony.

"Aaaah!" Kinich pulled out and dropped to his knees, groaning.

I reached out, but he shirked away. "Don't touch me!"

"What? Oh my God. What did I do?"

"Fire. I'm on fire," he grunted.

*Oh no...*

# Thirty-Four

"Well, that was interesting," I said, still dripping wet, with a towel wrapped around my body.

Kinich emerged from his walk-in closet with a duffel bag in one hand and a pile of clothes in the other, wearing a pair of soft, faded jeans. Although he appeared to have recovered from his penis sizzling, he was visibly not okay.

"What happened?" I asked.

He slipped on his trademark white linen shirt and quickly fastened the bottom two buttons. "I should have seen this coming," he grumbled.

"What?"

He ignored me and slipped his clothes in the bag, mumbling about his dumb effing luck.

"Dammit, Kinich! What is going on?"

He froze and looked at me. "By some miracle or sick twist of fate, considering it couldn't have happened without the Maaskab's dark powers, my soul has returned, but I am no longer as I was."

"English for nondeities, please!"

He huffed. "My powers have remained inside you, and judging from the small burn I have on my penis, which has yet to heal, I am but a soul with a mortal shell."

"What? You're human?" I exclaimed. Would his penis eventually be okay? That was important.

"More or less."

"Are you sure?" I asked.

"I believe the only way to know for certain is to die, an experiment I'm not willing to conduct at this juncture."

"But how? How can that be possible? Fate said breaking the bond would put everything back."

His brows furrowed. "No. She said it would send me back to my mortal shell or to the cenote. She was correct, as was my brother Guy, who appropriately pointed out that the Maaskab's dark powers are unpredictable as demonstrated by my current situation."

Oh, great. Frigging fantastic, joy of all joys, lucky day, and whoop-de-do! I was still the Sun Goddess.

"This can't be happening."

He shoved more clothes in the bag and began collecting items from the nightstand. "It is done," he said coldly.

"I don't think so! I'm not getting stuck being the Sun God."

"I can relate to your sentiment," he replied.

I watched him cross the room, heading for the door.

I ran after him and grabbed his arm. "Where are you going?"

He stopped with his back to me. "I-I . . . there is something I must do."

*Of course. He's waited his entire existence for this.*

"I get it. You're human now. You have what you want, so you're leaving. To hell with all this! With me! That's your answer."

He turned and looked down at me, his eyes filled with a subtle rage. "Wrong. I planned to leave all along. As soon as I had my body back. Now I do."

"But not until you slept with me first?"

"Of course," he said bluntly.

I slapped him. "You pig! You never cared about me, did you?"

He didn't flinch. "No. It is quite the opposite. I do not expect you to understand, Penelope."

"Wow! What a way to show it. Leaving me to deal with your fucked-up life! I'm twenty-five! I can't be the leader of the gods. I don't have a clue about your world."

"You underestimate yourself, Penelope. You were clearly born for this role. It is your destiny."

*Well, thank you, Obi-Wan Kenobi. Do I get a blue or green light saber?*

"If you leave, Kinich. After everything that's happened, everything I've been through for you, if you leave...don't expect to get me back."

He stared with intense, emotionally charged eyes, but did not speak.

There was a jolting knock on the bedroom door. "Guys! We need you in the living room...Cimil is back."

"I'm going to kill her," I grumbled and quickly slipped on a pair of sweats and a T-shirt.

"No. That honor belongs to me," Kinich countered.

I was about to remind him that he no longer had any powers, but thought better of it. He opened the bedroom door and charged off in the direction of the living room, and I followed close behind.

"I can't believe the other gods don't beat her up on a regular basis," I said under my breath.

"We have become accustomed to her devious ways, but this is different. She abandoned her duties when we most needed her. We will not go light on her this time."

We rounded the corner and found Cimil sitting in the armchair next to the flagstone coffee table. The other gods and Gabrán, Emma, and Brutus stood near her. From their body language—arms crossed, eyes narrowed—I surmised they were about to jump her and give her a good old-fashioned LA gang-style ass whooping.

As Kinich moved through the large, open room, Zac frowned at him, then gave me a wink. I pretended not to see the gesture.

When I finally had a clear view of Cimil, I instantly knew something was wrong. She had dark circles under her eyes; her usually perfect bob was matted and unkempt. Her clothes, a plain gray T-shirt and black leather pants, looked dirty. Definitely not her usual lively pink ensemble.

She stared straight ahead as if completely checked out. Well, that part was, I guess, pretty normal for her.

"Cimil has not spoken," Bees instantly offered.

"What's wrong?" I asked.

The moment I spoke, Cimil's eyes blinked and shifted toward me. "Oh. Penelope. It's you," her voice was muted and lacking its usual boisterous inflection.

"It's me? It's me? Is that all you have to say? For

Christ's sake, you drugged me! My mother has been taken by those Scabby things. And where the hell have you been?"

Cimil shrugged. "Where I always am: everywhere. Nowhere. Here and there."

Kinich looked at me. "That means she's been doing one of her garage sale marathons again."

"Yep. That's pretty much it," she admitted.

I stepped around the coffee table. "You selfish, childish bitch!" Unexpectedly, a grapefruit-sized fireball burst from my palm and smacked Cimil squarely in the chest. The armchair, with Cimil in it, tipped backward. "Did I happen to mention that I'm now the Sun Goddess?"

A collective gasp swept across the room; then Belch rushed to Cimil's side and poured red wine from his leather bota onto her smoking shirt.

Cimil's tiny voice grumbled, "Of course, I know. That was the plan all along."

"Bloody hell," said Guy in his commanding baritone voice, "Kinich didn't get his powers back?"

Belch plucked Cimil off the floor.

"Yes," Cimil replied. "That is correct. Kinich is now mortal." She attempted to smooth down her frazzled red hair and then picked up the armchair and sat back down, clasping her hands in her lap.

"So, you knew?" I asked. "You knew this would happen?"

Avoiding eye contact, she gave a nod.

Guy stepped in closer to the coffee table, looking like he was going to launch himself over at Cimil. "Then you will tell us how to restore him. Immediately! Or I swear by my brethren, Cimil, I will drag you to Mexico by your innards and shove you down that hole with Chaam."

Kinich turned to leave.

"Wait! Where are you going?" I asked.

"To finish packing," he replied.

I began to follow, but Zac grabbed my arm. "Let him go, Penelope," he whispered. "You are needed here to keep the order. We cannot afford to have the gods divided by another petty spat. We must remain united."

"Kinich, please," I whispered.

He glanced over his shoulder, then kept moving.

My anger won out over all other emotions. "Tell me how to fix this!" I commanded Cimil.

She shook her head. "I cannot."

Oh, I had so had it with her cryptic bullshit and this entire chaotic circus. "Yes! You can and you will."

Her eyes darted around the room. "No. You're not listening. I can't. That's the problem."

"Sorry?"

She wiggled in her chair. "I can't tell you what to do."

"But, but you have to! This is all your fucking fault!"

My mind shuffled between fear and anger. I'd hoped and prayed all along that Cimil would return, help us figure out how to fix this giant mess, and get my mother back. After all, she was the one who'd orchestrated the events that got my mom trapped in the first place—the fake medical center and treatment for her illness, the need for money that had gotten me mixed up with all of them.

"Holy shit! Did you make my mother sick? Was that part of your twisted plan?"

Her eyes lit up. "No. I would never do something so

horrible. I cannot harm humans…unless your name is Günther and you sing the 'Ding Dong Song.' Then you're fair game."

I shook my finger at her. "It's still your fault she was captured. You have to know how to get her back!"

Cimil bobbed her head and then shook it from side to side. "Yes. No."

"What do you mean, 'Yes. No'?" I was going into full-blown panic mode.

Cimil stood and bit down on her lower lip. "It's my fault! Yes. She was supposed to be rescued by Viktor—a good thing, trust me. I've taken that bicycle for a ride and *rarrrr!* But that went all wrong, too. It's all one big fucking mess! Just like the time I wore the red glittery platform shoes when I should've worn blue!" She threw her hands in the air. "Of course, my date changed his tie to red, gotta match, which made the bull very, very angry." Her head sagged. "Poor, poor Estevan. *La vida es tan corta.*"

She looked up at the ceiling. "I told you! Shut it or I'll take you down, bitch!"

All heads rotated toward the tiny black spot on the ceiling. *Oh, for heaven's sake. A fly? Not this again.*

I stomped my foot. "Oh. My. God. Would you focus! Tell us how to undo this mess."

"That's the problem. I can't. I can't see a thing. It's all gone."

Within the span of a heartbeat, Guy was holding Cimil up in the air by her shoulders. She reminded me of a tiny rag doll about to be demoted back to a rag. "Cut the crap, Cimil. What is going on? Where the hell have you been?"

"Consulting the book of the Oracle of Delphi, trying to understand where it all went wrong. But now the pages are blank. Blank!"

Guy asked why she of all people would be consulting a book that foretold the future when she had the gift of sight, but she simply mumbled something about retracing her steps. "I think it happened when I was watching that *Love Boat* marathon. I was entranced by Isaac's pearly-white smile and witty humor. I couldn't stop watching," she said. "That's when I must've missed something I was supposed to do, a step I was supposed to take to keep everything on track. A letter I was supposed to write? Or maybe it was that Hungry Hungry Hippos tournament I needed to schedule. I don't know! Then they stopped. Just"—she snapped her fingers—"like that. Every last one of them gone! It's been weeks now."

"The *Love Boat* reruns?" I asked.

"No! The dead! The dead!" She began to cry, which literally freaked me out. Because if someone like Cimil was upset, that meant something bad, very, very bad, was going down.

"Mind elaborating? Some of us are new to the deity club."

"I can't see the future. I never have! I need *them* and they're gone!"

Guy's eyes went wide along with everyone else's. "Wha-what are you saying?" He set her down.

"I lied." She pressed her hands to the side of her face. "That's what I'm saying. I can't see the future—well, not the way you think. I see snippets, little clues, but they are usually meaningless."

"Then how do you always know so much? For

Christ's sake, you even watch television in the future," Zac said.

"I am Goddess of the Underworld, not that there really is an Underworld. Although there is the Short Hills mall near the Jersey Turnpike; they have Chanel and Dolce! That's why the dead like to hang out there. Fashion never goes out of fashion. Yanno?"

*Holy mother of broken brains, this goddess is so bat-shit crazy. How in the world did she get this job?*

"No! We don't know, Cimil! We have no clue what you're talking about!"

Her eyes darted around the room in a paranoid manner. Then she whispered, "I look after the souls of the dead, and they see everything: future, past, present. The dead exist in the place beyond time or dimensions. Everything they knew, I knew. Everything they saw, I saw."

Hands down, this had to be the weirdest thing I'd ever heard. In fact, if they took every episode of the *Twilight Zone*, put them in a blender, and simmered them for ten hours into a condensed soup of weirdness and the unthinkable, that wouldn't come close to competing with this funky concoction.

There were several moments of angry grumblings among the gods.

"Cimil," Guy finally said, "make no mistake, you will be punished for your deception when we are through with this crisis."

"Don't you get it?" Cimil howled. "There is no after. It's over! Over! If the dead have moved on, it's because this world is going to end! The blank pages in the book of the Oracle confirms it. There is no future. We lose the Great War!

I heard the simultaneous mental *click* of everyone in the room.

*Oh. No. Oh, oh, oh . . . no.*

"You mean, it really is the end of the world?"

She covered her face with her hands. "Damn that stupid *Love Boat* and Isaac's glorious Afro!"

# *Thirty-Five*

The gods scrambled back to the summit room. Gabrán followed with his cell phone glued to his ear, issuing some kind of "code red." Guy called Niccolo and did the same.

*Sweet. Thank you,* Love Boat *and Cimil.*

I shook my head. "Be right there. I need to catch my breath." *Or jump off a bridge. Or binge on egg rolls. Something to pull me back into the gravitational pull of planet Earth.*

I sank down on the couch next to Cimil, who'd returned to her semicomatose state.

"Well, I certainly didn't see that one coming," I said.

"Nobody ever expects the Spanish Inquisition," she mumbled.

*Huh?* I mentally sighed. *Whatever. Doesn't matter.*

What did matter was figuring out what to do next. The funny thing about finding out the world is really, truly going to end is that your priorities suddenly shift in ways you wouldn't expect. For example, now more than ever, I needed to find my mother. If it was the last thing I did, I'd find her. I'd hug her and tell her I loved her.

I also wanted to see my friends Anne and Jess again. I hadn't called or spoken with them in over a week, but I wanted to thank them for everything they had ever done. I couldn't count the number of times they'd come to my psychological rescue in one way or another after my mother got sick. They were like my personal angels. How could I have taken them for granted?

Then there was Kinich. I still couldn't believe he was leaving. Did he truly care so little about me? Was I simply the object of his sexual fantasies, but nothing more?

I didn't want to accept it. I was too smart to give my heart away to someone like that. Wasn't I? There had to be a reason he was so hell-bent on leaving. Maybe I wanted to think that because it tasted less bitter going down.

Cimil looked at me and placed her hand on top of my stomach. "I'm sorry, Penelope. I know this can't be easy. The baby won't suffer when the time comes. I promise."

*Oh, good. That's nice to hear!* "What?"

She cocked one brow. "Baby. As in yours."

"Mine?" I sat up straight.

"Uh, yaaah. Don't you remember what I told you in the cab?"

My brain began to sift through the wild memories.

Hmm. First, there was her wild jibber-jabber about everything going wrong. Then there was something about how she hated champagne because the bubbles tickled her nose and how she'd bought an original 1980s Atari set still in its box at some garage sale. Then we were attacked by that Maaskab and a few nasty vampires.

"No. Not exactly," I replied.

"I said, 'Congratulations on the baby.' Don't you remember?"

"No. Not exactly."

"Oh. Maybe I forgot." She scratched her head.

She had to be joking. "But...but—I took a test; it was negative. I saw it!"

"Nope. I tossed yours in the trash when I cleaned your place. Did you like the air freshener I used to get rid of the Scabby smell? It's new! I call it..." She waved her hand through the air like a magician doing an amazing trick. "Sun God! The Odor of a Thousand Suns." She scratched her chin. "Or did I use my new fav perfume, that cat urine cleaner? Hmmm. Can't remember."

"Cimil, focus!"

"What?" she responded defensively.

She must've been confused, a state she seemed to be chronically afflicted with. "If it wasn't my pregnancy test, then whose?"

Her gaze fluttered toward the ceiling for a moment. "Oh, I know! It was mine! And boy, let me tell you, I was worried. Those clowns and I had one crazy night after my party. Just say no to tequila and animal tranquilizers, if ya know what I mean."

Shock waves barreled down. The entire time I'd been reliving memories of my night with Kinich? They weren't simply dreams? I mean, I knew it was a possibility, but now...now it felt all too real. Or surreal. "But I—But I... This can't be right. I mean, wouldn't I have known if we slept together?" I certainly felt the effects after our little episode in the shower.

"Oh, believe you me! You two did it all right. Here.

Let me show you the video." She reached into the pocket of her dingy black leather pants, pulled out a smartphone, and made a few taps. "See!" She held up the tiny screen.

"You filmed us having sex?" I sprang from the couch.

A coy little smile swept across her face. "What? You two were hot. Really. I mean haaawt. Especially when the midgets showed up. And thank goddess they did."

No words could ever...*ever!*...describe the horror I felt. There, on the screen, Kinich and I were making out on his couch like wild, horny teenagers. Arms and hands flew in every which direction, tearing away clothes and groping. Then two tiny men in suits came into view, both held a spritzer bottle.

"What the hell?" Oh, the horror! The horror!

Cimil giggled. "Great idea, right? They were exactly the right size to really get in there and put out the flames. You didn't even know they were there, and I figured Kinich's first time would be," she cackled, "on fire! And let me tell you, wow! Was I right."

Seething with anger I never knew possible, I felt myself heat up. Tiny beads of sweat broke out all over my body. I felt scorching, painful flames flickering beneath the surface. But I didn't care. I'd kill her! I'd just kill her!

I was about to lunge when she held out her hands. "Whoa, whoa there, cowgirl. I don't have any midgets handy, and I'm not sure bursting into flames is good for the baby or that body. You're still mortal for the most part."

Shit! I took a deep breath and exhaled. A billow of smoke escaped from my mouth. *Great. I'm Puff the Magic Dragon. And a porn star. Who's pregnant.*

*Crappity crap!* "Am I really pregnant? Are you sure? Kinich said I needed to wear that necklace to be able to carry a baby."

She nodded. "The ring your mother gave you, you're still wearing it."

I looked at the silver ring with tiny black stones. "The stones are onyx."

"No. Jade."

*Wait! Oh my God! How does she know about the ring? It's a gift from my mother.* I stood up. Maybe I couldn't turn into a fireball, but I could still throw one. "You sold it to her! Didn't you?"

She smiled and wiggled her digits in the air. "Guilty as charged."

"Then you did something to it so I couldn't take it off! I'm going to kill you! How can you mess with people's lives like this?"

"You mustn't take it so personally, Penelope. I merely facilitated that which is meant to be. It's like being the host of *The Bachelorette*. I merely create the set for the love to happen. And the scandals. And commercials every five minutes that drive everyone insane. But I don't actually participate in the drama. Yanno what I mean? Besides, you may remove the ring at any time."

"I can't. I tried fifty times. Soap, lotion—"

"The ring is bespelled to only come off if you truly wish it. You clearly wanted to have this baby with Kinich, although you may not have admitted it to yourself yet."

I plopped down on the couch, toying with the ring. Could it be? Could she be telling the truth? But there was no way. In fact, I'd had my . . .

I covered my mouth.

No. No, I hadn't had my monthly monster for...

"I'm three weeks late." Why hadn't I realized it?

So much had happened, I guess it slipped my mind.

I suddenly recalled what Andrus had told me that morning outside of Cimil's home: Cimil was a person who knew what you wanted even before you did. "So, this baby was part of your master plan? The one that's now gone sideways?"

She gripped my hand. "That's why I don't understand, Penelope. I did everything right except for the doomsday *Love Boat* incident."

I never imagined the words *doomsday* and *Love Boat* would be used in the same sentence.

"Aside from that," she mumbled. "I was steering the cruise ship in the right direction, toward our port of call: love. And toward the gods' eternal happiness. You must believe me! You must! I don't know where it all went wrong." She blubbered uncontrollably.

I almost liked the old Cimil better. At least she was sort of entertaining in a really twisted and inappropriate way. But Drama-Cimil was kind of sad. Hysterical was not a look she wore well.

She continued on. "You were supposed to be the surrogate, the stand-in for Kinich's power. Kinich got his wish of mortality so he'd finally stop his incessant yapping—'I want to be mortal, I want to be mortal. Waaaah!'" she whined mockingly. "He needed to learn the grass isn't greener. And then, when he saw the baby, he would finally believe that Payals were meant to be, paving the way for the rest of us to live happy existences. And once we are all happy..."

She zoned out completely.

I shook her by the shoulders. "What? We what?"

Eyes glossed over, she replied, "I can't remember. I'm useless without my dead. Especially Estevan and Günther. And my unicorn." She held her hand over her heart and sighed. "I can't even remember the words to my favorite song, "Pop! Goes the Weasel.'" She sprung from the couch and began clapping. "Oh! Oh! But I do remember this one from the Stones!"

Cimil began howling the words to "You Can't Always Get What You Want."

"Oh my God. Please stop," I said pressing my hands over my ears.

She halted her oratory assault. "It's so true!" she said. "Sometimes you only get what you need. It's sort of ironic, isn't it?"

Not as ironic as finding out I was pregnant. "Why me?"

"How the hell am I supposed to know? I just follow the signs, I don't make them. Well, I used to follow the signs. Now they're gone. No more world. Poof!" She sighed. "No more garage sales. No more used picnic baskets, golf clubs, and exercise equipment. Bad times. Bad times."

"Wow. Yeah. Useless crap. Such a loss for humanity. Especially when compared to... losing humanity."

*Nut bag.*

Then a new panic attack hit me. "Wait. Will the baby be all right? I mean, I have Kinich's powers, will it be safe? Am I even human anymore?"

Her eyes filled with tears. *Tears!* This was too much.

"You can't ever go home if you've never lived there." She began to blubber again and sank into the couch.

"No more gibberish. Answer me!"

Her head dropped. "The last thing the book showed me was a date. The final day. We have eight months."

There were no words for the despair I felt. There was no point of reference for the darkness that threatened to consume me. This couldn't be happening.

"Penelope, you are needed. Acan and Camaxtli are strangling each other."

I looked up at Zac hovering in the doorway. If only I could remember who the hell Acan and Camaxtli were. These Mayan names were a mess. If we didn't have bigger fish to fry, I'd call a vote to rename everyone with simple, easy names: Bob, Carol, Jenny. We'd keep Belch. Zac, too. Those were good names.

Then I remembered. *Dammit! I need to find Kinich.* I needed to tell him about the baby before he left.

*Wait. Think. Do you want him to stay with you because you're pregnant? Don't forget, the world is going to end; you don't have a minute to lose.*

I froze in my tracks with that thought. I didn't want to spend my last days on Earth with a man, uuuh, ex-god, who didn't want me. Yes, I loved him, but sulking and crying and withering away wouldn't save the world. It wouldn't save me.

*It won't save... my baby.*

*Oh, hell. Am I really pregnant?*

Then, and I don't know how it happened, but it did. I chose. I chose not to crumble. I chose not to let the hurt of rejection or the anger of the crappy hand I'd been dealt pull me under and sink me. I chose to fight. I chose to win or go down trying.

So there it was. I ate the lemons, swallowed them whole, and spit out the seeds.

Well, I'll be damned. I *was* strong enough.

I looked at Cimil and Zac. "Get ready boys and girls, because there's a new sun god in town."

Guy was the first to echo the sentiment that most of the gods were thinking. "We fight and attack as planned. Every last one of us."

"All of us?" Bees, who wore a shades-of-summer camouflage jumpsuit, asked as she petted the hive on her head. The bees purred with delight.

"The Great War is the turning point," Guy replied. "If we do not win, the apocalypse is inevitable. So we must use every means we can to win. Your bees can assist with monitoring the Maaskab's movements during the battle."

The bees made a cheery little buzz. *Such little warriors.*

Gabrán, who stood at my side, arms crossed, chimed in. "We should make the final decision when Niccolo arrives."

"Niccolo answers to me," Guy barked.

Gabrán frowned like a disapproving parent. "Yes, but he still leads the vampire army and is the de facto king. We must have his support."

Guy growled. "The vampires will do as they are told or perish with the rest of the mortal world."

The rest of the conversation sounded like:

*…Blah, blah, blah. I'm right and you're wrong.*

*Blah. Blah. Am not. You're wrong.*

*No, I'm right. Blah, blah.*

*Blah, blah…oh yeah? Prove it, blah, blah.*

I realized that the species was irrelevant; male posturing was universal.

"Both of you, can it!" I barked. "We're sticking to the protocol, which is..." I looked at Gabrán.

"We list the options, debate the pros and cons of each, and then take a vote," Gabrán stated with a disappointed sigh.

Very pragmatic. "Thank you."

"Let's start with thinking this through." I glanced around the table. "Options?"

Bees spoke up. "We stay the course as Guy suggested. The gods will also fight, except for Cimil, Penelope, and Zac."

That made sense, Zac said he was strong, but didn't really have any gifts. I was pregnant—*crappity crap! Really? Really?*—and Cimil was about as useful as a lump of dog poop.

"Okay, that's one option. Others?"

"We do nothing," Suicide suggested in a blasé voice.

I stared at her, wondering if she ever had the urge to apply her skills to herself.

"What?" She shrugged.

I shook my head. "Nothing." I wrote down "Do nothing" on my magic tablet, and then looked around the table again, hopeful that someone else might have a better suggestion. "Fate, how come you haven't said anything?"

She waved her hand through the air. "Because whatever we choose, this is our fate."

Wow. Another shocking answer. No wonder the world was about to go down the crapper.

I thought about the tiny life in my belly. It didn't feel real, but somewhere, buried beneath the layers of raw emotion, was a gnawing urge to fight like hell to protect it.

Zac offered, "If the course we are on is the one that leads to the end, then we need to make a turn."

"This is the problem," K'ak pointed out, ever so carefully turning his head so as not to cause his enormous, two-foot-high turquoise-encrusted headdress to tip. "Without the book or Cimil's powers, we do not know which action is truly the one we wish to avoid. What if the turn you suggest is the one we must avoid and the original plan is the one we must follow?"

"I have a coin," Bees offered. "We could let Chance decide."

"Chance is on vacation," Ah-Ciliz, God of Eclipses, said in a dreary voice.

I looked at Zac, who stood by my side like a deadly sentry. "Who is Chance?" I whispered.

He leaned in and spoke quietly in my ear. "A friend of the family." His warm breath sent a shiver down my spine.

As he pulled away, I couldn't help but study Zac. His size matched Kinich's, as did his confidence. His perfectly shaped body, packed with powerful muscles, only appeared fiercer in his black leather pants and dark tee.

"Seriously, you don't have any powers?" I asked.

*God of Seduction, perhaps?* 'Cause . . . wow. I knew Kinich had given me the anti-deity whammy; nonetheless, this guy still packed a punch. Pretty damned impressive, if you asked me, because I wanted nothing to do with men, and I'd just had my heart trampled.

He smiled. "Like I said, you'll be the first to know."

It pleased him that he was inspiring very inappropriate and unwelcome feelings at this time in my life when I was hanging on by a thread.

Interesting.

Belch, who still wore his shiny green running suit, which now boasted several nasty-looking stains down the front, chimed in. "Does anyone have vodka? I need more vodka."

"Amen to that," said Suicide.

"You are the biggest group of misfits I've ever seen," I scolded.

Several of the gods looked at each other and nodded in agreement, the only exceptions being Zac and Votan.

Christ. We were all in so much trouble.

I took a deep, calming breath. We were flying blind, so any choice we made could be the exact choice we wanted to avoid. Not easy. So many lives depended on us, on our every move.

I ran my hands over my face. "So our options are to fight or do nothing? That's it? Can't we try to negotiate with the Mobscuros"—I decided the time had come to name our evil Reese's Peanut Butter Cup treat—"or cripple them and buy some time?"

The group debated for a moment and came to the unanimous conclusion that the more time we gave, the worse off we were, and that the Mobscuros were not interested in negotiation.

I closed my eyes. We were missing something. Something big. It didn't make sense that the Maaskab or Obscuros, Mobscuros, would want to end the world. Give it a yucky, evil makeover? Sure. But destroy it completely?

Regardless, the gods were right; we didn't have many options: wait, fight, do nothing. The only one that felt right was to take out as many bad guys as possible. If we were going down, we'd go kicking and screaming.

"If no one has any other suggestions, then it's time to vote. All in favor of initiating the Great War?"

I looked around the table. It was unanimous. Even Suicide raised her hand. Maybe we could send her ahead, and then the Mobscuros would be too depressed to fight.

It was worth a try.

# Thirty-Six

⌒

I didn't know exactly what to expect when I entered Kinich's room. Part of me had pathetically hoped he'd changed his mind and stayed. Part of me kicked myself for wanting him to stay at all. I deserved better. I deserved to come first. Or even in the top three.

It didn't really matter anymore how I felt because his bag was gone, the room empty.

I walked to the glass door and looked outside. The miles of lonely desert now seemed bleak instead of calming. The sky, a perfect, crisp blue, only reminded me of what we were all going to lose.

I needed to take a walk and clear my thoughts.

Still barefoot, I turned to retrieve my boots in the closet and ran straight into Zac. I jumped from my skin.

"Jeez, you scared me." I placed my hand over my thumping heart.

"My apologies. I came to tell you that Kinich paid me a visit."

"You saw him? He's still here?"

Zac shook his head. "No. He left me a note with instructions and asked me to give you this." He held out a clean white envelope.

"Any clue what it says?" I asked.

"No."

"What did yours say?" I asked.

"He requested I care for your...needs in his absence."

"Needs?" The way he'd said that word implied all sorts of things. Very sexual things. Doubtful.

"There was also mention of making the asshole who burnt the inside of his one-point-seven-million-dollar car pay dearly."

*Yikes. One point seven? Well, serves him right!*

I took the envelope. "He didn't say anything else?" There was that dang lump in my throat again.

His ice-blue eyes turned to azure blue. "I'll be in Kinich's study if you need me." He gave my shoulder a squeeze, then turned to leave.

"No. Wait. Don't go." I suddenly didn't want to be alone for this.

I ripped open the envelope. Inside was a small sheet of crisp paper and the words:

*Forgive me for not saying good-bye. I leave you in the care of my brother. Zac has sworn to protect you and be your Right Hand.*

*May the sun always shine upon you.*

*Kinich Ahau*

I looked up at Zac. "So, he made his choice. He left. He really left."

Zac reached out and clutched my hand. "I am...sorry."

"Did he say where?"

Zac shook his head. "We know not. Perhaps he left because he is ashamed. In his new fragile state he is unable to be of use in battle. Perhaps he simply wishes to enjoy his new life as a human."

My knees trembled, threatening to give out.

I quickly pulled it together and straightened my back. "Fate has spoken."

His head dipped. "I see you're catching on."

I unexpectedly felt dizzy again and the room turned black.

# *Thirty-Seven*

"She's coming around." I heard a female's voice off in the distance. "Penelope! Can you hear me?"

Someone tapped my cheek. "She's in shock," I heard the same female voice whisper. "I can't believe he left her. What kind of moron leaves a pregnant woman?"

"He was not informed of the news," argued the man.

"She didn't tell him?" said the woman.

"She did not have the chance," the man replied.

"You idiot. Why didn't *you* tell him?" she asked.

"I did not see him, and if I had, it is not my place to meddle."

My mind fell into place. As it did, I wondered if I really wanted to come around. Reality was waiting for me, and it was a place far too painful to be at the moment. I'd had about all I could take.

"Penelope. Please wake up." I realized it was Emma speaking. "They're getting ready to attack. I'm going to the command center to monitor everyone on the satellite."

I lifted my lids slowly; they felt like they had lead weights attached.

"Did he really leave? Or was it a dream?" I asked, my mind foggy and slow.

Emma brushed the hair back from my forehead. "Yes, honey. He's gone. I'm sorry. And I'm even more sorry because I know your heart's been broken. But you have to be strong. Too much is at risk."

The bedroom came into focus, and as it did, the starkness of the situation hit home. But I'd already had a heart-to-heart with myself, so I knew I couldn't let my broken heart distract me.

"Well, I guess the bright side is," I mumbled, "that now I have one less problem. I'm down to four."

Emma chuckled. "That certainly is something."

Zac appeared behind Emma, his blue-green eyes glowing with warmth. "I happen to agree. I once tried to count mine but got bored after number five thousand two hundred and twenty-two. Four is good. Very manageable."

Sure. I'd accidentally become the "surrogate" Sun God and was carrying the real Sun God's baby, my mother was still a captive of the Mobscuros, and the world was ending. Not that I was complaining. *'Cause it's still just four*.

"Piece of cake." I sat up slowly. The room still wobbled unnaturally, but at least now I understood why.

*Pregnant. Wow.*

"Is everything ready?" I mumbled.

"Everyone is almost in position. Every Uchben soldier, vampire, and allies of the gods. Even the others."

"You keep mentioning the others. Do you mean leprechauns?"

Zac chuckled. "No. They don't fight; they are peaceful people."

"Maybe you should try taking away their clothes. I hear that makes them angry."

He raised both brows. "I do not wish to know how you came into possession of that knowledge."

"Who are the others?" I questioned.

"Why don't we save the debriefing on immortals for another day? You need nourishment," he replied.

"I'm not hungry."

"Penelope," Emma pointed out, "you can't think just about yourself."

She was right. I'd almost forgotten. It was all very new. "All right. I want egg rolls, sourdough bread, and spinach salad."

"I will obtain your meal," Zac said and disappeared.

"I think he likes you, Pen," Emma whispered.

I rolled my eyes. "I think I'm pretty much done with men for eternity."

"All right. But he's hot."

"Emma! I'm not exactly on the market. Kinich has been gone for an hour; the world is going to end in eight months; I'm also pregnant."

She held out her hands. "Actually, you were out for five hours, so . . . Kinich has been gone a little longer."

I growled.

"Okay. But Zac's really hot. And ain't nothin' wrong with a little rebound romp."

"Emma. Seriously?"

"I'm just sayin'." She smiled with a goofy grin.

No, she wasn't serious, but I appreciated the effort to make me laugh.

"All right, my little goody-goody." She stood up. "After you eat, Zac will drive you to the camp. I'll see you in the control room."

"So this is it? We're going to attack? This fast?"

"The troops were already on standby. They mobilized five minutes after the meeting concluded. They should be hitting the Maaskab village any minute."

Emma turned to leave.

"Hey," I called out.

She froze with her back to me. I noticed that today she wasn't wearing one of her usual girlie outfits, but the standard Uchben uniform: black tee and cargos.

"Are you okay?" I asked. "I mean, with what Guy's about to do?" Yes, Guy was a god and immortal, but that didn't mean going head-to-head with the Maaskab wasn't dangerous. Who knew what those monsters had up their sleeves? After all, look what they'd done to Kinich.

She shrugged without looking my way. "A god's gotta do what a god's gotta do. Especially the God of Death and War." She left without letting me see her face. I understood why. Tears didn't serve any purpose at this point.

I took a slow breath, trying not to let it all tear me up. The world now hung on a razor-sharp edge.

Selfishly, I could only think of Kinich.

At twenty minutes to midnight, I followed Zac through the vacant lobby of a two-story office building situated at the edge of the Uchben camp. This didn't seem like the sort of place where strategic world decisions were made.

We walked down a long, narrow hallway with glass walls and empty, dark conference rooms on each side. We turned the corner and encountered two heavily armed guards next to a harmless-looking elevator.

"Sir." One of the men nodded stiffly when we stepped inside.

Zac, like the other gods, towered over any human. Hardened, battle-seasoned men looked miniature sized in his presence.

"God of Intimidation?" I asked.

He smiled with that knowing, insanely charming smile. "Your guess is as good as mine."

He pressed the Down button, and I realized that the modest structure we'd entered was a facade. The heart of the operation was buried twenty stories belowground, given that he'd pressed B-20.

After a short ride down, the doors slid open. As we stepped out, perhaps due to the absolute silence of the long, dark hallway illuminated by red bulbs, I felt intensely aware of Zac—a god who didn't know his path or purpose, yet glowed with confidence. He exuded absolute comfort with his place in the universe.

Funny how one man could flourish in the face of uncertainty while it crippled others.

"How do you make the whole 'not knowing' thing look so easy?" I asked.

He gently placed his hand on my lower back to guide me along. "When we each came to light, most knew right away which gifts they carried, while others merely felt power but were unable to command it. Over many centuries, those gods spent all of their time honing their gifts."

"But not you."

We continued along the eerie, dark hallway until we reached an iron door.

"No," he replied. "This is why I spent my time developing in other ways. Finding peace was one of them."

He truly had a Zen-like outlook on life. I was jealous.

"Are you saying," I asked, "you're okay with never finding your gifts?"

"No. It will happen when it is meant to be. And I believe I am close."

"Really?" I asked. "How do you know? Do you get a tingle or a special feeling?"

"A god finds his powers when he or she experiences the strength that they house. Acan didn't know he was the God of Wine until he tried it about two thousand years ago."

Zac punched several numbers into a keypad beside the steel door. The pad beeped and the panel door slid open.

"How exciting. So, if you took a stab, what would you guess your power will be?"

He looked straight ahead. "It is something I've only recently discovered: love."

Zac's little comment boggled the mind, *my* mind.

*The God of Love?*

It made sense. From the get-go, I wasn't able to articulate or rationalize how it was physically possible for me to feel anything for a man I didn't know from Peter or Paul, but I did. I felt nothing but warmth and affection in his presence.

Yes. It made perfect sense. Suicide made me angry and depressed. Acan made people want to party, though not me for some weird reason. Zac made me feel loved.

*Except that Kinich gave you the anti-god whammy. You're immune to their powers.*

*Nooo. It must've worn off.* I wasn't that sort of girl, the kind that hopped from one lily pad to the next. Kinich was, without a doubt, the one I loved.

*He left you. Don't forget that.*

"Ready?" Zac's towering frame turned to the side as he held the door open.

I shook my head. "Not really." I paused in the doorway and looked up into his arctic-blue eyes. They had specks of green that seemed to dance around the pupils.

Mesmerizing.

"Zac, can I ask you something?"

"Of course," he replied.

"Do you really think this is the end if we don't win?"

His warm smile melted away. "Yes."

"I see." I turned away and continued until we reached yet another door. "Then we better kick ass."

The door swung open in front of me. "Penelope! Where have you been?" Emma barked. "They've started! Oh my God, it's a fucking mess!"

"Shit!" I followed her into a large stadium-style room. There were ten tiers, each one about ten feet wide. Each tier had a station every five feet with a computer bank, monitors, and a person frantically speaking on a headset or typing into a keyboard. A giant floor-to-ceiling screen was situated in the front of the room, displaying an infrared satellite feed with little moving colored dots.

Emma darted to a station at the top tier's center, where a woman with golden spirals stood frantically talking with a man.

"Helena. Andrus. This is Penelope," Emma said.

"We've already met." We exchanged polite nods.

Helena, a petite, little thing, looked up at me with her bright blue eyes. "They are getting their asses handed to them. We have to do something! The Maaskab are sifting in and out of their portals so fast we can't kill them."

Andrus shook his head. "They must have turned. Every last one of them—only vampires move that fast."

Yes, we'd known that the Maaskab had joined forces with the Obscuros, but that they'd all turned into vampires? Christ, that was bad. According to Gabrán, the Uchben were a strong match against the Maaskab, and Niccolo's vampire army could take down any Obscuro. But we were unevenly matched if the enemy had all turned into this hybrid army of sorts.

"Where's Guy?" I asked Emma and pointed to the screen. The dots were moving so fast I couldn't tell who was who.

"He went inside a portal with Niccolo and two hundred vampires to flush out the Scabs."

"Why can't we see them?" I asked. "I thought the satellite could pick them up from anywhere?"

Emma bent over, panting. "We don't know. They faded off the screen the minute they jumped inside. Then the Scabs started flooding out of their portals like angry swarming bees."

This was without a doubt an occasion that called for a very, very strong word. "Fuckity fuck."

I leaned over and wrapped one arm around Emma. "It's okay, Emma. He'll be all right."

She shook her head. "No. No. It's over."

I spoke in a low voice so only she could hear. "I'm here for you. Your sister. Remember? Whatever happens, we'll face it together."

She pushed out a long, steady breath. "I can't lose him, Penelope. I can't face—"

"I don't believe it!" Helena pointed at the screen. In between the purple, green, and blue dots, red ones began appearing in droves.

"What are those?" I asked.

Andrus replied, "Not what. Who. The purple are the gods. The green are our vampires. Blue are Scabs. And the red dots...are humans. Hundreds of them."

As clear as day, little red dots were popping up all over the center of the screen. I cupped my hand to my mouth. "The Payals...it's got to be them," I whispered in amazement. Niccolo, Guy, and the vampires must have found them and gotten them out. Was my mother there, too?

I noticed Gabrán standing on the bottom tier toward the front of the room, frantically screaming into his headset. I darted down the stairs to my left. "Gabrán! Look. Look at the screen. People!"

His head snapped up. "Christ almighty. Humans? They won't stand a chance if we can't get them out of there."

"Do something!" I screamed. My mother could be with them, I thought.

"I cannae, lass. We've got every last man fighting, and they're dropping like flies."

*Shit. Shit. Shit.* I was supposed to be the leader, but I had no clue what to do. I had no battle experience. None. But one thing was clear. We were losing. If we didn't do something fast, there would be no one left.

"Call them back. Retreat," I ordered.

Gabrán looked at me. "Guy and Niccolo command the army, lass. I cannae without their orders."

"Well, what the hell did they tell you to do if they both got captured or injured or something?"

"Well," he said, "the issue never came up."

*Ugh! Stupid, arrogant men.*

"Look at me," I said in a stone-cold voice. "Look deep into my eyes. They have disappeared. I rule the House of the Gods, and I'm in charge now. Call them back; have your soldiers grab the Payals and run. Tell them to regroup at the fort."

There was an old Spanish fort about one and a half miles away where we'd set up a small armory and triage.

He paused for a moment as the noise and commotion swarmed around us. He knew we had to do something.

He gave a nod and the expression in his eyes spoke volumes. "Let's hope you're right, Sun Goddess."

He spoke into his headset, and the dots on the screen began shifting away from the fight, but then something very unexpected happened.

"The Maaskab are falling to the ground," someone screamed out from across the room. The entire room fell silent, and everyone stared at the infrared satellite feed on the screen.

Each and every blue dot, the Scabs, stopped moving.

"What does it mean?" I asked Gabrán, as he stared at the blinking satellite image and listened on his headset.

"Lass, it's a bloody fucking miracle." He looked at me, his green eyes sparkling with excitement. "Brutus says the Maaskab are dropping to the ground. Giant black holes are appearing in their bodies."

Andrus appeared at my side. "Holes? That means their vampire blood is dying."

Whatever the hell was happening was completely lost on me.

"We must attack!" Gabrán looked at me. "They are vulnerable now."

I had to trust that whatever was going on, they knew what they were doing. "Do it."

Gabrán turned and faced the men and women in the room. "Tell everyone tae go back in! Do nae stop until the priests are dead."

The dots blipped back toward the middle of the screen.

A wide smile stretched across Gabrán's face. "They cannae even fight back, lass; the Scabs are completely crippled. We've won. We've bloody fucking won."

*We won? We won?* An enormous weight lifted from my shoulders.

I just prayed my mother was with the group of humans they'd freed—she had to be!

I began to jump up and down with excitement. I ran up the stairs to the top tier and grabbed Emma. "We've won!"

Emma's eyes were filled with tears. "I can't believe it! Oh my God."

We hugged each other tightly. I turned and found myself looking straight up a mountain of muscles. Zac's blue eyes glowed with joy. He bent down and kissed me.

My cell phone rang, startling me. I pushed away and blinked several times.

He smiled with that devilish grin. "Sorry. I guess I got carried away."

I shook my head and turned away.

*Caller Unknown.* It was very strange because very few people had my number.

"Hello?" With all of the commotion, I had to cover one ear to hear.

"Penelope."

My heart skipped a beat.

*Kinich.*

"Where are you?" I asked.

He spoke, but I couldn't hear him. "Speak up! There's too much noise! We won, Kinich! We won. The Maaskab are dropping like flies. It's a miracle."

There was no sound, none that I could hear above all the cheering anyway.

"Kinich? Are you there?"

"Yes. I am glad to hear the news." His voice didn't sound happy. He sounded distressed. He sounded like I'd told him we'd lost.

"Kinich, where are you?"

"Is Cimil still there with you?" he asked.

Why did he want to know?

"She's at your house, staring at a wall, I think. What's going on?"

"If we do not speak again, I wish you to know that..." His voice broke up.

"What? I can't hear you! Speak up!" I walked through the cheering crowd, out the exit and into the hallway. "There. I can hear. What do you want me to know?"

No response.

I pulled the phone from my ear. Call Ended flashed across the screen.

"Who was it?" Zac leaned in the doorway.

I looked at my feet. A cold sensation filling me with dread hit like an avalanche. "Kinich. But we got cut off."

I dialed him back but got a busy signal.

"Do not worry, Penelope. I'm sure he will call back."

I wasn't so sure. Something told me that the call wasn't him checking in. No, he sounded like a man saying... good-bye. *Really* saying good-bye.

I followed Zac back inside and noticed that not everyone was cheering. Helena's eyes stayed glued to the screen.

"What is it?" I asked.

"Niccolo and Guy never came out of the Maaskab's portal," she muttered.

Emma froze at my side. "There must be some mistake."

Helena shook her head. "No mistake. One of Niccolo's men, a vampire, attempted to sift inside to look for them. It's closed."

*Oh, God. No.*

# *Thirty-Eight*

The next thirty-four hours were a bittersweet whirlwind. I'd never felt so polarized in my entire life. Our army—the Uchben soldiers, ten gods, and the vampire army—easily took down thousands of evil vampire Scabs as they helplessly flailed on the ground while their vampire blood died.

Reports then began pouring in from all over the world of Obscuros dropping in their tracks, turning to dust.

Andrus explained that whoever had been their maker, two things were absolutely certain: first, he or she was an Ancient One, an original of the six first vampires, and second, that Ancient One had been killed.

So who killed the Ancient One? How? No one knew, and frankly, we didn't care.

It was the miracle we needed. The added bonus being that for any regular Maaskab who still lived, they lost the upper hand without their vampire blood. They would no longer be able to sift or hide "in the spaces."

Fate. It was fate, everyone said.

But victory did not come without a price. We'd lost over one thousand Uchben and vampires in those first twenty minutes. Had the "miracle" not occurred, our entire army of twenty thousand would've been wiped out in a few hours.

We got off lucky. Except for Emma and Helena.

Of the two hundred who sifted inside the Maaskab portal, Guy, Niccolo, and forty vampires never came out. The Uchben team in the control room had carefully analyzed the satellite footage and confirmed it.

Even worse, we'd learned it wasn't only the Maaskab portals that had been sealed shut. The entire sifting dimension had somehow closed. Not one of our vampires could sift. They said it was as if the "spaces" had been filled with cement. Impenetrable.

Emma and Helena were devastated, but like the strong women they were, they kept it together and focused on finding a way to rescue the men, as did everyone else.

Now it was my turn to face my worst nightmare.

"Ready?" Zac asked.

I stared at the morning sky and stretch of flat desert. No, I wasn't ready. Sadly, there was no getting around it.

The Uchben and vampires who still stood after the battle had their hands full dealing with the injured and taking inventory of the dead from both sides. The only thing we knew was that there were approximately two hundred humans—Payals we assumed—coming our way. The Uchben medics in the field had said they were physically okay. But mentally? We didn't have a clue. Was my mother one of them? No one knew that either because the women weren't able to speak.

Emma, Helena, and Zac stood at my side inside the small, glass-windowed room attached to the hangar. We watched quietly as the camouflaged carrier touched down over the dusty landing strip at Camp Uchben.

I tried to maintain my composure, to be strong like Emma and Helena, but I had to face facts: I was at my tipping point. Who could blame me? Watching as the world's fate had hung in the balance; finding out I was pregnant; Kinich's leaving; my becoming something I didn't want to be, the Sun Goddess; and now I was supposed to pretend I was all right if my mother, the one person in the world who really loved me, my only real family . . . I was supposed to pretend I was okay if she wasn't on that plane?

No. I wouldn't be okay. I just wouldn't. A person can only handle so much.

*Please, please, be on the plane. Please be on the plane.* I closed my eyes tightly as I heard the engines wind down.

"They're coming out," Helena whispered. "There are so many."

I opened my eyes and felt overwhelmed with sadness. Their eyes were so empty, their expressions so bleak and forlorn. What had those monsters done to them? God, my heart cried out for each and every one while my eyes desperately searched the line of women in tattered clothing, marching toward the hangar. Soldiers and medics rushed to their sides and began taking them to the underground hospital.

The nameless faces continued passing. "She's not here." I turned away and began to sob. I couldn't bear it.

Zac wrapped his arms around me, and I buried my face in his chest. I wished it were Kinich, but it wasn't, and now I hated him for it. I hated him for leaving me to deal with everything on my own. I hated him for not loving me enough to stay with me. I hated the Maaskab for robbing me of my world. I never knew there could be so much hate inside me.

Zac stroked the back of my hair. "Don't lose hope, Penelope. Another plane with more humans is still on the way."

"I don't effing believe it!" Emma darted out the door and launched herself on top of a large man who had been walking with the Payals into the hangar. She began beating the fallen man in the face. "You bastard! I'll kill you!"

Two soldiers rushed in and pulled her off. With her red hair a wild mess, I couldn't see her face, but I sensed she was getting ready to unleash her Payal power.

I rushed outside. "Emma, calm down!" I yelled.

"I'm going to kill him, Penelope! Kill him!" She looked down at the man who lay on the ground, writhing in pain. "Do you hear me, Tommaso? Do you? You're a dead man. You fucking traitor!"

*Tommaso?* This had been the man who'd betrayed her.

"Lock him up," I commanded the two Uchben soldiers, who suddenly resembled deer in the headlights.

"We were given orders to take care of him," the taller of the two spoke up.

Emma screamed at the top of her lungs. "No! I get that honor. Me!"

The soldier shifted his weight. "No. We were given the order to *care* for him, make sure his wounds are bandaged."

The soldier helped Tommaso stand. I could tell he was a man who'd seen better days; he was very thin and haggard. His dark hair was straggly and his eyes—*hell, they're turquoise*—could only be described as desolate.

"Who? Who told you to take care of him?" I asked the soldier.

Unexpectedly, Tommaso reached for Emma's hand. "I would never betray you."

She snapped it away. "Liar! It should be you who's trapped. Not Guy!"

Zac chimed in. "Emma, he tells the truth. Guy told me before he left in case anything happened. Tommaso did not betray you; he went back as a spy to prove himself to us and the Uchben."

Emma froze. "What are you trying to say?"

Tommaso, a braver soul than I, stepped toward her. "Guy had me free your grandmother to gain her trust and get me back inside the Maaskab. But I got caught when I saved that woman—they said she was an angel and were torturing her with their sick fucking experiments."

Um. Wow. I wasn't sure which part of the story was more shocking, the freeing of Emma's grandma or the part about the angel.

I went with the latter.

"Angel? Like, as in fluffy wings, lives in heaven, yada yada?"

Tommaso gave a nod.

Hmmm. So we had gods, vampires, ex–vampire demi-gods (like Andrus and Niccolo), evil priests (Maaskab), vampire evil priests (Mobscuros)—*or are they now dead ex–vampire evil priests?*

*I think we call those "dead."*

*Oh yeah.*

Then there were the gods' mortal daughters (Payals); demigod Payals who were immortal (like Emma); a half-vampire, half-human baby (Niccolo and Helena's baby);

an ex-god who's now mortal (Kinich); a human who's now a god with no dang clue about her mortality status and is pregnant with the ex-god's baby (*that one is me, in case you were wondering*); leprechauns; and—*deep breath*—angels.

Well, goody. Now the only thing missing from our little paranormal soap opera were the magical talking animals.

*You forgot about Cimil's unicorn.*

I wondered if it talked.

"I don't fucking believe you!" Emma screamed. Her face was wrath personified. No, wait. Devastated. Nooo...*Shit! Pissed!* I jumped in front of Tommaso to shield him because there was no doubt in my mind she was about to split the man down the middle like a baked potato about to receive all the fixings.

"Emma! Stop!" I yelled.

"Goddamn him! How could Guy lie to me like that? How could he?" she screamed.

I brushed her shoulder. "I don't know, Em."

But I did know.

And I guessed so did she.

When all was said and done, the gods couldn't help being who they were; their hardwiring would *always* win, always take precedence over personal loyalties. It was exactly as Kinich said, Guy had been a fool to think he could have a relationship because sooner or later he'd put his role first and break Emma's heart.

*Goddammit. Kinich was right.* I didn't want him to be. I wanted to believe there was hope for us still.

Emma reached around me, clawing for Tommaso. "Where the fuck is my grandmother?"

He stepped back, avoiding Emma's deadly hands. "Emma, you need to know, your grandmother, she—"

"Where! Where is she, you motherfucker! And where the hell is Guy?" Emma's face turned redder than a beet.

Tommaso stared at the ground, speaking softly. "The last time I saw them, they were facing off. Guy was winning. I don't know if she's still alive."

Oh, man. Maybe it wasn't such a bad thing that Guy was trapped somewhere. Because if he'd been there inside this cavernous airplane hangar with Emma, she'd have it decorated with his man parts by now.

Emma's face, still filled with an unspeakable rage, turned paler than a scoop of vanilla ice cream. She threw up on the cement.

I steadied her so she wouldn't fall over. "Are you okay, Emma?"

She slowly rose and wiped her mouth with the back of her hand. "Morning sickness," she mumbled.

*Oh. Add half-immortal Payal, half-god baby to the list.*

Not knowing what else to say, I went for cheery. Not the best call of my life. "Wow! Congratulations," I said. "Does Guy know?"

"Uh-uh," she replied.

Wow again. This was turning out to be one giant cluster.

"You need to rest." I turned to one of the two Uchben standing with us. "Take her to her room." I glanced at Tommaso. "And take him down to the hospital."

The soldiers nodded. Then, from the corner of my eye, I saw a large blond man approaching us. He was covered in dirt and dressed in black. "Viktor!"

He looked like he'd been through the vampire-Maaskab ringer. "Oh my God!"

Then I noticed he held a woman in his arms. The hole in my heart filled up.

It was her.

"You brought her back," I whispered, not believing my eyes.

The smile on his face said it all.

"Mom." I stroked her cheek. "It's me." Her heavy lids parted. "Is she okay? What did they do to her?" I asked Viktor.

With deep regret, he replied, "They tortured her."

Simultaneously, my blood boiled and my heart sank. They had tortured her. My mother. What kind of sick, sick beings would torture someone so sweet and kind? For what purpose? She had nothing to give them, no information to share. The only explanation was that they did it for their enjoyment.

I would kill every fucking last one of them.

"Penelope? Baby, is it really you?" my mother mumbled.

"Yes, it's me. You're safe now."

I looked into Viktor's cobalt-blue eyes. They were filled with the deepest joy I'd ever seen in a man.

"How can I thank you for saving her?" I asked him.

"Actually, it was Tommaso who saved her life."

I froze. Hadn't Tommaso just said that he rescued a . . . ?

*Nooo.*

I looked at Tommaso, who now stood by my side. Then I looked at my mom still cradled in Viktor's arms. Then at Tommaso. Then at her.

*Nooo.*

# Thirty-Nine

*Eight Days Later. New Year's Eve*

Hell certainly wasn't something delivered in a hand-woven Easter basket, as Cimil liked to say. No. Hell was delivered in the form of helplessness and unanswered questions. Hell was spending every minute of every day wondering when the end would come, obsessed with stopping it but not knowing how.

Why did I say this? The plain and simple truth was that we'd won the battle, but not the war. Cimil continued to hear nothing from the dead, and since people died all the time that meant their souls were still moving on to another plane of existence. She likened it to rats jumping off a sinking ship. So when or how would the world end? She couldn't say.

Still, we weren't giving up. Not now. Not ever. We would focus every resource on finding any remaining Maaskab and crush them. We had a few solid leads, but without Guy and Niccolo leading our military, we were no longer a well-oiled machine. More like a rusty tractor that would get the job done, just not as quickly or efficiently.

So, after eight long days of heartbreaking drama (sprinkled with intermittent joy because we'd rescued my mother—the best Christmas present I'd ever received— and Viktor, her new BFF, who spent every waking moment by her side), I realized we were getting nowhere in our daily summits.

"I am calling for a two-day recess. I need to rest." I stood at the head of the summit table, rubbing little circles over my temples. "My brain is officially mush."

"There is one more topic we must address," said Fate, "before we take our leave."

I was too tired to snap at her for breaking protocol and not flagging the agenda topic when we'd opened the meeting. "What?"

"We must formally recognize the interim leaders of the Uchben and vampires."

"How does that work?" I asked with a long sigh.

"Our laws are clear," Bees stated. "The right hand for each leader is automatically chosen. We need only record the transition of power."

That sounded easy. "Okay, Gabrán and who else?" I said.

Zac stood and shook his head. "No. Helena will now be the leader of the vampires. Emma will rule the Uchben."

*Huh?* "You can't be serious," I said.

"It is law," Bees said, plucking one of her loyal subjects from the lapel of her yellow blazer and popping him back atop her head.

Well, weren't Emma and Helena going to be happy? I

wondered if they even knew about this law. "Doesn't any-one think it's a little strange?"

The gods exchanged glances.

"I rule the House of the Gods," I clarified. "Helena is essentially the vampire queen. Emma the leader of the Uchben?" I was about to add that little tidbit about Emma's grandmother leading the Maaskab, but couldn't bring myself to say the words aloud.

They all mumbled no and shook their heads.

*Okeydokey.* Well, I thought it was weird. Really weird.

"Fine. Let me break the news, though." With their men missing, this wasn't going to be a fun conversation.

# *Forty*

⌒

I closed the meeting and snuck out quickly. I wanted to make my daily rounds—to see my mother, Emma, and Helena—without my loyal and dedicated bodyguard, Zac. After eight days of staring at his annoyingly masculine body, I needed a break. No, he hadn't tried any of his moves, but the tension unmistakably infused with love spewed from every pore of his body. And the way I caught him staring at me when he thought I wasn't paying attention—well, I knew it was only a matter of time before he'd say or do something. I wasn't ready to go there. Not with him. Not with Kinich. Not with anyone. There simply wasn't time for distractions when so much hung in the balance.

*Funny, you sound just like Kinich now.*

*Ugh…Kinich. Where are you?*

I placed my hand on my lower belly and rubbed it in a little circle over my T-shirt. Why did it all still feel like a dream? I certainly didn't feel pregnant except for being tired and passing out a lot, and my body looked the same. In any case, I started taking vitamins right away. Emma had bought some for herself and insisted I take them, too.

I knocked on her bedroom door, hopeful she might have moved from the bed where she'd been the last week, eating junk food and watching reruns of *Lost*.

"What?" she called out.

I popped my head inside.

Nope. There she was, curtains drawn, a large bowl of popcorn on her lap, her large eyes fixed on the television.

"Did you at least take a shower?" I asked.

"I took one yesterday," she said between bites.

I didn't believe it; her short red hair was matted into curly clumps.

I sat down at the edge of the bed. "I have some news for you."

"Oh yeah?" She continued chewing like a cow enjoying its cud.

"Emma, this is important."

"Yeah?" Her eyes remained locked on the TV.

"Emma. We need to talk."

Chomp, chomp, chomp. "So talk."

But she wasn't listening. She was wallowing. I marched over to the TV and shut it off.

"Hey!" she protested. "I was watching that. Put it back on."

"We need to talk." I walked over to the window and pulled open the curtains.

Her eyes narrowed into little slits. "Get out."

"No. You said we were sisters. So as your sister, I'm not going to let you self-destruct—"

"I'm not self-destructing!" she screamed. "I'm mourning!" She pounded her fists into the bed.

"Dammit, Emma. Guy isn't dead. We will find him."

"No! You don't get it." The tears poured from her red, swollen eyes.

I walked over to her nightstand and handed her a box of tissues. "Then try explaining."

She sopped up her tears and threw the balled-up tissues into a large pile on the floor next to an even larger pile of dirty clothes. "Even if we free him, it's over. Over. He lied to me. He betrayed me."

I lowered myself next to her. "He couldn't help himself, Emma. You know that. He loves you. He loves you so much that it makes everyone around you feel sick with jealousy. Even me. I'd do anything to have a man want me that way. It...it's like no one in the world exists, except you."

She shook her head. "It doesn't matter. He made a choice, one that resulted in his killing my grandmother."

"We're not sure about that, Emma," I argued. "Tommaso just said Guy was fighting her." Then I recalled what Guy had said about his standard policy of killing Maaskab. Would he have really spared Emma's grandmother's life? Not likely.

"I'll never be able to trust him again," Emma whispered. "And without that, I can't be with him. I'll always be wondering and questioning his motives. His role, being a god, will always come first. I get it now."

She was right. Ironic really, because it was the exact same point Kinich had made. It was the reason my heart now sat inside my chest, begrudgingly beating, shattered in a million tiny pieces. How could the universe be so damn cruel? I'd never asked to love Kinich. It happened. And it wasn't a crush or infatuation. It was the kind of connection that makes your soul ache, that makes you crazy inside your head because from the moment you meet, you realize how alone you were all along but never knew. Because suddenly, there's this other being out there you can't live without. You can't breathe or eat or think of anything but him, of being in his arms and hearing his voice.

So what was the point? Did the universe want to teach me how to feel hollow? Or what it was like to have my heart decimated? I simply didn't know. I just...didn't. Sadly, I no longer cared. Whatever I had with Kinich disappeared the moment he'd left me to deal with this mess all alone. My heart was in a place so dark, broken, and sad that no sunlight would ever touch it again. And it didn't goddamn matter. Not one little bit. Because the world would end, along with everyone in it, if I didn't find a way to suck it up.

I patted Emma's hand. "I understand. I do. But right now, we have bigger things to worry about." I glanced at her stomach.

"I know." She sniffled and grabbed another tissue. "I can't stop thinking about it. I wanted a baby so badly, and now I'm faced with losing him before he's ever born. It's really effed up."

"It's a him?"

She nodded. "I can feel him. It's like I'm linked to the baby through my bond with Guy."

Amazing.

"Well, *he* needs us to keep going," I said quietly. "We can't let it all end. We have a lot, and I mean a lot, of people depending on us," I pointed out.

"I don't know how you do it, Penelope," she said. "How can you keep going after everything?"

Oh, boy. Here goes. "That's why I came to see you. I'm going to have help. You."

She pointed her finger at herself. "Me?"

I explained the law and the outcome of the summit. Stunned, she stared at me in silence.

I knew exactly how she felt. But who better to save the world than us? We had everything to lose.

"So what's your move?" I asked, using her line.

She frowned in silence for several moments. "I guess there's only one option: fight."

I felt a huge weight lift, knowing Emma would be at my side. "Great. We reconvene in two days."

I hugged her and then wrinkled my nose. "Can you take a shower before the meeting? You smell kind of funky."

She laughed a little as I stood to leave.

"Penelope? Is it true? About your mom?"

Good frigging question. It had been gnawing at me these past eight days, but my efforts to get the gods to talk came up empty-handed. They flat out refused to speak. That meant I'd have to get the truth from my mother, but she'd been in a vegetative state for the last eight days. I was beginning to worry she wouldn't make it, a thought I didn't dare say out loud.

"I kind of hope so," I replied. "Then maybe she could call in a few favors for us." We were going to need all the help we could get.

"Well," she said, "if she's not, maybe we can call in the naked leprechauns."

My next stop was the Uchben hospital, where I received my usual debriefing from the doctors and made my rounds to check on the women, the Payals, who were now up and about, ready for release.

What would we do with them? That was pickle number one. The women collectively suffered from amnesia. Maybe it was for the best because heaven only knew what the Maaskab had done to these poor souls. Surely they had loved ones looking for them or who believed they were dead. Discovering their identities was a must, and we'd work around the clock until we did that.

That brought us to pickle number two. We hadn't killed off all the Maaskab and believed they had sects around the globe. The women wouldn't be safe until we'd exterminated every last Scab.

Total effing pickle.

*One pickle at a time, Pen. One pickle at a time.*

I sighed and pasted on a bright smile. Viktor's distinctive voice, deep with an unrecognizable accent, was rambling away when I entered my mother's hospital room.

My pasted smiled became a real one. She was awake and sitting up in bed. "Mom? Oh my God! Look at you," I said.

Her long, golden hair was elaborately braided and her hazel eyes were bright and lively.

"Penelope! Baby!" She held out her arms for a hug. I rushed to her side and gripped her tightly. It felt so good to hold her, to see her awake again, that I wanted to cry. I decided not to ruin the moment with any blubbering.

"You look fantastic," I said.

"I feel exceptionally great. Must be the company." She glanced at Viktor, who sat in his usual place next to the bed.

He also looked different. Maybe because he wore a cream-colored turtleneck, brown suede boots, and soft, faded jeans instead of his customary black getup.

*Wow. He cleans up nicely.* I'd never really gotten a good look at the man before, but with his high cheekbones and strong chin, he reminded me of that actor who'd played Thor—Chris something-or-other. In fact, Viktor could've been his very large older brother. Pretty dang gorgeous. But what was going on with that hair?

"Matching braids?" I asked.

Viktor, a well-built man I often heard others refer to as the Viking tank (because he really used to be a Viking), squirmed in his chair. "I—uh...wanted to show her the traditional braid from my village."

Viktor braided her hair?

"I didn't know they had metro Viking vampires." Of course, I didn't know there were gods, vampire gods, offspring of gods, evil priests, and leprechauns, either. Oh. And add angels.

"Penelope, how rude," my mother said.

Viktor chuckled and looked at my mother. "She is correct, Julie. I am metro and proud. I much prefer fashion and fine fabrics to weapons and killing. It gets old after a thousand years. My new favorite pastime is shopping. I will take you next week now that you are completely healed. We can stay at my Italian villa near—"

"Whoa! Whoa! You're healed? And you two are planning a vacation together? You're going to leave? What's going on?"

My mother looked at Viktor. "Can we have a minute alone? I need to talk to my daughter."

He bowed his head and stood. "I won't be far if you

need me." I could tell he was about to sift, but then he realized he couldn't. "Damn, this is annoying," he grumbled as he walked from the room.

"This is going to take a lot of explaining, so why don't you sit, honey." She pointed to Viktor's chair.

"You mean the Viktor part, the healing part, or the angel part?" I asked and took the seat.

Her face froze. "All three."

Hell. I really wasn't ready for this. "So it's true? You're not human?"

She wrung her hands and then placed them neatly in her lap. "I am human. I mean, I was. But I wasn't always."

Oh, great. It was going to be another of *those* stories. The ones that left my head feeling like I'd taken it for a spin on a lazy Susan.

"Go on."

"First, I must tell you it is forbidden to talk about my past life or where I came from." Her eyes flashed toward the ceiling. "*They* will punish me if I do. So you must be careful, Penelope. You must keep what you already know a secret."

*Oh, great! More crap to worry about. Just put it right on top of this other giant pile over here.* Dammit! I couldn't believe there was a gag order on her. I had so many questions.

*Find the silver lining, Pen. Your mother is alive and healed.*

"My lips are sealed," I said.

My mother smiled and began telling me how twenty-six years ago while she was "on duty," she'd met a man and fallen in love. At first, she tried convincing herself that her feelings weren't real, but the more she resisted, the stronger her feelings became.

"I had to choose. Him or my job; they don't allow both."

"You chose him obviously."

"Yes," she replied. "And we were very happy, Penelope. Your father was…magnificent. His laughter, his thirst for life, he made me feel so alive."

"Then why did he leave?" I wondered.

Her eyes dropped. "He died the day I found out I was pregnant."

I wanted to gasp, but there were no gasps left inside my body. All gasped out. "Why didn't you tell me?"

"I didn't want your life to be marked with such a tragedy. He was murdered, killed by a very evil man who hunts people like me."

This was where the story got weirder. To protect me, my mother ran. And she kept running for the next ten years, finally settling us in New York. "I thought we were safe. Or maybe he'd forgotten about me, but I was wrong. One year ago, he found us."

"What did he want?"

"What he always wanted: my blood. He believes it has powers, ones he can use to create an unstoppable army. I explained again and again that I was completely human, but he spent the next year drinking from me, anyway. I think he enjoyed making me suffer."

I was horrified. "A vampire?"

"Yes. The most evil vampire of them all."

Holy crap. The entire time I thought she'd been sick, when really, some psycho vampire made her his personal blood bank. And to boot, it had been the vampire who killed my father. She must have gone through hell. "I'm so sorry, Mom."

"He said if I didn't give him what he wanted, if I tried to run, he'd come after you. I had no idea what to do until the goddess Cimil came to me with her plan to get you somewhere safe with her brother and make it look like I'd gone to a clinic so you wouldn't worry."

Okay. Now that was just messed up. "Mom, *you* made a deal with Cimil? *You?*"

She reached for my hand. "I'm so sorry for deceiving you. Cimil said it had to be this way. Of course, everything went wrong. Probably because she's batshit crazy."

"You have no idea," I responded.

"I'm so sorry, honey. Sorry for all the lies. The truth wasn't an option. Can you ever forgive me?" Guilt filled her big hazel eyes. I wanted to be angry, but somehow couldn't. Not when I knew she'd done what she thought was best for me and acted out of love.

"Kinich left me and I'm pregnant—thanks to Cimil, by the way," I bitterly confessed.

"I know. Viktor told me everything. Have faith, honey. Have faith that everything will work out as it should."

I wasn't ready to do that.

"Let's not talk about it now," I suddenly blurted out. "I want my year to end on a happy note. Who is this bastard that's hunting you?" Revenge qualified for happy, didn't it? Sure felt like it. I was definitely going to look him up, because now...*now* I knew "people." Oh yeah, a lot of really fucking deadly people.

"Philippe. He is what they call an Ancient One. That's not important, though. If he finds me again, he won't touch me. I've made sure of it."

Of course. She had one of the toughest vampires roaming the planet, obsessed with saving her, and now he was apparently her personal guard dog. "Viktor, he told Kinich that he dreamed about saving you for five hundred years. Do you know why?"

She nodded. "He believes he was destined to love me. That I am his soul mate."

"So he loves you?"

"Yes," she replied. "Very much."

"And you? Do you love him back?" *How very strange it would be if Viktor became my stepdad.*

She ran her fragile, pale finger over her heart-shaped lips, giving the question some thought. "I can't remember what happened when we were imprisoned, but I know I love him, too."

*Well, there you go. Munsters, watch out! We've got a vampire dad, fallen-angel mom, and pregnant sun goddess daughter.* We were just missing someone with fur and perhaps a reanimated human or two to complete our cast of zany characters.

But in all seriousness, after everything that happened, this was the one part that made me happy. She'd found love.

She sighed. "Philippe will never bite me again."

"No. I'm sure Viktor would never allow it."

"Likely not," she said. "Even so, Viktor turned me last night. Philippe won't want to drink me, anyway."

*Wha-wha-what!?* "Vampire? You're a vampire?"

"Surprise?" she said with an awkward smile.

"Okeydokey."

*Add fallen angel turned vampire to the species list.*

# Forty-One

After a very long drive to clear my head, I pulled Kinich's Jeep into the garage, trying to make as little noise as possible.

I looked at my watch.

*Eleven forty-five. Almost midnight.*

I'd successfully avoided Zac the entire evening and wanted to keep it that way. I'd had just about enough drama for the day and was seriously looking forward to celebrating New Year's by calling Anne and Jess, who were likely about to pass out. Not only were they two hours ahead, but they generally started celebrating New Year's in November.

Heading for my room, I tiptoed through the living room.

The front door abruptly flew open and in sauntered a tall man dressed in a tailored black suit, his jet-black hair pulled into a ponytail. His black eyes resembled voids of light against his pale skin.

*Oh, gods. Please. No more! No more drama for today!*

I immediately readied to pummel him with a nice ball of fire when I noticed he held an unconscious man, wrapped in a cloak, in his arms.

"Who the hell are you?" I spoke with a sigh. More drama wasn't what I wanted, but I knew a heaping helping was coming my way.

Cimil, wearing pink pj's with yellow duckies, appeared at my side, glaring with an unspoken fury. "That piece of shit is Narmer."

The sinister man smiled, displaying two sharp incisors. "Oh, now, do not forget, my dear Cimil, you made me change my name to Roberto. Right after you had me tattoo your portrait on my back and move into your Spanish abode to be your love slave."

"I was going through a phase! You can't hold that against me!"

His eyes narrowed. "I vowed to return the favor, to repay you for the humiliation I endured, my sweet, darling Cimil." He strolled to the center of the room, where we stood, behaving like he owned the place.

"That video is awesome!" she exclaimed. "It's a triple-X classic! You're just mad because I stole the show with my hot-pink chicken suit!"

"Ha! Don't you wish!" He chuckled with sadistic arrogance.

Cimil scowled. "Whatever! What the hell do you want?"

He blew her a kiss. "I told you, Cimil: revenge. Eye for an eye. Tat for a tat."

"Roberto, I wasn't aware that you'd made taking hallucinogens into a competitive sport. How very unvampy of you."

He made a little pout with his lower lip. "Very well, if you do not wish to play, then I will let your brother die."

*Brother? Die?*

Roberto tossed the man to the floor like a lifeless sack of potatoes.

My eyes filled with horror as I realized who it was. "Kinich! Oh my God!"

I scrambled to the immobile bundle and rolled it over. Kinich was pale and emaciated. I put my ear to his mouth. "He's not breathing!"

Emma appeared in the room and rushed to my side. "What the fuck does *he* want?" she screamed at Cimil.

Apparently everyone knew Roberto—*uhhh, Narmer*—but me.

"You dirty son of a vampire bitch!" Cimil barked.

Roberto tsked. "Language, my dear. Language. There are children present." His gaze flickered toward me and then Emma.

"Language?" Cimil cackled. "I've got language—"

Roberto raised his palm to silence her. "Cease with the posturing, my little dove. The clock is ticking. So what will it be?"

She growled, looked down at Kinich and then back at Narmer.

"I'll get you for this. And if I don't, my clowns will. And if not them, then my unicorn."

He laughed. "Oh, my little turnip, how I love you so. I would expect nothing less."

"Quit your yapping and save my brother," she ordered.

He dipped his head. "Very well."

I wanted to kick that smug smile right off his pasty face.

He floated over and motioned for me to move.

Protectively, I hovered over Kinich's body. "What's he going to do?" I looked at Cimil.

"He's going to make Kinich a vampire," Cimil explained all too casually for my taste.

"*What? No! I won't let you touch him!*" I didn't want Kinich to die—gods, no. The one and only thing he'd ever wanted was to be mortal. And after seventy thousand years, he finally had it.

Roberto made a theatrical bow. "As you wish. But it is Kinich who came to me and struck the bargain."

"Bargain?" I asked.

"Yes, he and I have been in negotiations for over a month. I was to kill my brother Philippe and he would deliver Cimil. Kinich came to me last week to finalize the deal. He offered his new mortal life as insurance."

My mind scrambled. "Kinich had you kill your own brother? He let you do this to him? Why?"

Cimil gazed upon Kinich's limp body with affection. "Very clever, my dear brother. We shall engrave your portrait in the summit room, right next to Kathy Griffin."

"I'm not following," I said.

"Philippe, who we'd been hunting for eons, was the maker of the Obscuros," Cimil explained. "Roberto killed him, thereby snuffing out his bloodline, including any Maaskab who'd been turned."

Philippe? *The Philippe? My mother's tormentor was the maker of the Obscuros?* Son of a bitch was lucky to be dead because what I wanted to do was much, much worse.

*And Kinich gave his life to have him killed, to have all of the Obscuros killed.*

*Holy crap.* The sad irony started to sink in.

Why hadn't Kinich told anyone? Why keep it a secret? *Because . . .* you *would have stopped him.*

Christ! I would have. Since he had no powers, there would have been nothing he could do to fight me, either. But if he had stayed, we would have lost the battle. We would have lost everything. My mother included.

Now, more than ever, I felt low and unworthy of any affection Kinich held for me. Because he *had* put me first. He'd put us all first. I had just been too blinded by my own selfish desires to see it. I should have trusted him.

I moved out of the way. "Do it. Turn him."

Roberto leaned over Kinich and made a small gash across his wrist before placing the dripping wound to Kinich's mouth.

"There. It is done," he said.

I saw no movement. "Are you sure?"

"He will awaken tomorrow evening. Have some blood handy; he will be hungry." Roberto strolled casually over to Cimil and took her by the hand. "Come now. I wish to claim my prize immediately."

"Really, Roberto. You're such a horndog. Can't we do this later?"

"Wait!" Emma said. "Did *you* lock the portals?"

With a sinister smile, Roberto replied, "What will you give me if I answer your question?"

Cimil slapped his cheek. "Oh, quit it! You've won. I'm marrying you, isn't that enough?"

"Babies, too?" he asked.

*Oh, hell no! If there is any justice in this universe, Cimil will not be allowed to spawn. Especially with this evil bastard.*

"Whatever. Just leave the girl alone." Cimil looked

directly at me and winked. "Remember, it ain't over until the cruise ship returns to port and you hear the theme song."

*Andddd...thank you for those awesome words of wisdom, Cimil.*

"Let's go, leech." She took Roberto's hand and disappeared out the front door.

I dropped to my knees and placed my ear to Kinich's chest. There was no heartbeat, no breath, nothing. I looked up at Emma. "Now what?"

"Get some blood and pray."

## TO BE CONTINUED...

# A Very Important Public Service Announcement from Guy, God of Death and War

Humans,

I must inform you of some very troubling news: the apocalypse is indeed coming. While most of the gods were off doing our part for humanity, my sister Cimil, true to her useless and reproachable nature, decided that now—yes, now!—would be an excellent time to catch up on her favorite syndicated sitcom from the early '80s.

As a result, she neglected her duties—monitoring the future—thereby giving the Maaskab the opportunity to execute the next steps of their sinister plan. This plan included taking me and Niccolo as their prisoners.

I write you from a very dark and lonely place, hoping that my message may find its way to you. Please tell Emma I am sorry for betraying her. What

I did to her grandmother was unforgivable. I am now paying the price.

May the universe take pity on my soul.

GUY
*(aka Votan, God of Death and War)*

# Rebuttal from Cimil, Goddess Delight of the Underworld

Dearest People-Pets,

Please disregard my brother's whiny theatrics. Yes, it is true that I neglected my duties, and because of this, we are all going to cease to exist. But I ask you, what is the purpose of living if one cannot drop everything on a whim to enjoy the fruits of the late '70s and early '80s? Bad perms, Chia Pets, leg warmers, Duran Duran. And surely you must understand the importance of disco dancing and tacky sitcoms with men named Isaac bearing pearly-white smiles? Ah yes, *Love Boat.* Is there anything sweeter than something unexpected and new?

Anyhooo, I wouldn't hit the panic button yet. Suuure, the Maaskab are going to kick our asses, but these things have a way of working themselves out.

Maybe.

Okay . . . maybe not.

All right! All right. We're completely hosed. Go live your final days doing the things you've only dreamed of: kick the neighbor's cat (the one that wakes you at 2:00 a.m.), write a romance novel (make it a funny one, though), buy that really great pair of leather pants you've always wanted, or eat that entire box of Twinkies. Oh yes, live the dream! The clock is ticking.

Tootles,
*Cimil, Recently Retired Goddess Delight of the Underworld*

P.S. Sorry about causing the end of the world, but Roberto is ensuring I pay for my crimes.

# Note from Mimi J.

Hi, Everyone!

If you liked this story, don't forget to click those happy stars on the retailer's website, write a little review, or send me a note (contact info is in my bio). And if you have helpful critiques (and no..."Mimi, you suckity suck for writing another cliff-hanger" is not a helpful critique, LOL), don't hesitate to share. I'd love to hear from you, even if it's just to chat about our favorite paranormal hunky dudes or e-readers as we often do on my Facebook page.

Hugs,
*Mimi*

P.S. Hey, Mean People! You STILL suck. Yes, you know you do.

Dr. Antonio Acero is a world-renowned physicist whose life takes a turn for the worst—and the bizarre. In southern Mexico, he finds an ancient Mayan tablet that is said to have magical properties. But when he puts the tablet to use, he discovers that Fate has other plans. And her name is Ixtab.

Please turn this page
for an excerpt from

# *Vampires Need Not … Apply?*

# *Prologue*

⌐

*New Year's Day. Near Sedona, Arizona. Estate of Kinich Ahau, ex–God of the Sun*

Teetering on the very edge of a long white sofa, Penelope stared up at the oversized, round clock mounted on the wall. In ten minutes, the sun would set and the man they once knew as the God of the Sun would awake. Changed. She hoped.

Sadly, there'd been a hell of a lot of hoping lately and little good it did her or her two friends, Emma and Helena, sitting patiently at her side. Like Penelope, the other two women had been thrust into this new world—filled with gods, vampires, and other immortal combinations in between—by means of the men they'd fallen in love with.

Bottom line? Not going so great.

Helena, the blonde who held two bags of blood in her

lap, reached for Penelope and smoothed down her frizzy hair. "Don't worry. Kinich will wake up. He will."

Pen nodded. She must look like a mess. Why hadn't she taken the time to at least run a brush through her hair for him? He loved her dark hair. Maybe because she didn't truly believe he'd come back to life. "I don't know what's worse, thinking I've lost him forever or knowing if he wakes up, he'll be something he hates."

Emma chimed in, "He doesn't hate vampires. He hates being immortal."

Pen shrugged. "Guess it really doesn't matter now what he hates." Kinich would either wake up or he wouldn't. If he didn't, she might not have the will to go on without him. Too much had happened. She needed him. She loved him. And most of all, she wanted him to know she was sorry for ever doubting him. He'd given his life to save them all.

Tick.

Another move of the hand.

Tock.

And another.

Nine more minutes.

The doorbell jolted the three women.

"Dammit." Emma, who wore her combat-ready outfit—black cargos and a black tee that made her red hair look like the flame on the tip of a match—marched to the door. "I told everyone not to disturb us."

Penelope knew that would never happen. A few hundred soldiers lurked outside and a handful of deities waited in the kitchen, snacking on cookies; new vampires weren't known to be friendly. But Penelope insisted on having only her closest friends by her side for the moment of truth. Besides, Helena was a new vampire herself—a long story—and knew what to do.

Emma unlocked the dead bolt. "Some idiot probably forgot my orders. I'll send him away—" The door flew open with a cold gust of desert wind and debris. It took a moment for the three women to register who stood in the doorway.

The creature, with long, matted dreads beaded with human teeth, wore nothing more than a loincloth over her soot-covered body.

*Christ almighty, it can't be*, thought Pen, as the smell of Maaskab—good old-fashioned, supernatural, pre-Hispanic death and darkness—entered her nose.

Before Emma could drop a single f-bomb, the dark priestess raised her hand and blew Emma across the large, open living room, slamming her against the wall.

Helena screamed and rushed to Emma's side.

Paralyzed with fear, Penelope watched helplessly as the Maaskab woman glided into the living room and stood before her, a mere two yards away.

The woman raised her gaunt, grimy finger, complete with overgrown grime-caked fingernail, and pointed directly at Penelope. "Youuuu."

*Holy wheat toast*. Penelope instinctively stepped back. The woman's voice felt like razor blades inside her ears. Penelope had to think fast. Not only did she fear for her life and for those of her friends, but both she and Emma were pregnant. Helena had a baby daughter. *Think, dammit. Think.*

Penelope considered drawing the power of the sun, an ability she'd recently gained when she had become the interim Sun God—another long story—but releasing that much heat into the room might fry everyone in it.

*Grab the monster's arm. Channel it directly into her.*

"Youuuu," the Maaskab woman said once again.

"Damn, lady." Penelope covered her ears. "Did you swallow a bucket of rusty nails? That voice...gaaaahh."

The monster grunted. "I come with a message."

"For me?" Penelope took a step forward.

The woman nodded, and her eyes, pits of blackness framed with cherry red, clawed at Penelope's very soul. "It is for you I bring...the message."

*Jeez. I get it. You have a message.* Penelope took another cautious step toward the treacherous woman. "So what are you waiting for?"

"Pen, get away from her," she heard Emma grumble from behind.

*Not on your life.* Pen moved another inch. "I'm waiting, old woman. Wow me."

The Maaskab growled.

Another step.

"Don't hurt my grandmother," Emma pleaded.

*Grandma?* Oh, for Pete's sake. *This* was Emma's grandmother? The one who'd been taken by the Maaskab and turned into their evil leader? They all thought she'd been killed.

*Fabulous. Granny's back.*

For a fraction of a moment, the woman glanced over Pen's shoulder at Emma.

Another step.

Penelope couldn't let Emma's feelings cloud the situation. Granny was dangerous. Granny was evil. Granny was going down.

"We wish"—the old Maaskab woman ground out her words—"to make an exchange."

Penelope froze. "An exchange?"

The woman nodded slowly. "You will free our king, and we will return your prisoners."

*Shit. Free Chaam?* The most evil deity ever known? He'd murdered hundreds, perhaps thousands of women, many his own daughters. His sole purpose in life was to destroy every last living creature, except for the Maaskab and his love slaves.

No. They could never let that bastard out.

*But what about the prisoners?* She debated with herself. In the last battle, the Maaskab had trapped forty of their most loyal vampire soldiers, the God of Death and War, aka Emma's fiancé, and the General of the Vampire Army, aka Helena's husband.

*Dammit. Dammit. Crispy-fried dammit!* Penelope had to at least consider Granny's proposal. "Why in the world would we agree to let Chaam go?"

"A bunch of pathetic...little...girls...cannot triumph against us," the Maaskab woman hissed. "*You* need the vampires and your precious God of Death and War."

Penelope's brain ran a multitude of scenarios, trying to guess the angle. Apparently, the Maaskab needed Chaam back. But they were willing to give up Niccolo and Guy? Both were powerful warriors, perfectly equipped to kick the Maaskab's asses for good.

No. Something wasn't quite right. "Tell me why you want Chaam," Penelope said.

Another step.

"Because"—Granny flashed an odious grin—"the victory of defeating you will be meaningless without our beloved king to see it. All we do, we do for him."

*Ew. Okay.*

"You, on the other hand..." She lowered her gravelly voice one octave. "...Do not have a chance without your men. We offer a fair fight in exchange for our king's freedom."

Okay. She could be lying. Perhaps not. Anyone with a brain could see they were three inexperienced young women—yes, filled with passion and purpose and a love of shoes and all things shopping, in the case of Helena and Emma—but they didn't know the first thing about fighting wars. Especially ones that might end in a big hairy apocalypse prophesied to be just eight months away.

Sure, they had powerful, slightly insane, dysfunctional deities and battalions of beefy vampires and human soldiers on their side. However, that was like giving a tank to a kindergartner. Sort of funny in a Sunday comics *Beetle Bailey* kinda way, but not in real life.

"Don't agree to it," Helena pleaded from the flank. "We'll find another way to free them."

"She's right, Pen," Emma whimpered, clearly in pain.

Penelope took another step. They were right; they'd have to find some other way to get the prisoners back. Chaam was too dang dangerous. "And if we refuse?"

The Maaskab woman laughed into the air above, her teeth solid black and the inside of her mouth bright red.

*Yum. Nothing like gargling with blood to really freshen your breath.*

"Then," Granny said, "we shall kill both men—yes, even your precious Votan; we have the means—and the end of days will begin. It is what Chaam would have wanted."

Granny had conveniently left out the part about killing her and her friends before she departed this room. Why else would the evil Maaskab woman have come in person when an evil note would have done the evil job? Or how about an evil text?

No. Emma's grandmother would kill them if the offer was rejected. She knew it in her gut.

Penelope didn't blink. *No fear. No fear.* The powerful light tingled on the tips of her fingers. She was ready.

"Then you leave us no choice. We agree." Penelope held out her hand. "Shake on it."

The Maaskab woman glanced down at Pen's hand. Pen lunged, grabbed the woman's soot-covered forearm, and opened the floodgates of heat. Evil Granny dropped to her knees, screaming like a witch drowning in a hot, bubbling cauldron.

"No! No!" Emma screamed. "Don't kill her! Don't, Pen!"

*Crackers!* Penelope released the woman who fell face forward onto the cold Saltillo tile. Steam rose from her naked back and dreadlock-covered skull.

"Grandma? Oh, God, no. Please don't be dead." Emma dropped to her knees beside the eau-de-charred roadkill. "She's still breathing."

The room suddenly filled with Penelope's private guards. They looked like they'd been chewed up and spit out by a large Maaskab blender—tattered, dirty clothes and bloody faces.

That explained what had taken so long; they must've been outside fighting more Maaskab.

The men pointed their rifles at Emma's unconscious grandmother. Zac, God of Who the Hell Knew and Penelope's right hand since she'd been appointed the interim leader of the gods—yes, yes, another long story—blazed into the room, barking orders. "Someone get the Maaskab chained up."

Zac, dressed in his usual black leather pants and tee combo that matched his raven-black hair, turned to Penelope and gazed down at her with his nearly translucent, aquamarine eyes. "Are you all right?"

Penelope nodded. It was the first time in days she'd felt glad to see him. He'd been suffocating her ever since Kinich—

"Oh, gods!" They'd completely forgotten about Kinich! Her eyes flashed up at the clock.

Tick.

Sundown.

A gut-wrenching howl exploded from the other room. Everyone stiffened.

"He's alive!" Pen turned to rush off but felt a hard pull on her arm.

"No. You've had enough danger for one day. I will go." Zac wasn't asking.

Penelope jerked her arm away. "He won't hurt me. I'll be fine. Just stay here and help Emma with her grandmother." She snatched up the two bags of blood from the floor where Helena had dropped them.

"Penelope, I will not tell you again." Zac's eyes filled with anger. Though he was her right hand, he was still a deity and not used to being disobeyed.

"Enough." Penelope held up her finger. "I don't answer to you."

Zac's jealous eyes narrowed for a brief moment before he stiffly dipped his head and then quietly watched her disappear through the doorway.

She rushed down the hallway and paused outside the

bedroom with her palms flat against the hand-carved double doors. The screams had not stopped.

Thank the gods that Kinich, the ex–God of the Sun, was alive. Now they would have a chance to put their lives back together, to undo what never should have been—such as putting her in charge of his brothers and sisters—and she would finally get the chance to tell him how much she loved him, how grateful she was that he'd sacrificed everything to save them, about their baby.

This was their second chance.

She only needed to get him through these first days as a vampire. *And orchestrate a rescue mission for the God of Death and War and the General of the Vampire Army. And deal with the return of Emma's evil granny. And figure out how to stop an impending apocalypse set to occur in eight—yes, eight!—months. And deal with a few hundred women with amnesia they'd rescued from the Maaskab. And manage a herd of insane egocentric, accident-prone deities, with ADHD. And carry a baby. And don't forget squeezing in some time at the gym. Your thighs are getting flabby!*

"See? This Kinich vampire thing should be easy," she assured herself.

She pushed open the door to find Kinich shirtless, writhing on the bed. His muscular legs and arms strained against the silver chains attached to the deity-reinforced frame. He was a large, beautiful man, almost seven feet in height, with shoulders that spanned a distance equal to two widths of her body.

"Kinich!" She rushed to his side. "Are you okay?" She attempted to brush his gold-streaked locks from his face, but he flailed and twisted in agony.

"It burns!" he wailed. "The metal burns."

"I know, honey. I know. But Helena says you need to drink before we can let you go. Full tummy. Happy vamp—"

"Aaahh! Remove them. They burn. Please," he begged.

*Oh, saints.*

He would never hurt her. Would he? Of course not.

"Try to hold still." She went to the dresser, pulled open the top drawer, and grabbed the keys.

She rushed to his ankle and undid one leg, then the other.

Kinich stopped moving. He lay there, eyes closed, breathing.

Without hesitation she undid his right arm and then ran to the other side to release the final cuff.

"Are you okay? Kinich?"

Without opening his eyes, he said, "I can smell and hear everything."

Helena had said that blocking out the noise was one of the hardest things a new vampire had to learn. That and curbing their hunger for innocent humans who, she was told, tasted the yummiest. Helena also mentioned to always make sure he was well fed. Full tummy, happy vampire. Just like a normal guy except for the blood obviously.

Penelope deposited herself on the bed next to Kinich with a bag of blood in her hands. "You'll get used to it. I promise. In the meantime, let's get you fed. I have so much to—"

Kinich threw her down, and she landed on her back with a hard thump and the air whooshed from her lungs.

Straddling her, Kinich pinned her wrists to the floor.

His turquoise eyes shifted to hungry black, and fangs protruded from his mouth. "You smell delicious. Like sweet sunshine."

*Such a beautiful face*, she thought, mesmerized by Kinich's eyes. Once upon a time his skin had glowed golden almost, a vision of elegant masculinity with full lips and sharp cheekbones. But now, now he was refined with an exotic, dangerous male beauty too exquisite for words.

Ex-deity turned mortal, turned vampire. *Hypnotic. He is…hypnotic.*

He lowered his head toward her neck, and her will suddenly snapped back into place. "No! Kinich, no!" She squirmed under his grasp. Without her hands free, she couldn't defend herself. "I'm pregnant."

He stilled and peered into her eyes.

Pain. So much pain. That was all she saw.

"A baby?" he asked.

She nodded cautiously.

Then something cold and deadly flickered in his eyes. His head plunged for her neck, and she braced for the pain of having her neck ripped out.

"Penelope!" Zac sacked Kinich, knocking him to the floor. "Go!" he commanded.

Penelope rolled onto her hands and knees and crawled from the room as it was overrun with several more of Kinich's brethren: the perpetually drunk Acan; the Goddess of the Hunt they called Camaxtli; and the Mistress of Bees they called—oh, who the hell could remember her weird Mayan name?

"Penelope! Penelope!" she heard Kinich scream. "I want to drink her! I must drink her!"

Penelope curled into a ball on the floor in the hallway, unable to stop herself from crying. *This isn't how it's supposed to be. This isn't how it's supposed to be.*

Helena appeared at her side. "Oh, Pen. I'm so sorry. I promise he'll be okay after a few days. He just needs to eat." She helped Penelope sit up. "Let's move you somewhere safe."

Penelope wiped away the streaks of tears from her cheeks and took her friend's hand to stand.

The grunts and screams continued in the other room.

"I can't believe he attacked me, even after I told him." Tears continued to trickle from Penelope's eyes. Why hadn't he stopped? Didn't he love her?

"In his defense, you really do smell yummy. Kind of like Tang."

"Not funny," Penelope responded.

"Sorry." Helena braced Penelope with an arm around her waist and guided her to a bedroom in the other wing of the house.

Helena deposited Penelope on the large bed and turned toward the bathroom. "I'll get you a warm washcloth."

Ironically, Penelope's mind dove straight for a safe haven—that meant away from Kinich and toward her job, which generally provided many meaty distractions, such as impending doom and/or anything having to do with Cimil, the ex–Goddess of the Underworld.

"Wait." Penelope looked up at Helena, who'd become her steady rock of reason these last few weeks. "What happens next?"

Helena paused for a moment. "Like I told you, Kinich needs time to adjust."

Penelope shook her head. "No. I mean, you heard

Emma's grandmother; without Niccolo and Guy, we can't defeat the Maaskab. We have to free our men."

"Well—"

"I know what you're going to say," Pen interrupted. "We can't release Chaam, but—"

"Actually," Helena broke in. "I've been meaning to tell you something."

"What?"

"We've been looking for another way to free them, and I think we found it."

"Found what?" Penelope asked.

"A tablet."

# Glossary

*Black Jade:* Found only in a particular mine located in southern Mexico, this jade has very special supernatural properties, including the ability to absorb supernatural energy—in particular, god energy. When worn by humans, it is possible for them to have physical contact with a god. If injected, it can make a person addicted to doing bad things. If the jade is fueled with dark energy and then released, it can be used as a weapon. Chaam personally likes using it to polish his teeth.

*Book of the Oracle of Delphi:* This mystical text from 1400 BC is said to have been created by one of the great oracles at Delphi and can tell the future. As the events in present time change the future, the book's pages magically rewrite themselves. The Demilords use this book in Book #2 to figure out when and how to kill the vampire queen. Helena also reads it, while being held captive, and learns she must sacrifice her mortality to save Niccolo.

*Cenote:* Limestone sinkholes connected to a subterranean water system. They are found in Central America and southern Mexico and were once believed by the Mayans to be sacred portals to the afterlife. Such smart humans! They were right. Except cenotes are actually portals to the realm of the gods.

(If you have never seen a cenote, do a quick search on the Internet for "cenote photos," and you'll see how freaking cool they are!)

*Demilords:* (Spoiler alert for Book #2!) This is a group of immortal badass vampires who've been infused with the light of the gods. They are extremely difficult to kill and hate their jobs (killing Obscuros) almost as much as they hate the gods who control them.

*Maaskab:* Originally a cult of bloodthirsty Mayan priests who believed in the dark arts. It is rumored they are responsible for bringing down their entire civilization with their obsession for human sacrifices (mainly young female virgins). Once Chaam started making half-human children, he decided all firstborn males would make excellent Maaskab due to their proclivity for evil.

*Mocos, Mobscuros, O'Scabbies:* Nicknames for when you join Maaskab with Obscuros to create a brand-new malevolent treat.

*Obscuros:* Evil vampires who do not live by the Pact and who like to dine on innocent humans since they really do taste the best.

*The Pact:* An agreement between the gods and good vampires that dictates the dos and don'ts. There are many parts to it, but the most important rules are vampires are not allowed to snack on good people (called Forbiddens), they must keep their existence a secret, and they are responsible for keeping any rogue vampires in check.

*Payal:* Though the gods can take humans to their realm and make them immortal, Payals are the true genetic offspring of the gods but are born mortal, just like their human mothers. Only firstborn children inherit the gods' genes and manifest their traits. If the firstborn happens to be female, she is a Payal. If male, well...then you get something kind of yucky (see definition of Maaskab)!

*Uchben:* An ancient society of scholars and warriors who serve as the gods' eyes and ears in the human world. They also do the books and manage the gods' earthly assets.

# Character Definitions

## The Gods

Though every culture around the world has their own names and beliefs related to beings of worship, there are actually only fourteen gods. And since the gods are able to access the human world only through the portals called cenotes, located in the Yucatán, the Mayans were big fans.

The gods often refer to each other as brother and sister, but truth is they are just another species of the Creator.

*Acan—God of Wine and Intoxication:* Also known as Belch, Acan has been drunk for a few thousand years. He hopes to someday trade places with Votan because he's tired of his flabby muscles and beer belly.

*Ah-Ciliz—God of Solar Eclipses:* Called A.C. by his brethren, Ah-Ciliz is generally thought of as the party pooper because of his dark attitude.

*Akna—Goddess of Fertility:* You either love her or you hate her.

***Backlum Chaam—God of Male Virility:*** He's responsible for discovering black jade, figuring out how to procreate with humans, and kicking off the chain of events that will eventually lead to the Great War. Get your Funyuns and beer! This is gonna be good.

***Camaxtli—Goddess of the Hunt:*** Also known as Fate, Camaxtli holds a special position among the gods since no one dares challenge her. When Fate has spoken, that's the end of the conversation.

***Colel Cab—Mistress of Bees:*** Because really, where would we all be without the bees?

***Goddess of Forgetfulness:*** Um... I forget her name. Sorry.

***Ixtab—Goddess of Suicide:*** Ixtab is generally described as a loner. Could it be those dead critters she carries around? But don't judge her so hastily. You never know what truly lies behind that veil of black she wears.

***K'ak:*** The history books remember him as K'ak Tiliw Chan Yopaat, ruler of Copán in the 700s AD. King K'ak (don't you just love that name? Tee-hee-hee...) is one of Cimil's favorite brothers. We're not really sure what he does, but he can throw bolts of lightning.

***Kinich Ahau—God of the Sun:*** Also known by many other names, depending on the culture, Kinich likes to go by Nick these days. But don't let the modern name fool you. He's not so hot about the gods mingling with humans. Although... he's getting a little curious about what the fuss is all about. Can sleeping with a woman really be all that?

*Votan—God of Death and War:* Also known as Odin, Wotan, Wodan, God of Drums (he has no idea how the hell he got that title; he hates the drums), and Lord of Multiplication (okay, he is pretty darn good at math so that one makes sense). These days, Votan goes by Guy Santiago (it's a long story—read Book #1), but despite his deadly tendencies, he's all heart. He's now engaged to Emma Keane.

*Yum Cimil—Goddess of the Underworld:* Also known as Ah-Puch by the Mayans, Mictlantecuhtli (try saying that one ten times) by the Aztec, Grim Reaper by the Europeans, Hades by the Greeks...you get the picture! Despite what people say, Cimil is actually a female, adores a good bargain (especially garage sales) and the color pink. She's also batshit crazy.

*Zac Cimi—Bacab of the North:* What the heck is a Bacab? According to the gods' folklore, the Bacabs are the four eldest and most powerful of the gods. Zac, however, has yet to discover his true gifts, although he is physically the strongest. We *think* he may be the God of Love.

**#14 ???** (I'm not telling.)

## Not the Gods

*Andrus:* Ex-Demilord (vampire who's been given the gods' light), now just a demigod after his maker, the vampire queen, died. According to Cimil, his son, who hasn't been born yet, is destined to marry Helena and Niccolo's daughter.

***Anne:*** Not telling.

***Brutus:*** One of Gabrán's elite Uchben warriors. He doesn't speak much, but that's because he and his team are telepathic. They are also immortal (a gift from the gods) and next in line to be Uchben chiefs.

***Emma Keane:*** A reluctant Payal who can split a man right down the middle with her bare hands. She is engaged to Votan (aka Guy Santiago) and really wants to kick the snot out of Tommaso, the man who betrayed her.

***Father Xavier:*** Once a priest at the Vatican, Xavier is now the Uchben's top scholar and historian. He has a thing for jogging suits, Tyra Banks, and Cimil.

***Gabrán:*** One of the Uchben chiefs and a very close friend of the gods. The chiefs have been given the gods' light and are immortal—a perk of the job.

***Gabriela:*** Emma Keane's grandmother and one of the original Payals. She now leads the Maaskab at the young age of eightysomething years old.

***Helena Strauss:*** Once human, Helena is now a vampire and married to Niccolo DiConti. She has a half-vampire daughter, Matty, who is destined to marry Andrus's son, according to Cimil.

*Jess:* Not telling.

*Julie Trudeau:* Penelope's mother.

*Niccolo DiConti:* Ex-General of the Vampire Army. He is the interim vampire leader now that the queen is dead, because the army remained loyal to him. He is married to Helena Strauss and has a half-vampire daughter, Matty—a wedding gift from Cimil.

*Nick:* (From Book #1, not to be confused with Kinich.) Also not telling.

*Penelope Trudeau:* The woman Cimil approaches to be her brother's surrogate.

*Philippe:* Roberto's brother. An Ancient One.

*Reyna:* The dead vampire queen.

*Roberto (Narmer):* Originally an Egyptian pharaoh, Narmer was one of the six Ancient Ones—the very first vampires. He eventually changed his name to Roberto and moved to Spain—something to do with one of Cimil's little schemes. Rumor is, he wasn't too happy about it.

*Sentin:* One of Niccolo's loyal vampire soldiers. Viktor turned him into a vampire after finding him in a ditch during World War II.

***Tommaso:*** Oh, boy. Where to start. Once an Uchben, Tommaso's mind was poisoned with black jade. He tried to kill Emma. She's not happy about that.

***Viktor:*** Niccolo's right hand and BFF. He's approximately one thousand years old and originally a Viking. He's big. He's blond. He's got the hots for some blonde woman he's dreamed of for the last five hundred years. He's also Helena's maker.

## Which Gods Didn't Make the Cut?

Yes. It takes a lot to be a cover god for Mimi Jean. And while hundreds of men try out, only an elite handful make the cut. Don't forget to check out the studs who didn't make the final cover...

http://www.mimijean.net/paranormal_romance_
extras.html#rejects

BETTER LUCK NEXT TIME, BOYS!!

# Cimil's Mandatory Pop Quiz Answers

1. **An ancient society of warriors and scholars who serve as the gods' eyes, ears, and muscle.**
   A. The Smurfs
   B. The were-Smurfs
   C. The Uchben

*Answer: C. Although the Uchben's primary purpose is to serve as the gods' mortal army, they are also very active in investment banking, philanthropy, and politics.*

2. **A female descendant of the gods. Not immortal but does carry the gods' bloodline.**
   A. Snooki
   B. Betty White
   C. A Payal

*Answer: C. A Payal is a firstborn child who is female, descended from the gods, and carries their DNA.*

3. **An evil cult of dark priests, descending from the Mayans.**
   A. The Republican Party
   B. The Democratic Party
   C. The Maaskab (aka Scabs)

*Answer: C. The Maaskab are the powerful masters of the dark arts. Also, they do not believe in bathing and they cover themselves in their victim's blood, which makes them extra scary.*

4. **Evil vampires whose favorite flavor is innocence.**
   A. The Obscuros
   B. The Osmonds
   C. The Osbournes

*Answer: A. The Obscuros are a group of evil vampires who dine on Forbiddens (innocent humans) and do not live by the laws of the Pact.*

5. **Now that Chaam, the God of Male Virility, is locked away, I lead the Maaskab army.**
   A. The Dos Equis "Most Interesting Man in the World"
   B. Kathy Griffin
   C. Gabriela, Emma Keane's grandmother

*Answer: C. I really, really want the answer to be A, but it is Gabriela, who is one of the original Payals, was captured by the Maaskab, and injected with black jade. Now she is one of the most evil humans on the planet. How ya like me now, kids?*

6. **Mimi Jean's favorite slang term for a man's private parts.**
   A. Man-treat
   B. Man-sicle
   C. Man-fritters
   *Answer: All of the above.*

# THE DISH

*Where Authors Give You the Inside Scoop*

*From the desk of Marilyn Pappano*

Dear Reader,

One of the pluses of writing the Tallgrass series was one I didn't anticipate until I was neck-deep in the process, but it's been a great one: unearthing old memories. Our Navy career was filled with laugh-out-loud moments, but there were also plenty of the laugh-or-you'll-cry moments, too. We did a lot of laughing. Most of our tears were reserved for later.

Like our very first move to South Carolina, when the movers lost our furniture for weeks, and the day after it was finally delivered, my husband got orders to Alabama. On our second move, the delivery guys perfected their truck-unloading routine: three boxes into the apartment, one box into the front of their truck. (Fortunately, Bob had perfected his watch-the-unloaders routine and recovered it all.)

For our first apartment move-out inspection, we had scrubbed ourselves to nubbins all through the night. The manager did the walk-through, commented on how impeccably clean everything was, and offered me the paperwork to sign. I signed it, turned around to hand it to her, and walked into the low-hanging chandelier where the dining table used to sit, breaking a bulb with my head. Silently she took back the papers, thumbed through to the deduction sheet, and charged us sixty cents for a new bulb.

There's something about being told my Oklahoma accent is funny by multi-generation Americans with accents so heavy that I just guessed at the context of our conversations. Or hearing our two-year-old Oklahoma-born son, home for Christmas, proudly singing, "Jaaangle baaaa-ulllz! Jaaan-gle baaaa-ulllz! Jaaan-gle *alllll* the waaay-uh!"

Bob and I still trade stories. *Remember when we did that self-move to San Diego and the brakes went out on the rental truck in 5:00 traffic in Memphis at the start of a holiday weekend? Remember that pumpkin pie on the first Thanksgiving we couldn't go home—the one I forgot to put the spices in? Remember dropping the kiddo off at the base day care while we got groceries and having to pay the grand sum of fifty cents two hours later? How about when you had to report to the commanding general for joint-service duty at Fort Gordon and we couldn't find your Dixie cup anywhere in the truck crammed with boxes—and at an Army post, no less, that didn't stock Navy uniforms?*

Sea life was great. We watched ships leaving and, months later, come home again. On one homecoming, the kiddo and I watched Daddy's ship run aground. We learned that all sailors look alike when they're dressed in the same uniform and seen from a distance. We spied submarines stealthing out of their bases and toured warships—American, British, French, Canadian—and even got to board one of our own nuclear subs for a private look around.

The Navy gave us a lot to remember and a lot to learn. (Example: all those birthdays and anniversaries

Bob missed didn't mean a thing. It was the fact that he came home that mattered.) I still have a few dried petals from the flowers given to me by the command each time Bob reenlisted, as well the ones I got when he retired. We have a flag, like the one each of the widows in Tallgrass received, and a display box of medals and ribbons, but filled with much happier memories.

I can't wait to see which old *remember when* the next book in this series brings us! I hope you love reading A MAN TO ON HOLD TO as much as I loved writing it.

Sincerely,

Marilyn Pappano

MarilynPappano.com
Twitter @MarilynPappano
Facebook.com/MarilynPappanoFanPage

*From the desk of Jaime Rush*

Dear Reader,

Much has been written about angels. When I realized that angels would be part of my mythology and hidden world, I knew I needed to make mine different. I didn't want to use the religious mythos or pair them with demons. Many authors have done a fantastic job of this already.

In fact, I felt this way about my world in general. I started with the concept that a confluence of nature and the energy in the Bermuda Triangle had allowed gods and angels to take human form. They procreated with the humans living on the island and were eventually sent back to their plane of existence. But I didn't want to draw on Greek, Roman, or Atlantean mythology, so I made up my own pantheon of gods. I narrowed them down to three different types: Dragons, sorcerers, and angels. Their progeny continue to live in the area of the Triangle, tethered there by their need to be near their energy source.

My angels come from this pantheon, without the constraints of traditional religious roles. They were sent down to the island to police the wayward gods, but succumbed to human temptation. And their progeny pay the price. I'm afraid my angels' descendents, called Caidos, suffer terribly for their fathers' sins. This was not something I contrived; these concepts often just come to me as the truths of my stories.

Caidos are preternaturally beautiful, drawing the desire of those who see them. But desire, their own and others', causes them physical pain. As do the emotions of all but their own kind. They guard their secret, for their lives depend on it. To keep pain at bay, they isolate themselves from the world and shut down their sexuality. Which, of course, makes it all the more fun when they are thrown together with women they find attractive. Pleasure and pain is a fine line, and Kasabian treads it in a different way than other Caidos. Then again, he is different, harboring a dark secret that compounds his sense of isolation.

Perhaps it was slightly sadistic to pair him with a woman who holds the essence of the goddess of sensuality.

Kye is his greatest temptation, but she may also be his salvation. He needs to form a bond with the woman who can release his dark shadow. I don't make it easy on Kye, either. She must lose everything to find her soul. I love to dig deep into my characters' psyches and mine their darkest shadows. Only then can they come into the light.

And isn't that something we all can learn? To face our shadows so that we can walk in the light? That's what I love most about writing: that readers, too, can take the journey of self discovery, self love, right along with my characters. They face their demons and come out on the other end having survived.

We all have magic in our imaginations. Mine has always contained murder, mayhem, and romance. Feel free to wander through the madness of my mind any time. A good place to start is my website, www.jaimerush .com, or that of my romantic suspense alter ego, www .tinawainscott.com.

*Jaime Rush*

♥ ♥ ♥ ♥ ♥ ♥ ♥ ♥ ♥ ♥ ♥ ♥ ♥ ♥ ♥ ♥

*From the desk of Kate Brady*

Dear Reader,

People ask me all the time, "What do you like about writing romantic suspense?" It's a great question, and it always seems like sort of a copout to say, "Everything!" But it's true. Writing novels is the greatest job in the world. And romantic suspense, in particular, allows my favorite elements to exist in a single story: adventure, danger, thrills, chills, romance, and the gratifying knowledge that good will triumph over evil and love will win the day.

Weaving all those elements together is, for me, a labor of love. I love being able to work with something straight from my own mind, without having to footnote and document sources all the time. (In my other career—academia—they frown upon letting the voices in my head do the writing!) I love the flexibility of where and when I can indulge myself in a story—the deck, the kitchen island, the car, the beach, and any number of recliners are my favorite "offices." I love seeing the stories unfold, being surprised by the twists and turns they take, and ultimately coming across them in their finished forms on the bookstore shelves. I love hearing from readers and being privy to their take on the story line or a character. I love meeting other writers and hobnobbing with the huge network of readers and writers out there who still love romantic suspense.

And I *love* getting to know new characters. I don't create these people; they already exist when a story begins and it becomes my job to reveal them. I just go along for the ride as they play out their roles, and I'm repeatedly surprised and delighted by what they prove to be. And it never fails: I always fall in love.

Luke Mann, the hero in WHERE EVIL WAITS, was one of the most intriguing characters I have met and he turned out to be one of my all-time favorites. He first appeared in his brother's book, *Where Angels Rest*, so I knew his hometown, his upbringing, his parents, and his siblings. But Luke himself came to me shrouded in shadows. I couldn't wait to write his story; he was dark and fascinating and intense (not to mention gorgeous) and I knew from the start that his adventure would be a whirlwind ride. When I put him in an alley with his soon-to-be heroine, Kara Chandler—who shocked both Luke and me with a boldness I hadn't expected—I fell in love with both of them. From that point on, WHERE EVIL WAITS was off and running, as Luke and Kara tried to elude and capture a killer as twisted and dangerous as the barbed wire that was his trademark.

The time Luke and Kara spend together is brief, but jam-packed with action, heat, and, ultimately, affection. I hope you enjoy reading their story as much as I enjoyed writing it!

Happy Reading!

*Kate Brady*

♥ ♥ ♥ ♥ ♥ ♥ ♥ ♥ ♥ ♥ ♥ ♥ ♥ ♥ ♥

*From the desk of Amanda Scott*

Dear Reader,

The plot of THE WARRIOR'S BRIDE, set in the fourteenth-century Scottish Highlands near Loch Lomond, grew from a law pertaining to abduction that must have seemed logical to its ancient Celtic lawmakers.

I have little doubt that they intended that law to protect women.

However, I grew up in a family descended from a long line of lawyers, including my father, my grandfather, and two of the latter's great-grandfathers, one of whom was the first Supreme Court justice for the state of Arkansas (an arrangement made by his brother, the first senator from Missouri, who also named Arkansas—so just a little nepotism there). My brother is a judge. His son and one of our cousins are defense attorneys. So, as you might imagine, laws and the history of law have stirred many a dinner-table conversation throughout my life.

When I was young, I spent countless summer hours traveling with my paternal grandmother and grandfather in their car, listening to him tell stories as he drove. Once, when I pointed out brown cows on a hillside, he said, "Well, they're brown on this side, anyhow."

That was my first lesson in looking at both sides of any argument, and it has served me well in my profession. This is by no means the first time I've met a law that sowed the seeds for an entire book.

Women, as we all know, are unpredictable creatures who have often taken matters into their own hands in ways of which men—especially in olden times—have disapproved. Thanks to our unpredictability, many laws that men have made to "protect" us have had the opposite effect.

The heroine of THE WARRIOR'S BRIDE is the lady Muriella MacFarlan, whose father, Andrew, is the rightful chief of Clan Farlan. A traitorous cousin has usurped Andrew's chiefdom and murdered his sons, so Andrew means to win his chiefdom back by marrying his daughters to warriors from powerful clans, who will help him.

Muriella, however, intends *never* to marry. I based her character on Clotho, youngest of the three Fates and the one who is responsible for spinning the thread of life. So Murie is a spinner of threads, yarns...and stories.

Blessed with a flawless memory, Muriella aspires to be a *seanachie*, responsible for passing the tales of Highland folklore and history on to future generations. She has already developed a reputation for her storytelling and takes that responsibility seriously.

She seeks truth in her tales of historical events. However, in her personal life, Murie enjoys a more flexible notion of truth. She doesn't lie, exactly. She spins.

Enter blunt-spoken warrior Robert MacAulay, a man of honor with a clear sense of honor, duty, and truth. Rob also has a vision that, at least for the near future, does not include marriage. Nor does he approve of truth-spinning.

Consequently, sparks fly between the two of them even *before* Murie runs afoul of the crazy law. I think you will enjoy THE WARRIOR'S BRIDE.

Meantime, *Suas Alba!*

Sincerely,

*Amanda Scott*

www.amandascottauthor.com

♥ ♥ ♥ ♥ ♥ ♥ ♥ ♥ ♥ ♥ ♥ ♥ ♥ ♥

# From the desk of Mimi Jean Pamfiloff

Dear People Pets—Oops, sorry—I meant, Dear Readers,

Ever wonder what's like to be God of the Sun, Ruler of the House of Gods, and the only deity against procreation with humans (an act against nature)?

Nah. Me neither. I want to know what it's like to be his girlfriend. After all, how many guys house the power of the sun inside their seven-foot frames? And that hair. Long thick ribbons of sun-streaked caramel. And those muscles. Not an ounce of fat to be found on that insanely ripped body. As for the...eh-hem, the *performance* part, well, I'd like to know all about that, too.

Actually, so would Penelope. Especially after spending the evening with him, sipping champagne in his hotel room, and then waking up buck naked. Yes. In his bed. And yes, he's naked, too. Yeah, she'd love to remember what happened. He wouldn't mind, either.

But it seems that the only one who might know anything is Cimil, Goddess of the Underworld, instigator of all things naughty, and she's nowhere to be found. I guess Kinich and Penelope will have to figure this out for themselves. So what will be the consequence of breaking these "rules" of nature Kinich fears so much? Perhaps the price will be Penelope's life. But perhaps, just maybe, the price will be his...

Happy Reading!

Mimi

♥ ♥ ♥ ♥ ♥ ♥ ♥ ♥ ♥ ♥ ♥ ♥ ♥ ♥

## *From the desk of Shannon Richard*

Dear Reader,

I knew how Brendan and Paige were going to meet from the very start. It was the first scene that played out in my mind. Paige was going to be having a very bad day on top of a very bad couple of months. Her Jeep breaks down in the middle of nowhere Florida, during a sweltering day, and she was to call someone for help. It's when she's at her lowest that she meets the love of her life; she just doesn't know it at the time. As for Brendan, he isn't expecting anyone like Paige to come along. Not now, not ever. But he knows pretty quickly that he has feelings for her, and that they're serious feelings.

Paige can be a little sassy, and Brendan can be a little cocky, so during their first encounter sparks are flying all over the place. Things start to get hot quickly, and it has very little to do with summer in the South (which is hot and miserable, I can tell you from over twenty years of experience). But at the end of the day, and no matter the confrontation, Brendan is Paige's white knight. He comes to her rescue in more ways than one.

The inspiration behind Brendan is a very laid-back Southern guy. He's easygoing (for the most part) and charming. He hasn't been one for long-term serious relationships, but when it comes to Paige he jumps right on in. There's just something about a guy who knows exactly what he wants, who meets the girl and doesn't hesitate. Yeah, it makes me swoon more than just a little. I hoped that readers would appreciate that aspect of him. The diving in headfirst and not looking back, and Brendan doesn't look back.

As for Paige, she's dealing with a lot and is more than a little scared about getting involved with another guy. Her wounds are too fresh and deep from her recent heartbreak. Brendan knows all about pain and suffering. Instead of turning his back on her, he steps up to the plate. He helps Paige heal, helps her get a job and friends, helps her find a place in the little town of Mirabelle. It just so happens that her place is right next to his.

So yes, Brendan is this big, tough, alpha man who comes to the rescue of the damsel in distress. But Paige isn't exactly a weak little thing. No, she's pretty strong herself. It's part of that strength that Brendan is so drawn to. He loves her passion and how fierce she is. But really, he just loves her.

I'm a fan of the happily ever after. Always have been, always will be. I love my characters; they're part of me. They might exist in black and white on the page, but to me they're real. At the end of the day, I just want them to be happy.

Cheers,

ShannonRichard.net
Twitter @Shan_Richard
Facebook.com/ShannonNRichard